DEAD BEDROOM

DEAD BEDROOM

STEVEN R. BROOKS

Limner
Books

ISBN: 979-8-9857103-0-4 (ebook)
ISBN: 979-8-9857103-1-1 (pbk)

Published by Limner Books
P.O. Box 5644, Athens, Ga 30604

www.LimnerBooks.com

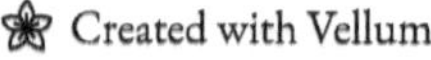 Created with Vellum

For Shannon,
who knocked me off my feet,
and showed me where to put the commas

WEDNESDAY

1

JACKSON BRUTUS BOOTH loved his job. At forty, he'd finally found his calling. Driven and focused, he knew he was putting his own unique stamp on the world.

Sadly, Monty—the man duct-taped to the kitchen chair—must have mistaken the zest in Jackson's eyes for anger because he was on the verge of tears.

Jackson found this miscommunication disturbing. He wasn't angry with Monty. He felt sorry for the little guy. The Montys of the world often had trouble expanding their horizons and, despite Jackson's best efforts, remained blind to the wondrous world before them.

Still, Monty, like all losers, deserved a chance.

"Tell me, man. No harm, no foul, if you just tell me," Jackson said.

"It's not here. Why the hell would I keep it here?"

"We both know it's here."

"I swear to God it's not."

Jackson reached down, grabbed the handle of the Bowie knife stuck in Monty's thigh, and twisted the blade.

Monty screamed.

"Let's be honest," Jackson said. "You're a dumbass. Ain't no shame in that. I did piss-poor in school. Had that whole dyslexia thing going on, but did I quit? No. I found me a mentor. I modeled behavior. I studied NLP."

He caught the flicker of confusion in the man's broken eyes and clarified, "Neuro-linguistic programming."

Satisfied Monty understood, he continued, "I learned to read and enjoy it. Now look at me. Good job, steady paycheck—I've even got my own place. And the women? They cream in their panties when I come around. You want the women to cream their panties, don't you?"

Monty nodded like a dog begging for a treat.

Jackson smiled. This was what he lived for—a teachable moment.

"You're not a hopeless case, Monty. You've got potential. We all have potential. Now it's time to come clean. Time to wash those sins away, my friend. You stole something that didn't belong to you, and we can continue down this path of pain, or you can repent. Give it back. Start anew."

Jackson reached for the knife.

"Okay, yep, whatever, whatever, man," Monty sputtered, spittle flying from his lips. "Downstairs. Fuck, man, it's downstairs."

"Smart move, my friend. Smart move. Where downstairs?"

"Behind the water heater, there's a large black plastic container. It's in there."

"Let's hope so." With a swing in his step and a whistle on his lips, Jackson strolled out of the dismal kitchen and into the living room. His heart sank a little when he caught sight of the droopy plastic Christmas tree crammed in the corner. The red and green lights on it were blinking out of time, and the despair in the house hung on him like a heavy coat.

A black cat bolted out from under the tree, whipping between his legs so fast Jackson almost went down face first. With a bit of luck—or skill, as he preferred to call it—he regained his balance by grabbing the Christmas tree. Surprisingly, it didn't tip over.

The cat took off down the hallway. Jackson followed him. As he passed an open doorway, a nauseating stench stopped him cold. He leaned in the bathroom and spotted a litter box in the corner. Ugh, it looked like no one had emptied it in weeks. His eyes began to burn, and he stepped back into the hall.

He tried the knob on the door next to the bathroom, but the door wouldn't budge. With both hands he yanked on the doorknob, and the plywood screamed in protest as the door relented.

He flicked on the light and let out a quiet gasp. Cardboard boxes, junk bursting from each, filled the small concrete room. He scrambled down the tottering wooden stairs. How did people live like this? he wondered. All it took to keep a clean house was a little discipline, but discipline was the last thing Monty had. The man was a druggie, a thief, and a liar—a train wreck trifecta.

Jackson, on the other hand, was the master of self-control. Take coke, for example. Sure, he'd done a few lines before he got here, and sure, he'd do a few more in the car later. But he could handle it. He didn't need it, and that was the key.

He didn't need it.

He just liked it.

Pushing the boxes left and right, he made his way toward the water heater in the corner. He stepped into an unseen spiderweb and furiously wiped the webs off of his head and torso. When he was absolutely certain he was spider-free, he continued on. Suddenly it dawned on him: Monty was alone in the kitchen. Best to keep the man focused.

"Monty?" he yelled. "You still with me?"

"Uh, yeah," a raspy voice echoed down the hallway.

"Okay, good, because I just want you to remember that there is no free ride, my friend. No free ride. But that's a good thing. So don't be discouraged. A man needs to work for what he gets in life, you know, and let me tell you, brother, I'm out there earning it every day."

He found the plastic container, opened it, pulled out a black gym bag, and unzipped it.

Success.

This deserved an extra line of blow later.

"See, that's what you need," Jackson yelled. "You need to find your passion. What makes your heart sing?"

Silence.

"Monty?"

Was that a chair leg scraping across the floor?

"Monty?" Bag in hand, he bulldozed through the boxes.

"Yeah?"

"What makes your heart sing?" He charged up the stairs.

"I don't know. I never thought about it."

"Well, find that, and you will find true bliss. But remember, stealing is not a vocation."

Jackson stepped into the kitchen, dropped the bag on the floor, then bent down and searched it.

"We're good?" Monty said, lines of sweat creeping down his boney, pale face.

Jackson looked up and flashed his million-dollar smile. "We are good." He zipped the bag close and stood up. "Got any soda?"

"In the fridge."

He stepped around Monty, opened the refrigerator, and scanned the shelves. "Mountain Scream?"

"Yeah, it's like Mountain Dew, but a hell of a lot cheaper."

"Hmm...okay, I'll bite." He grabbed a can and popped the top. The hiss echoed throughout the house.

Monty cleared his throat.

Jackson chugged the drink. When he was done, he asked, "Ever been in the military?"

"No. Asthma."

"Shame. Joining the Marines really turned my life around. You know, when I was a kid, I chased a lot of pussy and had some crazy mind-altering experiences in the Chihuahuan Desert. Peyote... wow...highly recommended, by the way. But Afghanistan and Iraq...that shit put me on the road to righteousness. What I learned over there gave my life meaning."

He sat the can on the counter and gazed at the back of Monty's head. The sun was coming up, and the light streaming through the kitchen window illuminated his bald spot like a bull's-eye. "Wouldn't you like to have some meaning in your life, Monty?"

He didn't respond.

"Monty?"

"Hey, man, uh, like, no offense, but I don't know what you're talking about."

"Okay, fair enough." In one quick motion, he reached inside his leather jacket, pulled out a Glock 22, and put a bullet right through Monty's bald spot.

Chunks of brain shot across the room, spraying all over the torn, faded wallpaper. Blood ran down the wall, turning the washed-out yellow daisies red.

Monty slumped forward.

Jackson slid the gun back in his jacket pocket, grabbed the half-empty can, and picked up the bag. Fingers on the sliding glass door handle, he stopped and turned back toward the lifeless body duct-taped to the chair.

Jackson raised the can in a toast. "Merry Christmas, my friend."

And then he hustled out the door.

2
____

Diane Hancock raced through the parking lot, the wind whipping her hair into a frenzy and her heels clicking up a storm on the pavement.

She stopped next to a silver Lexus and glared at the massive red-and-yellow logo on the brick wall in front of her: *WRBB Radio 580 News. Weather. Talk.* Fighting back a scream, she got in the car. She couldn't wait to get her husband, Hilton, to Hartsfield-Jackson for his morning flight to Albuquerque and then back home for a much needed nap. Even Ambien had failed her the night before.

She started the car and turned on the heat. For the middle of December it was about ten degrees colder than normal but, like an idiot, she hadn't bothered to grab her coat when they'd left the house earlier.

Leaning forward, she eyed the ashen sky through the front windshield. Rain? She checked her phone. No, but the sun wasn't coming out either. Winter in Georgia was cold, gray, and, more often than not, wet.

The passenger door opened and Hilton climbed in, the top of his head grazing the ceiling. "What's the rush?"

"You don't want to miss your flight."

"We've got time."

"Says the perpetually late man. It's nine thirty. We're gonna hit rush hour traffic on 85."

She backed out and cruised through the parking lot toward the exit.

"I'm dying for a cup of coffee. You?" he said.

"You're gonna miss your flight."

"We have time."

"Okay, it's your flight."

When a hole opened in the traffic, she floored it, took a left onto Old Kings Road, and headed to Jittery Express, a locally owned shop with some of the best coffee she'd ever had.

Hilton grabbed a pack of chewing gum from the console, took a piece, and popped it in his mouth.

They rode in silence for a few minutes. She waited for him to ask.

Finally, he did. "So, how did I do?"

"The interview was fine. Brenda always treats you with kid gloves."

"Kid gloves? I thought she got a little rough when she started asking about Richard."

Diane wanted to say, *Better toughen up, honey. People in politics play to kill*, but forced a smile.

"What do you think of my chances?" he asked.

"Of being elected mayor?"

"Well, yeah..."

"Hard to say. You have an honest face, and you're tall. That helps. And most people think you're a good person."

"Not really the answer I was hoping for."

"Did you want me to say how magnificent you are?"

"Why are you mad at me?"

"I'm not."

She took a left onto Four Winds Boulevard.

"You sure?"

"Well, it would have been nice if we'd discussed it first before you announced your candidacy to the world."

"We did."

"No. You told me last night, and honestly, I thought you were joking."

"Why would you think I was joking?"

"Because I didn't want to believe you were crazy."

"So you are mad at me."

"Don't do that to me," she said. "I'm not mad. But this is a big decision that affects both of us, and I simply would have liked to have been involved."

"It's just Mulberry Grove, honey. It's not like I'm running for mayor of Atlanta or anything. It'll be fun," he said, smiling.

"Fun? You have a strange idea of fun. What if I'd said no? That I didn't want you to do this?"

When he didn't answer: "You knew I'd say no."

His smile—Diane thought it was more of a smirk—slid off his face.

"It's a part-time job, honey, if that. It's good community relations. It helps the stores. It helps us. It's a win-win."

"You have a full-time job. You run a company. So what's up?"

"Okay, look, Dewey Prescott is retiring next year. I have a fantastic shot at this. You know I do. If Ray Dillard runs and I don't, he'll walk away with it, and it's another four years before I can try again."

"So wait four years. What's the rush? You're not even forty."

"It's closing in fast. Maybe you should trust me a little more, Diane. I know what I'm doing."

She stopped at a light. After a minute, it turned green. She pressed the gas. "Are you a Republican?"

"What?"

"Are you a Democrat?"

"What's your point?"

"I don't think I've ever heard you talk politics. In fact, I can't remember you ever expressing any interest in the state of the world."

"Religion and politics, two things my dad always said a man should keep to himself."

"I'm your wife."

"I don't need a party affiliation to run for mayor. I can always make that decision before I run for—"

"What?"

"Forget it."

"Run for what?"

He took the gum out of his mouth, rolled down the window, and tossed it.

"Hilton?"

He rolled the window back up, inhaled through his nose, and said, "State senate."

"Oh, my. That's ambitious."

"Well, state senate is a good stepping stone to the House of Representatives."

"And then what? Senator? President?"

He grinned. "I wouldn't go that far. I'm sick of running Crazy Dick's. I don't want to spend the rest of my life living Richard's dream. He's gone."

Crazy Dick's Chicken Town.

She remembered the night Hilton and Richard unveiled the name for their new restaurant. *Crazy Dick's Chicken Town?* Had they lost their minds? She'd lobbied them for weeks to reconsider, but Richard was adamant. Hilton wasn't sold on it either, but he always deferred to his older brother when it came to marketing, so Crazy Dick's Chicken Town it was.

She gave it six months before Richard realized it was the worst name ever and changed it.

Ten years and seven locations in Georgia later—with more on

the way—she had to admit she knew nothing about naming a restaurant.

"Is this because of what happened to Richard? Do you have something to prove?"

"No," he replied. "But you know me. I think big."

"Too big."

"Maybe. Sometimes. But Crazy Dick's ain't too big, is it? It was my drive that built that. My drive."

"You and Richard—"

"Richard was the front man, the funny guy in the commercials. He didn't build anything. Once I become mayor—"

"Become?"

"Oh, you know I'll win. Come on, this is me we're talking about. When I become mayor, I might hate it. That's always a possibility. I mean, I'm not necessarily a team player. One term and I might go back to frying chicken. But I have to try. You understand? I've got to take my shot."

She looked into his green eyes. He always had beautiful eyes, even if he was a shit. What happened to the man she'd married? Maybe he wasn't her husband at all. Maybe it was like that movie *Invasion of the Body Snatchers* and some weird alien pod thing had replaced Hilton. A clone with no soul. Or common sense.

She turned into Jittery Express. As usual, the drive-thru line wrapped around the building. It'd always baffled her that Wendy and Charles didn't turn this into a franchise. Hilton told them plenty of times they were sitting on a gold mine. Even offered to go in together.

They quietly moved through the drive-thru line.

"Tell you what," Hilton said after a few minutes. "When I get back, I'll make some 'we time'. Just you and me. We can go to the mountains or the beach or...hey, you know where we could go?"

Diane smiled. She heard the words before they flew out his mouth.

"Europe. We could take that trip you've always wanted."

Good old Europe. He'd been promising that one for longer than she could remember.

"Sounds great," she said.

"Whatever you want to do. I just want you to be happy." He opened the door and got out.

"What are you doing?"

"This line's gonna take forever. I'm going in. Your usual?"

She nodded.

He closed the door, and she watched him walk inside. He had a bounce to his step she hadn't seen in a long, long time. Something was going on with him. Maybe he was coming to terms with his brother dying or an early mid-life crisis. Or...maybe he was having an affair.

An affair?

She laughed out loud. What a ridiculously stupid idea. Hilton might be a lot of things, but he was not a cheater.

How in the world had she ended up here? This wasn't the life she'd imagined for herself.

Choices, baby, choices.

That's what her sister, Nicole, liked to say. But what did she know? She slept with anything that moved, and so far all it had gotten her was a lot of heartache and a mess of trouble.

3

———

BLACK SUNGLASSES INCHING DOWN her nose and her hair in a ponytail, Nicole Robinson opened the back hatch of her red RX-7. The car was practically an antique and needed a new paint job, not to mention some engine work, but she loved it. Once she finished bringing it back to life, it'd be her little dream machine.

She grabbed as many grocery bags as she could, closed the hatch, and started up the winding gravel path toward a dilapidated trailer. A headache was brewing, and she chastised herself for deciding to be so charitable this early in the morning.

"Let me go! Let me go!" a woman yelled.

Nicole froze. Did that come from inside the trailer?

"Aw, come on, angel cakes. Who's your daddy? Who's your dada?" a deep, ragged voice bellowed, clearly from inside the trailer.

"Janice!" Nicole flung the bags to the ground and took off like a banshee.

Halfway to the trailer, she tripped on an empty beer bottle and tumbled sideways into the tall weeds. Her sunglasses went flying as she came down hard on a pile of rocks.

"Son of a bitch!"

She rolled over onto her back, clutched her right side, and tried to take a breath. Did somebody smash her in the ribs with a baseball bat?

Fighting the pain, she got to her feet and looked around for her sunglasses. They were nowhere to be found. Damn it, those were her favorite. She'd gotten them for a steal at the Dollar Store. For a brief second she considered turning around, climbing back in her car, and getting the hell out of there. She didn't need this, especially after last night. She found her breath, brushed the dust and muck off her T-shirt and jeans, and looked back at her car.

Family *was* family.

With a shrug of resignation, she charged up the flimsy steps, raced through the front door, and came to a screeching halt.

"Janice?" was all she squeaked out, her eyes forever scarred by the sight before her.

On the other side of the living room, a bald, skinny man in his early sixties had a middle-aged woman bent over the edge of the couch. His pants and boxers were down to his knees, and he had his hands under her skirt. Her blouse was unbuttoned, and her hair was a mess.

"Hey! Hey, buddy!" Nicole said. "What are you doing to her?"

In unison, they looked up.

But the expression on the woman's face was one of surprise, not relief, while the man's face sported a mixture of embarrassment and confusion.

"Janice? Are you okay—"

"Baby girl, what are you doing here?" the woman said in a sweet and innocent tone, as if Nicole had walked in on her while she was having a little Christmas party, not getting ready to give an old man the ride of his life.

The geezer crept back and pulled up his boxers and pants. He hid his eyes and zipped up his fly.

Janice adjusted her clothes and moved away from the couch.

"What the hell are you doing?" Nicole asked.

"Come on, now," she whispered as she walked toward Nicole, a wry grin on her leathery face. "You're a big girl. I think you can figure it out."

She was a small woman, with fake lips, fake breasts, and short gray hair that had once been strawberry blond. Back in the day she was a knockout. Now, in a dimly lit bar, after a few shots, she was still quite the looker.

"Was he hurting you? 'Cause if he was—"

"No...honey, no. Not at all," Janice said, smiling. "Not yet, anyway."

As she got closer, Nicole saw the red streaks in her eyes and smelled the alcohol and nicotine on her breath. Would she be like this in twenty years? Nicole cringed at the thought.

"This is Roger. Roger, this is my youngest, Nicole. Nicole doesn't know how to knock. Do you, Nicole?"

"Now wait a minute. When I got here, you were screaming bloody murder. I could hear you in the driveway. I thought he was killing you."

"Honey, does he look like he could hurt a fly?"

Roger lifted one hand and waved. Then he glanced at Janice, his eyes waiting for her approval. "Maybe, you know, I should get going?"

"Sure thing, dear."

He edged past Nicole and scooted out the door.

Janice winked at him and mouthed, "Call me."

Nicole paced around the room. "I came by to drop off some groceries, and to see how the meds were working."

Janice grabbed a cigarette out of the pack on the coffee table and lit up. "So far, so good."

Nicole ripped it out of her mouth. "Trying to kill yourself?"

Janice's eyes lit up like a house on fire. "I can smoke if I want. You do it all the time. Glass houses, you know."

Nicole marched into the kitchen, put the cigarette out in the sink, and tossed it into the overflowing trash can. She returned to the living room to find Janice at the coffee table pulling another one from the pack. "You have lung cancer."

"And I'm in remission."

"Fine. Whatever."

Nicole looked around, letting herself see the trailer. Usually she kept her eyes on the floor when she came by and pretended it wasn't as bad as it was. And it was bad: trash littering the floor, window blinds falling apart, stained carpet, dishes overflowing in the kitchen sink, roaches scurrying around on the counter. The air reeked of pot, beer, and mothballs.

"Got any air freshener?" Nicole said, trying to keep from bolting out the door.

"All out."

"What are you doing?" Nicole turned toward her.

"Excuse me?"

"I thought you wanted my help. You said things were going to be different this time."

"What do you want me to do? I'm in remission, baby girl. I deserve to have some fun, 'cause you never know. It could come back. That could have been my last time."

"I doubt it."

Janice gave her the finger.

"Where did you find him?"

"My AA meeting."

"Figures." Nicole watched a fly trapped in the window blinds. It was buzzing like a chainsaw. "I got you some groceries. They're in the driveway."

NICOLE LEANED DOWN, grabbed the box of Cheerios lying in the grass, and tossed it in a plastic grocery bag. She stood and looked up at the empty blue sky.

No good deed goes unpunished, right, big guy? Or big girl. Or whatever you are.

Her entire body was shaking. She wanted to punch something or somebody.

Two grand...two fucking grand.

That was how much she lost last night.

She had spent the last twelve hours getting her ass handed to her in an all-night poker game, and now her body ached, head to toe. With a gig in less than nine hours, she should be home sleeping. Instead, here she was, mothering her mother.

She walked over, leaned down, grabbed a bag of pretzels off the gravel driveway, and tossed it along with a can of chicken noodle soup into the bag.

The two grand was to have gone toward her mom's cancer meds for the next few months. She had hoped to double or triple what she had saved up, but she'd lost it all. Every dime.

And it wasn't like she had blown it all on a racehorse or lottery tickets or some other pipe dream; Nicole was a damn fine poker player.

Back in her misspent youth, when she lived out in LA, she kept herself fed by playing cards. But last night something was off. Maybe it was because she needed that money. Maybe it was because she was rusty. Whatever it was, she screwed the pooch big-time.

Why am I putting myself through this?

Diane could pay for all of Janice's medical bills, no problem. But her sister had written their mother off a long, long time ago. Who knows, maybe Diane had the right idea. It wasn't like Janice gave a damn about them. She was the one who left when Nicole was two and Diane was seven. They were the ones who hoped and prayed she'd come back, until one day realizing that was a waste of time.

All Nicole cared about was rebuilding whatever relationship she could before something bad happened. But Janice sure as hell didn't make it easy, and sometimes she thought maybe they'd all be better off if the bad thing happened.

She hated herself for thinking that, but there it was, plain as day.

Oh, well.

On the bright side, she had a gig tonight. That was the important thing. She had a gig.

Hallelujah.

She stood up, grabbed the bags, and glimpsed herself in the fractured full-length mirror propped against her mother's trailer.

She burst out laughing.

An armadillo splattered on a two lane looked better.

NICOLE SAT the grocery bags on the kitchen counter. Behind her, Janice opened the refrigerator and pulled out a can of Pabst Blue Ribbon.

"How about you put these away, okay? I gotta run," Nicole said without looking at her.

"Got a show tonight, huh?"

"Yep."

"I'm so proud of my baby girl. Picking on that guitar like a rock star." With the can of beer in her right hand, she played air guitar with her left. "You get it from your mama, you know. In middle school I played violin in the orchestra. Probably could have done good too, if I hadn't gotten knocked up with Diane."

"So I've heard." Before she could stop herself she said, "You can come out to the show, if you feel up to it."

"Thanks, but I'll pass. I'm pretty wiped out already, and it ain't even noon."

Nicole breathed a sigh of relief and opened the front door.

"Sorry you walked in on that," Janice said.

"Doesn't matter. I just don't understand what you're doing."

"I think it's pretty obvious what I was doing."

"Janice...?"

"Don't tell me you don't get around."

"Maybe, but I don't throw it in everybody's face."

"I wasn't doing it in the front yard, honey. Give me a little credit. You barged in without knocking. Last I checked, this was my home."

"I'm not talking about whatever the hell you and that old fart were up to. I'm talking about your life. Aren't you tired of living like this? Isn't it time you grew up?"

Janice's big brown eyes turned to slits, and through tight lips she said, "Honey, I've been grown up longer than you've been alive."

"Uh-huh. Take your meds...please? And lay off the beer and the cigarettes." She stepped out the door.

"Maybe I don't want to change. Ever think of that? Maybe I'm happy the way I am."

Nicole ignored her and raced down the steps. Charging along the path, she spotted her sunglasses in the grass and shot her fist into the air. "Yes!"

She ran over, grabbed them, and headed to her car.

As she opened the car door, she could hear Janice scream after her, "Thanks for ruining my morning! Merry fucking Christmas."

4

————

THE FIRST THING Diane noticed was his ass. It filled out his jeans in a way that made her wish there wasn't a wedding ring on her finger.

After dropping Hilton off at the airport, she'd stopped by Betsy's Book Nook to get a travel guide to Europe. If he was going to play the Europe card, then she was going to make damn sure he took her this time. But instead of the travel section, somehow she'd found herself in the sex and relationships area. As she perused the pages of the *New York Times* bestseller *Getting the Sex You Crave*, she glanced up and saw him.

He was standing in the mystery section, two aisles over.

Diane's eyes moved from his butt to his shoulders. Not bad. He didn't look like he worked out, but still; he had a nice build. Between five eleven and six foot with black hair, he was maybe forty-five and had a dark tan, which was unusual for this time of year. Either he wasn't from Georgia or he went to a tanning salon.

She tried to picture the face that went with the ass, but a twinge of guilt came over her and she put the book down. She looked up to catch a parting glimpse.

Tight Slacks was gone.

A sigh escaped her lips.

Wandering through the aisles looking for the travel section, she hummed along to "Jingle Bell Rock" as it blared over the speakers.

Christmas was only seven days away. She couldn't believe it. Normally she would have been super-extra excited because she loved—emphasis on *loved*—Christmas. The cold weather, the decorations, the holiday songs, the presents, everything about it made her happy.

Nicole, however, was not a fan and teased her mercilessly each year. Halloween was more her style.

But this year Diane didn't care about Christmas at all.

The past six months had been hell, and she wanted the holidays over with. Now with this nonsense of Hilton's, she wasn't even looking forward to the New Year. She wasn't looking forward to anything.

Why wait until the last minute to tell her about this idiotic mayoral idea? She was his wife. Running for mayor was something you discussed and decided on as a couple. You didn't spring it the night before you announced it to the world. None of it made sense. She wanted to be angry—and a part of her was livid—but mostly she was just sad.

They had never had what you would call a passionate relationship, but at least the love was real. Now they were just two people living in the same house, never touching, never kissing, never laughing, never making love. Married in name only.

Diane picked up the *Lonely Planet Discover Caribbean Islands* travel guide. As she flipped through the pages, she imagined herself and Hilton lying on the beach, Hilton on his phone doing business while she was deep in a paperback, each lost in their own world. What would be the point? Same problems. Different location.

It had been almost a year since they had made love.

A whole year.

A whole damn year.

She looked up.

There he was again, skimming the shelves of the automotive section. Except this time she could see his face. It was quite a face. She ran her thumb across her bottom lip and imagined the tip of his tongue on hers. It sent goosebumps up her spine. She glanced at his hands, wondering how they would feel on her hips, caressing her skin. His breath on her neck as his fingers undid her bra. His hips pressed into hers. Her hands running down his chest—

Their eyes met.

He smiled at her.

She tried to smile back, but her lips refused to move. She might have put her hand to her cheek to see if she could feel her face, but she wasn't sure.

He knew. She could see it in his eyes. He knew.

The *Lonely Planet* guide slid from her hand. It hit the floor with a loud thud. She waited for every head in the store to turn and look at her. No one did.

Her body caved in on itself, and she snuck back down the aisle. Her face was warm, and she resisted the urge to run screaming out of the store. Poised, but with a mixture of excitement and embarrassment, she made her way to the front entrance.

Steps from the exit, she stopped.

Come on down...

She glanced left.

Come on down...

She glanced right.

...to Crazy Dick's Chicken Town...

It was the Crazy Dick's Chicken Town radio commercial. But where was it coming from?

She looked up. The bookstore's sound system. They were playing one of the local FM stations that ran the commercials like clockwork. Another reason she didn't listen to the radio.

She yanked the front door open and stumbled out onto the sidewalk, the jingle ringing in her head.

Come on down, come on down to Crazy Dick's Chicken Town...

She thought she was going to vomit.

Come on down, come on down...

5

WITH ONE HAND on the wheel and the other outside the window riding the air, Jackson cruised I-10 singing along to Billy Squier's "Christmas Is the Time to Say I Love You." He wasn't much for the holidays, and he wasn't much of a singer, but this year Christmas got to him in a way it hadn't in forever.

Lost in song, he swore he could taste sugar cookies and hot cocoa and feel the warmth of the fire from the fireplace against his back, and damned if he couldn't feel his mother's arms wrapped around him and her kisses on his forehead. For one fleeting second he remembered exactly how happy he'd been at Christmas when he was six years old. Just his mom, his dad, and him.

Then one day it all went tits up.

His sister was born. Deborah. He could still hear their voices in his head as if it were yesterday. Complete strangers approaching his mom and dad whenever they were out, fawning over his baby sister. *Isn't she just the cutest little thing?*

Jeez, it made him sick.

Suddenly the boy who could do no wrong—the apple of his mother's eye—could do no right. He had to be responsible and set an example. There were expectations to live up to. Christmas, along with everything else, was never the same again.

He roared up on a delivery truck hogging the center lane just as Nat King Cole began crooning "O Little Town of Bethlehem."

"Damn it." He slapped the dashboard. "I got places to go. People to see. I got a life to live."

He veered left and floored around the truck.

The glare from the morning sun hit the front windshield, blinding him. He grabbed his sunglasses from the passenger seat, slapped them on just in time to see a blue Fiat 500 dead ahead, moving like a turtle in the passing lane.

"Oh, shit." He slammed on the brakes and jerked the wheel to the right.

The tail end of the black '67 Camaro swung back and forth as it skidded into the middle lane, missing the front end of the delivery truck by inches.

He pulled the wheel to the left, righted the car, and power shifted from third to fifth. As he roared past the little blue toy, he yelled out the window, "Get a real car, asshole."

He shook his head and looked back over his shoulder at the carnage that almost was. Why the hell did people drive so damn slow in the fast lane? It pissed him off almost as much as somebody riding his tail. He rode with the anger for a minute and then let it go. Anger was an insidious poison. A poison he refused to swallow. He smiled. That felt better. He liked to smile. "Turn that frown upside down, mister," his mom used to say.

Cole's voice faded away, and the ringing intro of Chuck Berry's "Run Rudolph Run" came blaring out of the speakers. He had a soft spot for Mr. Johnny B. Goode. As far as Jackson was concerned, Chuck was the real King of Rock 'n' Roll, not that loser Elvis. The poser didn't even write his own songs.

He glanced down at the speedometer and realized he was closing in on ninety. I-10 ran from Houston, Texas, to Baton

Rouge, Louisiana, and there was little doubt the state troopers were lurking about like banditos, ready to pounce. He slid his foot off the gas and let the car ease on back down to seventy.

It would turn out bad for everyone involved if he got pulled over.

The hours passed. The sun moved up high in the sky, and he crossed over the Mississippi-Alabama state line.

He grew bored and replayed the events of the past few days over again in his mind. After a job it was his habit to study it from every angle, every nook and cranny to see any area in which he could improve.

Jackson was big on self-improvement.

He felt guilty about Monty. No, that wasn't true. He felt guilty about not feeling guilty. He didn't want to kill him, but what choice did he have? If he hadn't, well, it'd be a bullet in *his* head.

Why the dumb bastard thought he could get away with it, Jackson had no clue. Everybody in the Southeast knew you didn't steal from Fisher McAllister. Monty didn't even work for McAllister—his buddy Dwane Long did. But Dwane got shit-faced one Saturday night and, instead of making a delivery, drove his Chevy pickup into a Dairy Queen. Monty knew where Dwane kept his product and decided everybody would figure it went up in flames along with Dwane and his Chevy.

He was wrong.

Jackson tracked Monty down to his sister Ellie's place in Houston. It wasn't difficult; the dude wasn't the sharpest knife in the drawer. Hell, he practically invited Jackson to find him by using his debit card instead of cash for gas and not ditching his cell. Thank God for Le Deuce's dark web buddies or finding Monty would have been a lot harder.

With Monty's sister gone for the weekend, it was the perfect opportunity. The boy was so stoned he barely put up a fight. Jackson wished he would have. It bothered him to think someone could give up so easily. That they had so little life left in them it wasn't worth the effort.

Oh well, there wasn't much he could do about it now.

Dead is dead.

6

____

THAT'S WEIRD. Diane ended the call and slid her phone into her coat pocket. *Hilton's plane landed hours ago. Why isn't he answering?*

She poured herself some wine and, glass in hand, moved from the kitchen to the veranda. Leaves crunching under her feet, she walked across the yard and marveled at the lake—her beautiful, spectacular lake—sitting at the foot of their property. Above her, the vast sky was awash in red and orange as the sun bid the day adieu. She couldn't believe all this was hers. Growing up, she never would have imagined she would live in a million-dollar house with a lake in her backyard.

A gust of wind whisked past, and she savored the feel of the cool breeze against her skin and the smell of the crisp winter air. Hands down, October to December was her favorite of all the seasons. Problem was, it didn't last long enough. If only she could live in a place where it was like this year-round. That would be absolute heaven.

She closed her eyes.

And pictured Tight Slacks.

Her breath quickened. Try as she might, she couldn't put him out of her mind. It wasn't Tight Slacks himself who got under her skin. It was the *idea* of him, of being wanted, of having wild, crazy, no-strings-attached sex with a stranger. That's what intrigued her.

Because she'd never done that before.

Ever.

She wasn't the life of the party when she was young. Unlike her sister, Nicole, Diane had little time for boys and their frivolities. Instead, she kept her nose to the grindstone and her focus on college. Her life would not be a train wreck like Janice's.

Once she got to the University of Georgia, there were a few casual boyfriends but nobody she remembered with any sense of wistful longing, and when she took the plunge, she found the experience awkward, unfulfilling, and overrated.

Then she met Noah. He was a skinny, blond boy from California with a rambunctious smile, a wicked sense of humor, and kisses that to this day got her all hot and bothered if she dared to think about them. Right from the get-go he seemed to know where all her hot spots were and how to work her into a frenzy. And he did it with such ease.

Now she knew what all the fuss was about.

But they didn't even make it a year. It was one of those moments in life she cherished without regret. She adored Noah but never loved him. Maybe it was because for all his charm, she knew deep down he wouldn't be there when she needed him most. Someone having her back was far more important than all the magical kisses.

Hilton was different. He didn't set the world on fire, but he also didn't burn it down. He protected her, and she protected him.

What changed? She wished she knew. Another woman? That was ridiculous. Richard's death? They were drifting apart well before he died. Because they couldn't have a baby?

She let out a sigh.

Thirteen years was a long time, and she hadn't been on the pill in ages. She had seen a fertility specialist, but all the tests came back normal. According to her doctor, there was no reason she couldn't conceive. Multiple times she'd tried to talk to Hilton about it, but he would shut down and flat out refused to have his sperm checked. After a while she realized the idea that he might be defective was too much for him to bear, but what stuck in her craw was that he was the one always going on about having a "successor."

Now that she was a hair's breadth away from thirty-seven—two-and-a-half weeks, to be exact—she wasn't sure she wanted to be a mother anymore. She couldn't imagine having a baby at forty, not with a man whose mind always seemed a million miles away.

In the end, did it matter *why* Hilton had pulled away? Did it matter why he didn't include her in something as important as running for mayor? Did it matter why their marriage was falling apart?

No, all that mattered was that it hurt, and it hurt like hell.

Her phone pinged.

Hilton?

She yanked it out of her coat pocket.

Nicole.

She swiped on the notification, and the text opened: *What are you up to?*

Diane's back stiffened. Why couldn't she just call? She knew Diane hated texting. She tapped on Nicole's contact.

A moment later her sister answered. "You hate texting."

"I really do," Diane said.

"Sorry. What are you doing?"

"Right now I'm enjoying this beautiful sunset with a glass of wine."

"Where's Mister Chicken?"

"You mean Hilton?"

"Yes, Hilton. The chicken miser."

"In Albuquerque," Diane said.

"Business?"

"Always."

"Uh-huh."

"What does that mean?"

"It means uh-huh. If he's gone, then you're free, right?"

"What exactly are we talking about?"

"Well, my band is playing tonight at The Wicked Hand—"

"The Wicked Hand? Sounds enchanting."

"It's a club. It's great, actually. Anyway, I was hoping you might want to come out and see the show."

"It's been a long day."

"Diane, come on. It'd mean a lot to me. You've been promising for years."

"I know. I know."

"It'll be fun. I promise. You won't regret it."

Did she want to spend another night by herself? Maybe she needed a change. What would it hurt? "Okay, you win. I'll be there."

"Sweet. I'll text you the directions later." *Click*.

Diane hated that. No "Goodbye," just *click*. Her sister needed to learn some manners.

She eyed her phone. Where was her husband, and what kind of business did he have in Albuquerque anyway, a week before Christmas?

Could there be someone else?

It was the only thing that made sense and yet made no sense. This was stupid. Hilton was the least sexual man she knew.

Still the question hung in the air. Was he having an affair?

Okay, she reasoned, if he was, who was the mystery woman? She couldn't think of anyone in their circle who'd ever shown the slightest bit of interest in Hilton. Of course, it didn't have to be someone she knew. Many people worked for him, and you could order an affair on your phone the same way you ordered pizza these days.

She tapped on Hilton's contact and typed: *Where are you? Are you at the hotel?*

Instead of hitting send, she read it again. And again. Then she backspaced it to oblivion.

Screw him. If Hilton didn't want to talk to her, then she didn't want to talk to him. She put her phone back in her coat pocket and finished her wine as she watched the darkness descend over the lake.

"SON OF A BITCH." Hilton stared at the phone lying at the bottom of the toilet bowl like it was a two-headed calf.

Without batting an eye, he yanked it out of the water, grabbed some toilet paper, and furiously wiped it off. Glancing down, he realized he hadn't flushed.

He let out a screech and tossed the phone up in the air like it had Ebola. It hit the side of the stall, bounced off, and swan-dived to the floor.

"Son of a bitch!" he reiterated louder, just in case there was somebody in the airport men's room who didn't hear him the first time.

Pants at his ankles, his little buddy swinging in the wind, he stared at the chunk of gray-and-black aluminum lying at his feet.

He pulled his pants up, got some more toilet paper, bent down, and with extreme care picked up the phone. The impact had shattered the screen beyond recognition.

"Perfect," he said, laughing. "Absolutely perfect."

He grabbed his backpack off the stall door and stepped out into the crowded bathroom. Avoiding eye contact, he walked over to the sink and sat the broken phone on the counter. He lathered up his hands and went to work, washing them like they were on fire. Diane always made fun of his focus on good hygiene, called him a germophobe.

Germophobe, my butt. Doesn't she watch the news? Doesn't she understand the risks? We are all just one germ away from death. One germ.

Satisfied his hands were pristine, he tossed the phone in the sink, ran it under scalding water, and berated himself for being a complete idiot. He knew better than to answer the phone when he was going to the bathroom. And to top it off, it was a damn spam call.

He glanced to his right and caught the man at the sink beside him, eyes wide, staring at Hilton as he washed the phone. Hilton gave him a nod and smiled. The man turned and moved to another sink. Hilton shrugged. *Hey, pal, accidents happen.* He wrapped the phone in paper towels and tossed it in his backpack.

Frustrated, more with Diane than the phone, he walked out of the bathroom and merged with the crowd moving through the Albuquerque International Sunport concourse.

He'd spent the entire flight trying not to think about his wife's utter indifference to his political career, but the anger had burrowed in deep. What the heck was her problem? The woman he married wouldn't have gotten so bent out of shape over this. She used to be fun. She used to take chances.

Okay, maybe, just maybe, she had a point.

He shouldn't have told her the night before the interview with Brenda, but if he'd told her a few months ago, she would have done everything she could to talk him out of it. He just couldn't win with her.

Screw it. She'd come around.

Or not.

It didn't matter. Peggy would be here in a moment.

The memory of their first kiss engulfed him so fast he about came to a complete stop. He'd always believed Diane was a good kisser, but Peggy—*oh boy, Peggy*—she was in a different league alto-gether. She kissed almost like she'd invented it. The night it happened was a shock, but it shouldn't have been. Everything had been leading up to it. He had just been too blind to see.

His heart leapt when he spotted her waiting near the baggage claim, and he picked up the pace. Engrossed in her phone, she didn't notice him, but she must have felt his eyes on her because she looked up, caught his gaze, and broke out in a dazzling smile.

Right then he understood why he hadn't told Diane he was running for mayor earlier. Because then she'd find out about Peggy—what choice would he have? He'd have to introduce her to his campaign manager—and the moment she saw them together, Diane would know. She'd know everything.

It'd be as clear as the nose on his face.

8

DIANE TOOK a sip of her drink as she watched Nicole tune up a battered black-and-red guitar. It looked a bit like the one that weird little man in AC/DC played, but what did Diane know. John Coltrane and Mozart were more her speed.

Nicole glanced up. "What's that?"

Diane looked at her glass. "It's supposed to be a Manhattan."

"Can I?"

"Sure." Diane handed her the glass.

Nicole took a sip and gave it back. "Tastes like Long Island Iced Tea. Good God, Ian can't even make a Manhattan."

"It's not half bad."

"Yeah, but he's been a bartender for years, and he's from New York. He should know how to make a Manhattan."

"So what time does all the rockin' start?"

Nicole hit a chord on the guitar.

BBBBOOOOMMMMMM!

Everything in the ramshackle dressing room, including the ratty old couch Diane was sitting on, shook. It surprised her the green concrete walls with all the graffiti and handbills didn't crumble to the ground.

Nicole ran her fingers along the neck of the guitar. Impressed, Diane nodded along. Her sister usually got loud and crazy, but this had a nice jazzy feel. Of course, it didn't last long. She took off, and the guitar screamed. Diane watched her hands moving at lightning speed around the neck. She had to hand it to her, the girl could play.

Nicole clicked a foot pedal and went into overdrive.

Diane rolled her eyes. Her sister was showing off again. "Enough, already," she shouted, her fingers in her ears.

"What?" Nicole looked up.

"All that noise."

"It's not noise," Nicole shouted. The guitar screeched and belched its last notes and whimpered to a stop. She flashed a Cheshire cat grin. "Fuddy-duddy."

Diane stuck her tongue out.

Nicole laughed, took her guitar off, and sat it on a stand. Then she grabbed the cigarette smoldering in the ashtray atop the little amp beside her.

"Thought you quit?" Diane said.

"Me too."

Diane looked at the amp. "I'm surprised that tiny thing can get so loud."

"Yeah, it's crazy. Twenty years ago it would have been up to my waist."

"What is that?" Diane pointed to the foot pedal.

"A wah-wah."

"A what?"

"A wah-wah pedal. Remember *Shaft*? The theme song? Isaac Hayes?"

"Uh, maybe."

"Wacka wacka wacka." She paused. "You have no idea what I'm talking about, do you?"

"Nope."

Nicole picked up a half-empty beer bottle from the floor,

finished it, and placed her skinny butt on the rickety sofa table behind her. Diane waited for it to crash to the floor, taking Nicole with it.

Diane hadn't seen her sister in ages and couldn't get over how beautiful she was. Five foot three, with dirty blond hair, piercing blue eyes, a mischievous grin, and legs up to her neck, Nicole was a head turner. Even with her numerous tattoos, she still had a cheerleader vibe going on. And yet, as far as Diane could tell, Nicole's looks had never brought her happiness.

"Nice brunch look you got going on there," Nicole said.

"Thanks and screw you too."

"I'm just saying that skirt, boots, silk blouse, and jacket are more business lunch than The Wicked Hand."

"So you want me to leave?"

"No. I'm not saying you look bad. I mean, come on, you look great, but you do kinda stand out like a sore thumb. Do you even own a pair of jeans? Or any T-shirts?"

"Do you know how long it's been since I've been in a club?"

"Years?"

"Exactly."

"You should get out more."

"I should." A long pause and then, "Did you hear Hilton's running for mayor?"

"What?"

"Oh, get this. He wants to be president."

"President? Of what?"

"The United States."

Nicole burst out laughing.

"Yeah, you believe that? Last night, out of the blue, he tells me he's running for mayor and that he's going to announce it today on Brenda Clarksdale's show. I thought he was joking, but he wasn't."

"What did you do?"

"Nothing. I was in shock. Honestly, I'm still angry but, I don't know, maybe I'm just overreacting. You think I'm overreacting?"

"Hell, no. I'd be totally pissed. Like extremely pissed. I mean, you guys are married. He can't just run for mayor without talking it over with you first. If Timothy had done that, I'd punch him in the balls."

Diane nodded like she agreed but didn't see herself ever punching Hilton in the balls. She wanted to know who Timothy was but let it go. Nicole had so many boyfriends it was hard to keep track.

Diane nursed her drink as Nicole stared off into space. Sometimes her sister would just zone out in the middle of a conversation. Diane always found it odd.

"So how's the book coming?" Nicole asked.

"Book?"

"Your new novel?"

"You mean the one I've been working on for years? Probably be a bestseller if I'd put my keister in the chair and actually did some writing."

"I'm sure it would be a bestseller. You're really good."

"From your lips to God's ears."

Her *new* novel was the last thing Diane wanted to think about. When her first one received rejection after rejection, she went into a deep depression and didn't write a word for years. Her new novel —all thirty-two thousand words of it—was her hanging on to her dream by her fingernails.

"I checked on Janice today," Nicole said.

Diane peered at her sister over the rim of her glass.

"Aren't you going to ask me how she's doing?"

"Nope."

"She's our mother."

"Nana is...was...our mother."

"True, but—"

"Nana was our mother," Diane said.

"I can't just sit around and watch her die."

"Isn't she in remission?"

"Yeah, but she needs her meds. I can't pay for them. I don't have the money." Nicole grabbed her guitar and strummed a few chords, her bottom lip sticking out like she was three years old.

Diane wanted to say, "She's never going to love you," but what would be the point? Nicole wasn't going to give up on the woman.

The door creaked open, and Diane glanced up. A gangly man with short bleached-blond hair and tattoo sleeves waltzed in and plopped down on the couch beside her.

He leaned back, spread his legs, and put his boat-like hands behind his head. "Hunny bunny, we are on in ten."

"Timothy, you haven't met my sister, Diane, yet, have you?"

"Nope"

"Diane, this is Timothy. He's my bass player."

He looked at her and whispered, "She's my guitar picker."

Diane laughed.

He gave them each a quizzical look. "You girls are sisters?"

"Hard to believe, but yes, we're related," Diane said. "Although, I've always suspected she might have a different dad."

Nicole glared at her, and she immediately regretted the comment. "You know I'm just kidding."

Nicole turned to Timothy. "Babe, where are Max and Rita?"

"Last I saw, they were outside by the van with Gary doing shots."

"Great." Nicole looked down and strummed her guitar.

Timothy pulled a small ziplock baggie out of his pocket and rolled a joint. Diane watched him in amusement. She'd never understood the appeal of drugs. Alcohol, yes. Drugs, no.

He held it up, eyes full of pride, and looked at her as if to say, "Wanna toke?"

Diane shook her head.

"Can't you wait until after we play?" Nicole said. "You know it chills you out too much."

"Hunny bunny?"

"You know it does."

"But?"

Nicole glared at him.

Diane pitied the poor boy. She'd been on the receiving end of that look plenty of times.

Timothy put everything back in the baggie.

Diane stood up, smoothed out her purple blouse, and grabbed her Coach purse and drink. "Restroom?"

"Down the hall, on the right," Nicole replied.

"I'll let you guys do whatever it is you do." She walked out of the dressing room, ready for this night to be over so she could get back home, crawl into bed, and enjoy a good book.

She was too old for this.

9

———

"Baby?" Nicole purred as she eased down on the couch next to Timothy.

Hunched over his bass guitar, hands moving up and down the fretboard, he glanced up.

"Does all *this* look like it belongs to a 'girl'?" She ran her hands down her curvy body.

"No, but what the hell?"

"You called me and Diane 'girls' earlier, and I just wanted to remind you I'm not a girl, okay?"

"Sorry, my bad."

She snuggled close. "Think you could do me a favor?"

"Depends." He continued to practice.

She put one hand on his thigh and kissed his neck. "Depends on what?"

"What it is," he replied without looking at her.

"My sister needs to get laid." She ran her hand down his chest and stopped when she got within inches of his crotch. She loved teasing him like this, and she knew he loved it too. He was all about being dominated.

"Okay. You want me to—"

"No, dummy. Not you. I was just thinking that after the show, maybe you could introduce her to one of your buddies."

"Hunny bunny, have you seen my buddies?"

"She's in a bad way right now," she whispered in his ear. "She needs something wild, something crazy."

"Your sister seems a little uptight."

"A little?"

"A lot. She ain't gonna go for anybody I know."

He was right, but it was worth a try. She couldn't remember the last time Diane had seemed happy. Not that she would ever own up to it. She wasn't one to let anybody get too close, even her own sister, but Nicole could see it in her eyes. And she knew exactly who was causing her pain.

"Her husband's been a real dick lately. She's lonely."

"She's married?"

"You know Crazy Dick's Chicken Town?"

"Ooh, that's some good chicken."

"Her husband, Hilton, owns it."

"For real?" He stopped playing. "You think after the show we could swing by and get some free chicken?"

"Timothy. Baby." She put a hand on each cheek and turned his face toward hers. "Do you ever think about anything else but food?"

"Yeah, sure. Sometimes. Lately, I've been reading about masonic rituals."

She held his face in her hands and looked him in the eyes. *Who's flying your plane, babe?* She had no clue why she was wasting her time with him. Probably because he was a damn good bass player, and boy, are those hard to find. Plus, he wasn't too bad in bed and didn't give her a lot of lip. She wasn't big on lip, and he was funny as hell.

"Find Diane somebody to fuck tonight. Okay?"

"Sure thing."

She pulled his face to hers and kissed him on the lips. "Good boy."

When he stood up, she slapped him on the ass. He looked back at her, a twinkle in his eye. She knew what he liked.

"Maybe later...if you do a good show, I'll get out my whip," she added with a wink.

He grinned, all teeth, and leaned the bass against the couch. Then his expression turned serious. "She's a Capricorn, right?"

"Um, maybe?"

"You don't know your own sister's sign? Come on, babe."

"Hey, I don't know your sign."

"Cancer. When's her birthday?"

"December."

"The date?"

He looked at her like she had to be the dumbest person he'd ever met. It sent her blood boiling. "I'm not into all that shit, remember?"

He shook his head and headed toward the door.

"I know it's after Christmas 'cause she always hated that," Nicole said.

"Okay. Okay. That's good. She seemed like a Capricorn." He stopped and thought for a second.

"What does it matter?"

"You told me to find her somebody. Hunny bunny, I'm trying to do my job." He threw his hands up. "Jeez."

She grabbed another cigarette and watched him storm out the door. Yep, good bass players were *really* hard to find.

10

J ACKSON POURED a line of cocaine out on the dashboard of his Camaro with all the finesse he could muster, rolled up a dollar bill, and snorted the white powder up his nose.

Riding the rush, he closed his eyes, shook his head, and clenched his shoulders.

"Whoa..." He opened his eyes. A guy could get addicted to this stuff.

After a few moments, he reached behind the passenger seat and pulled out a little black travel bag. He took out a toothbrush and a tube of toothpaste and brushed his teeth.

Finished, he reached over and grabbed the water bottle lying in front of the passenger seat and rinsed his mouth out. He spit the water out the window, closed it, climbed out of the car, brushed the potato chip crumbs off of his black button-down, and strolled across the parking lot. Most of the parking lot lights were out, and he nearly plowed face first into a Chevy van.

Ian needed to get on the ball. The place was turning into a dump.

After disposing of the gun in Alabama, he'd decided he needed a pit stop before his rendezvous with Le Deuce. He might be exhausted, but he was too damn young to call it a night.

Le Deuce wouldn't mind waiting. And even if he did—well, too bad. It wasn't his fault the old man didn't have a life.

Normally Jackson would invite him to come on down, but lately Le Deuce had become a real whiney son of a bitch, always going on about the "lying, thieving government," the "goddamn Federal Reserve," and the "end of the world."

Tonight there would be no political diatribes. He just wanted to hang for a while, down a few beers, play some pool, and, if he got lucky—which he almost always did—get a blow job in the parking lot.

If the universe provided more, so much the better.

And if it *was* the end of the world, Jackson was going to party like it was 1999.

11

—————

Victor Le Deuce thanked God, the Son, and the Holy Ghost for the good piss he was enjoying. Lately they were few and far between. According to his urologist, a sniveling little man Le Deuce despised, his prostate was enlarging. At least that's what he'd said after he shoved his finger up Le Deuce's ass. "Your prostate, it is *huge*. Take zis Flomax."

His doc didn't speak in broken German, but since Le Deuce pictured him as a Nazi, complete with monocle, black boots, and a Luger pistol, that's how he remembered it.

He knew the little prick was full of shit, probably just wanted to get him hooked on some high-priced sugar pills. Fuckers were all about the money.

Of course the junk was going to take a hit. He was getting old. But he still had his moments, like right this second, where he pissed like a racehorse.

Ah, the little things.

He zipped up his fly and walked out of the woods. Rubbing his hands together, he cut across the deserted gravel lot and headed for the dirty green Volvo parked behind an old, dilapidated barn.

He pulled his trench coat tighter and picked up the pace.

Christ on a bike, it was getting cold. Christmas was around the corner, but he didn't give a rat's ass. His mother had bit the dust twenty-something odd years ago, and if he had any other family around, he didn't know about them.

For Le Deuce, Christmas was just one more day to get through. One more day to bide his time until his ship came in. Or sailed. Or sank. Or whatever.

One more day until he could tell his captain and the rest of the force to shove it where the sun don't shine. Twenty-four years of being a detective was enough.

He climbed into the car and planted his rather sizable butt in the driver's seat, fired up the engine, cranked the heat, and checked the time: 10:22 p.m. He still had time to swing by Sophie's Donut Hole, get a chocolate iced glazed with sprinkles, a hot cup of joe, and flirt with Monica.

Damn, she was hot for a grandmother. Actually, for a grandmother, she was smokin' hot. His trousers tightened in the crotch. Sure, she had a few extra pounds on her and she smelled like a chimney, and her right eye was a little bigger than her left one, but he knew she could rock his cock. The more he pictured her in his mind, the hotter it got in the car.

He was tempted to whip it out right here and rub one out. Who would know? He was in the middle of nowhere, and there wasn't a soul for miles. Why drive all that way just to get worked up when he could work it out now?

He did all the flirting, anyway. Monica only took his cash and listened to his stories. Laughing, and smiling, and slapping him on the arm. "*Le Deuce*"—nobody called him by his first name—"*Le Deuce, yousocrazy.*"

He had to give it to her. The lady worked hard for her tips.

Women. Screw 'em. At least his hand didn't yak all the time and drain his bank account. At least it didn't whine when he came too quickly. At least it couldn't leave him for another man.

The bitch would be damn lucky to have him.

He decided to skip Sophie's Donut Hole. He needed to lose weight. Once his ship came in, he'd be rolling in the dough, and with the prime pussy he'd be getting, it might not be a bad idea to get his body into shape. Right now, rubbing one out left him breathless. Imagine if he had to make love to a woman?

No more donuts. Time to invest in the new, improved Victor Le Deuce.

He cued up Hank Williams's "You Win Again" on his phone and grabbed a beat-up paperback copy of *The Hound of the Baskervilles* off of the floorboard. He pulled out the McDonald's receipt he'd used as a bookmark and began to read.

Hopefully Jackson would be here soon enough. But if not? That was okay too, because Le Deuce was used to waiting. He'd spent his whole life waiting. Why should tonight be any exception?

12

DIANE COULDN'T BELIEVE her eyes or her ears. Was that her baby sister up on stage?

Planted in one spot—legs apart, guitar held like a weapon, her blond hair hung over her face—Nicole wasn't bouncing around pretending to be a rock star, she was pounding out the music like it was life or death.

On the other side of the stage, Timothy grinned as he swung the bass around. Diane thought he looked like a big goofball in his bright red T-shirt and purple pants and yellow sneakers.

Between the two of them, a shirtless, tattooed bundle of energy roamed the stage, belting out the vocals, working the crowd into a frenzy.

At the back of the stage, hidden behind a massive drum set, a blasé brunette pounded out the beat like she was a human drum machine.

This wasn't Diane's type of music, but she knew it was good. She could feel it, and so could the rest of the crowd. Seated by herself at a table in a dark corner, she was watching their reaction as much as she was watching the band. The crowd was much larger than she'd expected. Sixty people, at least, and they were going crazy.

She considered moving up closer to the stage, but the thought of being sandwiched between all those hot, sweaty bodies made her stomach turn. She wasn't claustrophobic, but she was big on personal space. Some of these people she could smell a mile away. Did everybody in here smoke? And did they ever take the trash out? Something must have died in here.

She pulled her phone out of her purse. Not a word from Hilton. Where was he? She had a good mind to text him and tell him to kiss her ass. Bet he'd call her back then.

Eyeing her empty glass, she saw two possibilities—call it a night after Nicole finished and head home to her big empty house, or get other drink, relax, and enjoy the evening. But what if she got too drunk to drive home? Getting pulled over by the police was one of her biggest fears, that and being buried alive. She'd never even gotten a speeding ticket. The obvious thought danced through her head.

Nicole could drive her home.

Yes, she could.

She got up and stumbled over to the bar. The Manhattan, along with the glass of wine from earlier, was already having an effect. She put her elbows on the counter and leaned forward, resting her chin on her hands. She smiled and waited for the bartender—*didn't Nicole say his name was Ian?*—at the opposite end of the bar to notice her. Since he was flirting with some pretty young thing, Diane figured it would be a while. *Don't mind me, Ian, I'm almost forty. Take your time.*

She turned back to watch the band. After a couple of minutes, she looked back. Was Ian's pretty young thing gone yet? She was, but now a man was banging his hand on the bar top.

Tight Slacks?

Ian turned around, let out a huge laugh, and made a beeline for the man. When they met, each leaned across the counter and vigorously shook hands. They tried to hug, but the gulf between them was too wide.

Diane strained to get a better look and felt a wisp of disappointment when she realized he wasn't the man from the bookstore. Oh, well, it was probably for the best. If he had been Tight Slacks, there's no telling where this night might have ended. Hoping to catch Ian's eye, she stood up straight and raised her hand like a kid in school who needed to go to the bathroom. It was pointless. They were too deep into their love fest.

"Excuse me! Excuse me!" she said as she made her way down the bar.

Ian and the man looked over at her.

"Can I get a drink? I've been waiting down here for a while."

"Oh, I'm sorry. I didn't see you." The bartender headed toward her.

"Ian, you're snoozing on the job," the man said. "How on earth could you not notice a beautiful woman like this?"

She fought back a smile. She couldn't remember the last time someone had called her beautiful. "Gin and tonic, please."

"Coming right up." Ian nodded and got to work.

She took a seat on one of the barstools, positioning herself toward the stage so she could watch Nicole. Out of the corner of her eye, she gave the man the once-over. He was tall, dressed in black with short dark hair and broad shoulders. His nose was a little bent, and his jaw square. Not Tight Slacks, but damn close.

Behind her, Ian sat the drink down. "Here you go."

Before she could reach in her purse, the man laid a twenty down on the bar and said to Ian, "I got this one. And how about a bottle of Miller High Life?"

Diane took a sip. "Thank you."

The man smiled at Diane and said, "Hey, it's Christmas, right?"

Ian grabbed the bill, giving the man a quick wink as he walked back to the register. The man nodded and smiled.

Diane caught the exchange and raised an eyebrow. *Not so fast, mister.*

She turned and watched the band. They were pulling out all the stops.

BOOM. The symbols crashed, and the guitars landed on a giant chord.

Diane put her fingers in her ears.

BOOM. Another hit.

BOOM. And another.

Each hit grew further and further apart until with a loud crescendo the music staggered to a halt.

And sixty plus people with their hands in the air roared.

"Hey, motherfuckers, we're The 8 Ballers. Thanks. And follow us on Facebook and Twitter and all the other social crap, all right? On second thought, get off your damn phones and get out and live life. Peace," the singer said as the house lights came on.

Nicole and Timothy, both drenched in sweat, leaned their guitars against their amps and shuffled, half-dazed, off the stage. The singer and the drummer followed.

Within seconds, two beefy guys were onstage breaking down the drum kit and putting the guitars in their cases.

Diane beamed from ear to ear. She was so proud of her little sister. Maybe things were finally going right for her. She could only hope.

"Here by yourself?" the man asked.

"Huh?" Diane glanced over her right shoulder.

"Are you here by yourself?" he repeated louder.

"No."

"So where's your boyfriend?"

Diane held up her hand and showed him her wedding ring.

"Ah, I see. When he comes back, will he kick my ass?"

Diane laughed so hard she almost choked on her drink. "No, no, I can't picture that happening."

"What's so funny?"

"You haven't met my husband."

He smiled. Their eyes met and held each other for a few seconds longer than they should have.

Diane glanced back at the stage. "The guitar player. She's my sister."

"She's damn good." He took a seat on the barstool next to her. "I'm Jackson."

She glanced over at him, gave him a slight smile. "Diane, and she is amazing."

"The bass player, we go way back."

"Timothy?"

"Afghanistan."

"He was in the military?"

"Marines."

"Timothy was a Marine?"

Without looking at her, he leaned close and said, "Not was. Is. And would you believe it? The kid was good at it."

Diane could feel her heart beating a little faster. It had been a long time since she had flirted with anyone. It wouldn't go anywhere. How could it? Soon one of these young college girls would catch his eye and he'd be off like a kid in a candy store, but for now it was invigorating.

"So where is your girlfriend?" The words fumbled out of her mouth.

"Tonight, I am solo."

"Tonight? So last night you weren't?" She frowned.

"No, last night I was solo too."

"But not for long, huh?"

"What makes you think that?"

"Please."

"Smooth?"

Diane shook her head. "*Smooth* would not be the word I would use."

"You don't strike me as a woman who hangs out in bars."

"No?"

"No."

"And why not? What gave me away?"

"Well, let's see." He swiveled around on the stool so that he was facing her.

"Is that a good thing? That I don't hang out in bars?" She felt light-headed. She placed the back of her hand on her forehead. Was she sweating? No. No sweat.

"Yes," he said, smiling.

"But you hang out in bars."

"Sometimes. Wait...let me clarify. Not bars. This bar. I don't hang out in bars, I hang out in *this* bar. Not often, but I do drop in from time to time."

"Why? So you can pick up strange women?"

"What? Me? Madam, you have the wrong impression," he protested in a mock French accent.

Diane brushed her hand against his knee. "No, I think I have the right impression."

Jackson laughed. Confident and relaxed.

She didn't get it. He wasn't that good-looking, but something about the tone of his voice and the way he moved and the way he smelled—he didn't have that musky scent most men had—made her want to rip his clothes off and—

I'd better get ahold of myself. This is the alcohol talking, isn't it?

"So what gave me away?" she asked again as she gazed into his eyes.

He leaned in closer and whispered, "Okay, for starters—"

"Hello. What's going on here?" A loud voice cut through the din.

Diane looked up to see Nicole and Timothy walking toward them. "Oh, hey." She could feel her face getting flush.

"Jackson?" Timothy said. "How did you know we were playing tonight?"

"I didn't. I dropped by for a drink and to shoot the shit with Ian."

Jackson stood and gave him a big bear hug. He was about two feet shorter and his face landed in Timothy's chest.

"Wow. It's been a long time," Timothy said as he sat down on the stool next to him.

"Damn, son, you guys sound good. Your girl there, she has some chops."

Nicole walked over to Diane, leaned against the bar, and quietly asked, "What are you doing?"

"Nothing." Diane giggled.

"Did you just giggle?"

Diane put her hand over her mouth. "Maybe. I need to go to the bathroom. You?"

"I'm good."

"I think you need to go." Diane stood up.

Nicole stared at her.

"Please?"

"Hey, boys. Oh, boys," Nicole said.

Jackson and Timothy, oblivious to the world, looked up.

"We'll be right back."

13

———

JACKSON WATCHED Diane and Nicole wade into the crowd. It was clear Diane was interested in him, but he wasn't sure if he wanted to pursue it. Sure, she was sexy as all get out, and just his type—long brown hair, big brown eyes, not too tall and with curves in all the sweet places. She looked like a real woman, not some photoshopped Barbie doll.

But he'd always had a disdain for sleeping with married women. He didn't enjoy playing in another man's sandbox.

On the other hand—and there was always the other hand—he could see she needed help. The desperation he heard in her laugh, the sadness in her eyes, and the touch of her hand on his knee were clear signs she was lonely.

Yes, he could provide sex. Any man in this room could do that. But she was looking for something more, and he didn't know if he had the time or the inclination. That was why he liked college girls. A few drinks, a line of coke, and boom—down on their knees in the parking lot. He gets off, and they get lost.

Easy peasy.

Dollars to donuts, she had never done this before. Had never allowed herself to be so vulnerable. He couldn't believe it, but he felt protective. Odds were she was taking *someone* home tonight. Better him than one of these wolves.

He took a swig of beer, closed his eyes, and relaxed his mind. Shut out all the surrounding noise. Timed his breathing.

And it came to him. Like a gift.

Maybe, just maybe, he could open the door for her. If this was the path that she wanted to take, at least he would show her the respect that she deserved. At least in the morning she wouldn't feel used or degraded. Unless *that* was what she wanted. Jackson always aimed to please.

He was so excited he almost jumped off the barstool and screamed to the heavens. He had a mission. Tonight could be a teachable moment.

He turned to Timothy and with a twinkle in his eye said, "So tell me about Diane."

14

"WHAT AM I DOING?" Diane stopped and spun around so fast Nicole and two other people almost ran into her.

Nicole grabbed her by the arm and pulled her to a corner. "I don't know. You tell me. I can tell you what it looks like."

"You were fantastic tonight, by the way."

Nicole broke out in a wide grin.

"Do you know this guy Jackson?" Diane asked.

"No, I've never met him before—"

"He was in the Marines with your boyfriend."

"I wouldn't know. Timothy doesn't say much about that."

"Jackson's interesting. Don't you think?"

Nicole took a step back and shook her finger. "You naughty girl. You're thinking impure thoughts, aren't you?"

She grinned. "Okay...yes. Is that wrong?"

"You are the most unhappily married woman I know."

"I'm probably the only married woman you know."

"Not true, a lot of my clients are married."

"Okay, but is it wrong?"

"Technically? Sure. But where is Hilton right now?"

"New Mexico. Albuquerque."

"Doing what?"

"Business."

"Yeah, I'll bet. Call him." Nicole shuffled from foot to foot. "You mind? I need to—"

"I have been calling."

"And?"

"No answer."

"Is it wrong? I don't know. Is it wrong your husband doesn't seem to want you anymore? Is it wrong he doesn't think enough of you to involve you in a major decision, like running for mayor? Sweetheart, the clock is ticking. Seize the moment. Or not. I don't care. I have to pee."

"I thought you didn't have to go."

"Well, I do now."

"Then go." She stepped out of the way so Nicole could get to the bathroom.

"Call him. Call him one last time. Give him one more chance."

Diane tapped her foot and tugged on her earlobe. Getting her sister's permission, or lack of it, shouldn't change how she felt. But it did.

"Call him."

Diane pulled out her cell phone and tapped on Hilton's contact. Put it on speaker. It rang and rang and rang and then, "You've reached the voicemail of Hilton Hancock. At the tone—" She ended the call.

"There you go," Nicole said.

"Why is it so easy for you?"

"What are you talking about?"

"It's always been easy for you." Diane twirled a rogue strand of hair.

"Easy? To do what?"

"Men."

"What about men?"

"Nicole, men are drawn to you, like moths to the flame."

"Seriously? Moths to the flame? Am I a femme fatale or something?"

"You're beautiful," Diane said. "And you know it."

"So are you."

"Don't, okay? Just don't."

"Look, if I believed Hilton really loved you—like, really, truly loved you—then I'd say go home and forget about this, but I know that's a crock of shit. Hilton only cares about himself. How long have you two been living in a dead bedroom?"

"A what?"

"You know, a dead bedroom."

"What are you talking about?"

"Technically, a dead bedroom is when a couple has sex less than six times a year. When's the last time you guys...?"

Diane didn't want to tell her. It was embarrassing.

"Exactly. You deserve a good lay for that mayor stunt alone. And it's not what he's doing in New Mexico, it's who he's doing in New Mexico. Now, if you don't mind..." Nicole charged into the bathroom.

Her sister had a point. Hilton was selfish. And she still couldn't shake the feeling he was having an affair. For all she knew, he was with another woman right now. Holding her. Kissing her. Loving her.

She blew the wisp of hair out of her face, and a slight smile crossed her lips. What could one little fling hurt? In the scheme of things, it was just sex, right?

Not that it would even get that far.

15

DIANE PRIED HER EYES OPEN. A bit of light poured in. It felt like little shards of glass tearing into her pupils. She flinched, closed them, and tried to focus. The last thing she remembered was—

"Ahh, sleeping beauty awakens."

She tilted her head to the side, gave Jackson a lopsided smile, and shook her index finger at him.

He shook his finger back at her. "You dozed off there for a few minutes. Don't drink much, do you?"

She tried to shake her head, but it was too heavy, so she rested her chin on her chest. "Just a glass of wine now and then." She thought on it for a moment and then added, "I read on Bookface that a glass of red wine is as good as exercising."

"Well, I'll be damned. I had no idea." Jackson turned off the ignition switch and slipped his car keys into his pocket. "Bookface, huh? I'll have to check that out."

"You know what I mean."

He grinned.

"Are you laughing at me?"

"No, I'm smiling at you."

Diane stuck out her tongue at him.

"Careful, now," he said.

The slow death rattle of the Camaro cross-faded into the quiet musical hum of crickets singing in the distance. Above it, all Diane could hear was the blood racing through her veins. It felt late. Very, very late. How long had she been out? Why was she in his car?

"Where are we?" She swallowed hard. Her mouth was so dry her tongue stuck to the roof.

"Your house. Your sister asked me to drive you home. Remember?"

Diane glanced out the passenger-side window, turning her head right to left in a sweeping motion as she did. "My car?"

"Back at the bar."

Diane tried to replay the evening over in her mind. She remembered coming back from the bathroom. Jackson bought a round of drinks. Everybody got pretty silly, especially Nicole. Jackson made Diane laugh. And laugh. And laugh. She remembered him teaching her how to play pool. As he strutted around the table, she marveled at the grace with which he moved, and she knew she had to be careful. For the first time in a long time, she really wanted to get—

"I need some air." Diane grabbed the door handle and pushed the passenger door open. She fell out onto the driveway, throwing her palms out front to keep from landing on her face. "Shit."

She hung her head and took a deep breath. Tossing her cookies in front of Jackson would not be too smooth.

"Diane?"

She glanced over to see him kneeling beside her, an impish grin on his face.

"You're not going to puke on me, are you?"

"Now you *are* laughing at me." She blew her hair away from her face.

"Come on." He held his hand out.

She grabbed it and let him help her to her feet.

"I feel like such an idiot," she said, brushing the dirt from the driveway off of her hands.

Jackson leaned against the Camaro, crossed his arms, and said, "You know where this is headed, don't you?"

"Maybe." Diane shook her head. "Maybe not." She liked the way he was looking at her. Like he wanted to make a meal out of her. It made her feel good. Made her feel sexy. She couldn't remember the last time she'd felt sexy.

"For argument's sake, let's just say...I get in my car and head out...we call it a night. No harm, no foul. We flirted a little, had a few laughs...you know. Would you be cool with that?"

She moved closer to him. What was she doing? He needed to leave. Before she did something stupid.

"You haven't done this before, have you?" he asked.

"Done what?"

"Brought a guy home while your husband was out of town." He smiled, but his eyes were serious, probing.

"Oh, yeah, yeah, I do it all the time. Can't you tell?" Diane moved even closer until they were inches apart. "I'm curious." Her voice shook. "It's been obvious all night that I'm interested. Right? I don't think I'm *that* out of practice."

"True."

"But you haven't tried anything. You haven't tried to kiss me. You haven't touched me."

"I like to think I'm a gentleman."

"Jackson, I don't need a gentleman."

"I believe in the karmic laws of the universe. You, ma'am, are married. I am not. If I were to make the first move—"

She leaned up on her toes and kissed him. For a moment she thought he wasn't going to kiss her back and her body withered in embarrassment, but he placed his hand behind her head, pulled her closer, and kissed her like she hadn't been in years. It was a kiss that went on forever.

"Don't do this because you're drunk," he said as their lips parted.

"I'm not drunk," she whispered and kissed him again. This time savoring the feel of his tongue on hers. She loved how he smelled. He wasn't neat, he wasn't clean, and he didn't smell like Hilton. He was a little sweaty, a little raw. Noah, she thought. Like Noah, he smelled like sex.

He wrapped his hands around her hips, grabbed her by the small of her back, and pulled her into him. He felt so good pressed up against her. She knew this was the point of no return. If she reached down and opened that door, there would be no way of stopping. No turning back. A million thoughts raced through her head. Yes? No? Maybe? What did she have to lose?

Everything.

But it didn't matter. The little voices in her head couldn't compete. She wanted this. She needed this. And if she didn't do it—

She pulled her lips from his, letting the tip of her tongue linger, and looked him in the eye. They stared at each other for what seemed like an eternity. She slid her hand into his jeans. He moaned, deep and throaty.

"Diane. Ohhhhh..."

She put her lips to his ear and, in a breathless voice she didn't recognize, said, "It's getting cold out here. Do you want to come inside?"

16

———

"This chick is wearing you out," Jackson muttered to himself as he washed his hands. "Who's getting schooled here, bud, you or her?"

He splashed cold water on his face and studied himself in the mirror. It had only been seven months since he'd hit the big four-oh, and already the wrinkles were creeping in around his eyes and the corners of his mouth.

He looked like a ghost, a pale copy of the man he used to be. He needed a new line of work. A new calling. He was too damn young to feel like this. He remembered reading that your body changes completely every seven years. Every cell. By his count, he'd be brand new in two years.

Climaxing early was a shock. It shook the foundations on which he'd placed a great faith. He couldn't remember the last time *that* had happened. High school? It sent a chill up his spine thinking about it.

The look of disappointment in Diane's eyes was so strong, for a moment he thought she was going to punch him. Instead, she said, "This was a mistake," and quietly asked him to go. He understood. She was embarrassed for him and herself, but he couldn't leave her like that. So, he poured on the charm and the frown on her face blossomed into a smile, and they moved from the kitchen to the lavish great room.

On the rug in front of the fireplace, he got his mojo back, and Diane got everything she wanted and more. At least that's how he saw it. He didn't like to brag, but sometimes it is what it is, and damn, he was a rock star in the saddle.

But that premature ejaculation fiasco gnawed at him. He knew things like that were just a blip on the radar screen of life. No big deal, right? Just as long as it didn't happen again. Ever.

He pulled a pack of Marlboros out of his jeans pocket along with a lighter. He lit one up, took a slow drag, and—

Son of a bitch. Le Deuce.

He'd forgotten all about the poor bastard. He yanked out his phone and checked the time. Nearly four a.m. Holy shit! And look at all the texts.

He shook his head. There wasn't anything he could do about it now, might as well get his groove on again before he hit the road. There would be hell to pay in the morning. At least he could face Le Deuce with a big shit-eating grin. That would piss the old bastard off.

He slid an orange-colored glass vile out of his pocket and sprinkled a tiny pile of coke onto the bathroom counter. With the pinky on his right hand, he broke the pile into lines and sorted each one up his nose. He clenched his shoulders tight and rode the lightning.

He sat down on the edge of the bathtub and finished his cigarette and admired the bathroom. It was beyond immaculate.

The chick was obviously filthy rich. Maybe he could parlay this little romp into a semi-permanent arrangement. A man like him could use a sugar mama. Take the burden off his back.

He stood up, tossed the cigarette into the toilet, and headed out into the hallway. He was ready to rock and roll.

17

———

BUNDLED up in a patchwork quilt her Nana had made for her when she was six or seven, Diane sat on the couch and contemplated the clothes strewn about on the floor. She should be ashamed. A few years ago she would have been, but not now. Not tonight. She felt good. She felt alive. She was on fire, and she wanted more. No, she deserved more.

You can only push a person away for so long. You can only be told it's all in your mind so many times before you say, "Screw it" and find yourself here. She wasn't crazy; Hilton had changed. The soft kisses had become pecks on the forehead, the warm hugs had become awkward and ended with a patronizing pat on the back as if his body language was saying, "Enough, let me go."

"I love you" was just an empty phrase uttered through gritted teeth. Her marriage had ended tonight, and she didn't give a damn.

"This is...uh...quite the little palace you got here," Jackson said tripping over the oriental rug. "You must be loaded."

"Oh, this isn't my place." She stood up and met him in the middle of the room. "I'm house-sitting for a friend."

"Well, your friend must be loaded." He brushed the hair out of her face.

"She is."

"So how are you feeling? Better?"

She looked at him. What was he talking about?

"You almost threw up in the driveway," he said.

"Yeah, I'm definitely over that."

"Energy level good? You need a snack?"

"I'm good." She smiled.

"God, you're beautiful," he said.

"I think you need to have your eyes checked." She could feel her face getting warm. When was the last time Hilton had told her she was beautiful? She couldn't remember.

"Oh, come on, you know you're hot."

"I'm not bad on a good day, but hot? Nicole, she's hot."

"She can't hold a candle to you."

She leaned forward and wiped something off of his upper lip.

"What are you doing?"

"You've got something on your face."

"Oh." He rubbed his lip. "Better?"

"Yes."

"So, think you're up for another—"

Diane dropped the quilt, kissed his lips, and whispered, "Please shut up." She took his hand and guided his fingers. "You talk too much."

"I know. It's a personality flaw."

18

WHAT THE HELL is that noise? Nicole pulled the pillow over her head. *Why won't it stop?*

"Your phone," Timothy mumbled.

"My what?" She opened her eyes.

He rolled over to face her. "Nicole?"

"Yeah?" She closed them again.

"I think that's your phone."

"My what?"

"Your phone," he said louder. "Your phone is ringing like crazy."

"You don't have to yell." She rolled over, grabbed the phone off the floor, and checked the screen. Her bedroom was pitch black, and the bright light blinded her for a second. Then her eyes adjusted and she saw who it was.

"Diane? What's going on? Are you—"

"Nicole...oh, God...oh, God...oh, God, Nicole."

She sat up in the bed. "Diane...what?"

"Help," Diane got out between sobs. "Please, help me."

NICOLE SLID across the oriental rug and dropped to her knees beside Jackson's naked, lifeless body. He was facedown, inches away from the fireplace.

"Are you sure he's dead?" she yelled back at Diane and tried to turn him over.

"Yes, I'm sure." Diane, naked except for the quilt draped around her shoulders, paced in circles, her eyes fixated on the floor.

"Are you a doctor?"

"Nicole? Goddamnit!"

"Then how do you know? How do you know? Did you call 911?"

"No."

"Why not?"

"I can't do that."

"You can't? Or you won't?"

"Why are you yelling at me?"

Nicole glanced back over her shoulder at her. "Are you fucked up?"

"What?"

"Did he give you any drugs?"

"No."

"We need to turn him over."

"Why?"

"To see if he's still breathing. Help me." She tried once more, but he wouldn't budge. "I can't do this by myself."

Diane stopped pacing and glared at her.

For a minute Nicole thought her sister was going to run screaming out the front door and disappear into the night, never to be seen again.

"Diane, I mean it. Help me turn him over."

"Fine." She charged across the room, crept around Jackson, and bent down across from Nicole.

"Okay, ready..."

Together they turned his body over. Blood had caked under his nose.

"Nice." Nicole checked his pulse. Nothing. She got a hair tie out of her pocket, pulled her long hair out of her face, and put it into a ponytail. Then she leaned over him and performed mouth-to-mouth resuscitation.

"What are you doing?" Diane asked.

"What do you think?" She pounded on his chest.

"Do you even know what you're doing?"

"Hey, screw you, okay. I went to nursing school for a whole quarter, remember?"

After a valiant, no-holds-barred effort, Nicole threw up her hands in defeat. "Oh, he's dead all right." Flopping backward, she landed on her butt. "What in the hell happened?"

Diane stood up, tiptoed around the body, and headed back toward the safety of the kitchen. "We were...you know..."

"Screwing."

"Yes." Diane shook her head. "Then blood started pouring out of his nose and...God...he fell on top of me. It was horrible."

"Yeah, I'll bet." Nicole stumbled to her feet and strode past her sister and into the kitchen. "I need a drink. Something with a little kick. We have to call the police."

Diane charged after her. "Oh, no. Oh, no. We are not doing that."

"What are you going to do? Bury him in the backyard? Toss him in that lake back there?"

"Nicole? We can't call the police."

"He's dead. It's not like *you* killed him."

"I know. What do you think happened?"

"Brain aneurysm? I don't know." She ripped open the door to the liquor cabinet and pulled out a bottle of Scotch. "Nice."

She unscrewed the top and drank it straight from the bottle.

Diane crossed her arms, tapped her foot, and read her the riot act with her eyes. "We have glasses."

"You obsess over the weirdest shit."

"Oh, come on."

"You got a dead guy in the living room and you're pissed because I'm drinking out of the bottle?"

"I'm not pissed."

"Yes, you are."

"No, I'm not."

"Yes, you are."

"Okay, I'm pissed. It's trashy. Get a damn glass."

Nicole slammed the bottle down on the counter. "Did he do any drugs in front of you?"

"No."

"You're sure?"

"Do you think I'm a complete idiot? If he had, I would have told him to leave. I'm not into that. Why?"

"Walk through this with me. Okay?"

"I don't want to think about it."

"You called me, remember? Now, please, let's go through this together."

Diane let out a gasp of air in protest, rolled her eyes, and gave her sister a replay of the evening.

"So he went to the bathroom before you guys did it the last time?"

"Yeah."

Nicole took off across the kitchen, charged into the great room, and made a beeline for the hallway. Diane ran after her. They skidded to a stop in front of the guest bathroom.

"He used this one?" Nicole asked as she pushed the door open.

Diane nodded and followed her in. Nicole turned on the light and looked around the room. She ran her hand across the countertop.

"Oh, shit. You're kidding me."

"What?" Diane peeked over Nicole's shoulder. "What?"

"Cocaine."

"You're sure?"

Nicole licked the tip of her index finger. "Yep. I'll bet he poured it out here on the counter and did his thing. But he forgot—or didn't give enough of a shit—to wipe it down when he was done."

Diane sat on the toilet lid and buried her face in her hands. "I'm so screwed."

"We're running out of time here. We need to call the police."

"We can't."

"Diane?"

"I can't do it."

"You didn't do anything wrong."

Diane looked up at the ceiling as she fought back the tears. "Yes, I did."

Nicole needed another drink. No, she needed the entire bottle. She wanted to roll back time and start the night over. Highlight everything and click delete. This wasn't how it was supposed to go down. Her sister was supposed to get laid and have fun and—this was all her fault. She screwed up. She should never have let Jackson take Diane home. Nicole thought she was doing her a favor.

Some favor.

Diane wiped the tears from her eyes. "We could take him back to his place. Leave him in his bed. Nobody would know."

"Pretty sure moving a dead body is a crime."

"If they found out. How would they find out? This will kill Hilton. It'll kill him."

"So he won't be mayor? So what?"

"Mayor? I'm not talking about that. This will destroy the business. The restaurants. Everything."

"Sure, it'll be a big story for a few days, but then it'll all blow over. This stuff always blows over."

"This will not blow over. We're a family restaurant. You know how it is around here. This is the Bible Belt. We'll be pariahs. We will be the butt of every frigging joke on the internet. I'll be a meme!"

"I think you're overreacting."

Diane leapt to her feet and got in Nicole's face. "You owe me. Who has always been there for you? How many times have I bailed you out of jail? You really want me to list everything I've ever done for you, because we could be here all night."

"Go ahead, list them."

"I did them because I love you. And I've never asked for anything in return, but right now I need you to do this for me. I need your help. This would kill Hilton, literally kill him."

Nicole took a step backward into the hallway. Her fingers clenched into a fist. If it had been anybody else, she would have punched them square in the mouth, but Diane was right. It pissed her off, but she was right. "Okay, fine, what's the plan?"

She didn't reply for a few moments, and Nicole wondered if she was about to have a nervous breakdown.

Diane took off for the staircase at the end of the hallway.

"Where are you going?" Nicole asked.

"To see if I have some leftover gloves from the other night when I dyed my hair."

Nicole watched her charge up the stairs. "You dye your hair?"

"Funny."

19

———

"Thanks for all your help," Diane squeaked out between sneezes as she and her sister dragged Jackson's body through the kitchen.

"Hey, I'm sorry, but I wasn't putting his clothes on."

"God, you're such a baby sometimes."

Diane had him by the left foot and Nicole by the right, and they were almost to the garage door. They had laid him out on an old, shabby rug Nicole had found in the basement, and the dust mites had sent Diane's allergies into overdrive.

"Whatever." Nicole reached out, opened the door with her free hand, and stopped. "How are we gonna do this?"

"I guess we lay him down and then both of us get in the garage and pull him through the door?"

"Sounds like a plan."

They laid Jackson's body on the floor, making sure his feet hung over the threshold and out into the garage. One by one they stepped over his body and then each grabbed him by a foot and pulled him through the doorway. As he tumbled down the steps, his head slid off the top one, smacked the second one, and landed on the concrete floor with a loud crack.

"Crap," Diane said and sneezed again.

"Jeez, I'll bet that hurt."

"Did we break his neck?"

"I don't think so. We might have busted his head, though." Nicole leaned down and checked his head. "I don't see any blood."

"This night is getting worse and worse."

Diane dropped his foot to the floor and pulled the keys to the Camaro out of her pocket. She had exchanged her patchwork quilt for a pair of jeans, sneakers, a T-shirt, and a pink hoodie. Her hair was pulled back in a ponytail, tucked under a red Georgia Bulldogs cap, and her make-up had all but vanished. Before she dressed him, Diane had backed Jackson's Camaro into the garage and closed the garage door. The neighbors didn't need an eyeful.

"You think he'll fit in the trunk?" she asked.

"How about the passenger seat?" Nicole replied.

"No."

"If you get pulled over—"

"Don't say that. Don't you dare manifest that right now."

"What are you talking about?"

"You know, manifest. Bring into existence...call out to the universe...you know what I'm talking about."

"No, I don't."

"Don't roll your eyes at me."

"I didn't."

"Yes, you did."

"Whatever, Diane. All I'm saying is it's five o'clock in the morning, anything could happen."

"Well, I can't do it. I can't have him next to me. That's just...no."

"But if you get pulled over and they search the trunk—"

"I will not get pulled over."

"Fine, put him in the damn trunk."

"Thank you."

Diane unlocked the trunk, popped it open, and looked inside.

Nicole stood on her toes and peeked over Diane's shoulder. A black gym bag was lying next to the spare tire and jack.

"What's that?" Nicole asked.

"A gym bag."

"I know. What's in it?"

"What is your problem?"

"I'm curious," Nicole said as she tried to reach around her and grab the bag.

Diane elbowed her. "Would you stop it? What do you care what's in the bag?"

"I don't know. What if it's something important?"

"Like what? His dirty underwear?"

"I don't know. What if it's something that could screw this whole thing up?"

"Like what?"

"I don't know. But we need to check it out."

Diane knew her sister would never let it go, so she raised both hands in retreat and backed away from the car. "Fine. Go ahead."

Nicole popped her latex glove like a doctor getting ready to examine a patient and reached in the trunk and pulled out the bag. She unzipped it and peered in.

"Holy shit," she said, dropping the bag to the floor. "Oh my God!"

"What?" Diane rushed to her sister.

Nicole grabbed the bag and flipped it over. Out fell multiple stacks of cash along with ten or twelve white bricks.

"What is that?" Diane asked.

"These are obviously cash." She picked up one of the stacks, then gestured toward the scattered bricks. "And this, darling, is cocaine. Lots and lots of cocaine."

"He's a dealer?"

"Well, duh. Damn, Diane, you sure know how to pick 'em."

Diane clenched both fists, mashed them up against her cheeks, closed her eyes, and let out a horrifying scream.

Nicole ignored her and counted the bundles of cash. When the garage grew quiet, she asked, "You done?"

Diane hung her head. "Yeah."

"Okay, good, 'cause now we got a real big problem."

"How? It's not like we're going to keep any of that."

"Still, this...I mean...damn...you know this money could really help Janice. Hell, it could help me. There's gotta be at least a quarter of a million here. Probably more."

"Oh, no. No, no, no, no. Don't even think about it. Put it all back in the bag."

"But?"

"Put it back in the bag." Diane bent down and haphazardly picked up a few of the cocaine bricks and handed them to her. "We need to get out of here. It's going to be morning soon."

Nicole took the bricks and tossed them back in the bag, along with the cash. "This might be the most important drive of your life."

"Me?"

"Honey, if the cops pull you over, I'm gonna be long gone 'cause there won't be any explaining this mess."

20

———

TIMOTHY SCOOTED around in the driver's seat of his Chevy Silverado, trying in vain to tame his hemorrhoids. They had flared off and on for years, but the itching was bordering on suicidal. The last thing he wanted was for some doc to play whack-a-mole on them—*that* scared the bejesus out of him—but he couldn't spend the rest of his life with a burning ass.

He checked his watch. What was he doing in some fancy-schmancy neighborhood at five thirty in the morning?

Forty-five minutes ago, Nicole ran out of his house, flat out refusing to tell him where she was going. His sixth sense went haywire, so he followed her. Sometimes the girl could get up to no good, and it was better to put the brakes on before anything crazy happened.

Crescent Mill Plantation? What was she doing here? This place was way out of Nicole's league, and his too.

Was she screwing someone else?

That thought drove a knife right through his heart, because then he'd have to kill the dude; no ifs, ands, or buts. Since getting out of the service, he'd made it his life's mission to promote peace and to avoid violence at all costs. Unless some other prick was doing his girlfriend. Then he'd rip them to shreds with his bare hands.

Man, he hoped she wasn't cheating.

He picked up a pair of binoculars from the passenger seat and focused on the picturesque, three-story mini-mansion where Nicole had parked her red RX-7.

Who the hell does she know who lives in that house?

He tried to think, but after getting his skull smashed open in Afghanistan, his brain didn't function the way it used to. Before the injury, he was as smart as a whip. Now? Well, there was no point in dwelling on what he'd lost. Hell, he couldn't even remember what he'd lost. It was so damn confusing.

In the driveway, beside Nicole's RX-7, sat a black Camaro. He was trying to remember if he knew anyone with a Camaro when the garage door opened and a woman crept to the car.

Wait a minute, wasn't that Nicole's sister, Diane? Holy shit. Now it all made sense. Diane lived here. And the Camaro? Didn't Jackson have an old Camaro? He eased down in his seat, held his breath, and watched.

Diane craned her neck and looked up and down the street as if she were worried someone might see her and then climbed in the Camaro. The red brake lights lit up the darkness, and he heard the distant sound of the engine roaring to life. The Camaro eased into the garage, and a moment later the door rattled shut. Now all he could hear was the sound of crickets.

He didn't like this. The temptation to charge over there, bang on the front door, and demand some answers was overwhelming, but the part of his brain that still worked pretty well shot that idea all to hell. Best to see what was going on before he did something stupid.

Ten minutes later he knew something stupid was fast approaching. He could call Nicole, but when she found out that he'd followed her, she'd kill him. With her bare hands.

His stomach let out a guttural growl that sounded like "Feed me." In the console he found a half-empty bag of peanut butter M&M's, which he devoured. He washed them down with the last bit of a Dr. Pepper that had been sitting in his truck since yesterday afternoon. It was flat and syrupy and after a couple of minutes made him want to puke.

He opened the door, climbed out of the cab, put his hands on his knees, and leaned forward. He took a deep breath and waited. Timothy remained like that for a minute or more before he realized he wouldn't throw up.

He stood, popped his neck, and eyeballed the area. Diane lived on an unfinished street. Her house was in the back of the subdivision, and it looked like the developers had taken all their toys one day and gone home. There were two empty lots next to her house, and the three-story on the other side looked occupied. Across the street was a patch of trees, and the road ended in a paved cul-de-sac that had no lots, only woods.

Timothy had parked in front of one of the vacant lots away from the streetlights.

The freezing early morning air whipped across the back of his neck, bringing a jolt of pleasure. Most people hated the cold, but not him. He loved it. In fact, he'd been harboring a secret fantasy about chucking everything and moving to Norway if this band gig went south.

The gust of wind brought with it the smell of rain, and sure enough, a drop hit his forehead. Might as well take a piss in case the sky opened up.

As he unzipped his jeans, he heard the garage door open down the street. Spinning around, he saw the Camaro pull out of Diane's garage, followed by Nicole, who walked to her RX-7 and opened the door.

For a split second, he thought she looked right at him, and his heart went full bass drum—*boom, boom, boom, boom.* He was dead certain she was going to scream at him, but apparently she hadn't seen him because she climbed in the car, peeled out of the drive-way, and took off after the Camaro.

Where were they going? And where in the hell was Jackson?

Pissing as fast as he could, he watched their taillights disappear around a corner. Finished, he made a mad dash for the Silverado. Some crazy-ass shit might be about to go down, and he sure as hell was going to be there if it did.

21

———

Diane peeled her fingers off the Camaro's steering wheel and cranked the windshield wipers. The torrential downpour was making it difficult for her to see the road.

A white SUV came out of nowhere, careened past her, and charged into her lane. She jumped back and grabbed the wheel. Another inch and the idiot would have sideswiped her front end.

It took all she had not to floor it, catch up, and run the SUV off the road. Years ago she'd learned her road rage lesson when a crazy guy had followed her for miles after she'd flipped him off. She lost him, but it scared her half to death, and she realized screaming in the car (or in your head) was preferable to starting something that could spiral dangerously out of control.

"In three miles, turn left on Shallow Creek Road," Google Maps told her in an irritatingly helpful voice. She glanced at her phone lying in the passenger seat. Five minutes to go. Five long, excruciating minutes.

Nicole had gotten Jackson's address from his driver's license and put it in Diane's phone. Diane made a mental note to delete it when she got back home. Just in case. You never know.

Why am I doing this?

Make good choices, Nana used to say. This was not a good choice. And yet she couldn't see any other option. Should she go to the police? In the end, it'd save her a world of heartache, right? She was a terrible liar, and if some detective turned the heat on her like they did on *Law & Order*, she'd crack. Crack so fast it'd make their heads spin.

But she couldn't do it. She would not have her life dragged through the mud because of one mistake, and how would anybody know she was involved in Jackson's death, anyway? What proof would they have? The only thing anyone could prove is that he drove her home. They couldn't prove he went inside the house. Couldn't prove they had sex. Diane made another mental note to get rid of the oriental rug in the living room. It might have his stuff on it. And get rid of the condoms in the trash.

She had a lot to do when she got back home.

Okay, so maybe they could prove it. But not if she burned the evidence. And even if they could prove she and Jackson had sex, it's not like he had a bunch of bullet holes in his chest, or stab wounds. Whatever he died of, it wasn't murder. It was—

No.

No.

No.

Up ahead, flashing blue lights lit up the darkness. Diane's stomach spasmed, and she thought she was going to puke.

Was that a roadblock?

As she got closer, she could see through the rain-drenched windshield a police car had someone pulled over by the side of the road. The officer, raincoat flapping in the wind, was scrambling back to his patrol car.

Diane looked at the speedometer. Fifty-three. Just a hair under the limit.

"Everything's going to be okay. Everything's going to be just hunky dory," she whispered and pulled her cap down to hide her face. In the rearview mirror all she could see were two tiny dots of light, which meant Nicole was a good distance back. Or not. Those lights could be anybody.

To be on the safe side, Diane put on her blinker and drifted over into the left lane. The farther she could get away from the cop, the better. After a moment, she passed them.

Hello.

It was the same white SUV that had almost run her off the road earlier. Yelling "asshole" at the top of her lungs out the passenger window would not be a smart move, but it sure would feel good.

When she got farther down the highway, she checked in the rearview mirror. The SUV pulled back out onto the road. The lights on the patrol car died, and it eased out on the road behind the SUV.

Oh, God. What if the cop got behind her? What if he followed her? What if one of the brake lights was out? Damn, why didn't they check that before they left? What if he ran the plates?

And right on cue, she had to pee. Really bad. Her whole life, it'd been like this. Whenever she got extremely anxious, she immediately had to go, and boy, did she hate it. She wasn't even sure it was always a real urge. Sometimes she could push it to the back of her mind and it would go away. Other times, you better stand back because the flood gates were about to open.

Calm down, calm down, calm down, she told herself. She sucked in a deep breath, held it, and let it out. Waited a beat and did it again, and again, and again.

She didn't know if it would work, but it beat peeing all over the seat. She'd seen it the other day on Facebook: "How to stop panic attacks."

Once more she looked in the rearview mirror. She couldn't tell if the headlights behind her belonged to the police car or the SUV. But they were creeping up on her like a lion stalking his prey. Was he trying to read her plates? Diane pictured her mugshot on CNN. She saw herself on *Orange Is the New Black*.

This was so unfair.

I didn't do anything wrong. Officer, that's not my cocaine. That's not my money. I didn't kill him. I just wanted to get—

"In five hundred feet, turn left on Shallow Creek Road."

She almost leapt out the window.

"Dummy," she said with a nervous laugh. She wanted to reach over, grab her phone, call Nicole. But that would be the wrong move. He'd see her on her phone and pull her over. Georgia was a hands-free state.

The headlights veered to the right and disappeared off an exit ramp. She gave a sideways glance out the passenger window and saw that it wasn't the police car. It was the SUV.

"You're losing your mind. You better get a handle on it."

She peeked in the rearview mirror again. That meant that the two lights behind her could be Nicole, or they could still be—

BLUE LIGHTS.

The siren ripped through her like a bullet. She shot a quick glance at the speedometer. She wasn't speeding. This didn't make any sense. She wasn't speeding.

Did he run the plates? He'll know this isn't my car.

She fumbled around, unsure of what to do. She looked for a place to pull off the road, then over her shoulder, and back to the mirror.

The lights were getting closer.

Her body folded in on itself, and she gripped the wheel tighter.

"But I didn't do anything," she screamed.

The flashing lights overwhelmed the side mirrors, bathing the interior of the Camaro in blue. She eased off the gas, put her foot on the brake, and headed toward the grassy median on the left-hand side of the highway.

Please God, don't let him look in the trunk. Please. I'm begging you. Don't let him look in the trunk.

Her left front tire hit the dirt, throwing gravel everywhere, as she forced the car off the highway. She looked back. The police car was still in the right lane. Shouldn't he get over?

What the hell was he doing?

He flew right past her.

The Camaro shuddered to a stop. Diane put her hand over her eyes and sunk down in the seat. Everything went silent except the distant scream of the siren. She realized how close she'd come to having her life destroyed and waited for the tears.

But they didn't come.

She took in a big gulp of air and watched the police car, its blue lights setting the night on fire, vanish into the thick mist and rain. Over and over again, she thanked the Lord.

Diane had never been a religious woman, but like a soldier in the heat of battle, suddenly she'd found God.

22

———

"Damn, I about lost it when that dick turned on his flashers. You okay?" Nicole jumped out of her car.

"I'm fine." Diane shut the Camaro door and bolted past her.

"What are you doing?"

"I gotta go."

Diane charged toward the heavy bushes that ran alongside the apartment building.

"Oh, yeah. That. You should see a doctor." Nicole pulled her hoodie snug over her head. "I'm freezing. Thank God the rain slowed down."

Diane looked back, put her index finger to her lips. "Shh! You want to wake the whole place up?"

"I'm not that loud."

"Your voice resonates," Diane whispered as she slipped in between the bushes.

"Yeah, pretty sexy, isn't it? For a woman it is low—"

"Nicole, shut up."

Annoyed, Nicole pulled her fingers across her lips like she was zipping her mouth closed. Then she took out her phone, clicked on the photo she'd taken of Jackson's driver's license, and turned around to determine which apartment was his.

There were three buildings, each with a big letter stuck on the side: A to her right, C to her left, and B in front of her. All were three stories tall and in desperate need of repair. Nicole enlarged the photo. Apartment 9B. The parking lot lights near building B were out, which left some areas covered in darkness. That was good, since 9B had to be on the top floor. She slid her phone back into her pocket.

Hidden Pines.

Why did these dives always have such stupid names? It wasn't very hidden, and it didn't smell like pine trees at all. More like a garbage truck. She had imagined Jackson would live some place a little more upscale. But apparently he was a cokehead and a drug dealer, so she shouldn't have been surprised.

Tomorrow she was going to have a little chat with Timothy. Who was this guy? What had she gotten Diane into?

She glanced back at the bushes. Could Diane pee any slower? She was ready to get the hell out of here. This dive was ringing her alarm bells. *Run*, the little voice inside her head screamed. *Run while you can.* She told it to piss off, but it wouldn't go away. Her pupils danced across the various windows, and she considered how many eyes were staring at her right now.

Cameras.

Of course. Why didn't she think of that before? Apartment complexes have security cameras. Even a rathole like this one— scratch that—especially a rathole like this one.

Diane crept out of the bushes and whispered, "Where's his apartment?"

"We got a problem."

"What?"

"Cameras. Security cameras. Probably all over this place."

Diane glanced at the top of each building and the light posts. "I don't see any cameras."

"They could be hidden."

"We don't have a choice. We can't leave him in the trunk."

"No, but we could prop him up in the driver's seat."

"That would be even more suspicious. It has to look like he died in his sleep. If there are cameras, we're already busted. We can't change that. They'd wonder why we moved him from the trunk to the front seat. We have to walk him up the stairs, right? There's no way we can carry him. So if anybody sees us or asks about it later, we can say we helped him home because he was too drunk."

Nicole toyed with the idea; it could work. It had to. There was no other way. "Okay, but we need to move his car. We can't drag him across the parking lot."

"Which apartment is his?"

She pointed straight ahead. "That one. Third floor."

Diane's shoulders sank. "Third floor?"

"Yep."

"Great."

Thunder boomed in the distance, and the rain went from a drizzle back to a steady stream.

23

———

TIMOTHY PARKED his truck in the woods a few yards down from the Hidden Pines entrance and headed back to the complex. Plowing through the light rain, his curiosity gnawed at him. What were they doing *here?* And where was Jackson?

At the last moment before climbing out of his truck, he'd grabbed his binoculars. It was a gigantic risk. If anybody caught him out here with them, he might get his ass beat, or worse, the cops called on him. A man walking around with binoculars at the crack of dawn was never up to any good.

As he neared the front entrance, he crept down, sticking close to the bushes. God forbid Nicole saw him. She'd chew him a new asshole. He stopped behind one of the larger bushes and scoped out the parking lot.

There they were. Pacing back and forth near the RX-7 and the Camaro. He couldn't make out what they were saying, but they both looked half-crazed.

This was getting too damn weird.

He watched them talk a little longer. Then Diane got in the Camaro, and Nicole got in her RX-7. Both engines started within seconds, and one by one each car backed out. They drove across the lot toward the apartment building with the letter B hanging off the front.

Timothy was so mesmerized by what he was witnessing, he didn't notice that the rain had picked back up. A flash of lightning followed by a crack of thunder snapped him out of his trance. He glanced up. An avalanche of raindrops pelted him in the face.

After their taillights disappeared behind building B, he stepped out of the bushes and ran across the parking lot, sticking close to the shadows. This wasn't the place to be caught acting strange during the day, much less the middle of the night.

He wished he'd gotten his pistol out of the glove compartment along with the binoculars.

He made it to building B just in time to see the two women pulling Jackson out of the trunk of the Camaro.

The trunk? What the hell was he doing in the trunk?

They propped him up with Nicole on one side and Diane on the other and tried to walk him across the parking lot, but he didn't want to cooperate. His head kept falling forward and his feet kept getting entangled as they dragged him along. Was he *that* shit-faced? And if so, why bring him here? In the rain? At five something in the morning? The more he watched, the more Timothy realized Jackson didn't look drunk. He looked dead.

But that was insane.

Paralyzed with fear, he found it almost impossible to form a plan of action. Should he follow them up the stairs? Confront them? Call the police? If he followed, there was no way they wouldn't see him. If he called the police? Nicole could go to prison.

If Jackson was dead, that is.

But if Jackson was just drunk, then she'd be so pissed she'd probably break up with him. He fought back the flood of thoughts and focused.

All he could do was wait. That was it. Wait it out. Watch and learn. Once he knew the lay of the land, it would be time for answers. One thing he'd learned as a Marine, you didn't go charging into an unknown situation. You needed intel.

He pulled up his binoculars just as they made it to the second floor. But from where he stood, he couldn't see much. He tiptoed out of the bushes and stepped back a few feet.

Behind him it was all woods. Hidden Pines was out in the middle of nowhere, surrounded by forest. Further down the road there was a hodgepodge of industrial parks and after that, farmland for miles.

He looked through the binoculars again but still couldn't see Nicole or Diane on the second floor. To get a better angle, he turned and headed toward the woods.

"Uh, hey, dude, whatcha doing?"

A scarecrow of a man stepped out of the darkness.

Timothy almost dropped a load in his pants.

The man might have been forty, fifty, or even sixty; Timothy couldn't tell. His face was pockmarked, and deep creases ran from his cheekbones to the corners of his mouth. He needed a shave, and his eyebrows were like kudzu. A lit cigarette dangled from his lip. His yellow raincoat hung on his wire frame like a tent. Timothy wouldn't have been shocked if he had a hook for a hand.

"I said whatcha doing, boy?"

Timothy gawked at him, his mind racing for an answer.

"You a peeping creep?" the scarecrow asked as he blew out a cloud of smoke and watched it get taken down by the rain.

"No, I'm not, sir."

"Uh-huh."

Timothy looked down at the binoculars in his hand. "Oh, you mean these? I'm not peeping on anybody."

"Then what are you doing?" His voice went up an octave, and Timothy was afraid Nicole and Diane might hear him.

"I'm coming home from work. What are you doing?"

"Having a smoke. Then I leaned around the corner here and

see you watching those girls." He smiled big when he said *girls*, revealing a front row of loose and missing teeth.

"I live here and—"

"My ass! You don't live around here. I've been here eight years, and I ain't never seen you, boy."

"I just moved in. Last week."

The scarecrow stepped further into the streetlamp light, cocked his head, and studied Timothy's face.

Timothy pictured that hook coming up and slashing him to pieces.

"Which apartment?"

"Uh...I can't remember the..."

"Yep, I thought so. Maybe the poe-lease man can get some real answers outta ya." He pulled his phone out of his jeans pocket.

"Wait a second, just hang on. Okay, I don't live here."

"Tell me something I don't know."

"One of those women is my girlfriend. I think she's been cheating, so I followed her."

"You're a good-looking boy, why would anybody cheat on you?"

"Thank you, sir, but you know women."

"Hell, I do. Men too. A cheater's a cheater, don't matter if you're a woman or a man." Lightning lit up the sky behind him, and his face went dark except for his eyes.

Timothy nodded, raindrops rolling down his face.

"So, if the policeman showed up, that might mess up your night."

"Yes, sir."

Finished with his cigarette, the scarecrow tossed it on the ground and crushed it with the heel of his boot. He pulled a switchblade out of his back pocket, flipped it open, and used the knife tip to clean his remaining teeth.

Timothy thought he was going to vomit.

"How much would you be willing to contribute to the Ralph J. Thompson retirement fund?"

"What?"

"How much is it worth to you to keep the poe-lease man away?"

"Sir, I don't have any cash on me."

"That's all right." He pulled out a card swiper and plugged it in to the bottom of his phone. "I take Visa, MasterCard, or Discover."

Timothy pictured himself beating the hell out of the old man. "Would a hundred do?"

"How about one fifty?" The scarecrow smiled a big, toothless smile and cackled like he thought that was the funniest damn thing he'd ever said.

Timothy pulled out his wallet. "Fine, but I got a question for you. Anybody named Jackson live around here? Five-ten, dark hair. Couple of tats."

"Yeah, yeah, there's a fella named Jackson who lives up there." The scarecrow scratched his nose and pointed to building B. "Third floor. Same place your girl's headed."

24

DIANE PLACED a tentative foot on the second-floor hallway and steadied herself. Jackson's left arm was draped across her shoulder, his right across Nicole's. It had taken everything they had to make it up the flight of stairs, and Diane had no intention of falling backward and doing it all over again.

"Jeez, I think the bastard's gotten heavier since we left the house," Nicole said. "What do they call it when they go all stiff?"

"Rigor mortis," Diane replied through gritted teeth. "You got him?"

"Yeah, don't stop. Just makes it harder to keep going."

They moved in lockstep down the hallway. Diane kept waiting for one of the apartment doors to open and somebody to stick their head out and ask, *Whatcha girls doin' with that dead body?* But so far they'd not seen a soul.

"Why couldn't he live on first floor?" Diane asked.

"I don't know. Why did he have to die—"

Jackson's body wobbled and went sideways, sending Diane crashing into the wall. Her hand slipped from his arm, and Jackson went down like a boxer who'd just been KO'd. Getting to her feet, she looked up and down the hallway. What in the world?

Across the hallway, Nicole was facedown on the floor.

"My God, you all right?" Diane stumbled over Jackson and rushed to her sister. "Nicole?"

Nicole rolled over onto her back and locked eyes with Diane. Her breaths coming in short bursts, she replied, "Yeah...I'm alive."

"What happened?"

Nicole glanced up at the ceiling. Diane followed her gaze. Water, seeping in through a hole in the rusted-out roof, had left a puddle in the hallway.

"That plus my foot," Nicole said.

"You hurt?"

She rubbed her left wrist. "Nah, but this is the second time today I've busted my ass. It's pissing me off."

Diane stuck out her hand, but Nicole waved her away. With a bit of effort, she got to her feet. Diane watched her stagger to the railing at the end of the hallway, overlooking the parking lot. She leaned against the railing, closed her eyes, and clutched her wrist. The wind blew the rain in, soaking the back of her hoodie.

Diane joined her. "You're getting wet."

"I don't care."

"You sure you're okay?"

"Hand feels sore, but you know me."

"Tough as nails," Diane said.

Nicole managed a slight smile.

Behind them a bolt of lightning streaked across the sky, followed by an earsplitting thunderclap. Diane flinched and glanced over her shoulder at the parking lot. Soon the sun would be up and it would be full of people heading to work.

"We'd better hurry." She turned back and caught sight of Jackson's body. He was lying in a twisted heap in the middle of the hallway. She wanted to cry. How could this be happening?

"Can't we just leave him here?" Nicole asked. "He looks like a passed-out drunk."

"Are you crazy?"

"Like a fox," Nicole said and cackled.

THEY CAME TO A STOP. Every muscle in Diane's body cried out in agony, and she knew if they had to go one more floor, she'd take her chances and leave him on the stairs with a note pinned to his chest. *Had too much to drink. Please take me home.*

"We made it. Thank God. Okay, which one?" Diane asked.

"Huh?"

"Which apartment?"

"Uh, 9B," Nicole said.

"If I let go, can you hold him?"

"No, are you kidding?"

"I gotta unlock the door."

"Then we're gonna have to lean him against the wall or something."

"Okay, fine." Diane counted the apartment doors. "It's all the way at the end."

"It would be."

They waddled down the hallway and propped Jackson up against the wall next to the door of apartment 9B.

"Got him?" Diane asked.

"Just open the door."

Diane let Jackson go and waited a beat just to make sure her sister had him.

"Hurry up," Nicole said.

"Okay, okay." She pulled Jackson's enormous ring of keys from her pocket and tried to figure out which one opened the door. The first one didn't work. Neither did the second.

"What if there's no key here?" she said, her voice cracking.

"Why wouldn't there be?"

Diane stifled a scream and slid another key in the lock. Nope.

Below them, a door slammed. Followed by laughter. Panicked, Diane spun around and mouthed, "What the hell?"

Nicole held up her index finger and shushed her.

Voices echoed along with footsteps on the staircase. Diane couldn't tell if they were coming up to the third floor or down to the first. She tried another key. It didn't fit. She flipped through his key chain, her mind spinning. How many keys did he have? She picked one at random. Slid it in the lock and—the knob turned and the door opened. She almost threw her hands in the air and jumped for joy.

The footsteps and voices grew louder, and Diane realized they were coming up the stairs. In thirty seconds or less, they'd be joining Nicole and her in the hallway.

Together they pulled Jackson away from the wall, spun him around, and pushed him into the foyer. He slipped from their grip, stumbled forward, and went sliding face first across the floor. Nicole slammed the door shut behind them.

Diane ran over to his body and knelt down. She froze for a second and then giggled.

"Diane?"

"I'm sorry…" She put her hand over her mouth. The giggling got worse. Her abdomen started shaking. She put both hands over her mouth. Tried to hold it back. It was pointless. She burst out laughing.

"You're gonna wake up the whole place."

Through fits of laughter, "I'm sorry…" She fell backward and lay there, muffled giggles escaping between her fingers.

Nicole stormed over and peered down at her. "What is wrong with you?"

"Water…" Tears were running down her cheeks, she'd laughed so hard.

Nicole stormed into the small kitchen. "What is so damn funny?"

"I don't know. I think I'm losing my mind."

Diane pushed herself up and glanced around the room. Except for the furniture, it was void of anything that suggested somebody lived here, no books, empty glasses, or trash. Behind her sat a ratty old couch, a recliner, and a beat-up coffee table. The rug underneath her hadn't been cleaned in months, if not years. Everything looked like it was from a yard sale or Goodwill. The window beside the couch housed an air-conditioning unit that might or might not work, and the wall was wet from where the rain had blown in through the cracks between the unit and the window.

"Something's not right." Diane stood up.

"What do you mean?"

"It's like nobody lives here."

"Maybe it's his shag pad?"

"Shag pad?"

"You know, a cheap spot where he brings all his married girlfriends." Nicole handed her a bottle of water.

"I know what you meant."

Diane took a sip and slowly turned around as she scoped out the place. It was a one bedroom, one bath. The living room was a straight line from the foyer, the kitchen was off to the right, and the bathroom and bedroom to the left.

"He's a single guy," Nicole said. "He probably never even comes here. This could work out well for us. If nobody finds him for a few—"

"Don't say that. God, he's going to stink."

"I'm just saying, the longer it takes to find him, the better off we are. Memories get hazy. The police are going to question you, and me. We were all with him last night at the bar. It's going to come out that he gave you a ride home. You can't hide that."

Diane ignored her, slumped down on the couch, pulled her cap off, and ran her fingers through her hair. "Well, the key worked, but this doesn't seem like Jackson at all."

"What are you talking about? This place screams drug-dealing cokehead."

"Very funny."

"Well, sun's coming up soon. We gotta go."

"What about the money?"

"I don't know. You wanna keep it?"

"No, I meant should we bring it up here or leave it in the trunk?"

"I would say leave it 'cause I'm ready to get the hell out of here, but we should bring it up." Nicole motioned to the body sprawled out on the floor. "Put him in his bed?"

"I don't want to touch him again." She let out a sigh. "But I can't leave him like this."

"Okay, then get off your butt."

Diane stood up and walked over to Jackson's body. She stared at him for a minute, then looked back at her sister. "This was a stupid idea, wasn't it? We should've called the police."

"Too late. Can't go back now. We've already brought him here."

Diane inhaled and fought back the tears. What had they done?

Nicole walked over, put her arm around her shoulder, and said, "I wasn't sure until we found the coke and cash. But I am now. Trust me. We don't want the cops involved."

Diane hoped like hell she was right.

25

____

Water fills his lungs. He can't breathe.

Panicked, he looks up.

A blinding white light pours in from above. He races toward it.

Hilton awoke with a jerk.

A hand grabs his ankle. Yanks him back. He kicks with both legs, but the fingers tear into his flesh.

He looks back.

The thing's face is covered with seaweed. "Join me, Hilton. Join me."

He screams. Another hand grabs his other leg, pulling him into the dark depths.

For a split second, he didn't know where he was.

"It's so cold down here, Hilton. It's so cold."

The water turns to blood.

He sat up and wiped the sweat off his face. *Jesus, what a nightmare.* It was the same one he'd been having off and on for months, the one about his brother.

He reached over and laid his hand on Peggy. She was asleep on her stomach. Watching her back move gently up and down, a wave of guilt washed over him.

Maybe it was time to ask Diane for a divorce.

Or maybe not. The thought of throwing away all those years of marriage made him sick to his stomach. Yet, he couldn't imagine a world without Peggy. She understood him in a way Diane didn't. Knew what he wanted in life and how to help him get it. Without her, the whole idea of running for office was a joke.

It was so unfair. In France, most rich, successful men had a mistress and nobody batted an eye. Not the wife. Not the mistress. And certainly not the husband. Nobody cared. Do they like fried chicken in France? he wondered. Might be time to open a few stores.

He rolled back over and tried to find his phone on the nightstand, then remembered he'd left it in his backpack because he'd destroyed it earlier. He made a mental note to go get a new one in the morning and glanced at the clock: 2:35 a.m. Damn jet lag.

He slipped out of bed, careful not to wake Peggy, and shuffled over to the balcony window, opened the sliding glass door, and stepped outside.

The cool night air sent an exquisite chill down his back. He mulled going back in and grabbing his robe but didn't feel like it. So he leaned against the railing in his boxer shorts and T-shirt and took in the city. Albuquerque was a sea of lights before him. The spirit of Christmas was in the air, but not for him. It was time to get the whole damn holiday over with.

As he marveled at the cloudless sky, his mind drifted to Richard.

He loved his brother and missed him like crazy, but it was so much easier now that he was gone. That thought stuck a knife through his heart, but it was true. Everything was so much easier now that he didn't have to take care of Richard.

That's what his world had become the past few years, taking care of Richard. Making sure he stayed out of trouble. Making sure he didn't get himself killed. Richard's biggest strength was also his biggest weakness—he was a risk taker.

He was all in, all the time. Larger than life.

During their first year in business, when Hilton was convinced they wouldn't last another six months, it was Richard who made the decision to produce and star in a local TV commercial. The ones the Fred Borrows Agency had done weren't terrible, but they just didn't have an impact. People weren't coming in. Richard knew nothing about making a commercial, but he was funny as hell and knew how to get attention. Using money they didn't have, he made a spot that knocked it out of the park.

Fourteen years on and Crazy Dick's Chicken Town was poised to go regional, possibly even nationwide, and it wouldn't have happened without his brother.

Hilton's mind didn't work that way, and except for Peggy—and running for mayor—he preferred to play it straight down the middle. No highs. No lows. He was all about the numbers. Maximizing the profit and minimizing the risk.

Richard didn't care if he burned the whole thing down. He'd just build it again. No problem.

What he failed to understand, what Hilton desperately tried to explain to him, was that it's easy to start again when you're twenty-five. It's a whole other ball game when you're in your forties—and drunk more often than not.

What burns bright burns quick.

The day the horrible thing—as Hilton referred to it—happened, he and Richard were fishing on the lake. It was a ritual that began months after their parents were killed in a car crash when Hilton was sixteen and Richard nineteen. Twice a year they would spend all day out on the lake. Richard loved to fish, and Hilton loved to be outdoors.

After they opened the first restaurant, it turned into a getaway where they could be brothers, not business partners. Any discussion of the company was forbidden. They'd have a few beers, a few laughs, and in the process remember who they were and how much they needed each other.

That Saturday didn't start out well. It was overcast and windy, but it was a hot wind, and combined with the humidity, it made Hilton feel like he was submerged two feet underwater.

He could still hear his brother's voice as clear as day: "Rehab? You're joking, right?"

Hilton put the can back in the cooler and closed the lid. "No, I'm not."

"Goddamnit, just gimme the damn beer."

"What time is it?"

"Time for me to have another beer, asshole," he said and laughed.

"What time is it?"

"I don't know, Hilton. What time *is* it?"

He looked at his watch. "Nine fifty-two in the morning, and you're already drunk."

Richard leaned forward, a hand on each knee. "Do you even know what a drunk looks like? You've seen me drunk."

Hilton shook his head. *Too many times to count.*

"Then it should be clear as crystal that I am nowhere near three sheets to the wind." He jumped to his feet. The boat rocked back and forth.

Hilton dropped his rod and grabbed on to the side. He did not want to end up in the cold lake this morning.

"Want me to walk in a straight line?" Richard asked. "Do my ABCs backwards and forwards?"

"You're out of control. It's affecting the business."

"How? Sales are through the roof."

"Except for promotion, you're barely around. How many DUIs have you gotten? And how many women have you gotten—"

"First off, they make the legal limits so damn low you can't even have a glass of wine with dinner. Second, my last DUI was a year ago. And third, I'm not in jail."

"And you can thank Franklin for that. Can you just put a damn condom on? Is it that difficult?"

"Every one of those chicks said they were on the pill. And that money came out of my pocket." He paused, smiled, and stroked his chin. "Know what I think? I think somebody's jealous. I think somebody's jealous because while I'm out getting laid and having the time of my life, they're stuck at home with the Ice Queen."

Here we go, Hilton thought, *always dragging Diane into it.* "I don't want your life, Richard. At the rate you're going, you're going to end up in jail...or dead."

He laughed. "How about you handle your shit, and I'll handle mine?"

"You're not handling it. I am, and I'm sick and tired of cleaning up your mess."

"Do you even know how to have a good time anymore?"

"Yeah, and it doesn't include cocaine. Let's talk about that."

"Oh, fuck you, fuck you. I stopped that shit years ago."

"You want to lie to me? Fine. But don't lie to yourself."

"You know who you should have married? Remember Lisa? I'll bet you do 'cause she was hot. I know you tapped that. Oh, yeah, I see that grin."

"You are disgusting."

Of course Hilton remembered Lisa Hyde. How could he forget her? And yes, she was beautiful. Like an idiot, he let her get away. Lately he found himself thinking about her. Wondering if he'd made a mistake. She was probably happily married by now with a couple of kids like she'd always wanted. He wouldn't know. He'd never bothered to look her up.

"And what a personality," Richard said. "Don't get me wrong. Diane...she's a good-looking woman, but she's a total wet blanket, man. She's bringing you down. Hard. Rehab? Me? Nah, you need to get a divorce. Live a little. Get back in that saddle. Who knows how much time we got left in this world?"

"This is not about me, or Diane."

"Do you guys still even have a sex life? I'll bet your hand gets more action."

Hilton's fist clenched, and his face grew hot. "You need help—professional help."

"You think maybe she's getting it somewhere else? You ever think about that?"

"We're done." Hilton stood up, and the boat rocked a little. "Let's go back in."

"Maybe she's blowing some dude right now. You don't know."

"A few beers and you become a complete asshole. Or maybe you're always a complete asshole and hide it well."

"I never told you about Lisa, did I?" Richard asked, smiling.

Hilton looked him square in the eye. "Let me guess, you're gonna say you screwed her so I'll get all upset. 'Cause that's what you really want, isn't it? To hurt me. To piss me off."

Richard opened the cooler, pulled out a beer, popped the lid, and took a mouthful. It dribbled out the corner of his mouth.

Hilton headed toward the steering wheel. Time to get back to shore before he killed him.

"Everything you have, little brother—your house, your life—it's because of me. It's all because of me."

Hilton turned back. "Think so?"

"I could have hired an accountant to do what you do at a third of the cost."

"Wrong. Everything *you* have is because of me. I built this business. I found the money—"

Richard started singing softly, "Come on down, come on down to Crazy Dick's Chicken Town. Come on down, come on down..."—he took it up a notch—"...to Crazy Dick's Chicken Town."

"Shut up."

"Come on down, come on down to Crazy Dick's Chicken Town." Dancing back and forth, he belted it out as loud as he could.

"Stop it!" Hilton yelled.

"Hey, hey, calm down. I think you're starting to lose it. You know who wrote that little jingle? The one that sticks in everybody's head? Me. Not you. Me. You're just a pencil pusher, Hilton, you don't have a creative bone in your body."

"And you're just an asshole who thinks he can blow up the world and always land on his feet."

"I fucked Lisa."

"Liar."

"I did. After you guys broke up. I ran into her at Phil's. Took her back to her apartment and made that pussy sing all night."

"Liar."

"I'm just telling you the truth. You like honesty. Well, I can honestly say she told me I was way better in the sack than you."

"Stop it, just stop it. You didn't sleep with Lisa."

"You're right." He laughed. "We didn't sleep at all that night."

"I am this close to kicking your ass."

"Ahh, the threat of violence."

"It wouldn't be the first time," Hilton said.

"Yeah, but we're not kids anymore."

"And you're drunk off your ass. So, good luck with that."

"Remember that little tattoo Lisa had? The one on her inner thigh? What was it?" He thought for a moment and then snapped his fingers. "It was a butterfly. Remember?"

Hilton froze. How did Richard know about that? Obviously he must have told him at some point, but he couldn't remember.

"And how she came?" He grinned. "She'd grab a handful of your hair, hard, right? And then she'd scream, 'Take me, baby, take me, baby….' It was like riding a bucking bronco."

"You son of a bitch." Hilton raised his fist. "Another word and—"

"But you know who I didn't fuck? Because I am such good brother. Diane. She begged me, but I said no."

"Bullshit."

"Yeah, I came by one afternoon. You were gone, and she cornered me in the kitchen. Told me how horny she was. How you and her never did it anymore...started stroking me through my pants. I had to pry her off of me. It was embarrassing."

Hilton took off like a raging bull, sending the boat rocking back and forth. Feet off the ground, he landed a punch right across the jaw.

Richard stumbled backward, lost his footing, and went overboard. His head hit a mammoth rock that was sticking out of the water, and he went under.

"Richard? Richard?" Hilton yelled as he leaned over the side of the boat.

Watching the water spin round like it was going down the drain, he waited for his brother to come up for air, for him to come up laughing like he did when they were kids after a knock-down-drag-out fight.

He wanted to jump in after him, but his body wouldn't move. Time came to a standstill, and he saw his life without Richard. A life without embarrassment or frustration, pain or humiliation. It was beautiful.

He might have stood there for a second or an hour—to this day it was a big blank. All he knew was it was too long because when he finally dove in and pulled his brother to the boat, Richard wasn't breathing anymore. In a panic, he called 911 and tried mouth-to-mouth, but it was wasted effort. Richard was gone.

He'd let his brother die.

No one knew that. Things were whispered. Questions asked. Lawyers hired. He was a surprisingly good liar, he discovered. Ultimately, he walked away clean. Richard's death was ruled accidental, but Hilton knew better.

His eyes welled up. His hands shook. It would be so easy to go over the railing. They were on the twentieth floor. It'd be over in a heartbeat.

"Hey, honey, what are you doing out here? It's cold."

Peggy's hand touched his shoulder. He jumped back. She grabbed him by the waist. "I didn't mean to scare you."

He turned, wrapped her in his arms. "No, I'm fine."

She buried her face in his chest. "What are you doing?"

"I don't know. Couldn't sleep. Jet lag."

She kissed him. "It's warmer in the bed. If you can't sleep..."

"What did you have in mind?"

Giggling, she grabbed him by the hand and pulled him back into the hotel room.

THURSDAY

26

———

A BAG of donuts in one hand and a drink carrier with two large cups of coffee in the other, Nicole banged on the passenger window of her RX-7 with her elbow. A moment later the car door screeched open. Nicole handed Diane the bag and the carrier and closed the door.

Rubbing her sore-as-hell arm—which was getting worse, not better—she stumbled around to the driver's side and climbed in. She started the car, pulled her sunglasses perched atop her head back down, and savored a bit of coffee. As she was about to put the car in drive, Diane handed her a chocolate-covered donut.

"Oh, thanks." After a couple of bites: "Wow, I'm impressed. This is fantastic."

"Yeah, they are," Diane said with a rasp Nicole thought made her sound like a three-pack-a-day smoker.

By the time they'd left Jackson's apartment, Nicole's stomach was eating a hole through itself. She'd wanted to swing by Jittery Express, but her sister nixed that idea. "Too public," she'd said. "Everybody knows me there."

The compromise?

Sophie's Donut Hole.

Nicole had never heard of it before, but she'd be back. These little suckers were better than Krispy Kreme.

She drove out of the parking lot, and they headed toward Diane's house. For the next few minutes, she and Diane rode eating donuts and drinking coffee and saying nothing.

When the silence got on her last nerve, Nicole said, "We've got to figure out our story."

"Huh?" Diane turned and rubbed her eyes.

"You crashing on me?"

"No. No. I'm fine."

"We need to figure out what we're going to say if the police or somebody else shows up."

"You want to do that *now*?"

"No, but soon. Like later today. After we get some sleep. Who knows when they'll find his body?"

Diane sunk down in her seat, took off her cap, and played with it. "I'm so torn. Like you said, the later they find it...him, the better for us, I suppose, but...poor guy. He didn't deserve that."

"At least he went out on top."

"Nicole..."

"Hey, I'm sorry. I couldn't help myself."

Diane gazed out the window.

"Okay, that was a crappy thing to say, but he did it to himself," Nicole said. "The person I feel bad for is you. You didn't deserve this."

"I don't know. I was cheating on my husband."

"Who hasn't been a husband for a while now."

"Two wrongs don't make a right. Isn't that what Nana used to say?"

"Yeah, that and a lot of other folksy stuff like, 'That boy don't have a pot to piss in.'"

"I miss her so much."

"Me too." Nicole put on her blinker, slowed, and made a right turn. "Uncle Johnnie said she turned a lot of heads when she was younger."

"I'll bet she did. She was beautiful."

"And Papa was a pretty handsome guy too."

"You know that's where you get it from."

"My looks?"

"Guitar. Papa played in bands in high school and college, remember? Even went out to California for a while. Hoping to be a rock star. Pretty sure he was a hippie."

"That's right. That's right. You think he smoked pot?"

Diane burst out laughing. "Can you picture him stoned?"

"Remember when he found that joint in my room and got pissed."

"And said you were screwing up your life." Diane said it in a deep, loud voice.

"I'll bet he was pissed he couldn't get high anymore."

"'Cause Nana would have beat his butt."

"He was right, though. I am ruining my life, sorta…"

Diane coughed. "How's your hand?"

"Sore." She tried to make a fist with her left hand. "Real sore."

"You need to go to the hospital?"

"Nope, no hospital. Don't worry about it. Okay?"

"Okay."

"When did Papa go to California?"

"Mid-sixties?"

"Weren't they already married by then?"

"Well, according to Nana, they'd been married for a few years when he went out there. Almost got a divorce over it, but he came back and put the guitar away."

"I'll bet that was tough. Giving up something you love for someone you love."

"Could you do it?"

"Luckily, I am not a woman in love."

"But could you do it?"

Nicole shrugged. Her sister asked the weirdest questions.

"Well, I did. It sucks," Diane said.

"What did you give up?"

"Writing."

"You gave up writing for Hilton?"

"Not exactly, but maybe if I'd had to struggle more I'd still be writing."

"The struggling artist bit ain't all it's cracked up to be. A warm bed and roof over my head totally inspires my creativity. Seems to me if you want to do something, you do it. If you don't want to, you don't. I mean this in the best way possible, but you're incredibly lucky."

Diane turned, eyes narrowed. "How's that?"

"You have the one thing everybody wants."

"Money?"

"Time. How long has it been since you've had to work?"

"I left Blum & Pyne...?" She thought on it. "A few years ago?"

"And you could have written three books by now."

Diane sighed. "What have I been doing all this time?"

"Good question." Nicole cracked the window, and the cold winter air blew in. They cruised down the two-lane road in silence. The rain clouds were gone, leaving only gray sky.

After a few minutes, Nicole said, "I wish I could find someone who looked at me the way Papa looked at her."

"I don't think she ever got over it when he died."

Nicole glanced over at her sister. Diane's eyes were sunken and dark, hair wet and matted, and her lips parched. She had never seen her so broken down before. It was terrifying. Some people were built for the wild, out-of-control life. Diane wasn't one of them. Nicole hoped she could find her way back from this.

"Can we swing by the cemetery?" Diane asked.

"Now?"
"Yeah."
"Sure."
Nicole knew better than to ask why.

27

DIANE STOPPED in front of the gravesite. Engraved across the top of the headstone was the last name Scoggins. Beneath it, Betty Jean was on the left and William Charles on the right.

Billy and Betty. Betty and Billy. Together forever in eternity.

Diane hoped so. She'd never met two people more in love. Papa died first. Heart attack. Nana joined him six and a half years later of a broken heart. The pain of each loss still tore a hole in her heart.

Behind her, she could hear Nicole tapping her foot impatiently. Diane didn't care. Let her wait. She needed this moment. If only Nana were here, she'd know what to do.

Nana?

Can you hear me?

Please, Nana...

Help me...

Nana?

This was foolish, pleading with a slab of marble and a plot of grass and expecting some divine response. Her Nana was gone. She had to figure this one out on her own.

She looked around. Except for her and Nicole, the cemetery

was empty. The well-trimmed brown grass around the gravestone was still wet, and a light fog hung in the air. Sunlight rippled through the leafless trees, casting arcane shadows. Diane thought they looked like skeleton fingers clawing at her feet.

"Do you ever feel like you're being punished?" she asked Nicole.

"For what?"

"Living? Breathing?"

"By who?"

"God...the universe."

Nicole reached into her jeans pocket and pulled out a cigarette and lighter. "You know I don't buy in to all that."

"So you think this is it? This is all we get?"

"Pretty much."

"That's sad."

"Eh, maybe. Or maybe I sleep sound at night knowing I won't be judged."

Diane closed her eyes, took in the fresh morning air, and thought about the universe, about how massive and limitless it was. When she was a little girl, no older than five, she used to freak herself out by trying to imagine what was at the end of the universe. An infinite sea of white? A fathomless darkness? The harder she tried to picture it, the more frightened she became. Her mind couldn't process the thought of something that had no end.

Cigarette smoke yanked her out of her daze, and she rubbed her nose. "You know that'll kill you."

"A lot of things will kill ya." Nicole took another puff. "What are we doing out here?"

"How many random hook-ups have you had?"

"Random hook-ups? You make it sound like I'm a slut," Nicole whispered.

"Why are you whispering?"

"I'm not talking about this in front of Nana."

"But you don't believe in heaven."

"Or hell. But if you want to talk about this, let's go somewhere else."

Diane smiled. Nicole's logic often astounded her. "It's a piece of granite. She's not here."

"Then why did you want to come out here?"

"I don't know." After a long pause, Diane added, "Anyway, you're not a slut. You're just more fearless than I am."

"Or stupid."

"I'm not judging you."

"Maybe you should. God knows I've done some stupid shit in my life. Maybe there are consequences. Maybe there is a price for the things we do."

"Any of them ever go bad?"

Nicole raised an eyebrow.

"Your...encounters?" Diane waved the smoke away from her face.

Nicole grabbed her by the arm and hustled her away from the gravesite.

"What are you doing?" Diane yanked her arm free.

"I'm not answering these questions in front of her."

When they were a few feet down the pathway, Nicole said, "Define *bad*."

"Like last night."

"Well, no. Nobody ever died. At least not in the process."

"See?"

"So you think you're being punished by some angry God that didn't want you to have a good time last night? Who invented the vagina? Who invented the penis?" She pointed at the sky. "That dude. He can't get all bitchy 'cause he made it feel so good."

"This isn't about sex—"

"No, it's about a guy dying on top of you, okay? That's what this is about. But come on, that could have happened to anybody."

"But it didn't. It happened to me!" Her voice broke. "And it's horrible."

"I know. It is, and I'm sorry I encouraged you—"

Diane shook her head and cleared her throat. "I wanted to. I really did. And you know what? I'm glad I did it. 'Cause it was fantastic. I just wish..."

"Hey, it's over. It's over. Let's get you home. A hot shower and some decent food and the next thing you know it'll be Christmas and this'll be a bad memory."

"I don't think a week and some Christmas carols is going to wipe this out."

"You'd be surprised."

They headed down the path toward the parking lot.

"You ever dropped acid?" Nicole asked.

"Me?"

"Yeah, I didn't think so. You'd probably lose it, but it helps me. Clears out the cobwebs. If you ever want to try it..."

Diane stopped. "Oh, crap."

"What?"

"My car. We need to go get my car. I left it at the club."

28

———————

Sweat pouring down his face, Le Deuce trudged up the steps toward Jackson's apartment like he was walking the Bataan death march. He stopped halfway, grabbed the railing on each side of the stairs, bowed his head, and tried to suck in all the air he could. *Jackson better be here*, he thought. *He better be here or I'm gonna beat his damn ass when I find him.*

Who was he kidding? Jackson would kick his fat behind up one side and down the other. But he might shoot him in the foot just for making him climb these stupid stairs.

He couldn't believe he'd waited over three hours last night and the prick never showed. All morning he'd been calling and texting him. Zero response. Sometimes Jackson could be a flake, but he always showed up for a drop. And he always texted back. Jackson better have the money and the coke; if not, McAllister would have both their nut sacks.

With honey on top.

Damn, he could strangle the asshole. His earlobes were burning, he was so pissed. If he got any more pissed, he was going to have a stroke. After lunch he would head over to Big Planet

Fitness. It was time to get his fat ass into shape. He didn't want to die climbing the stairs at Hidden Pines.

First thing this morning he'd checked out Jackson's apartment over on 4th and Peachtree, but there was no sign of him. Then he'd remembered this shit-hole.

He made it to the third floor and found the apartment. He banged on the door with his fist as he glanced around to see if anybody was coming up the stairs or walking out of their apartment.

The coast was clear.

He waited a beat and knocked again. Silence. The bastard *was* inside. He'd checked out the Camaro in the parking lot before he came up. Probably passed out drunk. Knowing Jackson, he'd spent the night hanging out at The Wicked Hand getting his freak on.

That was the difference between the two of them. Le Deuce wasn't big on social contact. Jackson craved it.

He reached in his coat pocket and pulled out a lock-picking kit he'd gotten online. It was a great little tool set for when he couldn't get a warrant. Or didn't even want to ask for one.

When he grabbed the doorknob, he saw the door wasn't shut. It wouldn't budge, but it wasn't quite closed either. He knelt down and studied the base plate. Someone had used a crowbar to get the door open and pulled it shut when they left. Now it was jammed.

The hair on the back of his neck was tingling. Hand on the knob, he leaned his right shoulder against the door and with a heavy push forced his way into the apartment.

He walked into the living room and took in an eyeful. The place smelled like rotten cabbage or something. Beams of light streamed in through the jumbled up blinds, illuminating all the dust in the air. He covered his nose. The dust was going to wreak havoc with his allergies.

He moved down the short hallway and stuck his head in the

bathroom. Empty. He turned and headed across the hallway. The bedroom door was halfway closed. A gentle push swung it open.

Jackson was facedown on the bed.

"All right, get up. It's almost ten o'clock. Damn, boy, what'd you do last night?"

As he moved closer to the bed, he noticed something was off. Was Jackson breathing? He leaned down and with all his strength turned him over.

"Christ on a bike." He stumbled backward, crashing into the dresser.

Jackson's face had a bluish tint, his lips were white and his eyes lifeless.

He was dead.

LE DEUCE PLOPPED down on the couch and shot daggers at Jackson's phone. He'd torn the place to pieces, looking for the money and the drugs. Nada. He'd even looked in the Camaro. Zip.

There were no signs of foul play when he examined Jackson. Died in his sleep? It happens. But where was the money? The drugs?

He scratched his nuts. First things first. He had to retrace Jackson's movements last night. That required getting into his phone. And sure enough, Mister Neuro-Linguistic Programming had a password on it. Not a four-digit code—a password. Too many wrong attempts and he'd brick it. Before he stepped into that level of hell, he had an idea.

He got up, went to the bedroom, and sat down on the bed next to Jackson. He took Jackson's right thumb and laid it carefully on the home button.

The phone shook. No dice.

He tried Jackson's left thumb.

Same thing.

This was some real ding-dong shit.

He shoved the phone into his coat pocket and stormed out of the room. He couldn't dispose of Jackson's body until nightfall; that gave him eight to ten hours to get into the phone and find out where Stud-Muffin had been last night. He'd better hurry. The money trail was burning hot. It was now or never.

Who else knew Jackson was dead?

He paced the living room, a smile creeping across his face. A plan was taking shape. It was nebulous, but if he could bring it into focus, he might walk away with half a million dollars. Or more. And then the whole wide world, including Monica, could suck his little limp dick. Hell, with that kinda money he could buy himself a penile implant.

He strolled out the front door, his back straight, his step brisk. The morning was looking up.

29

Diane sped through her neighborhood, dreaming of the hot steaming shower she'd be taking in a few minutes. After that she'd have a glass of wine, a cashew bar, and pass out for a couple of days. She whipped around the corner onto Crescent Way and almost slammed on the brakes.

Sitting in her driveway was a rusty blue Honda Civic. Circa 2008.

"Are you kidding me?" She smacked the steering wheel and glanced at the dashboard clock: 9:23.

How could she be so stupid? She'd completely forgotten it was Thursday. Easing the Lexus slowly toward her house, she felt an overwhelming temptation to turn around and drive straight to Mexico. Or better yet, Canada. Mexico was too hot.

But running wouldn't fix anything. It would only delay the inevitable. Best to meet every snag head on.

Starting now.

She reached up and hit the remote. The garage door opened. She drove past the Honda and parked in the garage.

"TERESA?" Diane flung the door open and barged into the kitchen.

Deep in the house, a vacuum cleaner was humming along. She hurried toward the living room, her knees creaking as she walked. It was like she'd aged ten years in the last twenty-four hours.

"Teresa?" she cried out again. It was lost in the vacuum's racket. Skidding into the living room, her sneakers squealed on the hardwood floor.

Empty.

She paused and listened. The roar appeared to be coming from the guest bedroom. She took off down the hall.

Out of the corner of her eye, she glimpsed herself in the hallway mirror and came to an abrupt stop. What a disaster. She was twitching like she'd downed five cups of coffee. She inhaled and let it out. Tried to find her center. Inhaled and exhaled again. Took off her cap and tried to fix her hair. Decided it was impossible and put the cap back on. Satisfied she no longer seemed as crazy as she looked, she continued down the hall.

With a bit of poise, she entered the guest room. It was spacious with a twin bed, a dresser, and a nightstand. In front of the bed, a woman in her late fifties was methodically vacuuming the rug. A pair of earbuds in her ears, she was shaking her butt to the music as she worked.

"Teresa," Diane yelled.

Startled, the woman peeked over her shoulder. For a second Diane thought she was going to scream, and then her eyes lit up and her face broke out into an impish grin. Diane waved and smiled.

Teresa shut off the vacuum and pulled the earbuds out one by one. "Sweetheart, you scared the crap out of me."

"I'm so sorry. I didn't mean to."

"What's up?"

Diane wrapped her arms around her chest like a shield and

kept her eyes hidden. "Hey, I hate to do this to you, but...um... um...I don't need the house cleaned today."

"Uh, okay," she said, a hint of confusion in her voice.

"I'll still pay you. In fact, I'll throw in a little extra, but I couldn't sleep last night and I have a splitting headache. And I could really use a quiet day."

Teresa nodded. "Hey, it's good. It's all good. I can spend the day with the grandbaby."

"You sure?"

"Yeah, Lucy and Ron got into town last night, so...yeah, that would be great." Although her smile was inviting, her eyes had the hard-edged glare of someone who knew when two plus two wasn't adding up to four.

Diane forced her lips into a smile. If Teresa didn't believe her, there wasn't much she could do about it. She couldn't risk her finding something that might prove Jackson had been in the house last night.

"How far did you get?"

"Just the hallway and this room." She bent down and wrapped the power cord around the vacuum.

"When you're finished, meet me in the kitchen. I'll get your money." Diane backed into the hallway.

SHE STOOD at the front door and watched the Honda drive off. Teresa had been cleaning her house for over a year and yet Diane barely knew her. Born in Arkansas, she had four kids, a new grandchild, and she enjoyed hunting and fishing if the weather was right. And that was about it. Some people you have a rapport with. Others, not so much. But Diane didn't need a friend, she needed a maid, and Teresa excelled at that.

She prayed she hadn't made a critical mistake sending her away. On *Law & Order* it was always the little slip-ups that brought people down. That's why it was too risky to let her clean today. But making her leave was suspicious too.

Either way, Diane couldn't win.

She closed the door, locked the deadbolt, turned around, and faced the empty house. All she could hear was the tick-tock of the wall clock that hung in the living room. As she moved out of the foyer and headed for the kitchen, she made a conscious effort not to look over at the fireplace. Later she'd scrub the whole area from top to bottom, but right now she couldn't bear to see it.

She rubbed her palm across her forehead. Now she did have a headache. It felt like her face was being split right down the middle.

The shower could wait. She needed some wine. Maybe an entire bottle. She opened the kitchen cabinet and pulled out a crystal wineglass. It was from a set Richard had given them as a wedding present. Heading toward the fridge, she noticed the barstool Jackson had sat her down on last night.

Last night? It might as well have been a million years ago.

Her hand trembled. She glared at the quivering glass. "Damn it."

She threw it across the room. It smashed into the bay window, shattering both the window and the wineglass. Shards went flying. She turned and slammed her fist down on the kitchen countertop. Then in one fell swoop sent everything on it—salt and pepper shakers, stray utensils, various bills, and more—flying.

"Goddamnit! Goddamnit…" Her knees buckled, and she fell to the floor.

The floodgates opened, and the tears came. She sobbed. Sobbed like she hadn't in years. Not since Nana died.

A CARDBOARD BOX in her arms, Diane stepped out onto the veranda and trudged to the edge of the backyard where her property met the forest.

Because her house was at the end of the subdivision, miles of undeveloped woodlands separated her and the outskirts of Mulberry Grove. She enjoyed the privacy. She didn't think she could live in a big city like Atlanta, packed in like sardines in a can. Late in the afternoon, she would often sit on the swing, basking in the sun's glow as she read.

She opened the box and took out the crystal wineglasses Richard had given them. Flipping it over, she sat the box on the ground near a large oak tree and placed each of the five glasses on top.

She went back in the house and returned moments later with a 9mm Glock. She strolled out into the grass and stopped halfway between the house and the oak tree. With both hands on the pistol, she held it in front of her at waist level, safety on. After picking her target, she brought it up to eye level, arms extended, and released the safety. She aimed and fired a shot at the first glass to her left.

Boom! It shattered.

The gunshot, combined with the breaking glass, seemed to echo for miles.

Diane smiled. It had been months since she'd gone to the gun range, and she thought she might be a little rusty. Thanks to her Nana, she was a crack shot. Even better than her sister, which pissed Nicole off to no end.

Growing up on a farm in south Georgia, Nana had learned how to protect herself and was determined her girls learn the same. When they each reached the age of fifteen, she taught them gun safety and how to shoot. Diane took to it like a duck to water.

Standing there, the cold winter sun beating down on her face, the slow realization came—she was at the fork in the road. The middle of act two of her three-act journey.

Down this path lies great happiness, down this one doom and misfortune.

Decisions made over the next few days would affect the rest of her life, provided no one ever found about her and Jackson. That was another road altogether. The real question was, how would staying with Hilton do either of them any good? The marriage was over. If she hadn't met Jackson last night, the marriage would still be over.

She took aim and fired at the second wineglass. The bullet whizzed by, leaving the glass shaking, and ripped some bark off the tree. She recoiled. She didn't like to miss. Sometimes she could be very competitive, which is why Hilton didn't go to the gun range with her anymore.

She steadied her nerves and took another shot.

Boom. Without hesitation, she took out the three remaining glasses in rapid succession.

She walked down to the big oak tree and looked at the pieces of glass lying everywhere. The road to take couldn't be any clearer. Diane knew what she had to do.

30

———

Nicole stumbled out of the urgent care clinic, sunglasses on, hair in a ponytail, and her left hand in a cast.

If she could punch God, she would.

But she didn't believe in the Almighty, so she was thinking about punching her sister instead. Or maybe her brother-in-law. Or maybe she should head back over to Hidden Pines and beat the living shit out of Jackson's dead body for having the nerve to die last night.

Asshole.

Somebody was going to get one in the teeth for this. She still had a good right hook.

She tore through the packed parking lot, cursing her stupid luck. In two weeks—two short weeks—the band was going into the studio to do some recording, and now she had a broken hand.

It made no sense. After she'd landed on her hand earlier, it didn't hurt *that* much. But over the past few hours it had become more and more painful and swollen. By the time she'd dropped Diane off at The Wicked Hand to get her car, she could barely move her fingers, much less wrap them around a guitar neck.

She didn't tell Diane, but she knew something was wrong.

Hoping she'd just sprained her wrist, she went straight to the urgent care clinic only to find out she'd broken her hand instead.

"But I just fell on it," she'd insisted to the doctor, who informed her that using your hand to stop a fall is one of the most common ways to break it. Hell, if she'd know that, she would have let her face take the hit. A broken nose beats a broken hand for a guitarist.

"How long before I can play?" she'd asked as he was putting the cast on her hand.

He'd paused for what seemed to her like a lifetime before saying, "At least six weeks."

"But, but—"

"You've got to let it heal."

"Shit. But I won't have any problem playing again, will I?" For once her voice sounded unsure, weak, and terrified. She didn't like it. Not one bit.

He'd continued working and in a bored, reflexive tone said, "You should be fine. I don't see any reason you won't be able play again at some point."

At some point? That wasn't what Nicole wanted to hear. What she'd wanted to hear was: "No problem. It'll be like brand new. Don't worry about it. Eddie Van Halen broke his hand all the time. Didn't stop him." Those were the magic words.

She climbed into the car and, burning a little rubber, skidded out of the lot. Heavy bass thumping, she took a right onto Old Peachtree and headed for Winter Hawk Drive.

Since taking a shine to Timothy, her visits to her duplex had been few. But this morning it was the perfect spot to hide out while she tried to make sense of the last few hours. On the way, she stopped at the Quikie Shop and got a six-pack of Pabst Blue Ribbon, a pack of Marlboros, and some beef jerky. Time to drown her sorrows.

Careening onto Winter Hawk, she couldn't believe it. Timothy's Silverado was in her driveway. She figured he'd still be asleep.

The boy didn't open his eyes till at least noon. Sitting on the open tailgate, he was staring at the ground, his long legs swinging back and forth. He looked like a little boy waiting for his mommy to come home.

She zoomed in and parked on the grass. Not by choice. The big doofus had parked his green machine at such an angle it took up the whole driveway.

"What's up? Still haven't mastered that whole parking bit, huh?" she said as she got out, trying to sound like herself: calm, cool, and smart-ass. Fake it till you make it.

"What the hell happened to your arm?" Timothy rushed over to her.

"Oh, this?" She held up her left arm so he could get a full view of the cast. "Slipped in a puddle and fell."

"Fell...in a puddle...?"

"I know. Crazy, huh?"

"You okay?" He wrapped his arms around her and picked her up off her feet.

"Easy, tiger. Doctor Fantastic says it'll be good as new in about six weeks."

"I hope so."

"What are you doing here?"

He sat her back down and turned serious. "We need to talk."

"About?"

"Inside."

"Timothy?"

"Go on. I'll be there in a sec."

"What are you up to?"

"I just need to get something. Okay?"

"Okay, sure."

She opened her passenger door, grabbed the Quikie Shop bag, and walked inside. She glanced back over her shoulder at him. He smiled. Or at least his mouth did. His eyes didn't.

Something was up. She could feel it in her bones.

NICOLE STARED OPENMOUTHED at the pile of money and coke Timothy had dumped out on the kitchen table. She wasn't sure if she should scream or cry. Instead, she punched him in the face with her good hand.

"Ow!"

"You asshole!" she screamed. "You followed me?"

"You freaked me out, leaving in the middle of the night like that." He wiped the blood off his lip and rubbed his jaw. "Damn, I think you broke a tooth." He ran his index finger along the top row. "No...no, I think I'm okay." He did the same for the bottom. "Yeah, I'm good."

"How about I take another shot at it?" She pulled her fist back.

He jumped backward and held her at bay, both arms outstretched. "Nicole. Stop it. Just listen to me."

She continued to come at him. He ran to the opposite side of the table. They stood across from each other like two gunfighters at high noon—the pile of money and coke between them.

"I was worried about you," he said.

"So you stalked me? You can't just—"

"I wasn't stalking you, hunny bunny."

"No. Don't *hunny bunny* me, you bastard."

"I was trying to protect you. I trust my gut, and last night it told me you were in trouble."

"Sure it wasn't the Taco Bell?"

"And I was right. You could have gotten yourself killed. Do you realize where you two were?"

She tried not to look at the money. A few minutes ago she'd believed it was gone for good, and yet here it was again. She'd never seen this much cash before, all in neat little bundles. Keeping her eye on Timothy, she could hear the whispers in her ear. *No one would know. No one would ever know.*

"I don't need your protection," she said.

"Apparently you do."

"Okay, so you followed us. Fine. But then you went into his apartment and took the money? Why?"

"What happened to Jackson?"

"Why did you take the money, baby?"

"What happened to Jackson, Nicole?"

"He had a heart attack or something and died."

"Where?"

"Diane's. The house you followed me to. They were doing their thing, and then shit went sideways."

"So you guys didn't kill him?"

"You think me or my sister could kill anybody?"

"No, but you gotta admit—it looks bad."

"I wanted to call the police, but she talked me out of it. And she was right, it would have ruined her life. You still haven't told me why you took the money."

"I don't know."

"That's not an answer."

"I don't know. It didn't seem right leaving it there. That's 'fuck you' money."

Her eyes found the pile, and it transfixed her. "And it could get us killed."

"But it could also get the band going. You could stop cutting hair. We could go on the road. I saw an opportunity, and I took it."

He'd done this for the band? That was so incredibly sweet and so incredibly stupid.

"We can't keep it," she whispered as she came around to his side of the table.

He took a step back.

"I won't bite. Promise."

She reached out and touched his cheek. "Sorry I hit you. Between last night and this..." She held up her cast. "I snapped."

Timothy brushed the strands of hair out of her face. "I've had worse. You really want to take it back?"

"No. I want to keep it. I want to keep all of it. And I want to run away to some remote island, and I want to play my guitar again..." Her voice cracked, and she cleared her throat.

Ever since she was a little girl she'd avoided crying at all costs, but right now, she could feel the tears coming on like a freight train.

"This is such bullshit."

Timothy took her in his arms. "Hunny bunny, want some ice cream?"

"Yes."

———

CURLED UP ON THE COUCH, Nicole dug through a pint of Chocolate Chip Cookie Dough while Timothy, nestled beside her, diligently worked on a pint of Rocky Road. After she'd calmed down, he'd run to Piggly Wiggly and gotten the ice cream along with hot dogs, chips, and coleslaw for dinner later.

The duplex was a small two-bedroom with a kitchen and living room. She had lived here for the past few years, ever since she moved back from LA. It was a fixer-upper that still needed fixing. Diane called her "eighty-five percent" because she'd get something eighty-five percent done and then move on to something else. The place was temporary, much like Nicole's life.

"We can't go back until it gets dark," Timothy said between mouthfuls.

Nicole nodded and licked her spoon. "This is stupid crazy."

"What?"

"All of it, babe. I got...what? Couple hundred thousand in my house right now. Jeez, did you know he was a drug dealer?"

He shook his head.

"How did you know him?"

"We were in the Marines together, but that was another life-time. Then he started showing up at the club last year. Ian and him are buddies, I guess. It was just chance we ran into him last night."

"Does he have a job? Besides selling drugs?"

"Said he was doing some contracting stuff. Private security. Not my thing, but a lot of guys make good money doing it. I knew Jackson liked to party hard, but..."

"Why did you do it?"

"Huh?"

"Take the money, silly."

He dug through the container like he was looking for the perfect spoonful of ice cream.

She was tempted to elbow him in the ribs. His strong, silent type routine could wear on her nerves. "Babe..."

"'Cause my brain don't work right anymore."

"I doubt that."

After a long pause, he said, "He didn't deserve that money."

"Who?"

"Jackson."

"He's dead. And I can guarantee it wasn't his money, anyway." She leaned back and looked him up and down. "I thought you guys were friends."

"It's a long story."

"And you let Diane go home with him? Timothy?"

"He's not a monster. He can be charming as hell. Got his ups and downs like anybody else. I'm talking about something that happened in Afghanistan. Crazy shit. I knew he wouldn't hurt her, and he didn't. Way you tell it, she had a good time."

"She did...till he bit the dust."

"Ice water, hunny bunny."

"What? He died. I don't need to spruce it up."

He put a big spoonful of ice cream in his mouth and mumbled, "Well, you wanted your sister to have a good time. I made the best choice I could given what I had to work with."

"Diane made the choice."

"True."

They went silent for a bit. Nicole liked how they could be comfortable in their silence together. Maybe *that* was the real reason she stayed with him. She didn't have to be somebody else.

"I don't know why I took it," he said. "It's like I went in his apartment and the next thing I know, I'm driving away with the bag in my truck. That's why I came here. I figured you'd have a better idea what to do than me."

She turned and faced him. "Well, you know I want to keep it. Damn, I want to keep it. The money's one thing. That coke is a whole other world of shit."

"Maybe we could take the coke back and keep the money?"

"It don't work that way, babe."

She sat the ice cream down on the floor by her feet and stretched. She pulled her legs up underneath her, leaned into him, and closed her eyes.

After a few minutes, she mumbled, "We're such a kick-ass band."

"I know."

"I mean it. I've played in so many over the years, so many crappy-ass bands. We're like crazy good."

"Don't you have to work later?"

"No. I cancelled all my appointments. I'm not going to be able to cut hair for a few weeks, anyway." She rubbed her cast.

"Your arm's gonna be fine," he whispered and ran his fingers through her hair.

She smiled. His big hands felt good. She could stay like this forever. "I hope so. I really hope so..." Her words trailed off as her eyes grew heavy and the darkness overtook her.

31

"Yeah, he was here last night," Ian said. "You know him?"

Le Deuce nodded. He did indeed know Jackson, which was why The Wicked Hand was the first stop on his list.

He was standing in the parking lot as Ian and a younger man hung Christmas lights on the front of the building. Actually, Ian wasn't hanging anything, he was pacing back and forth—hands on his hips, cigar between his teeth—supervising.

"Little more to the right, Joey. Yeah, that's it. That's it," he yelled.

Ian Silver was a fifty-something New Yorker, his accent a muddle of Bronx and Dixie, who had found his way down South thirty-odd years ago. What Le Deuce's granddaddy used to call a "carpetbagger."

"Was he here long?" Le Deuce asked. The wind snuck up on him, scattering his comb-over. He quickly forced the hair back over his bald spot.

Ian took a puff off his cigar and kept his eyes on Joey as he said, "Hung out for a few and split with some chick."

"Got a name?"

"No, but they were playing pool together before they left. Playing with two of the kids from the band..." He stopped. "Joey, come on, damn it, lower, lower...that's better. Jaysus."

He turned back to Le Deuce. "Worthless kids can't even hang Christmas lights anymore."

"What band?"

"The 8 Ballers. Not bad. And they bring a nice-size crowd for some local cats. Although at my age, this shit is getting too loud for me. If you'd told me when I was a kid that I'd be digging Chet Baker and Miles Davis instead of Led Zeppelin and Black Sabbath, I'd have said, 'Get the fuck outta here.'"

"But you don't know who he left with?"

He thought for a second. "She might have been the guitar player's sister, but don't quote me on it. I will say that chick can wail on the guitar, man." He coughed, spit, and then after catching his breath wheezed out, "And she ain't too bad on the eyes either. The kind you'd like to bend over the table and smack on the ass while you're delivering the groceries, you know?"

Le Deuce smiled.

"Yeah, you know. You know. Of course, us old fuckers, we ain't delivering as many groceries as we used to. And most of the time it's a salad." He took another puff and wiped the sweat off his forehead.

It seemed to Le Deuce no matter how hot or cold it got, Ian was always sweating. The man must have a glandular problem.

"So what's the deal? Our golden boy in trouble?"

Le Deuce shook his head. "No. Just need to talk to him. It's not urgent. But he's not answering his phone. I checked his place. Figured you might know something."

"Probably sleeping off a drunk in some chick's bed. If he swings by later, I'll let him know you're looking for him."

He slapped Le Deuce on the back, reached out with his massive meat hook, and gave him a vigorous handshake.

"Thanks, I'd appreciate it."

Le Deuce turned and headed toward his Volvo, his comb-over dancing in the wind. As he did, he rubbed his right hand. The carpetbagger had squeezed the crap out of it.

Le Deuce sat in his Volvo, a burrito in one hand and his phone in the other, googling "The 8 Ballers." His first hit returned a book about WWII: *The Eight Ballers: Eyes of the 5th Air Force.*

Obviously not what he needed. Narrowing the terms to "The 8 Ballers band + Mulberry Grove Ga" brought up the band's website and Facebook page. He scrolled through the Facebook page, making notes in a little flip notepad as he went. Computers had their place, but he was old-school. Writing the facts out by hand was the best way for him to bring a situation into focus.

According to their bio, the band had been together for about a year and included Maximilian Hughes, singer; Nicole Robinson, guitarist; Timothy MacDonald, bass; and Rita Monroe, drums.

He clicked on the photos tab, scrolled through a few, and resisted the urge to puke. They were a motley-looking bunch— spoiled-rotten kids pretending to be bad asses. He bet they'd never had a bad day in their life. Everything about them was foreign to him. Growing up, he wasn't into rock and he wasn't into disco. George Jones, Conway Twitty, Merle Haggard, and Johnny Cash; those were real men singing about real things. And when he had the windows down and his foot on the gas, it was "Folsom Prison Blues" or "White Lightning" that would make his car shake.

Ian had said Jackson left with the sister of the guitar player, so he clicked on the link to her page.

Nicole Robinson.

He jotted that down. Ian was right, she was a little hottie. He went through her friends list and found Diane Hancock. Scrolling through Diane's pictures, he thought that while she was certainly a beautiful woman, she didn't look like somebody Jackson would go home with. She seemed a bit conservative, shy. Her selfies too forced. If anything, Nicole was more Jackson's type. She had that wild spark in her eyes, that up-for-anything look.

Over the years, Le Deuce had found most witnesses' memories weren't accurate. Not even close. Not even an hour later. Ian was probably too busy tending bar to see who left with whom. It'd make sense to question both women.

Getting into Jackson's phone could narrow down where he'd been, but even if that turned out to be a bust, at least Le Deuce had names, and that gave him a starting point. One of these ladies knew what happened to Jackson last night.

Now it was just a matter of finding out which one.

32

Hilton watched Peggy bite into her cheeseburger. He couldn't believe how beautiful she was, and he couldn't believe she was his.

Was this all a dream, and he'd wake up soon? Was Richard's death a dream too? Had his entire life been a dream?

He'd read in the *New York Times* recently about a group of scientists who believed that we were living in computer simulation. Hilton felt real, but then again, what did *real* feel like? He was a meat-and-potatoes kind of guy, and abstract ideas about reality only gave him a headache.

Computer simulation or not, Peggy felt real—every inch of her—and that was all he needed.

Earlier she had mentioned the D-word: divorce. It was the first time she'd ever brought it up, and it made him a little sick to his stomach. He thought he was the only one thinking about it. She looked up and caught him staring at her.

"What?"

He shook his head and took a bite of his ribs.

"I didn't freak you out earlier when I brought up divorce, did I?" Peggy said in her honey-drenched Southern drawl.

"No. Did I seem freaked out?" How could she read his mind like that? It was crazy.

"Maybe a little," she said with a smile.

When she smiled like that, it made him want to throw her on the table and make love to her right here. That probably wouldn't go over too well. Having sex on the table at Applebee's would definitely go viral. He bet it would be worth it, though.

"This isn't about us. I'm not trying to rope you into marriage, Hilt. I'm thinking about your political career."

"Hilt" had become her little pet name for him. He liked it.

"No, I get that." He looked around for the waiter. He needed a refill of his sweet tea.

"Let's say, for argument's sake, that our affair—which is what it is—ends soon. Not that it will." She gave him a wink. "Are you going to run back to Diane? Or eventually have another affair? If you weren't interested in having a life in politics, it wouldn't matter, but if you and Diane are as unhappy as you seem to be, it's only a matter of time before this becomes an issue that could derail everything you're working for. My advice, not as your 'mistress'"— she laughed—"but as your campaign manager is that it's best to confront it now. A divorce won't hurt you running for mayor of Mulberry Grove. Because frankly nobody is going to give a shit. But running for state senate? Governor? Then it could bite you in the ass."

When she put it that way, it made sense. Peggy always made sense. Maybe *she* should run for mayor and he could be her campaign manager.

The waiter appeared, refilled his iced tea, and disappeared just as quick. Hilton took a drink, followed it up with a piece of rib. "You should—"

He burst out coughing.

"You okay?" Peggy looked up from her plate.

He couldn't stop. He held up his right hand like he was a

traffic cop trying to halt an approaching car and tapped his chest with his left as he hacked up a lung.

Peggy was out of her seat and smacking him on his back before he realized it. He turned and looked at her, panic ripping through him, and clawed at his neck. He couldn't breathe. Something was stuck in his throat.

"Hang on, I got you," Peggy said. "Don't panic."

Without hesitation she wrapped her right arm around his waist, placed the heel of her left hand on his back, and did the Heimlich maneuver, hitting him between the shoulder blades with one hand as she thrust her other into his abdomen.

On the fifth try, a small piece of meat came flying out of his mouth.

Hilton gasped for air. "Oh...shit..."

She patted him on the back. Around them a small crowd had gathered, which included the waiter, two retirees, and a hipster.

"Is he okay?" asked one of the retirees.

"Yeah, he's all right," Peggy said, looking up at the group. Then to Hilton, "Breathe, just take a deep breath. Okay?"

"You saved his life," the waiter said in disbelief.

Hilton stopped coughing and caught his breath. "You did. You saved my life."

She grabbed her glass of water and handed it to him. He took a small sip. Now that the worst hadn't happened, the excitement around Peggy and Hilton left as fast as air escaping a balloon, and the crowd scattered.

As she walked away, the retiree said, "Better take him to the hospital just to make sure he's okay."

Peggy smiled at her. "Yes, ma'am. We will."

"Where did you learn that?" Hilton asked, rubbing his neck.

"When I was a kid, I was a lifeguard at my daddy's pool."

He took a drink of water. "Damn, that scared the shit out of me."

She hugged him. "Me too, babe. Me too."

He looked at the piece of meat lying on the table and found it hard to believe something that small could have changed everything.

They sat there for a few minutes as Hilton regained his composure. After taking another drink of water, he said, "I need to get a divorce."

Peggy looked at him, confusion in her eyes.

"Diane and I don't love each other anymore. All we're doing is hurting each other. Life's too short to live this way. I need to go back. Tomorrow. I need to sit down and talk it over with her. I'm not going to tell her about us, but you're right. I have to get a divorce."

"Honey, you know whatever you decide, I'm behind you a hundred percent."

He grabbed her hand. "I know."

She flashed that smile that made his heart stop. Despite his haggard breathing and sore throat and spinning head, he still wanted to throw her on the table and make love to her right here.

After the divorce and the election, maybe he'd rent out an Applebee's for a private party. Just the two of them. He'd take her on the table, and they could celebrate his victory.

Their victory.

33

––––––––

H ER WET SKIN glistening in the early afternoon sunlight, Diane stretched out on her king-sized bed.

She had an idea. It was silly, but it made her smile. She was going to get a tattoo. She'd never had much of a desire for one, but as she was cleaning up the house, it had hit her like a divine inspiration—a tattoo would be a milestone. A symbol of both her death and rebirth.

Diane was dead. Long live Diane.

The gentle wind from the open window washed over her, seeping into her soul. Normally, after a shower, she'd get dressed right away. Unlike her sister, Diane wasn't comfortable naked. Her body had too many flaws, but right now she couldn't care less. And were they flaws? According to whom? Her butt was a little too big? So what? Who cared if her breasts didn't perk up like they used to? There were men out there that still wanted to make love to her. Good-looking, sexy men. She could see it in their eyes when she walked past. Lying there, the future before her, she felt beautiful.

And damn sexy.

And after all, isn't it the imperfections that make us beautiful?

Probably not, but it made a nice meme on Facebook.

After scrubbing the living room, kitchen, and bathroom clean, she had hauled the oriental rug down to the dump. Tomorrow she'd buy a new one. Something ugly as a "screw you" to Hilton.

She was also entertaining the idea of getting her hair cut shorter and coloring it. What color, she wasn't sure. She reached over and grabbed her phone off of the nightstand. Hopefully, Nicole would be up for doing her hair tomorrow. Then she realized Nicole might be asleep and laid the phone down on the bed.

When Hilton got home, he wouldn't notice any of this—the rug, the tattoo, or the new hair. Whatever. Once she hit him with the divorce, it wouldn't matter, anyway.

She grabbed the blanket at her feet and pulled it up over her. Her thoughts drifted to Jackson. She missed him, crazy as it seemed. Missed how he made her feel. Like she was special. He might have been a horrible guy—or maybe not. She never got the chance to find out. But she was grateful that he helped her. Grateful he opened a door for her, one she might never have opened herself. One she would now have to step through on her own.

She snuggled with the warm blanket. Tomorrow was shaping up to be a big day—divorce lawyer, tattoo, haircut. She couldn't wait.

Long live the new Diane.

The thought terrified and thrilled her all at the same time.

Time slowed, and her eyelids grew heavy. Sleep welcomed her.

***

She enters the room. The walls are glistening white. It's so vast she can't see where it ends.

It is filled with people. So many faces they blur together, their laughter overwhelming, almost painful.

A casket is far off in the distance.

As she moves, it feels like she is trying to walk underwater, her arms reaching out slowly, pushing the heavy liquid apart.

She makes her way to the casket. It's closed. With a strength she didn't know she had, she slowly opens it. A man dressed head to toe in black lies still. He's a beautiful, distinguished man, she thinks. He opens his eyes. They're bloodshot. He smiles and has...

Fangs?

Wait a minute. He's a vampire?

Suddenly all the people in the room clap in unison like at a hoedown or a county jamboree, the kind Nana took her to as a child. She hears it, softly at first. An insistent whisper...

Come on down, come on down...

To Crazy Dick's Chicken Town...

The vampire sits up and is out of the casket in one quick motion. He lunges for her.

Come on down, come on down...

To Crazy Dick's Chicken Town...

She takes off, running through the crowd for her life, and the chant gets louder:

Come on down, come on down...

To Crazy Dick's Chicken Town...

Everything speeds up like a Benny Hill sketch.

Come on down, come on down...

To Crazy Dick's Chicken Town...

She runs faster and faster. Behind her, the vampire, who has morphed into a fireman swinging an axe, keeps the same distance, never gaining or losing ground.

Come on down, come on down...

To Crazy Dick's Chicken Town...

Suddenly she's in a field, the sun in the sky bigger than she's ever seen it.

Massive.

Overpowering.

She can smell the freshly cut grass. Her white dress blows in the wind.

Up ahead, a group of people are singing in joyous unison.

Come on down, come on down...

To Crazy Dick's Chicken Town...

She is in the group. It's a wedding.

Come on down, come on down...

To Crazy Dick's Chicken Town...

Her wedding.

At the end of the aisle, Hilton stands on one side of the pastor and Jackson stands on the other.

Come on down, come on down...

To Crazy Dick's Chicken Town...

COME ON DOWN...

———

DIANE ROLLED over and opened her eyes.

What was that?

Her phone vibrated. It was still on silent. She picked it up.

Hilton.

About time. But it was too late. He'd missed that window by about twenty-four hours and a couple of years. She wasn't ready to talk to him yet.

Maybe tomorrow.

But not now.

She declined the call, laid the phone on the nightstand, and looked at the clock. Twenty minutes? She'd only been asleep twenty minutes? It felt like hours.

In that time the room had grown dark as the wintery clouds outside her window had put a wall between her house and the sun.

34

———

HANDS IN HIS COAT POCKETS, Le Deuce paced the back row of Toytime.

"Dennis, I don't want to lock it up," he said. "I need to see what's on this phone. Besides, it's not a code. It's a password."

Beside him, a twenty-year-old in a red Santa hat knelt down, ripped open a large box, and pulled out a couple of action figures.

All around them, rambunctious children and anxious adults combed the aisles. The holiday spirit was palpable. Over the loudspeakers, Rudolph the Red-Nosed Reindeer was going down in history.

"Shit, man. That makes it even harder." Dennis sat the figures on a shelf.

"I thought—"

"Excuse me. Excuse me, sir." A tiny woman in a camo jacket charged up, dragging a young boy with a mullet along with her.

Le Deuce turned away and pretended to look at the action figures. He didn't want anyone to see him here.

He heard Dennis greet them with a smile in his voice: "Yes, may I help you?"

"My boy's about to burst his bladder. Where's your toilet?"

"Ma'am, I'm sorry, but we don't have a restroom. If you go out the front entrance, take a right, the restrooms are about two stores down."

"This is a toy store. You should have a toilet for the kiddies."

"You're right, we should. But we don't."

"Fine." She grabbed the child by the hand and dragged him down the aisle.

"Mama, I gotta pee now!" the little boy screamed. "I gotta peeeeeeeee!"

"You better hold it, Axel. Or you're gonna get a whupping."

Le Deuce turned and watched them leave. "There would be some dead kids if I worked here." He paused, eyeing the surrounding horde. "Dead parents too."

"You're all heart. It's Christmas. Smile."

Le Deuce got in his face. "*Never* tell me to smile."

"Hey, dude. Chill. I'm just jerkin' your chain."

"I'm not in the mood. That's it? That's all you got? What happens if I lock it up?"

"You're screwed."

"I thought you were the genius hacker. I can't erase the phone. I need to find out where he's been."

"When do you need it by?"

"Right now. Today."

Dennis shrugged, a look of shame in his eyes. "If I had a few days, maybe, but today? Ain't possible."

"How many times do I have?" He paced back and forth like a bull about to charge.

"Six before it locks it up for a minute, but after that each wrong password locks it longer and longer until it's a brick."

"Thanks for nothing."

"Hey, no problem, dude."

Le Deuce lumbered down the aisle. Almost to the door, he stopped and turned back. "Tell me, Mr. Genius Hacker, why the hell do you work here?"

Dennis beamed. "Because I get a great discount on the toys."

Le Deuce stomped out of the store. Was he the only sane person left on the whole damn planet? It felt like it.

AFTER PAYING for his hot chocolate, Le Deuce moseyed over to a bench and took a seat. Home to most of the big-box stores and a plethora of smaller retailers, Avenue on the Square was Mulberry Grove's outdoor shopping mecca, and, oh, how he hated this place. It was a snapshot of everything wrong with the world. Luckily, the foot traffic was light, considering how close it was to Christmas.

His feet were killing him, and he prayed his gout wasn't coming back. The attack last year had him out of work for an entire week and ready to slit his wrists. It always started with the ache in his big toe. He pulled off his shoe and massaged his foot. The loafers weren't cutting it anymore. He needed a new pair. Actually, some new feet would be nice. A blood transfusion wouldn't be bad either. He had a complete list of body parts that needed replacing. He put his shoe back on and took a taste of hot chocolate. The rich liquid coated his throat.

As he was running down the different passcode choices in his head, a woman sat down on the bench beside him. He caught sight of her out of the corner of his eye.

She was a knockout.

He could sense she had crossed her legs and angled herself toward him. He started to get up and head back to his car. Beautiful women made him break out in a sweat.

Before he could move, she asked, "Any luck finding Booth?"

An electric jolt shot through him.

He turned and got a good look at her. Five foot seven or eight, she had short black hair with white streaks, a brick house of a body, and legs to die for. She was wearing a black leather jacket, a black T-shirt, tight jeans, and boots and looked to be between twenty-five and thirty. Based on her accent, he thought she might be Australian. But he couldn't be sure. Accents were not his forte.

"Who the hell are you?"

"McAllister asked me to check on the status of his shipment."

"You, sweetheart? Is this a joke?"

With lightning speed, she reached across the bench, grabbed his left hand, and bent his middle finger back.

He screamed and dropped his hot chocolate, spilling it all over the sidewalk.

Everyone within shouting distance turned and looked at him. He didn't care. The pain was that intense.

"I'm not your sweetheart. Answer the question," the woman whispered.

"I'm working on it. Goddamnit!" He tried to clutch his finger. She slapped his hand away.

"How?"

"Shoe leather."

"What?"

"Shoe leather, police work, investigating. My job."

She let go of his finger and put her hands back in her lap.

"I could arrest you for assaulting a police officer," he said, rubbing his finger. "Christ on a bike, that hurt."

She put her wrists together, held out her hands as if to say, "Cuff me," and looked him square in the eye. "Officer, I'm all yours."

Angry as he was, she was really turning him on, and he hated himself for it. Sometimes he wished he had no sexual urges at all. They made him feel so weak. Either that, or he wished he was better looking so he could get some pussy. One or the other. The older he got, the more he seemed to repulse women. Might as well wear a bag over his head.

"You didn't have to bend my finger like that. You could have asked nicely."

"And you would have told me to go fuck myself."

He shrugged. "Maybe…"

"Don't call me sweetheart, darlin', or honey, and the rest of your fingers will be just fine."

"What do I call you?"

She scooted over, getting uncomfortably close. He tried not to, but he couldn't help but stare at her breasts. They were perfect—not too big, not too small.

"You can call me whatever you like," she whispered in his ear, "but the package better be delivered in the next forty-eight hours."

God, she smelled like pure heaven.

"Or?"

She put her hand on his inner thigh. "I'll bend more than your middle finger."

She stood, stepped over the puddle of hot chocolate, and walked off down the strip.

The lady was a killer in every way. Where the hell were women like this when he was thirty? He watched her for a second, but it was too much, and he glanced back at the puddle. He couldn't bear the sight of her ass. It moved in a way that wasn't human.

Once he was certain Miss Hot Chocolate was gone, he jumped up and raced to his car.

How the hell did she find him?

He'd taken a personal day today, so no one at the department should have any clue where he was. Which meant—a tracking device on his car, or they had hacked his phone.

McAllister had people everywhere. Still, this was too damn fast. He'd thought he at least had another day before anybody came looking. Hell, Jackson had only gone to Texas on Tuesday and texted him for a meetup yesterday. Jackson must have told somebody he'd found the package. Le Deuce sure hadn't. He never liked to say anything until it was a hundred percent for this very reason. Shit happens and then they blame him.

Not this time. This time he was going to beat everybody at their own game.

Coming to a stop in front of his Volvo, he bent down and looked under the back fender. Then he scooted around to the front. He didn't see anything, but that didn't mean diddly with today's surveillance equipment. For all he knew, there could be a robotic mosquito following him around.

It's a science fiction world we're living in.

Far more than most people even realized. If they did, they'd burn their computers and cell phones and lock up everyone in the government and put them on trial for treason along with the CEOs of every tech company in the world. The fact people were out Christmas shopping and not rioting in the streets should have amazed him. Sadly, it didn't. People were sheep.

With a grunt, he got to his feet and scanned the parking lot. He could feel the eyes of the world upon him.

He'd have to ditch the car and his phone, get one of those burner ones. And he'd have to find a place to stay for the next couple of nights after he got all the stuff he wanted from his house. There wouldn't be much. He was a simple man with little sentimentality. He didn't like to hang on to the past. And what would be the point? Either he'd find the money and get the hell out of Dodge or he was a dead man walking.

This was do or die.

Just the way he liked it. Finally, he'd get some excitement in his life.

LE DEUCE HANDED the woman behind the counter of the George Washington Inn three hundred-dollar bills and two twenties.

She thanked him, opened the register, and gave him his change. He forced a smile, nodded, and walked out of the office and into the rear parking lot.

The George Washington Inn was an off-the-beaten-path bed-

and-breakfast. He'd picked it over a regular hotel, like a Days Inn, because this was a slow time of year and there wouldn't be many Nosy Nancys around. Plus, the owner, Fred Hamilton, owed him a favor and knew how to keep his mouth shut.

Plus, they took cash. That was the critical thing.

He didn't want a paper trail.

Leaving his Volvo at his house along with his phone, he'd snuck out the back and walked two blocks over to the bus stop.

From there he took the bus to Levy's Used Cars, where he paid cash for a black 2008 Toyota RAV4. Getting the cash wasn't a problem—he kept large amounts hidden in different parts of his home because he didn't trust banks.

Before heading to the bus stop, he'd taken his money belt and filled it with all the cash he had. Now his house could burn to the ground for all he cared.

He'd left the Volvo in the garage so as not to be too obvious, but he hoped that by leaving his car and phone at the house they'd think he was staying there all night. To enhance the illusion, he'd left a few lights and the TV on, plus his laptop open and logged on to the internet.

He knew it wouldn't fool Miss Hot Chocolate for long, but it didn't matter. One of these two ladies, Nicole or Diane, would talk. He was sure of it.

And if they didn't?

He had never killed someone in cold blood before, but there was a first time for everything.

He limped across the parking lot toward his room, the big toe on his right foot burning like hell. Sure enough, his gout had to come back right at the worst possible time. Hadn't he read stress brought it on? Maybe he was wrong? Maybe it wasn't gout, just old age.

He found his room, closed the curtains, and locked the door, then plopped down in the chair by the bed, where he removed his shoes and massaged his toe.

Even without the gout, he would need some help to get rid of Jackson's body. It would be easier to leave it in the apartment, but that didn't jell with his scheme. McAllister had to believe Jackson disappeared with the money and the coke.

Who could he find to help him move the body? He thought on it for a few minutes but drew a blank.

He looked at his watch: 2:20 p.m. There was a lot to get done over the next few hours. He pulled out his notebook along with a pen and made a list. He was a master list maker.

Priority one was access to a computer or tablet. He needed some way to research the sisters. Worst case, he could hang out at the library, but he didn't like that idea. Too many prying eyes looking over his shoulder, plus they track those searches.

A cheap laptop would work, and then he could log in to his VPN. That would cover his tracks. Anything he needed to buy online, he'd use his Bitcoin account for.

He'd spent years hiding everything he could from the government. Hiding from McAllister and Hot Chocolate would be a piece of cake.

He would do all his research today, dispose of Jackson tonight, and "interview" Nicole and maybe Diane tomorrow. That would put him at the forty-eight-hour mark.

He pulled Jackson's phone out of his coat pocket. Without a doubt they were tracking this phone too, but he had to take the risk. Finding out where Jackson had spent his last hours would make this ten times easier. The more he knew, the quicker he could plan.

He cleared his mind as best he could and tried to think like Jackson, which should be easy—the man seemed to live only for pussy. While not friends, they had known each other and shared a beer or two along with tons of war stories for the past few years.

His first impression had been that Jackson was a smooth talker, full of piss and vinegar. Later he realized a good chunk of that bravado was an act, and that he was far shrewder than most people gave him credit for. However, the guy had a very warped world view.

Le Deuce saw the world as a cold and ruthless place one fought to survive. Jackson saw it as his stage from which he would educate the unwashed masses with the sheer force of his charisma.

The most important person in Jackson's world was Jackson. Everyone else came a distant second.

He wiped the sweat off of his lip and tried his first password guess. His hand shaking, he typed: *j-a-c-k-s-o-n*...

The text shook back and forth. Nope.

He tossed the phone on the bed, closed his eyes, and prayed. Not that he believed in God—he was a card-carrying agnostic— but he could use all the help he could get. Why wouldn't God want him to be rich?

It was thirty minutes later before he picked it up again. He inhaled, crossed himself, and typed: *p-u-s-s-y*...

The text shook back and forth. WRONG!

Christ on a bike.

Once he got the money, he was going to break this goddamn phone into a million pieces.

35

———

NICOLE GLANCED down at Jackson's dead body and pushed the toilet paper deeper into her nostrils.

It didn't help. The stench was nauseating.

Timothy stood beside her, toilet paper in his nose, holding a gray backpack.

Except for yellow dishwashing gloves, both were dressed in black.

Worried their fingerprints might be on the gym bag, Timothy had made an executive decision, gone to the Dollar Store, and gotten a backpack for the money and coke. He'd wrapped Band-Aids over the fingertips of his right hand and used only that hand to carry the backpack through the store just to be safe.

At her house they had wiped down all the bundles of cash before putting them in the backpack. On the way over, Nicole busted his balls about being paranoid, but now that they were in Jackson's apartment, she knew he was right.

They didn't want anyone tracing this back to them.

Jackson's bedroom was pitch black except the light from the parking lot coming through the window behind them. They'd debated on the best time to return the money and had to flip a coin before settling on two o'clock. *Was there a right time to do this?* Nicole thought. *Nighttime is nighttime.*

Timothy sat the backpack down beside the bed. "Well, I guess that's it."

"Yep."

"So, let's get out of here."

"Okay."

Neither one moved.

"We don't have to do this," Nicole said.

"So you don't want to do it either?"

"Well..."

"Don't you think it's odd that nobody has found him yet?"

"It hasn't even been twenty-four hours."

"I know. Still seems odd," Timothy said.

"We could look at it one more time."

"What?"

"The money. We won't see that much money again in our lifetime."

"That's a little glass half empty, don't you think?"

"You know what I mean." She picked up the backpack with her good hand and sat it on the bed. As she unzipped it, a loud noise came from down the hallway. She opened her mouth to speak. Timothy shut her down with a finger to his lips.

They froze. Waited. Listened.

The noise came again. Something screeching against the floor. A man's voice followed it. "It's back this way."

The front door slammed shut.

Someone was in the apartment.

They looked at each other. Nicole, seeing terror and confusion in Timothy's eyes, mouthed, "What the fuck?"

He pointed to the closet.

Moving fast, they made a beeline for it. Timothy got there first and slowly opened one of the two slatted bifold doors. Except for a few shirts and jeans hanging up, it was empty. He hunched down and stepped inside. Nicole snuck in behind him. As he pulled the door closed, she spotted the backpack lying on the bed and put her hand on his arm to stop him from closing the door. She tiptoed back to the bed, grabbed the backpack, and scurried back to the closet.

He pulled the door shut, and they waited.

The quietness was deafening. Nicole could feel her heart thumping in her chest. Her legs were shaking, and she tried hard not to breathe. She glanced over, noticed the Taurus Judge handgun holstered on Timothy's belt, and smiled. She was so glad he'd brought it. If she'd had half a brain, she would have brought her Glock too.

After what seemed like forever, footsteps on the hardwood floor rang out as someone walked into the room. Through the slats in the door, she could barely make out a figure in the darkness.

It was a shadowy blob. Short and fat.

A mountainous hulk joined it. Nicole almost gasped but covered her mouth in time.

We're dead. We are so dead.

"Damn, it smells rank in here," the hulk said. He had a broad Southern accent that reminded Nicole of the sheriff in *Smokey and the Bandit*, one of her Papa's favorite movies.

She watched as they moved over to the bed. When they stepped into the light from the window, she could almost make out their features.

The short fat one leaned over, inspected Jackson's body, and said, "You grab that side. I'll get this one."

"We gonna carry him? All the way to the car?"

"No, we're gonna walk him to the door and then down the steps."

Nicole looked up at Timothy. He shrugged his shoulders. She looked back through the slat just as the hulk went to pick up Jackson. After a second, he dropped him back on the bed.

"Shit, is this dude dead? You didn't say nothing about him being dead."

"Yes, I did."

"No, you didn't."

"Yes, I—"

"No, you didn't, Le Deuce. I might be fucked up, but my ears ain't fucked up, motherfucker. You said you needed my help to get a friend who was, and I quote, 'incapacitated' down a couple flights of stairs. I figured the motherfucker was in a wheelchair or something."

"All right. Yes, he's dead. And can you keep it down? These walls are thin."

"Shit, man, what the fuck is this? Goddamn, you want me to move a dead body?" he whispered.

"Just calm down, okay."

"Motherfucker, I want more money."

"Okay, sure. Whatever you need."

"A hundred dollars more."

"Sure." A long pause. "How about two hundred?"

"Three hundred."

"Really?"

"If you got two hundred, motherfucker, I know you got three hundred."

"Fine. Three hundred, but we need to get going."

"I don't like touching dead people."

"Me either."

"Yeah, but you're a cop. I'm sure you touch them all the time."

"But I still don't like it."

Nicole looked at Timothy. His eyes were as big as the moon. They mouthed in unison, "A cop?"

The short fat blob grabbed Jackson's arm and leg. "You ready?"

"Yeah, I'm ready."

"On the count of three...one...two...three..."

With great effort, they got Jackson to his feet.

"Damn, this sombitch is heavy," the hulk said.

"Just wrap his arm around your neck."

He did so. "Fuck, man, my skin is crawling."

Together they dragged him out of the room and into the hallway, their voices growing fainter.

"Where are we taking him, anyway?" the hulk asked. "Oh shit, we're gonna bury this motherfucker, ain't we?"

"If you shut your mouth, I'll throw in some prime heroin."

"For real?"

"For real."

Neither one of them spoke again.

Nicole and Timothy stood hunched in the darkness as the sound of Jackson's feet scraping across the wooden floor echoed throughout the apartment.

After a few minutes of grunts and groans, they heard the front door squeak open and close with a soft slam. Nicole went to open the closet door. Timothy reached out and stopped her.

"Not yet," he whispered. "They might come back."

Twenty minutes later, he opened the closet door. They stumbled out into the bedroom, Nicole shaken by what they had just witnessed.

Timothy ripped off his dishwashing gloves, pulled out his pistol, and moved like a panther into the hallway. Surprised, Nicole watched him carefully. She hadn't seen this side of him before. She threw the backpack over her right shoulder and followed him down the hallway.

When he reached the living room, he did a slow 360, gun extended, as he made sure they were alone.

Satisfied, he put the gun back in its holster and turned to her. "This is some crazy-ass shit. A cop? A goddamn cop? I can't believe it." He ran his fingers through his blond hair. "This is getting way out of control."

"Well, we gotta keep the money now."

Timothy looked at her.

"Insurance."

THE TOYOTA COROLLA roared down the pot-holed two-lane, sending leaves and debris flying in its wake, its high beams cutting into the fine mist. Timothy had insisted that they rent a car instead of using one of their own just to be on the safe side.

The full moon was waning but provided enough light for Nicole to make out the trees along the edge of the road.

They were on the south side about twenty minutes out from Mulberry Grove, where it was all trailer parks and farms.

Both hands on the wheel, Timothy was leaning so far forward in his seat it looked to Nicole as if he were trying to make the car go faster by sheer force of will.

"Man, that was close," he said as much to himself as to her.

She glanced over and noticed his hands were shaking. Odd. He didn't get worked up about much of anything except food and sex.

"Ease off on the gas there, babe. We don't need to get pulled over."

Her tone snapped him out of his trance, and he slowed the car down a hair. "Sorry, my bad. I just want to get the hell out of here."

"Me too, but in one piece. You okay? You seem kinda—"

"I'm not freaking out. I'm pumped up. There's a difference. The adrenaline...I can feel it flowing...and it's nuts..." He faded away, lost in thought. "Oh, shit."

"What?"

"Don't be mad at me."

"What?"

"Don't be mad at me."

"Timothy."

"Last night when I followed you to the apartment, somebody saw me."

"And? Details, babe."

"Wigged-out old dude, started questioning me and shit. Asking a lot of crazy shit, and he also saw you and Diane."

"Timothy? Why didn't you say—"

"I forgot. This whole thing has been a little weird."

"It's a clusterfuck."

"Yeah, problem is…"

Nicole sat there. Waiting. *Come on. Spit it out. You can do it.*

"He probably knows my name," he said, a hint of embarrassment in his voice. He began playing the drums on the steering wheel with his index fingers. A nervous habit of his that particularly irritated her.

"You told him your name?" She sat up straight in her seat, leaned over, and tried to catch his eyes. He kept them locked on the road.

"No, I'm not that stupid. I gave him my credit card."

"Wait? Why the hell would you—"

"He was going to call the police. I couldn't let him do that. What was I supposed to do? Kill him?"

"So you gave him your credit card?"

"He wanted money. I don't carry hundreds of dollars in cash on me."

"You gave him hundreds of dollars?"

"No, Nicole, I gave him a hundred and fifty. See, he had this swiper on his phone. So I…" He made a gesture like he was swiping a credit card in the checkout lane. "You know."

She buried her face in her good hand. "Oh my God. Baby? You have fucked us. Completely fucked us."

"Hunny bunny?"

Her hand in the cast came up so quick it surprised her. She held it like a wall between them. *Thou shalt not pass.* "I'm not mad at you, but don't talk right now. Okay? Just don't talk."

Nicole rubbed her temple. The mother of all headaches ripped through her skull, bringing with it a metallic taste in her mouth.

For a second she thought her brain would explode. She pictured bits of matter and flesh and blood splattering all over the windshield, splashing over Timothy like a tidal wave. She saw him screaming. Saw the car skidding off the road and into a tree.

Both of them dead: her head gone at the neck and Timothy sprawled out on the hood of the car after he'd flown through the windshield.

Sometimes her imagination was a bit much.

She ran her hand across the back of her neck and said in a slow, deliberate voice, "Two things I'm worried about. This cop— our cop—questioning this crazy old man and getting your name. And this crap making the news and the old man going to the police."

Timothy turned, eyes wide, and the words poured out. "Okay. First, this ain't gonna make the news, baby. No way. No way this makes the news. Nobody will know about this. Think about it. Whoever those two assholes were, they're burying Jackson, which means they don't want anybody to know he's dead."

"Which still sucks for us."

"Maybe, and maybe I'm wrong, but from their point of view —and one of 'em is a cop—it makes no sense to report this. See, baby, they want the money and the drugs. Money and drugs. That's it. Money and drugs."

"Which still sucks for us."

Timothy nodded.

It got quiet, only the sound of the tires on the road. Her headache had subsided. Thank God her head didn't explode.

She was entertaining different scenarios about who the cop was when Timothy looked at her and asked, "Are you horny right now?"

Taken aback by the question, she gave him a quick but confused smile. "Yeah."

He turned the wheel and skidded off the road, parking in a clearing near a large oak tree.

"What are you doing?" she asked, laughing.

He killed the engine and spun around, his eyes on fire with excitement. "If we don't make love right now, we're gonna miss the best moment of our lives."

Nicole looked deep into those fiery eyes to make sure he was serious and let loose the biggest grin she could muster. It made her heart swell when he got all romantic. It was so sweet.

Opening her door, she jumped out of the car and ran around to his side. He was out before she got there, sweeping her off her feet, kissing her. The wind whipped around them. It was freezing, but she didn't care.

He let her down, pushed her against the car and began caressing her breast with one hand and rubbing her ass with the other.

He mumbled something in French. When he got wound up, he liked to say dirty things in French. She didn't get it, but whatever. If it made him happy, that was all that mattered.

She couldn't believe how turned on she was. Moments ago she thought her brain was going to explode, and now she wanted him so bad she couldn't stand it. They hadn't had sex in days, and the last couple of times they did it was like they were going through the motions.

But not this time. This time they were going to—

"Wait," she whispered.

He stopped.

Headlights in the distance.

Timothy grabbed her hand, pulled her around to the front of the car, and they both sank to their knees. After a minute, the truck passed.

Once the taillights had faded away, she stood, gave him a smile, and with her finger, beckoned him to follow her into the woods. He moved so fast he almost tripped and fell on his face.

Thirty minutes later, a wide smile on her face, Nicole stumbled past the trees, through the tall grass, and back into the clearing. Timothy, pulling his shirt over his head, lagged a few feet behind her.

She came to a dead stop, and he slammed into her.

"Hunny bunny, what's up?"

"Babe?" Her voice trembled.

"Yeah?"

"Where's the car?"

"I don't know. It was right here." He looked up and down the highway.

"Where's the backpack?"

"In the car."

Nicole screamed.

36

—————

Hidden in the shadows, Le Deuce watched Beau roll Jackson's body into the shallow grave.

He shifted his weight from one foot to the other, trying to ease the excruciating pain. There was no point in denying it. His gout was back. With a vengeance.

He checked his watch. Time was running out. Another hour and the black sky behind him would be a sea of orange, pink, and blue. It had taken the two of them, mainly Beau, about forty minutes to get the hole deep enough. Hopefully, it wouldn't take Le Deuce that long to fill it back up by himself.

He put his hand on the Smith & Wesson on his belt and prepared himself for what he was about to do. What he had to do. But what he had never done before.

Shoot a man down like a dog.

If he were twenty years younger and fifty pounds lighter, he could have moved Jackson's body all by himself.

But he wasn't. He needed help.

Beau had been an informant for the Mulberry Grove Police Department until it became clear most of his information was junk, so he and Le Deuce had a history. Troubled, but a history.

Last night when he was scouring downtown Atlanta in search of a homeless helper, he'd spotted Beau digging through a dumpster. For a junkie, he was a hefty guy, six foot three and broad shouldered. Not too dumb, but not too bright either.

The right tool for the job.

So he bought him dinner, fed him a story, and offered him a hundred bucks. After that, Beau didn't need convincing. The next thing Le Deuce did was to score some heroin. His plan was simple, yet brilliant. He'd let Beau shoot up once they buried the body but would give him enough that he'd OD. A last meal of sorts. Then he'd bury Beau with Jackson and nobody would be the wiser. But finding this remote location and digging the hole had taken longer than he'd expected, and with the sun coming up soon, he'd run out the clock. Le Deuce hated it, but Beau was a loose end. And loose ends can—and will—come back to bite you in the ass.

He looked up. Beau had his back to him. He wouldn't get a better chance.

Without making a sound, he drew back his coat, unlatched his holster, and pulled out his gun. He had maybe ten seconds before Beau turned around, if that. With both hands he brought the gun up and took aim. He'd always been an excellent marksman, but that was against paper targets. Not a monster of a man who would break his neck if he missed. His heart racing, he couldn't keep the barrel steady.

Was there another way?

Maybe Beau didn't have to die?

Or maybe he'd be doing him a favor. The man's life was a living hell. He had no family. He lived on the streets, and most junkies OD'd, anyway. It was the law of averages. And a horrible way to go.

How much longer did Beau have in this world? Three years? Two? One? Six months? Anything might be better than the mud he was wallowing in now.

Beau turned his head and glanced back. Their eyes met, and they both knew.

Le Deuce pulled the trigger. The bullet went flying. He swore he could see it floating through the air, the world around him slowing to a crawl.

Swish...swish...swish...

Beau jerked his head to one side, and the bullet missed the space between his eyes, taking off most of his right ear.

Not the target Le Deuce had been aiming for.

Beau let loose a horrific scream that would haunt Le Deuce forever and looked up in shock—a confused, wounded animal. His face turned bright red, and he charged like a mad bull.

Le Deuce took another shot, missing completely. And then Beau was on him. Clawing at his face. Smashing him in the gut. Trying to tear him limb from limb.

Le Deuce struggled to pull his gun up. He tried to see where he was aiming so he didn't shoot himself, but the pain was too much. He could feel himself fading. In his wildest dreams he would have never imagined he'd go out like this, in the middle of the night, deep in the woods, a junkie beating the living shit out of him.

He was about to let go, about to close his eyes and stop fighting it, when a loud boom ripped his ears off. The jabs to his gut stopped, and for a minute he didn't know who'd been shot— him or Beau.

Warm blood hit his cheek. His eyes focused.

Part of Beau's face was missing.

"Christ!" He pushed him off and rolled across the ground like a man on fire trying to douse the flames.

After coming to a stop, he glanced over at Beau.

He wasn't moving.

Le Deuce scrambled to his feet and rushed over to him, his shoes slipping and sliding in the dirt. He checked Beau's pulse. Why he did that, he didn't know. The man was dead. Half his face gone.

He looked down. Blood covered his shirt. An overwhelming sense of disgust came over him.

What was he doing? He wasn't a killer. And yet here he was. Crossing the line, just like all the other losers he'd put away. And for what? Why did anyone kill?

In his experience it was always the same—money, happiness, sex, and power.

He couldn't stand the feeling of guilt eating at him. It made him uncomfortable. How many others would do the same thing in his position? How many would have shot Beau down without a second of remorse? The world was filled with people who could pull that trigger and not bat an eye. Why should he feel guilty?

Let he who is without sin cast the first stone.

He hadn't stepped inside of a church in years, but that one stuck with him. If God had wanted Beau to have a better life, why didn't he give him a helping hand? Send him an angel?

God knew from the moment Beau was born, his life would end tonight. He knew everything. So why didn't he do something?

This wasn't Le Deuce's fault. Hell, no. So fuck God! And fuck everybody else! Why was he sweating this idiot lying in the dirt? He was just a junkie who would have shot Le Deuce down for a fix.

Fuck this. Fuck this. FUCK THIS.

He grabbed Beau's feet and dragged him to the grave. Humming "Welcome to the Jungle," he pushed Beau's body into the hole and picked up the shovel.

Survival of the fittest, baby. Survival of the fittest.

FRIDAY

37

NICOLE TOOK a bite of hash browns as she surveyed the restaurant. Could she single-handedly take out all these people?

Sure, she was limited by the cast on her arm, but she did have the element of surprise. By her count there were eight people, including two waitresses and the cook. But there had to be a couple of employees in the back too. Best guess? Eleven? Twelve? For a Huddle House at five thirty in the morning, the place was light.

She didn't want to hurt anybody, but she knew if she took the knife in her hand and stabbed Timothy in the throat, she'd have to kill everybody else in the room too. After all she'd been through in the past forty-eight hours, she was not going to prison.

"Can we talk about it now?" Timothy asked, his mouth full of scrambled eggs.

"No."

He sighed.

For a grown man, he sure did know how to pout.

"What is there to talk about? Any way you look at it, we're screwed. That car..." She leaned forward and lowered her voice to a whisper. "That car could be in another state by now. It's gone, baby. Gone, gone, gone."

"You don't know that."

"You got any idea how to find it?"

Without answering, he cut into his waffle and made four perfectly shaped squares.

"I didn't think so." She pushed her plate away. She couldn't wait to get outside and light up a cigarette. Her face tightened as she watched him douse his waffle in syrup. "How can you eat like that?"

"With my mouth." Between bites: "I do know a guy."

"Really? Everybody knows a guy. The last guy you knew...well..."

"But he doesn't live here."

"Lot of good that does us."

"I'm pretty sure he's CIA."

"What is this, babe? A movie?"

"I'm just trying to think outside the box."

"Well, don't."

"Actually, he's probably out of the country right now."

"There you go."

Nicole poured more ketchup on her hash browns. "I know a guy. But I don't think it'd be a good idea."

"Come on, run it past me."

"He's a cop."

"Okay. Might work."

"He's an ex."

"Ex-cop?"

"No, ex-boyfriend."

Timothy chewed his waffle and looked at her.

"I told you it was a bad idea," she said.

"How ex?"

"What?"

"Ex like ten years ago or ex like right before we met?"

"It's been a while."

"A while?"

"Couple of years. Look, it's a bad idea."

"Wait a sec. Hang on now. Yeah, I get jealous, but we have to look at every option. This is too big a deal. Can you trust him?"

She shrugged.

"Did it end badly?"

"No. Just kinda fell apart. No crazy drama or nothing. It was one of those things that wasn't a thing. You know?"

"Was he good in bed?"

"Not even in the top ten."

He smiled. "Well, if he could help us find the car…"

"But what do we tell him?"

"We're sure as shit not telling him about the mon—"

She almost came across the table. "Hey, not here."

She glanced around. The people who came to Huddle House at five thirty in the morning were not the kind of people who needed to know about a backpack full of cash and cocaine.

"We say we have something in it that's embarrassing and we need it back," he whispered. "I dunno? Maybe a sex tape?"

Nicole smiled. He was so adorable, and he had no clue. As furious as she was earlier, she could never hurt him. She might want to, but she couldn't do it. He was too damn cute.

She'd been in love once. When she met Sean, she was twenty. He was thirty-one. It was the best year-and-a-half of her life, followed by the worst six months of her life. After that she swore up and down she'd never fall in love again, but damn, if the big goof across the table wasn't testing that vow.

She stood up and grabbed her phone and her coat. "I don't want to talk about this here. I need a smoke. When you're done annihilating that waffle, meet me outside."

She leaned over, gave him a kiss on the cheek, and whispered, "That might be the most expensive lay I've ever had."

"But it was worth it."

"We'll see," she said with a laugh. "We'll see."

IN THE DIM Huddle House parking lot, Nicole paced next to the dumpster, taking quick puffs of her cigarette. "Not in the top ten? Not in the top ten? The asshole was more like the one percent."

To anyone watching, she looked like a crazy woman—head down, hand with the cigarette flailing about—but this was her way of working through highly stressful situations: imaginary conversations with whomever she was having a problem with, which at the moment was herself.

"I can't do this," she mumbled. "I can't do it. He'll take one look at me and tell me to piss off. Or I'll tell him to piss off. I don't give a shit about the money. I really don't. What I care about... what is freaking me out is this—the police find the stolen rental with the backpack and we go to prison for a long, long time. Or the bad dudes find us—or worse, Diane—and want it back. So either we're in jail till we die or we just die."

She pulled her hoodie over her head and zipped up her jacket. Sunday's high of fifty started the downward slope, and each day this week seemed to get colder and colder. The wind didn't help.

That's because we're in Georgia, she thought. You never knew what you were going to get for Christmas in Georgia. It could be Frosty the Snowman or hotter than hell. Cold weather this early meant winter was going to be a bitch.

Once this nightmare was over, she was moving the band to Miami whether they liked it or not.

She watched the headlights whiz by on the highway. Where was everyone going at six o'clock on a Friday morning? Work? She scrunched up her face in disgust. She'd never had a nine-to-five job. Couldn't imagine the idea. Let somebody else call the shots in her life?

No way in hell.

Deep in thought, she didn't hear Timothy walk up behind her.

"The waffle is annihilated—"

Without skipping a beat, she spun around and punched him in the jaw.

NICOLE HELD the bag of ice up to Timothy's face as she rubbed the back of his neck. "Baby, I am so, so sorry."

She felt his eyes burrow in as he swung his head toward her.

"You're lucky I'm a gentlemen." He spit a drop of blood into his water glass.

"Gentleman."

"What?"

"You said gentle*men*, not gentle*man*."

"No. I didn't."

"Yes, you...look, it doesn't matter. I know you would never hit me."

He took the bag of ice from her and sat it on the table. "True, but some other dudes might. Future reference."

"There won't be any other dudes."

"You say that now."

"It won't happen again. Promise. You surprised me. I just...it's been a long night."

"I know. Been a hell of a night. Like one of those nights that flashes before your eyes right before—"

She put her finger to his lips. "Let's don't talk about that."

After she'd punched him, they had gone back inside Huddle House and returned to their booth, sitting side by side instead of across from each other. One waitress had been gracious enough to put some ice in a ziplock bag.

All eyes were on them as they'd entered, and Nicole could still feel their little sideways glances. She was half tempted to yell,

"What the hell are y'all looking at?" but knew better. Make a scene and people would remember.

She leaned into Timothy and put her head against his chest. "We need to get out of here. Everybody's staring at us."

"Screw 'em."

He pulled out his cell and opened the Uber app.

"Baby, no," she said.

"We gotta get home."

"That'll be a record of where we are and the time. We hitched a ride here. Let's get going and hitch another one. My house isn't that far."

"All right." He put the phone back in his pocket.

They got up, and Timothy led her by the hand toward the front door. As they stepped out into the early morning frost, Nicole turned and blew everyone in the restaurant a kiss. She just couldn't help herself.

38

Le Deuce found the deadbolt easier to pick than he imagined it would be at first glance. He'd scoped out the one-story ranch for over an hour before determining no one was home and the risk/reward ratio was in his favor.

After he buried Beau and Jackson, he'd gone back to his room at the George Washington Inn and taken a long, hot, scalding shower. Then he'd crawled into bed like it was his final resting place. He'd lain there shaking, his body an open wound.

Beau had done some damage, but not enough to force Le Deuce to the emergency room. Nothing at this point could force him into the emergency room. He knew there wasn't much fuel left in his tank, but he didn't give a rat's ass.

Getting that money, getting away clean—even if he didn't last a week down in South America—was the holy grail. A gigantic middle finger to the world that had been giving him one since the day he was born.

Viva Le Deuce.

He opened the door and stepped into the laundry room. The smell of incense and cigarette smoke hit him hard. The little room was dark, and once his eyes adjusted, he saw it was tidy and not at all what he had expected.

From the laundry room he dragged himself into the kitchen, propelled by the cane he'd picked up earlier at Walgreens. When his gout got too bad, he had to use one to walk or he wouldn't be walking at all.

The kitchen was also spotless, except for a few dishes in the sink.

"Is this guy a faggot?" he said aloud, his voice echoing throughout the house. "No, straight guy keeps his place this clean. Son of a bitch, I better not be in the wrong house."

He peeked around the corner into the den and realized he was indeed in the right place.

Sitting at the end of the couch was a large black amp with the word VOX emblazoned across the front. Leaning up against it, a beat-up guitar with red and green tape wrapped around the body. The same one Timothy had been playing in the photos on the band's Facebook page.

He moved into the den, the tip of the cane squeaking across the linoleum floor as he walked, stopping when it met the carpet.

This room was the central hub. A sixty-inch television sat across from the couch. Under it were multiple game consoles. Le Deuce had never been a gamer, so he wasn't sure which ones they were, but based on the sheer volume of game boxes overflowing around them, it stood to reason Timothy was an aficionado.

Deciding where to begin his search this morning hadn't been difficult. Since he still hadn't gotten into the phone, he didn't know exactly where Jackson had ended up Wednesday night when he left The Wicked Hand. But he knew he had to have gone with either Nicole or Diane. Le Deuce's money was on Nicole.

His research yesterday had painted a picture of two very different siblings. Diane Hancock, the oldest and the cleanest. No arrest record. No outstanding debts. Great credit score. Former paralegal with Blum & Pyne. A real peach as far as Le Deuce was concerned. Easy on the eyes but seemed uptight based on her Facebook page. Her husband, Hilton, a restaurateur, was loaded. The chick had it all.

There seemed to be no logical reason for Diane to leave with Jackson. Unless she was looking to get her pussy rode hard.

Le Deuce laughed out loud. God, he cracked himself up sometimes.

He was glad Jackson was dead. It always got stuck in his craw when women would throw themselves at Jackson. He wasn't even good-looking. Jeez, his face was kind of rough. Not that he took notice of how attractive another man's face was. Le Deuce liked the ladies, the longer the legs, the better. A tight caboose was nice too.

Nicole Robinson was the classic black sheep. Multiple arrests, but no long-term jail time. Misdemeanor drug possession. Lived in Los Angeles for eight years, moved back to Mulberry Grove three years ago. Hairdresser. Musician. Hot as hell. Judging by her Facebook page, she liked to party. So it made complete sense that Jackson left that night with her.

That's what Le Deuce would have done. Hell, that's what any red-blooded man would have done.

The only nagging question was if Jackson left with Nicole, what about Timothy, her boyfriend? Did they all leave together? Did she ditch Timothy to leave with Jackson? And if so, did that cause a rift between the two men?

There were no signs of physical trauma to Jackson's body. He wasn't stabbed, shot, or beaten. So an altercation between them was out of the question.

Why does a healthy man in his forties die? Heart attack? Stroke? Brain aneurysm? It had been eating at him since he found the body.

He wandered into the hallway, leaning hard on the cane. The house was a three-bedroom, two-bath ranch. Built in the seventies.

According to the property records, Timothy bought it three years ago.

To Le Deuce's left was the first bedroom. To his right, the bathroom. At the end of the hall, the master bedroom was on the right and the third bedroom was on the left. He searched all three rooms and both bathrooms.

Nothing.

No money. No drugs except for a few bags of pot, but who gave a shit? What was he going to do—arrest him for possession?

He knew it couldn't have been that easy. Nothing ever is.

He went back to the den and sat down on the couch. Propped his foot up on the coffee table, got out his notebook, and went through his notes.

Timothy MacDonald. Marine. Wounded in Afghanistan. Honorable Discharge. Did time in county for a drunk and disorderly at a Days Inn in Moultrie, Georgia. Owns Dr. Grass Lawn Care. *Dr. Grass, cute.*

Le Deuce realized he should have searched Nicole's house first, but something about Mr. MacDonald was ringing an alarm bell in his head. He was the odd man out. The piece that didn't fit.

What if they both left with Jackson? Perhaps to grab some food? Or come back here and get wasted? Maybe they were going to have a threesome? Jackson would be all over that. Le Deuce always figured Jackson might be into the dick. Guys who get tons of pussy, like Jackson, start thinking, "Hey, how about some dick." Everybody gets tired of eating the same meal all the time, right? Because of its scarcity, pussy was a prime commodity to Le Deuce. He would never get enough to get tired of it.

He jumped up and started pacing, playing it out in his head. Wherever they were or whatever they were doing didn't matter. At some point Jackson must have passed out or just keeled over, and they had to decide—call 911 or take him to the emergency room.

But they didn't.

Why?

Why hadn't they tried to save his life? And where did the money and coke fit in?

He paced even faster, the pain from his gout a distant memory. A breakthrough was coming on. He snapped his fingers. It was right there. So close, like honey in his mouth.

Then he heard the deadbolt on the front door turn as someone unlocked it.

39

TIMOTHY SAT in his truck finishing his cigarette. Next door, two boys who couldn't be a day over ten were horsing around in the front yard.

Shouldn't they be in school?

Then he realized: they were out for Christmas break.

Christmas? It was Christmas already. Wasn't that, like, a couple of months ago?

He rubbed his eyes. Time was doing a real number on him.

Watching the boys run wild in mindless circles, attacking each other with their light sabers, brought back memories of growing up in the Florida panhandle. He'd spent many glorious summer days on the beach raising hell. He'd give anything to be back there right now. No missing backpacks or loco cops. No crazy old men hiding in the bushes. And no dead bodies.

Life was good for ten-year-old Timothy MacDonald. Real good.

He tossed his cigarette out the window, climbed out of the cab, and headed up the driveway on a pair of wobbly legs.

Earlier he and Nicole had failed to hitch a ride, so they had walked the entire way to her place, and now his legs didn't want to do their job. He couldn't wait to get inside, light one up, and submerge himself in a warm bath until she showed up, hopefully with good news. After last night, they deserved some.

Persuading her to reach out to her ex hadn't been easy, but eventually she relented. She knew she had to take one for the team.

What was the dude's name? Mark Webb? Webster? Hell, he couldn't remember and didn't care. Just as long as What's-His-Name could help them find the money and didn't try to fuck Nicole. Timothy wasn't sure which was more important: the money or the dude not tapping his girlfriend. He wanted to have an open mind about sex. Wanted to be all twenty-first century. It shouldn't matter who she'd been with before.

But it did.

And that's why he didn't want to meet What's-His-Name. Picturing the two of them together—jeez, it was enough to send him right over the edge. Taking that money was the second-dumbest thing he'd ever done in his entire life. Losing it was the first.

He stopped and turned back toward his truck. Should he go back to Hidden Pines? Talk to the old man? What if he had something to do with stealing their car? Maybe he'd followed them and taken it when they stopped.

But that didn't make sense. Why steal the car? If the old man had been watching them at the apartment complex, he would have seen them carrying the backpack and stolen that, not the whole damn car.

He rubbed his face. Trying to sort this shit out was inflicting a serious pain behind his left eye. He needed to calm down. Clear his head.

He stepped up on the porch, pulled his keys out of his pocket, unlocked the front door, and entered the den. Spotting the amp and bass guitar, he smiled.

It was good to be home.

He plopped down on the couch, pulled his holster off his belt, and laid his gun on the coffee table. Absent-mindedly, he got his phone out of his pocket and placed it beside the gun.

He closed his eyes for a few moments. Then, out of habit, he reached out, grabbed the bass guitar by the neck, and sat it in his lap, the curve of the body resting on his thigh.

A click, and the amp hummed to life. He played a few scales and then ran through "Flashlight" by Parliament-Funkadelic. Even though The 8 Ballers were hard rock and metal, Timothy was a big Bootsy Collins fan. One day he'd always promised himself he would play in a funk ensemble complete with horns, keys, percussion, and some hot and nasty backup singers.

He stopped playing and studied the room. He'd lived here, alone, for the past three years. He knew this house.

Something wasn't right.

He laid the bass on the couch and stood up. Then he tiptoed into the kitchen. Turning the corner, his stomach rumbled. He had to go. Bad.

He rushed back into the den, down the hallway, and into the guest bathroom. Dropping his jeans and boxers in the blink of an eye, his butt landed with a thud on the toilet.

It was over in a matter of seconds.

Through clenched teeth he squeaked out, "Son of a bitch."

Sweat poured down his face as his stomach bunched up again, and he screamed in frustration. For the past year, his bowels had been in open rebellion. He'd chalked it up to anxiety, but it was getting worse. As much as he despised doctors, maybe it was time to see one. Between this and his hemorrhoids, he couldn't take much more.

He was trying to get the strength to stand when he heard the bathroom door creak open. Cocking his head to one side, he leaned forward to peer around the sink.

Standing in the doorway was a short, rotund man who looked to be in his fifties. Dressed all in black except for a red tie and tan raincoat, he was twiddling a cane in one hand. Timothy thought he looked like one of those little creatures from the *Lord of the Rings* movies.

"Damn, what died inside of you?"

"What the fuck?" Timothy came up off the toilet.

"Easy there, bud, why don't you just stay seated." He flashed his badge. "Detective Le Deuce, Mulberry Grove PD."

Timothy eased back down. "What the hell are you doing in my house?"

"Front door was open. I heard someone screaming."

"Bullshit. That door was closed."

"You were screaming, right? Passing a big one? Sometimes I get them so big it rips my asshole. Nasty."

"Fuck you."

The man smiled. Timothy wished he hadn't. He was already nauseous.

"Now that I'm here, maybe I can ask you a couple of questions about a mutual friend?"

"I don't think we have any mutual friends."

"Sure we do. Jackson Booth."

Timothy's stomach dropped again. Who was this asshole?

"Can you close the door? I'm trying to take a shit here."

"I'll wait." Le Deuce thumbed through his notepad.

"Are you fucking kidding me? You break into my house, and now you want to watch me...?" He couldn't find the words. "I want your badge number, freak."

He continued looking over his notes.

"Come on, asshole, shut the door or when I get up so-help-me-God I will beat the living shit out of you."

He didn't respond.

Timothy grabbed the plunger off the floor and threw it at him.

Le Deuce leaned back. It sailed past him, hit the wall, and landed with a crash in the hallway.

Laughing, he poked his head into the bathroom. "Watch that temper, son. Assaulting a police officer is a felony."

"Yeah? Well, I'm sure watching me take a shit is a felony too."

"I'll be in the den when you're done. Don't hurt yourself."

He closed the door.

Just as it clicked shut, Timothy's ass exploded and the taste of vomit came up the back of his throat.

In a panic, he reached into his jeans pocket for his phone. It wasn't there. Son of a bitch. He'd left it on the table next to his gun. He jumped up, wiped his ass, and pulled his boxers and jeans back up.

Thank God he hadn't gotten stoned yet. He needed as clear a head as he could get. He had to figure this out.

Who was this prick? Was he really a cop? Shit, was he the same one who moved Jackson's body?

That thought made his stomach rumble again, and he pulled his jeans back down and sat his butt on the toilet.

He wondered if he was ever going to get out of the bathroom.

"HEY, dude, can you put that down?" Timothy walked into the den.

Across the room, Le Deuce was admiring the bass guitar. He sat it back on the couch, but not before he plucked one string. A low tone rang out. "What kind of guitar is that? It's only got four strings."

Timothy gave him a blank stare and tried to keep cool. He didn't want the little prick to see he was shaking. "Wanna show me that badge again? How do I even know you're a cop?"

"Detective." He pulled it out of his coat pocket and held it up so the light from the window caught it. "Le Deuce. Mulberry Grove PD."

"Let's get one thing straight. I'm not into bullshit. You didn't hear anybody screaming. The door wasn't open. What do you want? What the hell is this about?"

"You were one of the last people to see Jackson Booth Wednesday night. You, Nicole Robinson, and Diane Hancock played pool and drank at The Wicked Hand until around two in the morning. Then Mr. Booth left with you and Ms. Robinson."

The room turned counterclockwise. Was this the same cop from earlier? Voice sounded similar, but it had been so dark he didn't get a good look. He took a deep breath and wiped his sweaty palms on his jeans.

"Last people to see him?"

Le Deuce paused, tapped his cane on the floor. "Mr. Booth appears to be missing."

"Missing? Who reported him missing? And no, we didn't leave together."

"What does it matter who reported it?"

"I don't know. How do you know he's missing? Who says he's missing? You obviously have a reason to think he is. So somebody had to report it. Look...sure, we hung out, played some pool. Shot the shit. Drank a few and then he left, and we left. I haven't seen him since."

"Son, you are a terrible liar. I've known some pros, and you suck at it."

"Whatever, dude."

Timothy walked over to the coffee table and reached for his phone. It was lying beside his handgun.

Le Deuce moved to the end of the table. "Hang on."

Timothy froze. "I'm not going for the gun."

"I would step back if I were you." He pulled his coat back, exposing the Smith & Wesson snug in the holster on his belt just like the bad guy in every cheap Western.

Timothy raised his hands and moved away from the table. "You got a problem with me calling your supervisor and making sure you're a real detective?" It came out *dick-tec-tive*.

"He didn't leave with you?" Le Deuce pulled his coat back over his gun.

"No."

"Who did he leave with?"

"Beats me. I didn't see him leave with anybody."

"How well do you know Jackson?"

"Do you have a warrant?"

"Wouldn't you say the warrant is an outdated concept in our modern electronic world?"

"You break into my house and tell me Jackson's missing, but how do *you* know he's missing?" Timothy opened the front door. "I'm not answering any more questions. Get the fuck outta my house."

Le Deuce marched over and stopped in front of him. He barely made it up to Timothy's chest. He shoved his finger in his face and let it rip.

"You don't like bullshit? Neither do I. You know way more than you're telling me. I can see it in your eyes. Right now, I'm the only one standing between you and the wrath of God. You know what I'm talking about."

A big smile crossed Timothy's lips, and he burst out laughing. He couldn't help himself. It was like he was being attacked by a Pomeranian.

"What's so funny?"

"Everything."

Le Deuce ripped a sheet of paper out of his notepad and wrote his phone number on it.

"I'm not the only one who's going to be coming around asking questions. I ask nicely, and my favorite game is 'Let's Make a Deal.' They won't play that."

He handed him the paper and stepped out the door.

Timothy stared at the number. Should he spill the beans? Come clean? No, that wouldn't be fair to Nicole or Diane.

He shoved the note into his pocket and watched Le Deuce shuffle down the sidewalk, his voice ringing out, "Wrath of God, son. Wrath of God."

Timothy slammed the door and ran for his phone. He had to reach Nicole before she talked to What's-His-Name.

40

———

THE FEAR WAS PALPABLE. It crept from the small of her back to the middle of her rib cage, sucking all the air out of her lungs. Diane couldn't remember ever being this terrified before. Not even when she was seven years old, waiting and hoping for Janice to come waltzing through the front door. *"Hey, baby girl. Mama's home."*

This was new and deeply disturbing.

She'd fallen asleep yesterday afternoon after her shower and slept like the dead until around five thirty in the morning. But from the moment she awoke, drenched in sweat, she'd been riding a tidal wave of apprehension. She'd lain in bed for over ten minutes, shaking from head to toe.

It took everything she had to get herself going and out the door. As she made her way through the rush hour traffic, one thought kept creeping back to haunt her.

What have I done?

She was chewing on her fingernail when she glanced up and caught the receptionist staring at her. So intent on the thoughts rampaging through her head, Diane didn't even realize she had the tip of her middle finger in her mouth.

She stopped and turned toward the front door of the lobby, hoping someone would walk in and change the dynamic in the room. She wanted to smack herself. Biting her nails was a habit she'd worked hard to break over the years.

She scooted back in her seat, ironed out her skirt, crossed her legs, and sat her purse on the floor next to the chair. With a sideways glance to her left, she peeked at the front desk.

The receptionist was juggling phone calls and data entry. Could she tell? Diane wondered. *I disposed of a dead body last night. I didn't kill him. Well, not exactly. Or maybe I did?* Was the guilt written all over her face? It was almost like when she'd lost her virginity at seventeen. Everywhere she went, she could feel the prying eyes. Did they know? Did the entire world know what she'd done?

She checked her phone. Nicole still hadn't texted her back. Probably passed out. That girl never saw the sunrise.

"Mrs. Hancock, would you like something to drink? We've got tea, coffee...water?" the receptionist asked, a polite but indifferent tone in her voice.

Diane brought her hands together around her knee and smiled. "Water would be nice. Thanks."

The young woman, a striking brunette in her early twenties, got up from her desk and disappeared down the hallway, her heels click-clacking on the hardwood floor. Franklin always did like them young and pretty. Personality needed a bit of work, though. A genuine smile now and then wouldn't hurt.

Diane leaned forward and took in the large room. It had changed little in the few years since she'd left the firm. Furniture and wallpaper were the same. And those green drapes? She'd helped pick them out. The enormous Christmas tree in the corner was a tradition, but maybe it was time to swap it out for a new one. It looked a little ragged. The high ceilings and hardwood floors reminded her of her great-grandparents' house. They'd had an old Victorian like this, except it wasn't anywhere near this pristine, and it had smelled like mothballs, not honeysuckle.

She'd tried to talk Hilton into renovating a three-story Victorian she'd found in Peachtree City right after they were married, but he wasn't interested. Said he wanted to start from scratch. Build something new. She couldn't complain, their house was beautiful, but her old soul still longed for something like this. A place with history.

Wait a second.

She could have slapped herself. This was where she'd met Hilton. Right here, in this very room. Fifteen-odd years ago. Those words were hard to take. She would have been...twenty-two? Twenty-three? Just a baby.

"Have mercy. Diane? What are you doing here, hon?"

She turned toward the sound of the booming voice.

Shuffling down the oak staircase was a tall, broad-shouldered man in his early forties. Decked out in khaki slacks, a rose-colored dress shirt, and suspenders, he had a full head of grayish-brown hair and a twinkle in his eye. His tie was loose at the collar and swung back and forth like a pendulum as he made his way toward Diane. He'd put on at least thirty pounds since she'd seen him last, all of it around his waist.

She grabbed her purse and stood up just in time. He wrapped his arms around her and gave her a robust hug. For a tough-as-nails lawyer, Franklin J. Blum was a big teddy bear.

"Everything okay? Stacy said it was urgent." He took a step back.

"Not, not really..." She fought back tears.

To the big man's left, she could see Stacy watching them like a hawk. Somebody was a little too nosy. Diane sucked it up. She wasn't about to break down in front of Ms. Personality.

Franklin turned and motioned toward the stairs. "Come on, let's chat in my office."

"Well, damn, darlin', that is a shame," Franklin said. "If you two can't make it, what hope do the rest of us have? I know Martha will be heartbroken to hear this."

"How is she?"

"Doing good. Doing good. Finally got her blood sugars under control." He leaned back in his chair and put his hands behind his head.

It was something Diane had seen him do so many times over the years, she'd lost count. It was like he was holding court.

"You sure he's got a little miss on the side? 'Cause that really don't sound like our boy."

She took a drink of water, found a spot amid the stacks of paperwork on his desk, and sat the bottle down. "No, it doesn't. It's crazy. But something's not right. Ever since Richard died…"

"That could be a big part of it. Have you tried to talk to him? I know he likes to play it close to the vest."

She got up from her chair, unbuttoned her coat, and walked back and forth in front of the massive oak desk. Like the downstairs lobby, his office had a high ceiling and big windows. The mid-morning sunlight blasting in made her squint.

"I have. He never wants to talk about it."

Franklin got quiet. She didn't prod him; she knew it was his nature when he was processing information.

After a few minutes, she got the feeling he was about to stand up and tell her to get the hell out. Richard, Hilton, and Franklin had grown up together. The three amigos, they called themselves. To everybody else they were the three stooges. Perhaps he didn't appreciate his former paralegal accusing one of the "boys" of an impropriety. Or maybe he knew all about it?

Then he said, "You could hire a private investigator. Dot your i's and cross your t's before you do anything rash. I'd hate for you to spy on Hilton, but…"

A private investigator? That gave her a jolt. This had been a giant miscalculation. "You know he's running for mayor, right?"

"I do. Been doing some prep for him. Spreading the gospel, so to speak. Your husband is a good man. Be good for this town. Cheating on you? That's just not Hilton's style."

"Don't you think that would be the worst thing to do? If he is cheating, I mean."

"At least you'd know the truth."

"It doesn't matter if he is or he isn't. It's over. Remember when you and Susan split? Didn't you know? Didn't you just know?"

He folded his hands and brought both his index fingers to his chin.

"Hilton and I are done, all right?" Diane said. "And if he is as serious as I think he is about politics, then I need to end it now. I don't want to be a political wife. I'm not looking for this to get nasty. I'm not going to drag his name through the mud. I don't want anything. I don't care about the money. I just want out. Obviously you're not a divorce lawyer, but I trust your opinion. I need a recommendation. Who's the best in town?"

"Have you tried counseling?"

"Did you and Susan?"

"Yes."

"Didn't work, did it?"

He smiled. "Well, that was different."

"Can I get a name? I know you're going to side with Hilton—"

He stood up and came around the desk. For a big man, he moved fast. "No. Not true. I care about both of you. Take it from one who's been there, hon. Divorce, it's a real pain in the ass."

She looked at him, tears welling up. "Franklin, I just need a name."

His eyes said, *This isn't a good idea,* but the words came out,

"There are a few I can think of, but at the top of the list, it'd have to be—"

"Everybody Wants to Rule the World" cut him off. Diane reached down in her purse and grabbed her phone. Talk about timing. "I have to take this."

She opened the door and stepped out into the hallway. Pulling the door shut behind her, she answered the phone. "Hey, what's up?"

"I've been trying to call you since yesterday," Hilton said.

"Well, I was trying to call you two days ago."

"My phone got wet. Would you believe I dropped it in the toilet?"

"And you couldn't message me? You have your laptop. And it took you a day to get a new phone?"

"You know how technology challenged I am." He threw it out there with a laugh.

"Yeah. So what's up?"

"What are you angry about?"

"I'm not."

"Okay."

"I'm not angry, I'm just busy."

"I need you to pick me up from the airport."

"Now?"

"No, tonight. I'm flying back."

"I thought you were staying until Sunday?"

"Things changed."

"Yeah, fine. Whatever. What time?"

"Seven."

"Okay."

The silence was deafening. So many things she wanted to say, but not yet. Not on the phone.

"Love you," Hilton said.

"Love you too."

She ended the call. The words felt fake in her mouth. She never wanted to say them to him again.

41

Nicole knocked on the door to apartment 10C. His GTO wasn't in the parking lot, but that didn't mean he wasn't here. It had been three years; he could have a new car.

She knocked once more and regretted it. "Please don't answer. Please don't be home," a little voice inside her head whispered.

That way she could go back to Timothy with, "Sorry, babe, I checked with the rental company, and Mark moved over a year ago."

She felt awful about lying to him earlier, but what could she do? Tell him the truth? That Mark had given her hands down the greatest orgasms of her life. Amazing in the bedroom, but a complete and utter piece of shit out of it.

A robust wind blew the Ray-Bans off the top of her head. In the distance, a crow squawked. Screw it. She spun around, picked up her glasses, and headed toward the exit, her sneakers squeaking on the concrete as she crept away.

She was almost home free when she heard his voice.

"Nicole? Is that you?"

It was a voice to die for. She turned around and flashed a smile, but not too wide. She didn't want him to get the wrong idea.

Their relationship had been one of late-night and early-morning booty calls.

"What are you doing here?" He stepped out into the hallway. Her heart skipped a beat. He was wearing a pair of washed-out jeans and a sweatshirt that said *Cops Do It By The Book*. He'd put on a little weight, but damn it, even chunky, he was still sexy.

Men have it so easy, she thought. Sometimes the older the bastards get, the better they look. Mark was in his mid-forties and his brown hair was turning a light gray, but he still had the boyish charm of a twenty-five-year-old. Most cops his age had lost that spark in their eyes, but not him.

"God, you still live here?"

"No, I was just hanging out for old times' sake. There's a bunch of illegal Mexicans living here now. What's going on?"

"I thought you'd be at work."

"What happened to your arm?"

She looked down at her cast almost like she'd forgotten she had it on and said, "I fell."

"That sucks. So what's up?"

She tried to find the words.

"Nicole?"

She walked to him, her shoulders pulled in and her head tilted to one side like a child caught lying about knocking over Mom's favorite vase. "I have a problem," she said in her little-girl voice. Where did *that* come from?

"Come on in."

She paused, then raised her voice an octave. "Actually, could I treat you to a Starbucks?"

He folded his arms across his chest and looked at her with piercing blue eyes. He still had it. The asshole still had it.

"Sure, let me get some shoes on." He stepped back into his apartment.

Her phone buzzed. She pulled it out of her pocket.

Diane. Again?

She'd been texting her all morning. Something about getting her hair done. Not today. Nicole didn't have time for that. She slid her phone back into her jeans pocket. She'd deal with her sister later.

"MAN, that's crazy. Like if I didn't know you, I'd swear you were making that up," Mark said, smiling, as he played with the remaining bits of his blueberry muffin.

"Well, I'm not."

She'd told him the story she and Timothy worked out. Timothy rented the car because his truck was in the shop. In the backpack was some cash, some weed, and a sex tape they had made. She knew Mark wouldn't care about the weed. He liked to smoke himself sometimes. A lot of cops did, or so she'd heard.

"So you guys were out on Church Road around five in the morning, and you just decided to pull off the road and get it on in the woods? In this weather? It must have been thirty degrees last night."

"Yeah, it was cold, but...I know it was crazy stupid." She laughed and took a sip of her latte. "Hey, I like to get a little wild sometimes."

"You're telling me." He gave her a wink.

She flashed a thin smile that disappeared just as quickly. There had to be some other way to find the car. This was excruciating.

"I hate to break it to you, but I'm not an officer anymore."

"What? Why? What happened?"

"Politics. Bullshit. Doesn't matter."

He leaned back in his chair and put his hands behind his head. When he did, she could see that despite the weight gain, his arms were still pretty solid. She remembered how they felt around her. His hands on her waist. His lips on hers. And how he would pull her hair when...

Enough. Just stop it.

She might have to go to the restroom and toss some cold water on her face. "So you can't help me?"

"I didn't say that." He stroked the three-day stubble on his chin. "I'm private now. Investigations. Cyber security. And I still have a few friends on the force. I could help, but first you have to be honest with me."

"There's always a 'but' with you."

"Nicole, that story is stinking up this whole place. Look around." With a wave of his hand, he motioned to the various customers. "You think any of these civilians would buy that?"

"They better, 'cause it's the truth. Why would I show up at nine thirty in the morning, when I haven't seen you in years, just to tell you some bullshit story?"

He leaned forward and looked her square in the eye like she was a suspect he was interrogating. She scooted her chair backward. The sound of metal on linoleum turned a few heads.

"Something's going on, but the question is what? I think you need my help. After the way it ended between us, you wouldn't be here if you didn't. But without knowing the truth, I can't do anything."

"I just need you to find the car and the backpack."

"Does that hurt?" he asked.

"What hurt?"

"Your arm. Does it hurt?"

"What do you think?" She hated when he'd randomly change the subject. Was he trying to throw her off? Sometimes she couldn't tell where Mark started and the cop ended.

"What happened?"

"Slipped and fell. Just my luck, I landed the wrong way. But it'll be fine."

"You still play guitar?"

She gave him a look.

"Does a bear shit in the woods?" He said and laughed. "So you haven't reported it stolen?"

"No, I can't. Timothy's on probation. There's enough weed in that backpack to send him to prison."

"Weed, a couple of thousand in cash, a sex tape—who makes sex tapes anymore? Shit, Nicole, everybody does that on their phone."

"It was a high-quality production."

"So you had, like, a crew and everything? Please. You never would make a video with me. Remember how I begged—"

"Can you not tell everybody in the fucking restaurant?"

The old man at the table beside them turned and gave Nicole the once-over. She puckered up her lips and sent him a kiss. He went back to his laptop.

Mark lowered his voice. "I'm just saying—you're a freak, but you never wanted to put it on tape."

"I was trying to make him happy."

"You want to lie to me? Fine. I'm sure I deserve it. But don't insult my intelligence. What's in the backpack?"

"Money."

"You said that."

"A lot of money."

"How much?"

She studied his face. She hated him so much, but damn, she wanted to kiss him.

"How much?" he asked again.

"Can we talk about this in the car?"

NICOLE CRANKED the engine to get the heat going. Through the windshield she spotted a white cat racing across the parking lot. *Hey, cat, wait for me. Wait for me.*

"Where did the money come from?" Mark, arms crossed and his face solemn, sat in the passenger seat of her RX-7.

"I can't tell you. Okay? I can't. But with the weed and the money, Timothy could be...this is serious. Really serious."

"So what's in it for me?"

"Paranoid" blared out of her phone. She flinched and glanced down. *Timothy*. She muted it. "I don't know. Gratitude? Money? You want to get paid? Is that it?"

"No." He smiled and flashed those baby blues.

Her eyes narrowed. She'd seen that look before. "I am not giving you a blowjob."

"I don't want a blowjob. I just...I miss you."

"You miss me? You? Miss me?"

"We had a good thing."

"Till you fucked it up. Did you miss me when you were screwing Donna? Or Marcy? Or Victoria?"

Now he wasn't so damn sexy anymore. And she wasn't thinking about his hands or his kisses or any other body parts. All the pain he'd inflicted on her was back like it'd never left. Yeah, he had it going on in bed, but so what? It was just sex. It couldn't hold a candle to what she had with Timothy. He might be a goofball, but he wasn't a liar, or a cheater. And he was a damn good bass player.

"You can't play bass," she whispered.

"Huh?"

"You can't play bass. Oh, you're good, but you can't play bass."

"What are you talking about?"

"Get out of my car."

"What?"

"Get out of my car."

"I'll help you."

"Get out of my car," she yelled.

"Nicole."

"What?"

"I will help you. No strings attached. I've changed. For real. And I'll prove it to you. I'll find this car and the backpack. Okay?"

He opened the passenger door. The icy wind gave her a chill.

"I'll call you when I know something. Just text me all the rental info." He stopped. "You still have my phone number, right?"

"No."

He pulled out his cell. Sent her a text. Her phone beeped. "There you go."

"Oh, okay. Thanks." But he'd already slammed the door shut. She sat there, mouth open, wondering what just happened.

"Paranoid" slapped her in the face again, and she answered the phone. "What?"

42

———

So THIS WAS how it ended. Pretty sad when Diane thought about it. But spending the whole weekend pretending was out of the question. She had to tell him. But how? And where? At the airport? On the ride home? At the house?

She could text him. Yes, it was cowardly, but it would get the job done:

Honey, I want a divorce. Please take Uber to a motel. There's a nice one on Fountain Head. You can pick up your things tomorrow. Promise not to take you to the cleaners.

Top it off with a heart emoji, and problem solved.

She pulled into Nicole's driveway.

She'd been texting her sister all morning about getting her hair done and gotten no response. After leaving Blum & Pyne, she'd called her twice. Of course, Nicole didn't answer.

Her RX-7 wasn't in the driveway.

Where was she? This wasn't like her sister. If she was awake, the phone was in her hand. And she always responded. Had something bad happened? Diane had been out of it for over fifteen hours. Nicole didn't have a nine-to-five job. She cut hair in a salon cubical she rented by the month. Outside of the cell phone, Diane had no way to reach her.

What time was it? Ten twenty a.m. Nicole didn't even see appointments until noon, so there was no point in driving over there.

Facebook?

She checked Nicole's page. Nothing had been posted for weeks. She opened Messenger and sent a message.

It was redundant—if Nicole didn't have her phone, she wouldn't be on Facebook—but you never knew. Maybe she'd see it.

She got out of her car and went to the front door, banged on it, and waited. After a couple of minutes, she peered in the dirty front window. With her sleeve, she wiped the grime off but still couldn't see inside.

She ran around back, found the key under the potted plant, and unlocked the back door.

"Nicole? Hello, hey, it's me. You home?"

She entered the house and closed the door. The house was freezing. Too cold for the heat to have been turned off within the last hour or two. Her sister was cheap and always kept the heat off if she wouldn't be home for any amount of time. Diane tried to explain that reheating the house cost as much if not more than leaving it at a consistent level, but—God bless her—she was as stubborn as Janice.

Nicole didn't spend the night here.

Most likely she was at her boyfriend's, wherever that was.

She could kick herself. She was overreacting again, but what else was new? Who wouldn't after the last two days? She went to the cabinet, found a glass, and got some water. To ease her mind, she checked all the rooms and then made her way back to the kitchen. As she was heading toward the door, something in the corner caught her eye.

She turned.

Lying on the kitchen floor next to the table was a black gym bag. She walked over and picked it up.

This can't be.

But it looked just like it.

But it can't be.

The room went sideways, and she grabbed the table to steady herself. She straightened up, got her bearings, and barged out the door, bag in hand.

She was going to kill her sister.

DIANE PUSHED the Lexus's speedometer past seventy-five. The morning traffic had dissipated, and Peachtree Parkway was wide open, just like her options.

She didn't know what to do or where to go.

She glanced down at the gym bag lying on the passenger-side floorboard. "What the hell, Nicole? What the hell?"

That couldn't be the same bag.

It looked exactly like it, but it couldn't be it. It just wasn't possible.

Her sister wasn't *that* stupid.

Once Diane found her, all this would get cleared up, and they'd have a big laugh. A fall-down, gut-busting laugh they would remember for years.

How about that time I freaked out because I thought you took the drug money, but you really didn't? Ha. Ha. Ha. Ha.

But what if she had taken it?

What then? Was Nicole gone? Was that why she wasn't answering her texts or her calls?

She could be in another state by now. With that kind of money, she could disappear. Would her sister do that to her? Leave her hanging like that? Come to think of it, it wouldn't surprise her. Nicole had a track record two miles long of screwing up her life and letting people down.

Bad boyfriends. Rash decisions. Drug problems.

Diane debated going back to Nicole's house and waiting for her, but that would be a waste of time if she'd left town.

She could call the police, but what would she tell them? "Hi, my sister took some drug money that we found after my one-night stand died on me. Can you find her?"

No. No. No.

Best thing to do was to go home. Relax and forget about it. There was no way Nicole took that money.

No way.

On second thought, the best thing to do was to go home, get on the internet, and find out where her boyfriend lived. What was his name? Jim? Tim? Timothy? Diane was terrible with names, but she'd figure it out. He had to be on Facebook.

She grabbed her coffee and took a drink.

Ugh.

Nothing she hated worse than cold coffee. This day was going to hell in a handbasket.

Canada sounded real good right now.

43

———

Disgusted, Le Deuce hobbled back to his RAV4. How could he have been so stupid? He forgot about the bag of pot he'd found in the bedroom. The kid was still on probation. Le Deuce could have played him like a fiddle.

Win some, lose some, but it sucked all the same.

Best he could hope for now was that the veiled threat he'd thrown out would provoke the kid into doing something rash, like leading him to the money.

If, in fact, Timothy knew where it was.

The driver's side door opened with a squeak. He tossed his cane in back and climbed in the front seat. The door closed with a more agonizing screech, and he made a mental note to swing by the store and get some WD-40. Not that it mattered. He'd be done with this vehicle soon enough, but that screech was like nails on a chalkboard. Even when he was a kid, discordant noises made him want to put a double-barrel in his mouth.

He'd parked at the farthest end of the street, behind a minivan. It gave him an unobstructed view of Timothy's house while providing some cover for his car. He would love to go back over and slip a tracking device on Timothy's Silverado, but it was too dangerous with those kids playing in the yard next door.

He watched them running around and around like a couple of idiots. They didn't have any jackets on. It must have been thirty degrees out, but they couldn't care less.

He tried to picture himself at ten years old but drew a blank. Even as a young boy, Le Deuce always been an old man. After he'd almost died at three, his mother spent her entire life protecting him from anything and everything, including himself.

The phone call was as present in his mind as the day it happened. His mother was driving home from work. The rain was pouring down like Noah's flood. The driver of the tractor trailer couldn't see the yellow line and crossed into her lane.

It was over in an instant.

She was the only family he had.

At first the pain had been incredible, but soon came a freedom he had never known before. It invigorated him and also brought tremendous guilt. He may as well have been a damn Catholic for all the guilt he felt.

He grabbed Jackson's phone off of the passenger seat and brooded over the password again.

The chances were drying up.

In reality, he didn't need the phone—his gut told him it came down to Nicole, Timothy, and/or Diane, in that order. But if he could see precisely where Jackson had spent his last remaining hours, it could put the wheels on the track.

Just looking at the login screen on the phone made him nauseous.

Enter Passcode.

Do it.

Do it and get it over with.

He couldn't spend the rest of the day obsessing over this. With the index finger of his right hand, he went to touch the screen. Aiming for the letter *B,* he slipped and hit the space bar. Damn it.

The login screen vanished, replaced by a selfie of Jackson. He was in a bathroom with no shirt on. Behind him, a gorgeous blonde was poking her head around the shower curtain and laughing like crazy.

Le Deuce couldn't believe it. He'd gotten in. But what was the password? He walked back through it.

Christ on a bike.

It was the space bar. The damn space bar.

God, he'd love to kick Jackson's ass.

Just to be sure, he went to Settings and tapped on Passcode. The "Enter the Password" screen came up with the keyboard.

He tapped the space bar.

The Passcode screen appeared.

Yes.

He removed the password and created a new one: *Fuckface.*

Nobody would figure that one out.

For a moment he debated scrolling through the photos. There had to be some naughty ones, and maybe he'd find out how tiny Jackson's penis was. Based on how much he overcompensated, it had to be a micro.

Reality whispered in his ear. Stop fooling around. Miss Hot Chocolate said, "Forty-eight hours." Twenty-four hours had already whizzed by. The clock was ticking.

On the phone he dug through the privacy settings, and sure enough, Frequent Locations was on.

For a genius, Jackson wasn't too bright.

He glanced up just in time to catch Timothy climbing into the Silverado.

Here we go.

He tossed the phone into the passenger seat, started the engine, and put the Toyota into gear. Once the truck disappeared around the corner, he pulled out and followed it, keeping a safe distance.

HE HAD BEEN TAILING Timothy for about ten minutes when he spotted the black van two cars behind him.

A black van? Could these people be any more obvious?

But it took a right when he and Timothy took a left.

The pain from the gout in his big toe jumped up a couple of notches. Christ. His nerves were getting the better of him. Although he'd wiped his tracks, that Aussie chick sneaking up on him yesterday still had him rattled.

Timothy continued on for a few minutes. As the road curved, Le Deuce noticed a silver Dodge Avenger a couple of cars back.

Something about it set his radar off.

Up ahead, Timothy slowed and made a right.

Le Deuce did the same.

So did the Dodge.

The hair on the back of his neck stood up.

A few more minutes passed. Timothy came to a stop sign and made a left onto Highway 315, a two-lane rural road.

Le Deuce stopped at the sign. A white SUV roared past and followed the Silverado.

Le Deuce turned left. He looked back.

A Subaru went right and a blue Ford pickup turned left onto the highway.

Then the Dodge turned left too.

This was getting creepy.

Was somebody tailing him? Or was this just a coincidence? And how close was Timothy to his destination?

Le Deuce didn't want to lead Hot Chocolate or anybody else to wherever Timothy was going. For all he knew, whoever was in the Dodge was following him and had no clue about Timothy, Nicole, or Diane.

He had to decide fast.

If the Avenger took the next turn with them, he would have to break off and forget about Timothy for now. Then he would lead it on a wild goose chase until he could double back and get the plates.

The Silverado stopped at a red light, as did the white SUV in front of Le Deuce. He glanced back. Behind him was the blue Ford pickup, followed by the Dodge Avenger.

As they sat there, waiting for the light, he tried to get a good look at the driver, but the sunlight bouncing off the Dodge's front windshield restricted his view.

He grabbed his phone, opened Google Maps, and clicked on Nicole's address that he had saved earlier. He wanted to see if that was where Timothy was headed.

Didn't look like it. Her house was a few miles south. Timothy was heading north.

The light changed, and the Silverado took off. The white SUV put on its left turn signal. About five cars had to get through the intersection before the SUV could turn, and they were all clearly in no hurry.

After the third car crept through, he smacked the steering wheel and yelled, "Come on, damn it."

The light was going to change any second, and he would lose Timothy.

Oh, to hell with it. He jerked the RAV4 to the right, sped around the SUV, and floored it through the intersection.

As he looked back in the rearview mirror, he saw the Dodge whip around both the blue pickup and the SUV and run the red light.

Gotcha.

He kicked the speed up a notch. He didn't want them to realize he had made them. How the hell had they found him?

Knowing his luck, McAllister had changed his mind and forty-eight hours just became twenty-four. Le Deuce grabbed his balls. The next conversation wouldn't be a bent finger.

He spotted the Silverado in the distance, zooming up a small hill. Over it would be Interstate 85, which went either south to Newnan or north to Atlanta.

Where was this kid going?

Le Deuce pushed the RAV4 up to seventy, ignoring the forty-five-mile-an-hour speed limit, and hoped there weren't any sheriff's deputies hanging around. This early on a Friday morning, he doubted it.

As he came over the hill, the ramp to I-85 North was on the right. He'd almost caught up with the Silverado.

He glanced back.

The Dodge was keeping a respectable distance.

Le Deuce brainstormed his options. Timothy taking I-85 North would play out best.

If the kid went straight and Le Deuce took the ramp and the Dodge kept following the Silverado, Le Deuce would be out of the loop. By the time he made a U-turn, they both would be gone.

He wished he had gone back and put a tracker on the truck when he'd had the chance.

For a split second he thought the Silverado was going to turn right, but it kept moving straight ahead.

Le Deuce slowed down. Timothy could still get on the I-85 South ramp further down. He watched with bated breath.

Timothy passed the entrance ramp and kept on going.

This was it.

His heart rate went off the charts. Ramp or straight?

Ramp or straight?

Ramp?

Or straight?

He took the ramp and lifted his foot off the gas. Seconds crawled by like minutes as he focused on the rearview mirror and waited.

Come on. Come on.

Nothing.

COME ON.

The Dodge turned onto the ramp.

This was going to be fun.

He slammed his foot on the gas and barreled toward the interstate. I-85 came into view. Traffic was decent for a Friday morning, busy but not a parking lot.

His plan was to lead the Dodge on a wild chase, zooming in and out of lanes, and drawing it out into the far left lane. Then at the crucial moment changing lanes, dropping back, and locking them in so he could get a good look at the driver and the plates.

He merged into the right lane and kept one eye on the rearview mirror.

Behind him, the Dodge merged into the same lane.

Le Deuce waited for the semi next to him to pass. Then he floored it and hopped over two lanes. At this point he was doing eighty.

The Dodge switched lanes and followed him for a few miles. He whizzed past exit 61.

In less than ten minutes he would have three options: I-285 East, I-285 West, or continue on I-85, which would take him to downtown Atlanta. He wanted to avoid downtown because the Atlanta PD were always out in force there.

Traffic was getting heavier now. Multiple semis in the far-right lanes.

He pushed the RAV4 to ninety and zoomed back and forth between vehicles, checking both side mirrors as he went.

The Dodge was about four car lengths back but shadowing his every move.

He saw an opening, scooted across two lanes to the far left one, and reduced his speed.

Eventually the Dodge pulled in behind him. Guess they're not playing around anymore, he thought. They had to know that he'd made them.

Question was, what were they going to do about it?

Up ahead near the I-285 exits, the traffic was slowing as

everyone tried to get on the bypass. Le Deuce was an old hand at the stop-and-go nature of Atlanta traffic, which could go from eighty to zero in a millisecond. He knew you had to stay on your toes or you'd eat the rear end of a tractor trailer.

In front of him a rusty old maroon pickup truck, its bed full of furniture, was weaving. The furniture wasn't strapped down very well, and he had visions of a hutch or a mattress flying back and smashing his windshield.

He glanced to the right.

Clear.

He scoped out the passenger-side mirror. A Nissan Rogue was heading toward him, but it wasn't moving quick.

Le Deuce roared over and eased on the brakes, causing the RAV4 to slow just enough so that the Dodge and his car were side by side. He was trying to make out the driver when the passenger window rolled down.

Hot Chocolate.

Damn, she looked even better than she did yesterday. He was so tempted to stop and let her have him. Maybe he would get lucky and she would give him a sympathy lay before she killed him.

Be a hell of a way to go out.

He rolled down his window.

"Hey, darlin', what you doing out here?" she yelled.

"Just taking you on a joyride," he yelled back, his comb-over flapping in the wind.

She flashed a beautiful smile that got him right between the legs, then flipped him off.

"I wish you would," he yelled louder.

She cupped her hand around her ear. "What?"

"I wish you would do me."

"I'll bet you do."

"We could split the money."

"You have it?"

He shook his head. "Not yet. But I will. Give me more time, then we'll talk."

"I'm not fucking you."

He smiled, gave her the thumbs-up, and slowed a little more so he could get the plates.

Florida.

Probably a rental. He etched the number in his mind.

He couldn't believe what he had just said to her. But what the hell? You never knew until you asked. Maybe if he would have asked years ago, he wouldn't be in this mess now.

The I-285 exit was coming up on his right. He planned to go east at the very last minute, forcing her to stay straight.

He peeked over.

There was just enough space between the two cars beside him for him to ease in and then hop over two more lanes.

He stuck his arm out the window, waved to her, floored it, and took off toward the exit.

She tried to follow, but a FedEx van cut her off.

As he zoomed across the lanes, he heard a thunderous crash and looked back.

Holy shit!

A semi was careening out of control, heading toward the concrete median and Hot Chocolate's Dodge. Behind him, all the vehicles were slamming on their brakes to avoid the truck.

He took the exit onto I-285 East. In his rearview mirror he thought he saw the Dodge speeding away as the truck crashed into the median, but he couldn't be sure.

Please let her be okay, he thought. He really wanted to work out a deal later.

44

Diane eased her foot off the gas as she approached her house. She couldn't wait to find out where Nicole's boyfriend lived. Nicole had better be there with him. If not? Well, she'd cross that bridge later.

She pulled into the driveway and slammed on the brakes. What the hell? She couldn't believe it. Janice was rocking back and forth in the swing on Diane's front porch.

"What are you doing here?" She about broke her neck getting out of the car.

"Merry Christmas to you too."

"What are you doing at my house?"

"Baby girl, now come on. Don't be like that." She stood and walked toward Diane, arms outstretched. "We gotta bury the hatchet sometime."

"I am not your baby girl. And you can just stay on that porch, okay? How did you get here?"

"Uber."

"Then we can just Uber you right on out of here." She reached in the car, grabbed her phone, and scrolled through her apps. She could feel a scream coming on that would shatter every window in a ten-mile radius.

"We ain't got much time," Janice said.

Diane ignored her as she searched the phone.

"Baby girl, I said we ain't got much time."

She clicked on the Uber app.

"Diane?"

"You're not dying. Nicole said you were in remission."

"I had a dream last night. An awful dream. You were in trouble."

"Well, I'm not."

"God told me to come here."

Diane looked up. "Are you high? Have you been drinking?"

"You can't hate me forever, kiddo."

The utter despair in Janice's voice shook her. The lady had always been a scrapper. A rocket launcher. Living way past the edge. How was this woman her mother? They were so different. Yet hearing her like that hurt.

"I don't hate you, Janice."

"Sure you do. I don't blame you. I was a terrible mother."

"You weren't a mother at all."

"Nicole doesn't hate me."

"Let me explain something. Hate is the opposite of love. Hating you would imply that at some point I loved you. I don't hate you. I don't love you. I don't care about you. I don't think about you. You don't exist. Understand? In my world, you do not exist."

"That kinda attitude only hurts you, baby girl."

"What is your problem?" With her hip, Diane pushed the car door shut. "You've been watching Dr. Phil, haven't you? And now you've got it all figured out. Let me guess, you're going to run over here, give me a big ol' hug, we'll cry a few tears, and everything will be all hunky-dory. Right?"

"The hell I've been through—"

"We've all been through hell, Janice. It doesn't make you special."

"I've seen the light."

"No, you haven't. Don't even. Don't you dare. You haven't seen the light. You are the eternal darkness."

"I don't want your money. I don't. Honest. You're my girl. I love—"

"Don't say it."

"You can't stop me. I love you. I may not be much of a mother, but that don't change how I feel."

"I will not stand out here in my front yard and argue with you."

She charged past Janice without so much as a sideways glance, unlocked the front door, and marched into the house.

"Uber's on the way," she yelled and slammed the door in Janice's face.

SHE PULLED BACK the curtains and looked out the front window. Janice was hunched over on the swing. It looked like she might be crying.

Diane felt like a coward and yet completely used. How dare Janice show up like this? She knew how Diane felt about her. It wasn't like it was a big secret. Once again, it was all about her. Her mother's entire life had been about her, everyone else be damned.

Go. Please just go. You're not my mother. You had your chance twenty years ago, and you blew it.

Janice disappeared when Diane was seven and didn't come back until she was eighteen. All that time and not a word. Diane spent years terrified that her mother had died. How could someone do that to their children? It took a long time for that pain to burn down to a small glowing ember, one that would reignite every time Janice came around.

Maybe that was why she hadn't had children yet. It wasn't Hilton's sperm. It was her mind. Her mind wouldn't let her get pregnant. She scoffed at the idea. But was it that crazy? Thousands of years on and the human brain was still a mystery. She recalled a story she had read about a man who hit his head in the pool and overnight could play piano like a virtuoso. Her mind not letting her get pregnant? Stranger things have happened.

The only reason Janice was out on that swing was because she wanted Diane's money. The joke was on Janice. It wasn't even Diane's money. It was Hilton's. She was just along for the ride. Hitched her wagon to the right train.

She paused at the sight of her living room, then glanced down and studied the hardwood floor beneath her feet. She'd put so much effort into this house. So much sweat and blood and tears. But it wasn't her home anymore.

Once Janice left, she was going upstairs and packing. Tonight she'd find a hotel, next week an apartment. Hilton could stay here. He could have this damn place.

Bam! Bam! Bam!

She spun around. What did Janice want now? She ripped the door open.

"Yes?"

Janice, her face drained of all color, stood there shaking. For a moment Diane thought she might fall over and braced to catch her.

"Sweetie, you got some water? I don't feel so good. My head is killing me," Janice mumbled.

"Yeah, okay. Come in, but just for a minute."

Diane took a couple of steps back and let her mother into the house. Her initial notion was that Janice was faking being sick to get some sympathy. A horrible thing to consider, but this was her mother after all.

Diane watched her stumble from the foyer to the living room and flop down on the couch.

It was the first time Janice had ever been inside her house, and she didn't even acknowledge it. Normally she would have made a big production about her humble life compared to her daughter's.

Instead she sat there staring off into space.

Diane hurried into the kitchen and grabbed a bottle of water out of the fridge. She ran back into the living room and handed it to her. "What's going on? You feel weak?"

Janice didn't say a word.

Diane stepped back, knelt down, and studied her, looking for any obvious signs of what might be wrong. "You're as white as a ghost. Maybe you're dehydrated?"

She tried to smile, but only the right side of her mouth behaved. "I don't...I...I don't...know."

Diane fell into the chair across from her, pulled up her phone, and googled "heart attack and stroke symptoms." The top hit listed some symptoms of a stroke: trouble speaking, dizziness, severe headache that comes on for no reason, trouble walking or staying balanced, numbness or weakness in your face, arm, or leg, especially on one side.

"You feel dizzy?" she asked.

Janice looked past her and said nothing.

Diane snapped her fingers. "Hey, look at me."

She continued to stare off into the distance. Diane jumped up and rushed over to her.

"Can you raise your arms?"

She didn't move. Diane grabbed her left arm and lifted it. It was like rubber.

"Okay, Janice, we need to get you to the hospital." Diane could hear her voice getting louder and louder with each word, as if her mother were deaf. She ran back to the chair, grabbed her phone, and dialed 911.

As she spoke to the operator, she watched Janice sway like a rag doll blowing in the breeze. A jolt of fear laced with heartbreak hit her.

Her mother had it right.

Diane hated her.

But what had all those years of hate accomplished?

Nothing.

Not a damn thing.

Something had to change. She couldn't keep living like this.

45

———

"Babe, you okay?" Nicole hugged Timothy so tight she pushed him back against the Silverado.

"I'm fine. Just freaked me out is all. What a weirdo."

She buried her head in his chest. His arms around her calmed her nerves, and the icy breeze blowing off the lake was heaven on the back of her neck. If she could freeze a moment in time, this would be it.

When Timothy phoned her, panic in his voice, all he'd said was "Starr's Mill" and she knew exactly what he meant. For the past few months this desolate old park that overlooked Lake Howell had been their late-night go-to spot to get stoned and have long philosophical discussions, which always led to sex under the stars in the back of his pickup.

"I swear it's the same cop from last night. Gotta be." Timothy let her go and pulled a piece of paper out of his windbreaker. "Detective Le Deuce. Bastard even gave me his number."

He handed it to her.

"Le Deuce? That can't be a real name."

"I'll bet he's not even a real cop. Who knows? I was hoping to catch you before you spoke to what's-his-name—"

"Mark."

"Yeah."

"You don't like him, do you?" she asked.

"I don't know him."

"Well, it doesn't matter because he's not a police officer anymore."

"What happened?"

"Don't know. Don't care." She debated how much to tell him. "But he does private security or something. Offered to see if he could find out anything about the car."

"Offered?"

"Paranoid" ripped through the tranquil park, startling them both. Nicole yanked her phone out of her pocket. It was her sister.

"I am not cutting your hair," she yelled and hit the power button twice. The call ended. "Damn, woman."

"What's going on?"

"Got a bug up her ass. Wants me to do her hair. Been texting all morning."

"Nicole? You need to call her back."

"Why?"

"Something could be wrong. What if Le Deuce found her?"

"No, I can't talk to her right now. I gotta figure all this shit out." She pulled her cast to her chest, held it tight with her other hand, and paced back and forth. "This thing is driving me crazy. Ugh, I need a cigarette."

Timothy opened the truck door, found a pack in the console, and handed her one. She took it, and he was right there with a lighter by the time she got it to her lips.

"Aren't you sweet." She sat down in the grass, the cigarette dangling from her mouth. Nicole took off her sneakers and her socks and pulled the legs of her jeans up to her knees.

"What are you doing?"

Ignoring him, she jumped up, tiptoed to the lake and stepped in, stopping when the water got over her ankles. It was freezing, but she didn't care. The shock of the cold water cleared her mind. Glancing back at Timothy, she blew out an enormous cloud of smoke and asked, "How the hell did this guy find you?"

He brushed the smoke away as he walked to the edge of the water. "Had to be somebody at The Wicked Hand. Only thing I can think of. I mean, it's the only place anybody could have seen us all together. I've gotta talk to Ian. See what he knows about this guy. Asshole tried to bullshit me. Said Jackson was missing. Then he threatened me."

"What?"

"Said if I didn't make a deal with him, there were other people who wouldn't be so nice or some shit."

Nicole took a puff and tried to picture Le Deuce. Tried to match the image from last night—a short, rotund blob—with the man Timothy was describing. She gave up. "We can't stay here. It's not safe."

"I'm sorry. I'm sorry I messed up so bad."

"Thanks, but you being sorry changes nothing, babe. I thought about taking that money too. If it wasn't for Diane, I would have taken it. Shit happens."

"What about Diane?"

"I guess we gotta tell her. She's going to be so pissed."

"Blame it on me."

"Don't worry. I will."

"Paranoid" screamed at them once again. Nicole ripped the phone out of her pocket so fast it slipped out of her hand, but she grabbed it just before it fell into the lake.

"Nice save." He laughed. "If it's your sister, you better answer that."

She scowled at the screen. This really, really sucked.

"Nicole?"

She accepted the call, handed the phone to Timothy, and mouthed, "It's for you."

Confused, he put the phone to his ear.

"Hello? Oh, hi, Diane. It's Timothy. No, Nicole's tied up. What? Oh, sure, sure. Wow. Sorry to hear that. Hang on." He handed it back to Nicole. "You need to take this."

46

WHERE WAS NICOLE? Diane stood at the window, scanning the hospital parking lot. It had been over forty-five minutes since they had spoken on the phone. On a busy day, it took less than thirty to get from one side of Mulberry Grove to the other.

A light rain was drizzling. She watched drops of water hit the glass and slide downward until they disappeared. They reminded her of her life. You hit the wall and down, down, down you go until you vanish forever.

She had followed the ambulance back to the Mulberry Grove Regional Medical Center. After they admitted Janice, Diane had taken a seat in the ER waiting room. Trying to relax proved impossible as her thoughts kept drifting back to the gym bag. Angry one second, calm the next, she could barely stay in her seat. The smart thing would be to forget about it—this wasn't the time or the place—but the horrible feeling that her sister had stabbed her in the back persisted.

And to top it off, her nervous bladder kept forcing her to trudge to the restroom every fifteen minutes or so to pee. She didn't really have to go; it was only anxiety, but she went anyway, mostly out of habit. On her last trip back, she decided to wait for Nicole by the entrance.

She was just about to call her when a green Chevy pickup truck pulled up out front. Diane peered through the rain-soaked window and watched as the passenger door opened and Nicole jumped out. The truck sped off, and she charged into the hospital, head bowed, shoulders forward, like she was ready to tear someone to pieces.

"Hey, Nicole, over here," Diane called.

"Wow, this is turning into, like, the best Christmas ever," Nicole yelled back.

As she came closer, Diane noticed something odd on her sister's left hand. "What's that?"

Nicole stopped, gave her a perplexed look.

"Your hand. What's that?" Diane asked again.

Nicole pulled her jacket sleeve up to reveal the cast. "Nice, huh?"

"Oh my God. Why didn't you call me?"

"What could you do?"

"But it seemed fine yesterday."

"Pain got worse, so I went by urgent care. Lucky me, guess I landed just right."

"Is it broken?" Diane led her into the packed waiting room and glanced around for somewhere to sit.

"Uh, yeah," Nicole said.

"Now I feel awful."

"It's not your fault."

"I know, but—"

"What happened? How is Janice? She okay?"

They found a couple of empty chairs side by side. Diane told her everything that had happened from the moment she came home until now. The doctor thought Janice had suffered a stroke, but she needed to run some tests to make sure. She had mentioned ministroke, but Diane didn't know what that meant. Apparently there were different types.

"Hopefully that one's better than the other kind, right?" Nicole asked.

"We'll see."

Diane's eyes welled up, and she spun toward the large-screen TV on the other side of the room, hiding her face from her sister. This was crazy. Why was she getting upset over Janice? Nicole was the one who should be in tears right now. Diane should be dancing in the street. *Ding-dong! The witch is dead. The witch is dead. The witch is dead.*

She cleared her throat, rubbed her eyes, and turned back to Nicole. "Where were you this morning?"

"Timothy's. Sorry I didn't answer. Long night."

"Having fun?" She forced a smile as she pictured Nicole sneaking back up the stairs, going into Jackson's apartment, grabbing the gym bag.

"Oh, it was insane."

"Well, good for you."

"Yeah..."

"I was getting worried. Was that his truck?"

Nicole nodded.

"He didn't want to come in?"

"He had some things to take care of."

What kind of things? Diane thought. The temptation to grill her about the gym bag was overwhelming, but instead she asked, "So you think anybody has found—"

"Shh, not here," Nicole whispered. "And no, I don't think so."

"Does he know?"

"Who?"

"Timothy."

"Know what?"

"Nicole? Did you tell him?"

"Why would I do something stupid like that?"

"I don't...sorry, I'm freaking out a little."

"You and me both." Nicole smacked her lips together. "Water?"

Diane pointed to a water cooler across the room. Nicole got up and headed over. Before she got there, a couple of out-of-control hellions surrounded her. Nicole gave their mother the evil eye, but the woman was too busy playing on her phone to notice.

Diane shook her head and mumbled under her breath, "Nana would have whipped our butts."

She pulled her phone out of her purse and searched for "ministroke." She had to take her mind off the gym bag. The search returned multiple articles, and she skimmed through them.

"Did you see that shit?"

Diane looked up. She hadn't realized her sister had sat back down. Nicole pointed to the kids running around.

"Yeah," Diane said. "I'm surprised you didn't smack that woman upside the head."

"Oh, it took everything I had."

She chuckled and returned to her phone. According to an article she found, the technical term for a ministroke was *transient ischemic attack*. Unlike a stroke where blood flow to the brain stays blocked, causing permanent damage, a TIA stops blood flow for a short period. Once the blood flow starts back, the symptoms go away. However, a TIA was a warning sign and could mean a stroke was coming. The next forty-eight hours would be critical.

If it *was* a TIA.

"You reading a book on that thing?" Nicole asked.

"Research."

"Oh, you're one of those?"

"One of what?"

"People who self-diagnose on the internet."

"No, I just want to see what we're dealing with," Diane said.

"We?"

"What are you talking about?"

"*We* haven't been dealing with anything. I've been dealing with it."

Diane sat the phone in her lap and turned to her. "And I'm a hundred and fifty percent sorry. I've been a real bitch with her. She left us both."

Nicole didn't respond. Drummed her fingers on her leg instead. Diane knew she hated it when people apologized. Said it robbed her of her best weapon, self-righteous anger.

"So now you want to be there for her?" Nicole asked.

"She's never going to change. I know that...but I don't want to be mad anymore. I'm so tired of being angry with her."

"See, that's funny, 'cause now *I'm* pissed. She's making it real tough for me to give a shit. When you called, I didn't even want to come over here. She's driving me crazy. Diane, you should see how she lives. It's disgusting. She's in remission. Re-mis-sion. And, damn it, still smoking, drinking—among other things." She laughed and turned serious. "It's like she's trying to kill herself."

"Maybe she is."

"Then I just need to get out of the way. What was she doing at your house?"

"Who knows? I come home and she's sitting on the swing."

"Oh...I'd love to have seen the look on your face."

"She wasn't making any sense. Told me she had some dream, and that I was in danger. Talking like she'd found God or something. Crazy."

"I won't even tell you what I walked in on her and some old dude doing—" The television caught her eye. "Hey, wait a minute...I know that chick."

"Who?"

"Sally Dupree. Wow, she got through law school?"

Diane looked over. On the screen, a woman was pitching a get-out-of-jail-free card for drivers who had gotten a DUI.

Nicole held up her crossed fingers. "We were like this before I moved to LA. Back in the day, she was a total cokehead. I'm amazed she graduated. Sally Dupree, Esquire. That's hilarious."

Diane sighed. Her sister had thousands of war stories about her vagabond life. She wore them like a badge of honor. "You sure we're related?"

Nicole leaned over, glanced around, and lowered her voice like she was about to tell her who actually killed Kennedy. "You really think George isn't my dad?"

"No, I don't."

"So why are you always making jokes about it?"

"I'm just messing with you."

"Well, if he wasn't my dad, wouldn't I have a right to know?"

"Sure, but honey, he *is* your dad."

"Then why have you been giving me shit about it for years?"

Diane took a moment. She didn't have an answer. Apparently she'd hit a sore spot. Was George Nicole's dad? Yes, but..."I guess because we're so different."

"No shit."

"Maybe I'm jealous?"

Nicole looked at her like, *You've gotta be kidding me.*

"Don't laugh," Diane continued. "Maybe I'm jealous."

"Of me?"

"You have a confidence I've never had. You want something, you go after it. You fall down, you get back up. I watched you on that stage the other night, and you were good. I mean really good. It was like you owned that stage."

"Wow, I'm speechless."

"You? Speechless? I'm shocked."

"Hey, it happens," Nicole said.

"Well, you owned that stage, and I wish I had something like that. Something I felt so passionate about."

"You write, what about that?"

"I'm a wimp. A couple of rejection letters, and I bailed."

"Come on, that is crazy. You are the most together person I've ever met, Diane. Nothing fazes you. You were the class valedictorian, for Christ's sake."

"What's that got to do with anything?"

"You've got a beautiful house. You don't *have* to work—"

"Hilton did all that, not me. He made that money. I just got lucky."

"Diane, we both know who the fuck-up here is, and it ain't you."

"Thanks, but..." She didn't know how the conversation had gotten here. The nagging question about the gym bag was killing her. She had to get some air. The walls were closing in.

She turned to Nicole. "Hungry?"

"Yeah, I guess. But what about Janice?"

"We can sit here and wait, or we can get a margarita across the street at El Campesino and wait."

Diane stood up, grabbed her purse, and headed toward the exit. She didn't look back to see if her sister was coming.

DIANE PICKED up her napkin and wiped off her mouth. She had gotten the enchilada-burrito-taco combo, but after a few bites felt like running to the bathroom, sticking her finger down her throat, and—she pushed her plate away.

"Thought you were hungry?" Nicole took a swig of Corona.

"Guess I just wanted to get out of the hospital."

"I hate those places. You know how I want to go out?"

"No, but I'm sure you're going to tell me."

"Heart attack. Boom. Bang. Done. No suffering. No hospital. Nothing. Just—ugh...I'm dead." She closed her eyes, stuck her tongue out, and tilted her head to one side.

"Charming."

"Yeah, I think about a lot of weird shit."

Diane didn't say a word. Every time she looked at her sister, all she saw was a giant gym bag.

"What's up?" Nicole asked.

Diane shrugged.

"I know when something is bugging you."

"I'm just worried."

"Never thought I'd see the day you'd be worried about Janice."

"I never thought she'd have a stroke on my couch. It's not just her. It's everything. You know what I'd planned to do today? Get you to cut my hair and dye it, and then I was going to—"

"Not today." Nicole tapped her cast with her fork. "No more haircuts for a while."

"For how long?"

"Weeks? I don't know."

"What about your bills?"

Nicole picked up her taco and took a big bite. After she finished, she said, "You could loan me some money for rent."

"How about I pay your rent until you can work again?"

"No, I'd prefer a loan."

"Okay..." If Nicole needed rent money, then maybe Diane was wrong about the gym bag. Or was she pretending she needed money to cover her tracks?

"What else were you going to do?" Nicole asked.

"Huh?"

"You said you were going to get me to cut your hair and then...?"

"Oh, yeah. A tattoo. I was going to get a tattoo."

"Get out."

"Isn't that crazy?"

Nicole reached across the table and put her hand on Diane's forehead. "Nope. No fever."

"Obviously, you're the tattoo expert. If I decide to get one, who's the best in town?"

"My friend Josh is amazing, but good luck getting in anytime soon. What are you thinking?"

"Something simple."

"Like?"

"Don't laugh."

"Okay."

"I'm serious," Diane said.

"Promise."

"A phoenix."

"On your back? Like a big phoenix?"

"No, can't they do something small?"

"Don't know. Where do you want it?"

She patted her right shoulder blade. "Here."

"Guess we'll have to ask him. That's nuts. My sister getting a tattoo. What's Hilton going to think?"

"Doesn't matter. When he gets home tonight, I'm going to tell him I want a divorce."

"Oh, damn."

Diane tilted her head and studied her empty margarita glass. Time for another drink? No, it was time to clear the air.

"You had me worried this morning when you didn't answer my texts or my calls. So worried, in fact, that I went by your house."

"Okay."

"After everything that had happened, I was freaking out. I thought something might have happened to you, but once I went in—"

"You went inside?"

"You do have the key under the plant. Anyway, once I went in, I realized you hadn't spent the night there and were probably at your boyfriend's house, and I calmed down."

Nicole nodded, her mouth full of food.

"But then, as I was leaving..." *Here we go.* "I found a gym bag in the kitchen."

Nicole leaned forward. "So?"

Diane whispered, "It looked like the one we found in his car."

"Gym bags are pretty generic looking. What are you accusing me of?"

"I'm just telling you what I found."

Diane watched her, looking for any sign that she might be lying. Her sister had a long history of massaging the truth.

"Okay, so you found a gym bag," Nicole said.

"Is it his?"

"I don't believe you. You think I went back there and took it? You do, don't you?" She looked around, spotted the server, and held up her hand for the check. "I didn't take anything."

"I'm sorry, I didn't mean to upset you."

Nicole took some cash out of her purse and laid it on the table.

"I got it." Diane pulled her wallet out of her purse.

"No, I pay my own way. I can afford it now, right?"

"Fine."

Nicole took a swig of her Corona and stood up. "And by the way, Diane, fuck you."

She marched out of the restaurant.

Now Diane was certain. Her sister was lying.

WALKING OUT OF EL CAMPESINO, the cold wind hit Diane hard, and she pulled her coat tight. The rain had stopped, and the sky was a mass of wintery gray, as if an enormous cloud was blotting out the sun. She smiled at the possibility of lying in bed, all snug and toasty.

If only I hadn't kissed him.

She pictured herself telling Jackson goodnight and walking into her house all alone. Listening at the window as his Camaro drove off. Spending the next two days wondering what could have been instead of slow-walking through a never-ending nightmare.

Coulda, woulda, shoulda, her Nana always said.

Diane looked around the parking lot. Where did she park? She spotted her Lexus.

Nicole was leaning against it. She held up her cast. "See this? I got it because I helped you out. Because when you called me in the middle of the night, I came."

Diane picked up her stride. If her sister wanted a fight, she was going to get one. Nicole wasn't that tough; she'd kicked her butt plenty of times growing up.

"And guess what? I might never play guitar again."

"You're being ridiculous," Diane yelled back, the sound of anger in her voice surprising her.

"You don't know, you're not a doctor. We were getting ready to go into the studio. And now I can't do shit. I can't even cut hair."

"What do you want me to do about it, Nicole? What do you want me to do? I'm sorry. I am so, so sorry. But I didn't break your hand."

An older couple coming toward her picked up their pace. Diane caught the woman's eye and smiled.

It's okay. We aren't really crazy. We're sisters.

It didn't work. The man wrapped his arm around his wife and charged past Diane, scurrying inside. She needed to stop yelling in parking lots. It was getting weird.

She got to the car, her heart pounding like a jackhammer. "Is that why you went back? Because you think you deserved the cash because you broke your hand?"

"I didn't go back. I didn't take anything. You know what really gets to me? What really pisses me off? You see that gym bag and you automatically assume that I took it. That I went back and took it. You didn't give it a second thought. Don't you have any faith in me? Just a little?"

"What would you think?"

"I'd think it was a gym bag because, you know, people, like, have them. It's not like it was a rocket launcher."

"A rocket launcher?"

"You know, like something—shit, I don't know—something odd that would never be at my house or whatever...you know what I mean."

"Okay, so you didn't take it. It's your gym bag, and I'm a horrible, horrible person."

Nicole's eyes turned red, and for the tiniest second Diane thought her sister was going to hit her. Then she said, "You're not a horrible person. I just...I didn't take it. That's not his gym bag. I didn't take the money." Nicole burst into tears. "I didn't take the money."

Diane's mouth dropped. She didn't know what to do. Stand there? Hug her? Get in her car and drive off?

The last time she'd seen her sister cry like this was when Nicole was in the seventh grade. She had desperately wanted to play drums in the Mill Creek Junior High band, but there weren't any open slots for drummers. Not that Nicole was a drummer, but she had wanted to learn. The band director had tried to talk her into either the flute or the violin, but she was adamant. It was the drums or nothing. The band director chose nothing. Diane came home from school to find her on the couch, a bowl of Count Chocula in her lap, sobbing her eyes out.

She decided to do what she did back then and walked over and wrapped her arms around her. Nicole withered and broke down.

Diane felt like a real shit.

Once more she'd screwed up.

Coulda, woulda, shoulda...

47

––––––

Hilton reread the text from Diane just to make sure he wasn't imagining it.

At the hospital. Janice had a stroke.

Janice? Since when did Diane have anything to do with her mother? His first instinct was to call her, but he knew that wasn't a good idea. For one, Peggy was in the car, and he didn't want her to say something and Diane ask questions. After this morning, Diane didn't want to talk to him, anyway.

He typed: *Sorry. I hope she's going to be okay.*

It's mild, but they're keeping her in for observation. I'm here with Nicole. I won't be able to pick you up from the airport.

No problem. I'll get an Uber.

Ok.

He typed: *Ok.* Then he hit send and waited.

That was it.

No *I love you.*

No heart emoji. Not that *he'd* sent an emoji, but still...

Nothing.

What did he expect? She hadn't ended a text with an emoji or *I love you* in ages. Still, it bothered him. He wasn't sure why. He wanted a divorce. The marriage was over. What did it matter if she didn't send him a frigging little heart on his phone?

"Something wrong?" Peggy asked as she steered the SUV into Albuquerque International Sunport.

Hilton looked at the text again and was glad she'd driven to the airport. He had been so scattered today he would have wrapped the car around a tree.

"Diane's at the hospital. Her mom had a stroke."

"Oh, honey, that's terrible."

He scratched his chin and studied the endless sky surrounding the airport. He'd never seen a blue sky like this back in Georgia. It seemed to go on forever. He pictured cowboys riding across these open plains over a hundred years ago. It must have been nice not being able to get some crazy text from your wife back then. Of course, it smelled like horse shit all the time too. But life, as they say, is a series of trade-offs.

"Yeah. Thing is, Diane hasn't spoken to her mother in years. I'm talking years. Guess her sister must have called her. Whole thing is bizarre. You know how you can tell something isn't right, but you don't know what it is. That's what I'm getting here."

Peggy found a space, parked, and shut the car off. She shifted in her seat toward him. He didn't want to look at her because he knew if he did, he might not get on the plane. He put his hands together, twiddled his thumbs, and said, "Maybe I should just stay here?"

"Baby?"

"It's a damn shame when your wife's mom is in the hospital and she doesn't even want you there."

"Do you want to be there?"

"No."

"You sure?"

"What does that mean?"

"Just asking. You seem upset."

"I'm not. I'm just confused. Diane hates her mother. Despises her. Won't even call her 'mom.' Calls her Janice. 'She's not *my* mother' she would always yell if I slipped up." He paused. "Would it bother you if I wanted to be there?"

"No." She crossed her arms.

He saw a darkness creep into her eyes. "That's a pretty weak 'no.'"

"It wouldn't bother me. She's still your wife."

He didn't like the way she said "wife." It had a bit of bite to it. In all the time they'd known each other, they had yet to have a real argument. Some playful back-and-forth, but nothing cutting. Was this going to be the first one? He hoped not.

"I lived with someone once. We weren't married, but we might as well have been," she said, staring out the window. "Ending it wasn't easy. Even if it was the right thing to do."

He reached over. Put his hand on her thigh. Tried to draw out a smile.

"I feel guilty," she said.

"Don't."

"I've never had an affair before. Told myself I never would. We've been having this whirlwind romance. And your wife? Who knows what she's going through?"

"That's on me. Blame me. Don't blame yourself."

She turned and found his eyes. He marveled once more at her. *She has no idea*, he thought. *No idea what she does to me.*

"You want to do this?" she asked. "Because if there is an ounce of doubt about us, get on that plane and let's call it a fun fling—"

He surprised her with a kiss. Passionate and lingering. As he held her, she ran her fingers through his hair. Her cheek caressed his. He closed his eyes and drowned in her perfume. He didn't want to let her go. Didn't want to go back to Georgia. To hell with being mayor. To hell with everything.

"You spend your entire life thinking you know what love is," he whispered. "You're young, you meet someone. Seems like the right thing, so you get married. Life moves on. It's comfortable, but not earth-shaking. You figure that's just the way it's supposed to be. But then one day—for the first time in your life—you fall in love. And you understand you were never in love before. In a strange way, because you care about the woman you married, you know you gotta let her go, so maybe she can find what you've found."

He put his hands on her cheeks and looked into her eyes. "I'm going to get on the plane, and tonight I'm going to tell her I want a divorce. And then it's going to be just you and me. Okay?"

"Okay."

Her lips quivered, and she kissed him. For a moment, the world was his.

48

"She knows," Nicole yelled. "Can you believe that? She knows."

"Can you tone it down?" Timothy set the windshield wipers to high, but the rain was pounding so hard it barely made a dent.

"Kiss my ass."

"Screaming in my ear ain't helping."

Nicole gave him her best bitch face.

"Nice. You gonna suck on your thumb too?"

She folded her arms and looked out the window. He was right. Getting angry wouldn't fix anything. But damn, it felt good. It was pretty much all she could do right now, anyway.

"How's your mom?" he said.

"I don't want to talk about it."

"Is she gonna be all right?"

"Later, please?"

"Sure." He reached over and cranked up the music. Judas Priest's "You've Got Another Thing Comin'" shook the cab.

They rode for a while—him playing the snare and bass drum on the steering wheel, her watching the cookie-cutter storefronts go by. No matter where you went anymore, it was all the same boring junk, she thought.

Once Nicole had pulled herself together, Diane had driven her back to the hospital, where the doctor informed them Janice, as they'd suspected, had suffered a mild transient ischemic attack and needed to be kept under observation. The doctor explained that the next forty-eight hours were critical in determining if it was the opening salvo to a full-blown stroke or an isolated incident.

When they checked on Janice, she was sound asleep. Diane left —didn't say goodbye, just walked out. Nicole stuck around for a while to see if she might wake up. She didn't want her waking up to an empty room.

Watching her mother in blissful slumber, she'd thought, *She looks so harmless. But don't be fooled. She's like a sleeping tiger. You can reach out and pet it and it might purr, or it might wake up and take your arm off.*

She tried to imagine how different her life might have been if Janice hadn't abandoned her. That one decision—which Nicole had zero say in—had shaped every aspect of her life in ways she couldn't even fathom.

However, if she took a step back and looked at it from another angle, maybe Janice had done her a favor by leaving. Perhaps it had been a gift. Her mother knew deep down she had no business raising two girls. Would her life have been any better if Janice had stayed? Odds were it would have been worse. Maybe her mother had made the ultimate sacrifice, and she and Diane hadn't even realized it. Or maybe not. But the idea brought her a bit of peace.

She reached over and turned the music down. "Where are we going?"

"Good question," Timothy said. "Can't go back to my house. Can't go back to yours."

"What do we do now?"

"Beats me. What does Diane know?"

Up ahead, the light turned red, and he brought the truck to a stop.

"Okay, so she doesn't *know* anything. She thinks I took the money. Oh my God, I can't believe I started crying in front of her. I mean it worked, but still, it was so embarrassing."

"You cried?"

"I had to do something."

"You? You really cried?"

"Not at first, but I got carried away and couldn't stop. That's what was embarrassing. I haven't cried like that in forever. It stopped her dead cold, which is good, but..."

"We both screwed up," Timothy said.

"I know."

"I shouldn't have taken the money—"

"And I shouldn't have made you take it back. And we shouldn't have fucked in the woods."

"Made love."

Nicole shot him a bewildered look.

"Baby, fucking is something animals do. We made love, and it was awesome."

She put her hand on his. "It was. But it wasn't three-hundred-thousand-dollars awesome. We've gotta find that money. What did Ian say?"

"Dude's a real cop. Been hanging out there for years. Lately it's been with Jackson, but Ian didn't think they were friends. More like business associates."

The light turned green. Timothy put his foot on the gas and took off.

"So he's one of those, huh? If it wasn't for this one asshole."

"I've been thinking—"

"We could kill him," Nicole said.

"Are you serious?"

"Sorta. I mean, it could be him or us."

Timothy jerked the Silverado to the right, skipped a lane, and floored it into a parking lot. He parked, cut the music, and turned to face her.

"You ever killed anybody?"

"No." She rolled her eyes and let out a weak laugh.

"Well, I have, and I have no intention of ever doing it again. Unless of course your life, my life, my mama's life, people I care about—if I gotta save 'em."

"I didn't know."

"Well, now you do."

She inched back closer to the door. She'd never seen him this angry. It scared her. "I wasn't trying to be funny, babe."

"Yeah, you were. But that's the world today, isn't it? People dying, nobody cares. It's in the movies. It's on TV. People getting blown away left and right. It's so funny. So goddamn hilarious. One big joke."

"Baby?"

"It's not an option. Not unless he tries to hurt you."

She reached over and put her hand on his shoulder. "I would never ask you to. But what do we do? This Le Deuce guy...what's he up to?"

"Like I said, I've been thinking, and it's pretty obvious. He found the body after I went back and took the money and the coke. He had to know about that stuff or else he could have called it in. Decided if nobody knew Jackson was dead, he'd take the money and drugs and everybody would think Jackson disappeared with it. That's what he was doing last night—getting rid of the body."

"Who was that other dude?"

"His partner?"

"They didn't sound like partners," she said.

"Either way, this cop's looking for the money."

"And we lost it. We are so screwed."

"Hang on. What if I told him?"

"Huh?"

"What if I told him everything?" he asked.

"Why?"

"I'm brainstorming here. I gotta do something. I can't sit around and wait for him to make a move."

"*We.* Whatever *we* do, we're doing together, and we leave Diane out of it."

"Okay."

Her brow furrowed, and her eyes lit up. "You know what we could do? Record him. Get him to admit that he moved the body last night. That would give us some leverage."

"Yeah, we could tell him you and me and Jackson went back to my place to party."

"And he passed out on the couch, and when we woke up, he had died in his sleep."

"Okay, this is good. This is working."

They sat there for a few minutes, the steady rat-a-tat of the rain mixed with the low hum of the engine to create a hypnotic pulse. Their eyes met. Timothy smiled. She returned it but looked inward as she explored all the angles to see what they were missing.

"So why did we move Jackson?" he asked.

She rubbed her cast, thinking. "Okay, get this...we found the money and shit in his car. Got scared, neither one of us wants the police sticking their nose into our business, right? There's no way we were calling the cops to your house. Le Deuce would buy that."

"So we don't tell him we took the money?"

"I wouldn't...I mean...I don't know. We can work out the details later."

"Devil's in the details, hunny bunny. Story has to be right as rain or we're—"

"Dead."

"You know, but before we do this, you need to talk to, um... what's-his—"

"Mark."

"Yeah, see if he found the Corolla. Might get lucky, get the money back." He put the truck in reverse, looked over his shoulder, and backed out.

Nicole slapped the dashboard and did a little dance in her seat. "You okay?"

"Hell yeah. We have a plan. Might not work, but hey, we have a plan."

The Silverado pulled out into the road, merged into the busy traffic, and sped off.

49

———

DIANE ORDERED a Manhattan and placed her phone on the bar. She was tempted to pick it back up and google: "Countries that don't extradite to the US." She was pretty sure Canada wouldn't be on that list.

After leaving the hospital, she'd had an epiphany—a little pick-me-up before the big showdown would be both proper and warranted, so she'd stopped at Murph's, a quiet, candle-lit restaurant and bar next to the Mulberry Grove Hotel and Convention Center. The place was sparse, but it was five thirty and the Friday night dinner crowd hadn't arrived yet. In the background, a familiar trumpet wailed. She tried to place the tune. After a moment it came to her. "You Go to My Head" by Chet Baker.

The bartender set her Manhattan down. Diane thanked him. Their eyes lingered on each other, and she grinned sheepishly as he turned and walked away. She felt like asking him for his number. She felt like doing a lot of things she had never done before.

Earlier, watching Nicole break down, she'd realized it was best to forget the whole gym bag fiasco. If her sister went back and took the money, there wasn't much she could do about it. On one level, the fact Nicole might have stabbed her in the back hurt like hell, but on another, it didn't even matter. She'd been abandoned so many times in her life that she'd grown used to it. Bathed in candle-light, nursing her drink, letting the music wash over her, she welcomed the pain like an old friend. At least it was something she could count on. It hadn't let her down yet.

"Mind if I sit here?"

Surprised, Diane turned to see a man standing next to the barstool beside her. He looked to be in his early fifties, a smidge under six feet, with light brown hair heading toward gray. If he lost twenty pounds and worked out, he still wouldn't be her type, but he had a nice smile and kind eyes, so she said, "No, not at all."

She picked her purse up off of the stool. He sat down and ordered a Heineken. She caught a whiff of his cologne. He smelled good; she'd give him that.

After a few moments of uncomfortable silence as they both played on their phones and pretended not to notice each other, he said, "Hi, I'm Ted."

She turned toward him, her hair revealing only a sliver of her face, and gave him a smile. "Diane."

"Nice to meet you." He stuck out his hand. She took it. His palm was nice and smooth. Obviously he didn't use his hands to make a living, she thought. She shocked herself and asked, "You do this often, Ted? Introduce yourself to strange women at bars."

He laughed. Adjusted his tie. "Sometimes. Depends."

"On what?"

"The vibe."

"I'm sending out a vibe?"

"Not exactly..." He took a drink of his beer.

"Does it work?"

"Sometimes. Depends."

She smiled. *I'll bet.* "So what do you do for a living?"

He started to answer, but she held up her hand. "Wait, let me guess..." She looked him over. "Accountant?"

"Nope."

"You don't look like a lawyer."

"That's good. I guess."

"Financial?"

"Medical."

"Doctor?"

"Gynecologist."

She arched an eyebrow.

"Yep." He smiled.

"Sorry, it's just usually they're women."

"Yeah, well, we gents do manage to get in there."

Diane burst out laughing and put her hand over her mouth.

His face turned red. "Oh, I'm sorry, didn't mean to phrase it like that."

"It's okay. No big deal." She glanced at his left hand. He wasn't wearing a wedding band, but even in the dim glow she could see the line from where one had been. She chuckled to herself. *I wonder where this is going?*

And then she did something she never would have done a week ago. "Maybe we should move somewhere where we can have a little more privacy?"

"Oh, okay. Sure."

She caught the smile in his voice and hoped she wasn't giving him unrealistic expectations. She just wanted to talk freely. Without any unwanted attention. They took their drinks and moved to a booth near the back where they sat quietly for a minute or two, exchanging awkward glances.

"Let me ask you something, Ted." She liked saying his name. It made her feel in charge. "And I want you to be honest with me because if not, I can get up and leave. Right now what I need is complete honesty, okay?"

"Okay," he said and looked at his beer bottle.

She could tell she was rattling his cage, but she didn't care. She didn't know if it was the alcohol or all the crap she'd been through the past few days, but right now she had a couple of questions and wanted some answers.

"Can I see your ring finger?"

He laid his left hand on the table.

"You're not wearing a ring, but I can see the lines from where you were. Are you married, Ted?"

He hesitated. Played with the Heineken bottle some more.

"Complete honesty."

"Yes. I am." He made eye contact.

She laid her hand on the table. Showed him her ring. "I'm sure when you asked me if you could sit down next to me, you saw my ring."

"Actually, at first I didn't."

"And if you had? Would it have changed anything?"

"Probably not. You're an attractive woman having a drink all by yourself in a bar at five thirty on a Friday afternoon. I figured you might be…available."

"Does your wife know?"

"She does. We have an open marriage."

She studied his eyes. He seemed to be telling the truth. But you never knew. Even if you were married to someone for thirteen years. You just never knew. "How does that work, exactly?"

"Well, she does her thing, and I do mine."

"You guys still sleep together?"

"Oh, yeah. It's not for everyone, but it works for us. Some people aren't meant to be monogamous." He flashed her a smile when he said it.

She found herself seeing him in a different light. He wasn't her type—if she had one—but she wondered how he kissed.

"The problem is," he continued, "when two people get married and one is monogamous and the other isn't."

"Or when one wants it three times a day and the other one twice a month. Do you tell your wife about these affairs?"

He smiled.

"I had a feeling," she said.

"I tell her. She tells me."

"So if you have a one-night stand when you get home, you tell your wife."

"Everything."

"And it turns her on?"

"Turns both of us on. It's pretty incredible."

"I appreciate the honesty. I really do."

"I've never told anyone that before."

"The other women. They don't know?"

"Not that."

"What would you tell her about me?"

He laughed. "Boy, I don't know where to start. I guess I would tell her how we met, what you looked like. How we got from here to my motel room..."

As he continued on, she put her arms on the table, rested her chin on her hands, and listened intently. *Do things really happen for a reason?* she thought. Was meeting this man a coincidence or fate? Was Jackson's death divine punishment for her indiscretion or just a case of poor timing and bad luck?

There was only one way to find out. She finished her margarita and in a sweet voice asked, "Maybe you could walk me through all this in your motel room?"

He smiled.

She smiled back.

DIANE CLOSED the car door and looked across the parking lot at Murph's. The rain had stopped, and the neon sign gleamed in the light mist.

"Did I really just do that?" she said aloud, shocked at the sound of her own voice. Perhaps she'd dreamed the whole thing.

Perhaps she'd never even gotten out of the car. Merely lost track of two hours sitting here fantasizing.

She reminded herself nothing bad had happened. Ted—if that *was* his real name—hadn't keeled over. He hadn't handcuffed her to the bed and cut her into little pieces. The police hadn't busted down the door and hauled her off to jail.

She smiled. She felt good. Really good.

She was in complete control.

Could she go back to a normal life? She wasn't sure. And what was a normal life, anyway? Who made those rules? She and Ted had fun. If he was telling the truth, his wife would enjoy it too. And if he was lying? Well, that was on him, not Diane.

Maybe this was what she'd always wanted.

But had been too scared to admit.

50

<hr>

NICOLE CLOSED HER EYES, turned her head, and popped her neck. She needed some shut-eye. Ten years ago, a couple of days without sleep would have been a cakewalk. But at thirty-two? It was absolute hell.

She glanced over at Timothy.

He yawned, smiled, and tipped his flask of Jack and Coke. She nodded and turned her gaze back to Le Deuce's house. Jack and Coke...yuck. She was a Southern Comfort gal.

They had spent the last hour parked down the street waiting for Le Deuce to come home. It was a miracle they had even figured out where the creep lived. Scouring the internet earlier revealed no Facebook, Twitter, or Instagram accounts. People Finder and the White Pages also came up blank. Victor Le Deuce was an online ghost.

Timothy reached out to his friend Billy—head tech at Computers & More—but all Billy could get was this address.

"What do you want for Christmas?" Timothy tossed his cigarette out the window and sat the flask down on the center console.

"Huh?"

"What do you want for Christmas? I'm one of those last-minute guys, but since this is our first Christmas, I need to make sure I do it right."

"Yeah, okay. Let me think. A backpack full of money? How about that?"

"You have to stop being so negative."

"What the hell are you talking about?"

"You don't know how this is going to turn out. You gotta think positive, hunny bunny. Use the law of attraction."

"You gotta lay off the weed, babe. It's messing with your brain." Her stomach growled. She placed her hands over it to stifle the noise.

"I heard that," Timothy said.

"We are not getting any food."

"I don't think the dude's coming home. We need to call him."

"And give him a heads-up? Not a good idea. Are we even sure this is his house?"

"Yeah, I'm sure. My boy knows his shit. There's only one Victor Le Deuce in Mulberry Grove. Hell, I'll bet there's only one Victor Le Deuce in the entire world. What kind of name is that? Le Deuce?"

"This was a stupid idea. He ain't gonna talk to us—"

"Okay, so what's Plan B?" He turned to her, a little smirk on his face.

"I don't know. Run like hell?"

"What about your sister?"

"She could come with us."

"Uh-huh, that would work."

"She's getting a divorce," Nicole said.

"Since when?"

"Since a little while ago. So she might be open to leaving with us."

"Running only postpones the inevitable, Nicole. Why don't you try what's-his-name again?"

She scrunched up her nose like he'd just farted. Calling Mark was the last thing she wanted to do. She still couldn't believe she'd been dumb enough to ask for his help.

Her phone rang. She grabbed it off the dash. "Speak of the devil. You psychic or something?"

"You're just now figuring that out?"

She stuck out her tongue and answered the phone with a curt, "Hey."

"Good news, bad news," Mark said. "Managed to locate the vehicle. It was abandoned at the Big Lots near Town Square."

"The backpack?"

"Nope. Not there."

"Shit. Thanks for trying." She put the phone on mute. "Should I ask him about Le Deuce?"

Timothy looked up at the ceiling for a moment. "Can't hurt."

She took the phone off mute. "Hey, Mark, do you know Detective Le Deuce?"

"Old Douche? Yep, I know him. Why?"

"Old Douche?"

"Yeah, the guy's a total douchebag."

"Well, anyway...he's been messing with Timothy."

"Like what, exactly?"

"Like harassing him and stuff."

"Nicole, what's going on?"

"Nothing. Do you know the guy?"

"I told you I did."

"Okay, so what's he like?" she asked.

"Crazy."

"Crazy nuts or crazy smart?"

"Both. Maybe we could grab a beer and I'll fill you in?" He chuckled.

She almost tossed the phone through the front windshield. "Can you just tell me about him?"

"Bit of a pit bull. Loner. Nobody in the department likes the guy, but he closes cases. One of those idiot savants. Thinks he's smarter than everybody else. Anti-government and all that crap."

"Is he a bad cop?"

"Bad?"

"You know...honest?"

"Well, there have been rumors. I don't like this. What have you guys gotten into?"

"Thanks for your help."

"I meant what I said. I'm sorry. I was a real scumbag. If you need anything, I'm here—"

Nicole ended the call. "He found the car. Backpack's gone."

"Damn."

"So we can't just sit here and hope for the best. We gotta get proactive."

LE DEUCE'S house sat on a small hill at the end of the street. A one-story brick with a one-car garage, there was a metal staircase leading up to the front porch. In the dark it was difficult for Nicole to determine the age of the house, but she guessed it had to be at least thirty to thirty-five years old. The grass was neat and trim along with the bushes lining the porch. A few lights were on, but the driveway was empty.

She and Timothy were strolling down the street, hand in hand, like two lovers on a quiet evening walk. The rain had left the asphalt glistening, and a haze hung in the air. A dog had pooped in the grass near them, and she grabbed her nose.

"Le Deuce is a scrooge," she said.

"What makes you say that?"

"No Christmas decorations."

"You're right. That is an excellent observation."

"Let me tell you, Jack, you don't get one over on me." She

made a little karate-chop move with her hand and waited for him to laugh, but he didn't.

They came to a stop in front of the house.

"Well, we can't go in the front door," he said. "And what if he has an alarm?"

"Run like hell?" She grinned, all teeth.

"Running like hell isn't the solution to everything."

"Always worked for me."

"What are we trying to do here? We break into his house and then what?"

"Find out who he is? Maybe there's something in his house that we can use against him? Find the child porn on his computer? I don't know. Like you said—we gotta do something."

While Timothy thought on it, she glanced up and down the street. Most of the houses—brick like Le Deuce's—were alight in red and green. Beaver Pond was one of the older subdivisions on the north side of town. They built it in the seventies to accommodate all the families moving in because of the new General Motors plant. Now the neighborhood was mainly retirees.

She checked the time on her phone. Closing in on eight thirty. *Good*, she thought. *Most of these old people should be in bed by now.* She looked up at Timothy. "We doing this or not?"

"Hell yeah, we're doing it."

He grabbed her, gave her a kiss, and took off up the driveway toward the back of the house. He zigzagged to the right and went across the walkway and up the stairs. She got to the foot of the stairs just as he stepped onto the welcome mat.

"What are you doing, dummy?" she whispered.

"Lights are on. He might be home." He knocked on the front door. After a couple of knocks with no answer, he came shuffling down the stairs. "I don't think anybody's here."

She followed him around to the back of the house, where they found a large broken down deck. They crept up the wooden stairs, trying to be as quiet as possible. Once they got to the deck, they found a sliding patio glass door that appeared to go to the kitchen or the living room.

Nicole peered inside. It was the kitchen.

"Shit," Timothy whispered.

"What?" She spun around, afraid something had happened.

"I left my gloves in the truck."

"So?"

"Fingerprints."

"Does it matter?"

"We need to do this right."

"So you want to go all the way back to the truck and risk being seen by one of the neighbors?"

"Yeah, you're right. You're right. Aargh! I'm so pissed at myself."

She pulled a pair of pink gloves out of her jeans pocket. "You can wear mine."

"Ha ha..."

"Suit yourself." She put the gloves on and looked around, but it was too dark to see. The mass of trees in Le Deuce's backyard were blocking out most of the light from the neighborhood behind the house. "Maybe he has a key hidden somewhere."

Timothy walked over to a group of withered potted plants tucked away in the corner and picked one up. He brought it back to where Nicole was, studied the door for a moment, and said, "Here goes nothing. Ready to run?"

"Yep."

"Hang on." He reached in his pocket, took out his car keys, and handed them to her. "If the alarm goes off, hightail it back to the truck. If I'm not there in two minutes, take off without me."

"Babe?"

"I'm serious."

He took a couple of steps back and held the pot two-handed like he was a quarterback about to throw the winning play. "You might want to move out of the way."

She went to the stairs and gave the backyard a once-over to make sure no one had snuck up on them.

Timothy took aim and sent the plant flying. The glass door shattered. Shards flew everywhere. He covered his face to keep from getting hit.

They froze, waiting for an alarm. But it never came, and after a minute they both giggled. Nicole glanced around to see if the next-door neighbors were looking out their window, but the blinds were closed.

Timothy reached in, unlocked the door, and swung it open. He stuck his head in for a moment, leaned out, gave her a thumbs-up, and stepped inside.

She chased after him. Entering the house, she thought she heard someone behind her and spun around, but it was only the wind blowing leaves across the deck.

51

———

Diane cranked up the Eurythmics' "Winter Wonderland" and sang along in all her tone-deaf glory.

Four simple words—*I want a divorce*—were about to rip her life apart. So why wasn't she freaking out? Cruising the glistening streets of Crescent Hill Plantation, she was calmer than she'd been in years. *I want a divorce.* She said them aloud. They felt right.

Seeing the neighborhood come alive with the glittering lights, ornate trees, plastic snowmen and reindeer, it broke her heart she hadn't put her tree up yet. Decorating for the holidays had always been a matter of pride. Usually she had everything up the weekend after Thanksgiving, but Christmas was six days away and she hadn't even bothered to get the decorations out of the basement. *This stinks. Maybe next year.* But there wouldn't be a next year. Not here.

She stopped in front of her house.

It was twenty minutes past eight. Hilton had to be home by now. She'd hoped to get there before him, but thanks to her little rendezvous, she'd lost track of the time.

A dark green Ford Focus, smack in the middle of the driveway, was blocking the garage door. Uber? Why wasn't the car running?

And why were the lights inside the house on? She was pretty sure they hadn't been on when she'd left earlier. Did Hilton invite the Uber driver in?

She parked on the street and got out of the car. She walked up to the Focus and peeked inside. Empty. She pulled her phone out of her purse and called her husband. He answered on the first ring.

"Are you home?" Her tone was more confrontational than she intended.

"Yeah. Where are you?"

"I just got here. Whose car is this?"

"Come on inside," Hilton said.

"What's going on?"

"Just come in."

She hung up and dropped the phone back in her purse. She clicked her tongue along the roof of her mouth and glanced back at the Lexus.

Just get in it and go. Just go.

No, only cowards run.

But I'm a coward.

Not anymore.

She stepped onto the porch and caught the swing out of the corner of her eye. So much had happened in the last few hours it made her head spin. She crossed her fingers and said a prayer.

Please God, don't let this day get any worse.

She opened the front door and went inside.

Hilton, standing at the end of the foyer, smiled but didn't meet her halfway. "Hey, thought you'd gotten lost. How's Janice?"

"Hanging in there. Should be fine, I guess." She sat her purse down on the rustic console table to her right. "What's going on?"

"Well, there is someone here who wants to talk to you."

She stepped past Hilton and into the great room to find a man sitting at the kitchen counter eating a Mr. Goodbar, a cane resting between his knees.

He stood and wiped his hand on his pants before extending it.

Through a mouthful of chocolate, he said, "Sorry, I'm starving. Haven't had a chance to grab a bite today, ma'am."

She shook his hand and gave Hilton a sideways glance to gauge his reaction. He had that same quirky smile on his face he always had. It was cute when they'd first met. Now it made her want to throttle him.

"I'm Detective Le Deuce of the Mulberry Grove Police Department." He pulled out his badge and showed it to her.

The air flew out of her lungs.

Don't panic. Don't panic.

Beside her Hilton whispered, "He just got here a few minutes ago."

"Mrs. Hancock, I hate to intrude like this. I realize it's late, but I'm investigating a missing persons case, and I just have a few questions."

"Missing person?"

"Jackson Booth. Disappeared two days ago. Last seen at The Wicked Hand bar."

"Who?" Her knees went weak, and her bladder did a little dance. Clenching her fists so hard her nails dug into the skin, she smiled and tried to act nonchalant. The last thing she wanted to do was pee all over herself, pass out, and wake up at the police station.

"Maybe this will refresh your memory." Le Deuce held up his phone and showed her a picture of Jackson. "You were one of the last people seen with him at The Wicked Hand Wednesday night."

This had to be a joke, she thought. This couldn't be happening. "I was there to see my sister play, but I don't remember him at all."

"Good-looking guy, huh?"

"Excuse me?"

He studied the picture and showed it to her again. "Do you think he's a good-looking guy?"

"He's okay, I guess."

"I hear he's a real ladies' man. Personally, I don't see it."

"I wouldn't know."

"But you were there?"

"Yes."

"And didn't meet or talk to Mr. Booth?"

"I think I would remember," she said.

"So he is hot?"

"No. I don't understand...what are you getting at?"

"Is this man attractive to you?"

"No."

Hilton stepped around Le Deuce and strolled into the kitchen. He opened the fridge and pulled out a beer.

Diane followed him with her eyes. Whatever was going on in his head, she knew he wasn't about to let it show on his face. She had to tread carefully. If he found out she'd had an affair, it would crush him.

"Did something happen—"

"He's missing." Le Deuce pulled out his notepad and scrolled through it as he spoke. "And I've got an eyewitness that says you and Mr. Booth, along with your sister, Nicole Robinson, and her boyfriend, Timothy MacDonald, played pool together for hours. And you seemed friendly with Mr. Booth. Very friendly."

"I wasn't very friendly with anyone."

Before she said another word, she had to speak to Nicole and make sure this wasn't some kind of sick joke. "You know...um...I need to go to the bathroom. Give me a minute, and then we can talk. Okay?"

Without waiting for the detective's response, she turned and headed down the hallway.

I'M GOING TO PRISON.

Forever.

Trembling, Diane closed the bathroom door and leaned against the sink.

Deep breaths. Deep breaths. Deep breaths.

When that didn't work, she went over to the toilet, lowered her skirt and panties, and sat down. While waiting to see if she had to go—or if it was just nerves—she reached down to get her phone out of her purse.

But her purse wasn't by her feet.

Panic-stricken, she looked around the room. It wasn't on the counter either.

Damn it. It was in the foyer, on the table. Right where she'd left it. Along with her phone. No way she could get ahold of Nicole now. It would be a little suspicious if she went back out and said, "Let me call my sister so we can get our stories straight."

Finished, she got dressed, washed her hands, and tried to figure out what to do. The whole thing didn't feel right. She couldn't believe Nicole would do something this nasty. There had to be another explanation.

Think. Come on. Think.

Missing? Why would somebody think Jackson was missing? Didn't it take forty-eight hours to declare a person missing? Had it been that long? Wednesday seemed like seconds ago and yet a lifetime.

She glanced at the counter. This was the same bathroom Jackson used that night. The same spot where he'd done the coke. The coke that killed him.

She wanted to cry. How did this happen? She went out to have some fun. It wasn't fair. Millions of people cheat all the time. Why her?

Calm down. Just calm down.

If someone thought Jackson was missing, the first place they would look would be his apartment, where they would find his body.

Unless someone moved it.

Another thought hit. She trembled.

What if that man wasn't a police detective? The badge he flashed meant nothing. You could buy a fake one online. For all she knew, he was some hit man flown in from South America. Although he didn't look like he was from South America. On second thought, he was kind of short and pudgy for a hit man. Usually they were pretty buff—shaved head, tattoos, sweaty—but what did she know? Maybe they drove him in from Alabama? Did it matter? Either way, he was here for the money and the drugs.

Which Nicole took.

Or didn't.

Diane's head was going to explode.

Next stop: psych ward.

She pictured Hilton on the floor, the detective—or hit man?—holding a gun to his head, screaming, "Where's the money, lady? Gimme the money, bitch, or I'll blow his head off."

She rushed for the door. She couldn't let him kill her husband.

52

Hilton drank his beer and kept his eye on Le Deuce. The man was hobbling around the great room, giving everything the once-over like some third-rate Sherlock Holmes.

This clown is a detective? With the Mulberry Grove Police Department?

The whole thing was ridiculous. When he became mayor, there would be changes. He wouldn't tolerate amateurs like this in *his* police department. He had half a mind to tell Mr. Le Deuce to get the heck out and come back with a warrant or something. Diane had no legal obligation to answer these questions.

Hilton had spent the entire flight home psyching himself up to ask her for a divorce, and now his mojo was blown. Time to speed things along and move Dick Tracy out of here. "Let me ask you something. By the way, can I get you anything? Water? Tea? Hot chocolate?"

"Nah, I'm good," Le Deuce replied.

"So, reading between the lines—if I'm hearing you—you think my wife had something to do with this gentleman's disappearance?"

"I wouldn't call him a gentleman." He flashed a smile.

Hilton cringed. *Please never do that again.*

"Just working out a timeline," Le Deuce continued. "After he left The Wicked Hand—"

"Wicked Hand?"

"It's a dive bar off of Marigold."

"Never heard of it." He stepped away from the kitchen counter and headed over to the fireplace. He placed his beer on the mantel and noticed the shattered window. What was going on here? He was stunned. How in the world had he missed that?

"Well, it's gone through a bunch of name changes over the years. Used to be The Lunch Paper, then it was Al Who's, then it was—"

"Mind if I see that photo?"

Le Deuce pulled his phone out of his pocket and handed it to him.

Hilton studied the picture for a moment. Shook his head. "I'm not seeing it. Diane and this guy? I don't think so. My wife...she's not going out to some bar and picking up *this* guy."

"He did have a way with the ladies."

"You make it sound like he's dead."

"My bad."

"Do you know him?" He handed the phone back to Le Deuce.

"We've met a few times. Being in law enforcement, you run into everybody in this town at least once. You probably don't remember, but we've met before."

"When?"

"Couple of years ago. Those multiple robberies at Crazy Dick's? I was the investigating officer."

Hilton did a double take and pretended to smack himself on the forehead. "I'm sorry. I thought I'd seen you before. Anyway... first off, Diane wouldn't cheat on me. I know a lot of guys say that, but trust me—she's not that kind of woman. And with this guy? Come on, give her some credit. If she was going to cheat, well, she could do a lot better."

"I'm not saying she slept with him, Mr. Hancock."

"Sure sounds like it."

"So far it appears your wife was one of the last people to see him. I'm just trying to determine what happened in his last hours."

Le Deuce continued to stroll around the room. Under his breath he sang, "Come on down, come on down to Crazy Dick's Chicken Town."

"What are you doing?"

"Sorry. I'll bet you get that all the time. It's the catchiest jingle. Who wrote that? You? Or your brother?"

"Richard."

"I was very sorry to hear about him. He was always good to the union."

"Thanks. Yeah, Richard had a soft spot for the police. Hey, think you could do me a big favor? That flight from Albuquerque—"

"New Mexico?"

"Yeah. It really wore me out. Could we talk about this another time?"

"How long were you out there?"

"I left Wednesday, so...two days. Why?"

"Consider me a curious fellow. Nature of the beast, I suppose. Heard you threw your hat into the mayoral ring. What prompted that?"

"I figured it was time to serve the community."

"Uh-huh."

"You don't believe me?"

"I'd like to, but come on, guys like you—once you get all your money—you just want the title. Mayor Hancock. Sounds good, doesn't it? What's next, Governor Hancock? President—"

Le Deuce's phone buzzed. "Excuse me." He pulled it out of his coat pocket and looked at the screen. His face went white, and he whispered, "Christ on a bike."

"Everything all right?" Hilton asked.

"Yeah...yeah. All good."

Hilton watched as he tried and failed to slip the phone back into his coat pocket. That must have been some text, he thought.

"You were saying?" Le Deuce asked.

"That flight about did me in, and I need to talk over some stuff with my wife. So you think we could push this off until tomorrow?"

Before he could answer, Diane appeared in the doorway.

Hilton's heart stopped. The sight of her brought a flood of memories pouring over him: grinning at each other like a couple of lovestruck kids on their first date, cuddling on the couch and binge-watching some dumb TV show, riding horses near Lake Rayburn, walking on the beach in Destin at midnight. Snapshots of a life together.

Was this how it was going to end?

"Sorry," she said. "I wish I could help, but I don't remember him. Honestly, I don't. And I wasn't being friendly with anyone. I watched Nicole's band play, then we had a few drinks, and after that I came home."

"By yourself?"

"Of course."

"You've got to stop insinuating that my wife and this guy—" Hilton interjected.

"See, that's odd. Because we found his phone," Le Deuce said to Diane.

"You did?" she asked.

Hilton caught the unease in her voice, and his heart sank.

"Yeah," Le Deuce replied.

"How the hell did you find his phone?" Hilton asked.

"Point is that we found his phone, and according to location services on the device, your house was the last place his phone was."

"That's not...that's impossible."

He held up his phone. "These modern miracles are pretty accurate. Question is—how did his phone end up at your house?"

She stumbled over to the chair and sat down.

Hilton pulled on his collar like he was about to rip his shirt off. This wasn't his wife. Diane wouldn't bring some random stranger back to their house—*our house*—would she? There had to be some other answer. There was some sort of mistake. Yeah, he was having an affair, but he'd never had sex with Peggy in their house. Peggy had never even been to their house. He at least had the decency to go to her place or a hotel. And Peggy wasn't some random person he'd met in a bar. She was a skilled political consultant instrumental in the governor of Georgia's election.

"He gave me a ride home."

"What?" Hilton charged toward her.

She shot him a look that said, *Back up*. He did.

"Okay, yes, we played some pool, and no, I wasn't extra friendly to him, but I'd had too much to drink and I needed a ride home."

Hilton smacked his thigh. "Uber, honey. Uber."

Ignoring him, she continued, "He drove me home. Dropped me off. And that was it. He left."

Hilton felt like an idiot. A complete and total idiot. Why did he even bother coming home to tell her he wanted a divorce? He could have saved himself the trip. And the plane ticket. Called her. He was so concerned about her feelings, and all the while she was screwing somebody in his house. The house he built. For her.

"Jesus, Diane."

"What? What are you freaking out about?"

"You let some guy drive you home?"

"He was a friend of Timothy's—"

"Who?"

"Nicole's boyfriend."

"I really don't like this."

"Well, if you'd been here, you could have driven me home."

"We can talk about that after Columbo here leaves."

Le Deuce snapped around. "Whoa, buddy—"

"Oh please, you can't tell me no one's ever called you Columbo before. You even have the rumpled old coat."

"You don't have to get nasty."

"I'm not. Columbo was a brilliant detective. Right, Diane?"

"I don't know who that is."

"Seriously? Peter Falk? Columbo?"

"It was before her time," Le Deuce said.

"No, it was too lowbrow for her. You don't know my wife."

Diane stood up and turned to Le Deuce. "Anything else?"

He pulled out his notepad. "Well—"

Hilton stepped between them. "Nope, we're done. If you have any more questions, you can talk to my lawyer."

"You sure about that?"

"Franklin Blum. Google it. But I'm sure you won't have to."

Le Deuce stuck his notepad in his coat pocket, grabbed his cane, and ambled toward the foyer.

Hilton charged past him and yanked the front door open.

Le Deuce stopped, glared at Hilton, and tapped his cane on the floor.

"You know, the big rumor in the department was that you killed your brother. We didn't have any proof, but that's what our collective gut instincts said."

"Get the hell out of my house."

"I hope you two have a pleasant evening. We'll talk more later." He laughed and walked out the door. Hilton slammed it behind him.

"What an asshole."

"Hilton?" She came into the foyer.

He kept his back to her. He couldn't bear to look her in the eyes. "Don't talk to me, okay? I can't believe this."

He heard her turn on her heels and walk back into the great room.

Yeah, go ahead. Walk away. That's what you always do. I'm ready to have a rip-roaring argument—ready to clear the air and you just walk out of the room.

If she wouldn't talk about this, he might as well drive to the airport right now, take a late-night flight back to Peggy, and let Diane figure this shit out on her own.

He couldn't believe she had sex with *that* guy.

She could have done so much better.

53

"Wait, babe, you hear that?" Nicole stepped through the shattered sliding glass door and into Le Deuce's kitchen.

In front of her, Timothy came to an abrupt stop and craned his head from side to side. "What?"

She stumbled to the right to keep from bumping into him and whispered, "Sounds like the TV's on."

"Shit." He pulled his jacket back and drew his gun.

"Timothy?"

"We don't know who's in there."

He was right. They didn't. She wished they had stopped by her place and gotten her gun. Being unarmed right now left her feeling vulnerable as hell.

She followed him into the den, her knees shaking with each step. As he rounded the corner, she peeked over his shoulder. The den was dark except for the pulsating glow of the big-screen TV.

And empty.

She found her breath. If you'd told her two days ago that she'd be slinking around a police officer's house at night, she would have laughed until she fell over.

Timothy pointed toward the hallway and tiptoed across the

room.

She glanced over her shoulder to make sure no one was behind them. The light from the TV was so bright she couldn't believe they hadn't noticed it in the window when they were on the back deck. But it was too late now. They were in the house. Turning back around, she realized Timothy had disappeared down the hallway and took off after him.

Fifteen minutes later they were back in the den. A thorough check of every room revealed Le Deuce wasn't at home. It also revealed nothing incriminating. Or even interesting. The man was neat, but not a freak. Had zero sense of style, and judging by the furniture selections, might even be color-blind. He lived alone, and the only thing he seemed to do was read. There were books every-where. Mysteries mostly.

She scratched her neck. Something about this place gave her the heebie-jeebies. The dark wood paneling in every room—which looked like it had been there since the seventies—made the walls feel like they were closing in around her. And the funky musty smell triggered memories of her great-grandparents' old house.

She couldn't have been more than five when she visited them for the last time, and it still gave her nightmares. Both of them should have been in a nursing home. Her great-grandmother was so thin the skin on her face looked like onion paper wrapped around a skull. Her great-grandfather, hunched over in a wheel-chair, never moved except for one eye, which seemed to follow her around the room. It was horrifying and sad, and being reminded of it put a lump in her throat.

"Wonder why he left the TV on?" Timothy whispered.

"Maybe he ran to the store?"

"Maybe. Hang on."

He rushed through the kitchen and ripped open the door to the garage. Tapped the flashlight on his phone and swung the beam around. She came up behind him and put her hands on his hips. Leaning up on her toes, she peeked over his shoulder.

"Nice Volvo," she said. "Always wanted one of those."

"His car's here, but he ain't?"

"So he owns two cars?"

He closed the door. "The guy seems paranoid and OCD but doesn't arm his house? Leaves his car. And the TV's still on, but nobody is home? We need to get out of here."

"Why?"

"It feels staged." He held up his arm and pulled his jacket and shirt sleeve back. "Look. The hair's getting all freaky. We need to get the hell out of here."

His arm hair looked normal to her, but he had a point. Time to go before Le Deuce came charging out of the darkness, meat cleaver in hand, to the sound of screeching violins.

Nicole rolled her eyes. She'd seen too many scary movies. Still, she grabbed Timothy by the hand and rushed to the sliding glass door.

THEY STUCK to the bushes as they came around the side of the house. The streetlight on the corner of Le Deuce's lot was fading in and out, and they waited for it to go dark again before they walked down the driveway.

"I can't believe we just did that," Nicole whispered.

"I can't believe he sleeps with a teddy bear."

"Did you notice there weren't any pictures? No family. No friends. No selfies. Nothing."

"Yeah, 'cause nobody likes him."

Once on the street, she wrapped her arm around Timothy and they ambled along, trying not to draw attention to themselves.

"You know," he said. "I think the dude wears the same clothes every day—black slacks, black dress shirts, red ties, black dress shoes. I couldn't find a pair of jeans, shorts, or T-shirts anywhere. And no sneakers. What the hell does he wear on his day off?"

"He's like Einstein or Steve Jobs."

"A genius?"

"No, they wore the same outfit everyday so they could focus on more important things."

"Like jerking off with teddy bears?"

She laughed. Sometimes he was such a goofball.

They stopped at his truck. The rain was gently coming down again. Nicole didn't care. She was happy to be free of that nasty place. Now she wanted to get somewhere warm and forget about the whole stinking nightmare of the past few days.

"Is it just me or is it getting colder?" She snuggled up close to him.

"Heard it might snow later tonight."

"A week before Christmas? That's crazy."

"So what do we do?" he asked. "Call him? I think we oughta call him."

"I need some sleep. You do too. We're not thinking straight, babe. Our neurons are blown. Let's find a motel and figure it out in the morning, but first we need to go by my place and get my gun."

"What about your sister?"

"In the morning." She yawned and pushed him toward the truck.

He slipped into the darkness and unlocked the doors with a click. She stumbled around to the passenger side. Reaching for the door handle, she got a nagging feeling that someone was watching her and glanced over her shoulder.

Across the street, a few yards away, a woman was sitting in a car, staring at her.

Nicole stepped forward to get a better look. The moment they made eye contact, the woman turned away. Her car engine revved, and the headlights shot on. Nicole watched her cruise to the end of the street, do a 180 in the cul-de-sac, and speed back past her.

She jumped in the cab and slammed the door.

Timothy put the truck into gear and pulled away from the curb. "I still think we should call him. Have him meet us somewhere. Lay out the story like we planned."

She looked out the back window and then out the front. The taillights from the car were tiny specks in the distance. "That was weird."

"Did you hear what I said? I think we should—"

"The chick in that car was watching us."

"What chick?"

"Across the street. I turned around as I was about to get in, and she was staring right at me."

"So?"

"When I looked at her, she acted like she was busted or something and drove off real fast."

"She was checking you out, that's all. She was like, 'Damn, now that's an ass.'"

"This isn't funny. She was watching us."

"You're getting paranoid."

"After all the weird shit we've been through? I don't think so. See if you can catch her."

"Hunny bunny?"

"Catch up with her, okay?"

"You trying to start some shit with this chick?"

She shot him a look. *That's not funny.*

"Shit." He laid on the gas, closing the gap.

She pulled out her phone and took a picture of the license plate.

"Sure it's the same car?" He slowed down, keeping his distance.

"I don't know. It looks like it. Can you tell what kind it is?"

"In the dark?" He studied it. "I think it's a Dodge, but I can't make the model."

Up ahead, at the top of the hill, the Beaver Pond entrance loomed.

"Now what? It's four lanes once we get out of here," he said.

"Follow her."

"And do what?"

"You're not helping. What if there are other people after the money? Remember what Le Deuce told you?"

"What?"

"He said he wouldn't be the only one coming around asking questions."

"Shit," Timothy said. "That's right."

"We need to follow her."

"Why?"

"To see where she goes," Nicole said.

"You don't think she knows we're behind her?"

"I don't care. We gotta follow her."

The Dodge came to a stop at the subdivision entrance. The right turn signal clicked on. It blinked in the darkness like a three-alarm fire. Warning. Danger. Danger.

Timothy eased off the gas and crept up behind the car. The traffic on US Highway 41 was light, and the Dodge had a clear opening to go but didn't move.

"What's she waiting on?" Nicole shuffled in her seat and peeked around Timothy. A swarm of headlights were moving in unison up the highway toward them but were still far enough out for the Dodge to make it.

"Go, bitch," she yelled.

Just as the swarm got close, the Dodge took off, burning rubber and skidding out onto the highway. The night turned red as the cars braked and swerved.

"Go. Go." She bounced up and down.

"I can't."

Multiple cars whizzed by before he got an opening and floored out. Zooming in and out of the left and right lanes, he pushed the truck to the limit as he tried to catch up to the woman.

"Drive it like you stole it," Nicole yelled.

"You wanna drive?"

"Nah, I think you got it."

"You've gotta be fucking kidding me," Timothy said.

In the distance, a cloud of dust appeared as the Dodge ripped across the grassy median and landed in the eastbound lanes.

"Nicole, I don't like this. We need to let her go."

"Don't be a pussy."

"I am not being a pussy. This chick is going to get us killed."

"Well, if you hadn't taken the money..."

He grabbed the wheel with both hands and took a hard left. The truck careened into the median, sending dirt and grass sky high. Nicole flew out of her seat, slammed against the dash, and fell onto the floorboard.

"Buckle up," he yelled.

Using her good hand, she pulled herself up and into the seat, grabbed the seat belt, and strapped herself in.

The truck slid onto the highway, and Timothy put the accelerator on the floor. The tail swung back and forth, and for a brief second, Nicole thought they were going to go sailing into the ditch. Then the momentum shifted, and they shot down the highway. She watched the speedometer climb from eighty to ninety to one hundred.

"Sorry I called you a pussy," she said, her voice vibrating from the potholes in the road.

"I just hope you're right, 'cause if this chick wasn't spying on us—"

A piercing wail cut him off. Nicole winced, swung her head around, and peered out the fog-covered back window. Flashing blue lights cut a swath through the darkness.

"Fuck me," she said.

Timothy looked over his shoulder and added, "Yeah, you said it."

54

———

You know, the big rumor in the department was that you killed your brother...

The big rumor...

Killed your brother...

You killed...

Le Deuce's words buzzed around Diane's head like an insistent fly. She poured herself a glass of wine. On top of everything else, now she had to deal with this?

Hilton murdered Richard?

Impossible.

Why would he kill him? He loved his brother. The day Richard died, Hilton was inconsolable. She'd never seen him break down like that. He did, however, seem to get over it pretty quick. But everybody grieves in their own way.

The little creep was clearly lying, but why? To put her on edge? Divide her and Hilton? Psychological warfare?

Brushing all that aside, she sat the bottle of wine in the fridge and remembered—*Nicole.* She needed to let her sister know about Le Deuce, just in case Detective Weirdo showed up on her doorstep.

She went into the foyer to get her purse. An icy wind chilled her cheeks, and she winced. Why was the front door cracked open? And where was Hilton? She ran into the dining room. Pulling the curtains back, she peeked out the window.

He was sitting on the swing, staring off into space, rocking in the dark.

For the third time today, she felt like a total piece of crap. It was getting old. She never meant for him to find out about Jackson. Her husband wasn't stupid. He knew if Jackson drove her home...

Well, it was obvious what he thought he knew.

Back in the foyer, she grabbed her purse and took out her phone. She ran through the great room out to the veranda. The smell of burning hickory warmed her heart. Somebody had a fire going. Hopefully, they were having a better night than she was.

She sent Nicole a text: *Call me. I must talk to you. It's IMPORTANT!*

Diane didn't want to go into detail with a text. They used text messages as evidence in court cases all the time now. The odds anybody would record her phone conversations, while possible, were remote. It was a chance she'd have to take.

After a few minutes, Nicole hadn't responded, so Diane went back to check on Hilton. He was still sitting on the swing, lost in his thoughts. Seeing him like that made her heart ache a little. The divorce conversation would have to wait. She couldn't bear to stick the knife in like that. She wasn't a total bitch.

"Hilton?" She stepped out onto the porch.

"Yeah?"

"You coming in? It's getting cold out here."

"In a minute."

"Okay. You want me to turn the porch light on?"

"No, thanks."

"Do you think he was a real police officer?" she asked.

"What makes you say that?"

"He was so odd."

"Remember the multiple robberies we had a few years ago? That right there was the lead detective. You believe that? Now that I think about it, he didn't do squat. Dropped the ball on the whole thing. He's real, all right. A real screw-up."

She stood in the doorway for a moment, watching him and wondering. Should she tell him? Spill her guts about everything? Jackson dying? Moving his body? The money? And the drugs? His life might be in danger now, too.

Her heart pounded. A tiny drop of sweat trickled down her cheek.

No. Not yet. Maybe after she talked to Nicole. She turned to head back inside.

One foot in the door, she heard, "What happened to the window?" and turned back around.

"Excuse me?"

"The kitchen window," he said. "It's broken."

"I tripped, and the wineglass in my hand went flying."

"Okay. That sounds plausible."

"You don't believe me?"

"Of course I believe you, honey."

"You sound like I'm lying."

"Did you break it because you were mad at me?" he asked.

"I wasn't mad at you. Are you coming in?"

She waited for him to answer. When he didn't, she started heading back into the house. "I'm going to bed."

"I want a divorce."

She stopped.

"Did you hear me, Diane? I said, I want a divorce."

Four simple words. And he beat her to it. She whipped around. "A divorce?"

"Come on, you know this isn't working."

"'Cause a guy gave me a ride home?"

"No, look, I flew back tonight because I'd already decided we needed to get a divorce."

She couldn't believe what she was hearing. "So, while you were hanging out in Albuquerque, you decided we needed to get a divorce? You think you should have been talking to me about this?"

"That's what I'm doing now."

"No, you're telling me. We're not discussing it."

"Don't you want a divorce?"

"What does it matter what I want? You've already figured it all out. Just like you always do. You never even included me in your stupid mayor fantasy BS."

"It's not a fantasy."

"Yes, it is. You've got a successful business. Why screw it up by getting into politics? I have never even heard you utter a political thought. What is wrong with you?"

He sat up straight, folded his hands, and lowered his voice. "You're being kind of bitchy about this."

"You just told me you wanted a divorce. How am I supposed to sound? Happy?"

"I don't know." He paused. "You were right. I should have been there to drive you home."

"Yeah, well...coulda, woulda, shoulda."

"Huh?"

"Nothing," she said.

"Did you sleep with him?"

"Did you sleep with her?"

"Who?"

"Whoever you're leaving me for?"

"I'm not—"

"Don't lie to me. That's all I ask. Please don't lie to me. I know you. You wouldn't just leave on your own. You don't have the guts."

"There's nobody else. Promise."

God, she wanted to kick his butt. But why? A few minutes ago she was all revved up to tell him *she* wanted a divorce. An hour ago she was with another man. So he got the words out first. This wasn't a contest. At least they didn't have to pretend anymore. And if he had a girlfriend? Then so what?

If he had a girlfriend?

Of course the bastard had a girlfriend. "Liar. Hilton Hancock, you are a liar."

"Diane?"

"I'm trying to be all compassionate, and you've been cheating on me."

"That's not true."

"Then let me see your phone."

"You're overreacting a bit, don't you think?"

"Tell you what. Here's my phone." She threw it at him. He flinched. It hit the top of the swing, bounced off, and went flying over the porch railing.

"Eight-two-three-one," she yelled.

"What?"

"That's my code. Eight-two-three-one."

"Everybody Wants to Rule the World" blared out.

She charged into the yard, got on her knees, and dug through the wet grass. After a moment, she found her phone. Despite the shattered screen, she could see it was Nicole. She tried to answer the call, but the screen wouldn't respond. "Great."

"You shouldn't have thrown it."

"Kiss my ass."

"Diane?"

She stormed back into the house. In the great room, she found her laptop, powered it up, and waited.

"Oh, come on," she said, slapping the coffee table. Finally it booted up, and she logged in. She opened the messages app and typed Nicole a message: *Just broke my phone. Can't answer calls. Urgent that I see you.*

She hit send and said a little prayer. So far her prayers hadn't amounted to much, but she figured it never hurt to ask.

55

———

Le Deuce made a U-turn, killed the headlights, and eased the Ford Focus back toward Diane's house.

After he'd lost Hot Chocolate earlier, he had ditched the RAV4 and stolen the Ford. Guilt whispered in his ear as he drove it away, but he didn't have a choice. There wasn't time to inspect the Toyota for a GPS tracker, and taking the bus or having an Uber drive him around was sheer madness. The Focus was old and on its last legs anyway, so fuck 'em. They shouldn't have left the keys in it. Maybe he'd send the owner a couple thousand when his ship came in. Maybe. But he doubted it.

He pulled up to the curb and shut off the engine. From here he could see Diane's house but felt confident neither she nor Hilton would notice him in the darkness.

He wiped his sweaty palms on his pants and got his phone out. His heart was about to blow a gasket, he was so livid. Some son of a bitch broke into his house.

During his "on the sly" interrogation of Hilton, a notification had popped up on his phone: his home security alarm had been tripped. When he left his house yesterday, he'd hacked the alarm to alert him only. Not his home security company and not the police.

Being behind the badge most of his life, he knew one truth—never, ever trust the cops.

He dabbed the sweat from his brow and opened the app. It had a live feed from the cameras he'd hidden in each room. He looked at the kitchen first.

Are you kidding me?

The bastard had shattered his sliding glass door. Every muscle in his body went into spasm—you spend your life working hard to provide for yourself, and then some asshole comes along and pisses all over your stuff. Even if he wasn't ever going back, it was still his home. His castle.

Miss Hot Chocolate. Had to be. Who else could it—

He smiled. She was alive. She'd gotten out of the way of that crashing semi. The sliding glass door didn't matter. Even the money didn't matter. He'd never met a woman so damn captivating before. He knew she'd have nothing to do with his sorry ass, but he could dream, couldn't he?

I wonder what her name is?

He looked back at the app. Clicked on the living room camera.

Christ on a bike.

It wasn't Hot Chocolate.

It was Timothy.

And Nicole.

How did they find him? And what were they up to? This was a bunch of ding-dong bullshit. If those two idiots could track him down, no wonder Hot Chocolate had found him. He scraped his nails back and forth along the plastic armrest console as the panic in him rose like water in the *Titanic*.

Time to bail? He had enough money to survive in Mexico for a while. He could live on next to nothing. Hell, he didn't have much longer to live, anyway. Heading across the border and drinking himself to death wasn't a bad way to go out. Maybe he'd die on top of some whore. Hope springs eternal.

He glanced up at Diane's house.

The two lovebirds were on the front porch. He could tell from their body language—even at this distance and with the porch light off—something was going down. Good. The more frazzled they were, the better for him. Princess couldn't lie her way out of a paper bag. It was a matter of applying the right amount of pressure before she told him everything. Once they went inside, he was going to sneak over and put a tracker on the Lexus. Just to be on the safe side. She wasn't going anywhere tonight, but if she did, he wanted to know where.

Up close and in person, Diane was a lot sexier than her Facebook selfies. It was odd how some beautiful women didn't photograph well. He saw the look in her eyes when he'd asked about Jackson. Damn it, the dead bastard had tapped that pussy. Le Deuce wanted to scream. He wished he'd strangled the piece of shit himself.

Why did life keep kicking him in the balls? How come he didn't have a palace like that? How come he didn't have a beautiful, hot, sexy wife? All Hilton did was make chicken. That was it—chicken. It was fantastic chicken, but Le Deuce saved lives. He made the world a better place. He brought closure to people in pain and put the bad guys away. And he had shit to show for it.

Hilton Hancock and Jackson Booth, two pricks built for this world. They always fucking won. Always. The asshole killed his brother. Everybody knew it. But Hilton had money, nice hair, and that stupid smile, so nobody gave a rat's ass. Maybe it was time Mr. Crazy Chicken got a taste of what life was like on the other side.

Then an idea hit. And boy, was it a good one.

Instead of following Diane, why not kidnap Hilton? Use him as leverage. Best-case scenario, she hands over the money to get him back—if she wants him back and if she has the money. Le Deuce wasn't sure about either. Worst case, Crazy Chicken opens his big fat wallet and pays through the nose to keep the universe from knowing what happened to his brother Richard.

Murderers don't get elected mayor.

Le Deuce broke out into laughter. Big-throated, gut-busting, knee-slapping laughter. He was on a roll. A motherfucking roll.

WHAT THE HELL is he doing? Le Deuce wondered. *Is he ever going back inside?*

Hilton had been sitting on the front porch swing for the past twenty minutes. A light rain had started to come down, and the windows were fogging up, which made it difficult for Le Deuce to see what was going on. All he needed was a good five minutes to run over, stick the GPS tracker underneath the Lexus, and boogie. He really didn't want to spend the rest of the night sitting here.

Diane came barreling down the porch, charged across the front yard, and jumped into the Lexus. The car roared to life, and she backed into the driveway, pulled out, and sped past him, smoke pouring off the rear tires as she skidded away.

Christ on a bike.

He had about ten seconds to make a life-altering decision: follow her or stick with Hilton. Now that he'd spoken to Diane—looked her dead in the eyes—he couldn't imagine she had anything do with Jackson's death. Yeah, she brought him here, and he screwed her, but that was it. Just another lonely woman looking for a wild fling. Whatever happened between Jackson leaving her house and Le Deuce finding his body yesterday morning didn't involve her. And why would she take the money? She didn't need it. It didn't make sense.

Hilton, though, he was a golden opportunity. Le Deuce could blackmail that son of a bitch for the rest of his life. All he had to do was get him to admit on camera that he killed his brother and *voilà*: a steady, never-ending stream of easy money.

Le Deuce reached in his pocket and pulled out a quarter. *Heads, Diane. Tails, Hilton.* He flipped it. Watched it go up and come back down in slow motion. It landed on the back of his palm.

Tails it was.

He caught Diane's taillights in the rearview mirror as she disappeared around the corner. He hoped he'd made the right call. He'd find out soon enough.

56

———

Diane tore through the Lexington County Jail parking lot like a woman on a mission. "Oh please, I wouldn't have freaked out."

"You would have lost your shit if I'd told you. And how did I know he'd show up at your house?" Nicole, cast held close to her chest, scrambled to catch up.

"I'd have been grateful for the heads-up."

"Really?" Nicole burst out laughing.

"I'm not freaking out now." She clutched her scarf as the wind made a mess of her hair. It was freezing.

"No, of course not. You never freak out."

"Okay, if I am—which I'm not—maybe it's because I just picked you up from jail. And your boyfriend is in there for doing a hundred and ten in a forty-five-mile...zone or highway or something. And our mother is in the hospital—"

"Our mother? Oh, she's *our* mother now."

"And my husband wants a divorce."

Without stopping, Diane unlocked her car with her key fob and climbed in.

"He does?" Nicole slid into the passenger seat and slammed the door.

"Yep." She started the engine. "You gonna buckle up?"

"Diane?"

"I'm not moving until you buckle up."

"Fine. Fine. Fine."

Diane watched her yank the seat belt across herself with as much drama as she could muster, but the weak click of the latch ended her performance on a flat note.

"Happy?"

"Yes."

"So what are you bitching about? You want a divorce."

"I know. I guess I just had this crazy idea that he might fight for me."

"Is he screwing somebody else?"

"Probably. Maybe. I don't know. Doesn't really matter. It is what it is."

"Unless it's not." Nicole laughed.

"What?"

"Never mind."

Diane gripped the steering wheel. Sometimes she just wanted to slap that smart mouth shut. She glanced in the rearview mirror, looked from left to right, and checked the back-up camera in rapid succession as she slowly backed out. Last thing she wanted was to hit a police cruiser. *That* would be the perfect end to her perfect day.

"Where are we going?" Nicole asked.

"Anywhere but here."

Diane took a right on Jail Road, and they traveled in silence along the winding two-lane. When they reached Vining Creek, she took a left and after a couple of miles merged with the heavy traffic onto Peachtree Highway. They headed south toward the belly of the Christmas beast—the Avenue on the Square.

Tired of the thoughts rampaging through her head, Diane turned and asked, "Who is this Le Deuce weirdo? Is he for real?"

"He is. He is a *real* Mulberry Grove detective."

"That's what Hilton said." She glanced at Nicole. Her face was awash in red from the sea of taillights in front of them.

"And he wants the money."

"So go to Jackson's apartment and take it."

"It's not there."

Diane almost slammed on the brakes. "Why would it not be there? And how would you know it wasn't there? We left it there, Nicole."

"You don't have to yell."

"I'm not yelling. You want me to bail your boyfriend out? You gotta tell me everything. What is going on? And why were you guys doing a hundred and ten miles an hour? And why did they arrest Timothy?"

She hesitated and then said, "After we left Jackson's apartment the other night...you're gonna be pissed."

"I'll be more pissed if you don't get to the point."

"Timothy went back and took the money."

"I knew it."

"Hey, I didn't take it."

"But you lied to me earlier." She could feel her breath coming in shorter and shorter bursts.

"He went back and took the money, okay? Not me. Him. I made him take it back."

"I think my head is going to explode."

Nicole cracked her window and pulled her cigarettes out of her pocket. "You mind?"

"Yeah, I do."

Ignoring her, she stuck one in her mouth and lit up.

"Nicole?"

"Sorry, I really, really need one."

A little cloud of smoke escaped her lips, and she continued. "When I ran out of Timothy's house that night—to help you, by the way—it freaked him out. Seriously freaked him out. And of course I didn't tell him anything, so he didn't know what the hell was going on. So he followed me to your house and then to the apartment, and after we left, he went up to Jackson's apartment, found Jackson's body, and took the bag."

"Why?"

"Ask him. I don't know. But when he told me, I punched him in the face."

"Classy."

"Hey, he deserved it. But I didn't try to keep it. I made him take it back. Last night we went to Jackson's and took it back."

"But you kept the gym bag?"

"Timothy bought a backpack at the Dollar Store, and we put everything in it."

"What for?"

"He was worried about our fingerprints on the bag and any hair or stuff from us. He was trying to do the right thing."

"Makes sense. I guess."

"We went back, left the backpack in his bedroom, and split."

"Okay, now I'm confused. You took the money back, but it's not there now?"

"Right."

"Where is it?"

"I don't know." She took a long drag, rolled the window down some more, and let out a big ring of smoke.

The cold hit Diane in the face, and she cranked up the heat.

Nicole tossed the cigarette, rolled up the window, and continued. "Look, here's the real scary shit. When we went back to Jackson's apartment, we were in his bedroom getting ready to leave the backpack, and we heard the front door open."

"What? My God, what did you do?"

"So I grabbed the backpack and Timothy and I hid in the closet, and these two guys came in. It was dark, but I could make out the shapes through the little slats in the door. You know those slats?"

"Yeah. What happened?"

"Okay, so these two guys took Jackson's body. One of the dudes was huge, like a freaking mountain, and they picked him up and carried him out."

"Why?"

She shook her head. "To get rid of the evidence? Maybe it would be better if certain people thought Jackson was still alive? Timothy thinks one of those guys was this Detective Le Deuce."

"What have we gotten into?" Diane grabbed Nicole by the arm.

"Crazy shit. Crooked cops. Drug cartels. Who knows?"

"Where is the money? And the drugs?"

"We left it there. But this guy comes to Timothy's house this morning, and he acts like it's not there."

"And he came to my house acting like Jackson had disappeared," Diane said. "I think I'm going to throw up. Really, I think I'm going to vomit."

"You want me to drive?"

Diane sped into the Kroger parking lot and skidded sideways into the first space she came to.

"You okay?" Nicole asked.

Diane opened the window and took in a lungful of cold, brittle air.

"Diane?"

"Give me a minute." She inhaled and exhaled a few times. Closed her eyes. She wanted everything to stop—just for a moment—so she could think. It seemed so hard lately to just think.

Finally she whispered, "Why were guys doing over a hundred miles an hour?"

Nicole pulled another cigarette out of the pack.

"Hey, I already let you have one."

She slid it back in the pack. "We went by Le Deuce's house. I know—bad idea. But we wanted to talk to him. Explain things. Reason with him."

"Why didn't you tell me? I don't understand."

"I didn't want you to get hurt."

"I could have gotten hurt by not knowing."

"Well, he wasn't home. But when we were leaving, there was this woman sitting in a car across the street. She was watching us. Pretty obvious. When I noticed her, she took off. So we started chasing her. That's how we got pulled over. Dumbass never mentioned he had a suspended license. And that flask of Jack Daniels didn't help either."

Diane didn't know what to say. What could she say? Some of it sounded like a load of crap. She knew her sister well enough to know that. But that detective showing up at her house was real and downright creepy. The guy gave her the willies.

"I need some coffee. How about you?"

"I don't care," Nicole said.

Diane pulled out of the parking lot and got back on the highway.

After a bit, she spotted Sophie's Donut Hole up ahead on the left. She smiled. A cup of coffee and a Boston Creme donut, and then she'd be able to think. If that didn't work, she was going back to Kroger and getting a bottle of wine.

DIANE TOOK her coffee and donut, got through the crowd, and found a table near the door. Over the speakers, Darlene Love was begging her baby to please come home for Christmas. It was sacrilegious, Diane knew, but she preferred U2's version. Something about it never failed to put a lump in her throat.

She watched the eclectic swarm move in and out with a wry smile. If only they knew what she'd been through. If she told them, they wouldn't believe it. She wanted to jump up on the table and scream, "Do you people know how tough I am? Do you realize how much crap I can take?"

Oh my God, I'm kinda enjoying this...

It was a startling admission.

I am enjoying this...

The last two days had been quite a ride. And as scared as she was of going to jail and as terrified as she was of dying—*don't put that thought out into the universe, okay*—she couldn't deny she felt more alive than she had in years. If ever.

It'd make a hell of a movie provided the ending worked. That, of course, remained to be seen. There were so many ways this could go it boggled her mind. Still, it would be one hell of a movie.

Or one hell of a book...

That got her blood going.

Nicole plopped down across from her, half a donut in her mouth. "What are you smiling at?"

"Nothing."

"Okay. How are we going to get Timothy out?"

"You got five thousand dollars?"

"No."

"Your boyfriend hit the trifecta—driving with a suspended license, drinking, and going over a hundred miles an hour."

"He messed up. I get it. I'll pay you back—"

"How?"

"I will. The how doesn't matter. I don't want him spending the night in jail. It's not right. He doesn't deserve it."

"If he hadn't taken 'it'"—she made finger quotes—"none of this would be happening. Maybe a night in jail would be good for him."

"You know that's annoying, right? That quote thing you just did with your fingers. It's, like, really annoying."

"Aren't you trying to talk me into bailing him out?"

"I shouldn't have to talk you into anything. When you needed help, my butt showed up. No questions." She glanced around and lowered her voice. "Drug a two-hundred-and-something-pound dude up three flights of stairs. Broke my fucking arm. Five thousand dollars is nothing to you. You probably wipe your ass with that kind of money."

Diane laughed and said, "You have a very inflated view of my financial situation."

"You know what I mean."

Diane took a good look at her sister. Past all the craziness, she was a beautiful woman with a big heart. Far bigger than Diane's. She'd always felt a twinge of jealousy about how pretty Nicole was, but it wasn't her sister's fault she won the genetic lottery. You toss the same sperm and eggs in a blender and sometimes you get her—not bad on a good day—and sometimes you get Nicole—drop-dead gorgeous. Same mom. Same dad? Maybe? Possibly. Who knows? But it was the same blood. She didn't understand her one bit, but...

"You're right."

"I am?" Nicole asked.

Diane grabbed her coffee cup and donut and stood up. "Let's go."

Nicole shot out of her chair.

"And google bail bonds. Hopefully there is a place nearby."

Diane charged out the door. Behind her, Nicole scrambled to catch up.

57

———

THE FIRST THING that hit him was the smell.

Gas? Gasoline? Motor oil?

Hilton took a whiff. And almost lost it.

Mildew? Dirty socks? Rotten eggs?

He held his breath. Another whiff and he'd toss his cookies.

The next thing was the cold. It was freezing.

He wrenched his eyes open, but the darkness remained. Something—*a bandana or a rag?*—was wrapped tight around his head. He struggled to move, and the horror crystallized: he was strapped to a chair and his wrists, along with his ankles, bound with handcuffs. Handcuffs? He tried to scream, but his jaw wouldn't move.

Duct tape covered his mouth.

(Don't)

He started hyperventilating.

(Panic)

The only way out of this—if there was a way out—was to clear his head and not do anything stupid or rash. He slowly counted to ten.

His heart was chugging like a freight train. He just knew a heart attack was imminent.

So he counted again.

And again.

His heart slowed down.

Where am I?

The last thing he remembered was backing out of the garage, realizing he'd left something in the house, getting out of the car, and then...

Nothing.

Complete blackness. He tried to piece it together, but his head ached so bad he couldn't grab hold of a thought. The only way you end up bound and gagged is if someone has kidnapped you. But who in the world would want to kidnap him?

Richard.

Come on, Richard is dead.

Was he? What if he didn't die in the lake?

Stop it.

His brother was dead. He'd seen him die with his own eyes. He'd pulled his lifeless body out of the water.

A friend of Richard's? Someone who blamed Hilton for his death and wanted revenge? Or maybe a disgruntled customer? Or even a political opponent? Maybe the Georgia elites had mapped out his political trajectory and decided to take him out now, before he became a threat? Anything was possible.

A gloved finger touched his cheek. Hilton flinched.

A familiar voice said, "This might hurt."

The duct tape came off in an instant, along with some facial hair.

"Ow!" Hilton yelled.

"Told ya."

"Who are you?"

"I'm your best friend. Or your worst nightmare. It's your call."

"What do you want?"

"Hilton, you know what I want."

"No, I don't."

"Sure you do, buddy. I want you to confess."

So it *was* a friend of Richard's. But which one? He tried to place the voice. "Confess?"

"Don't be an idiot. We both know you killed your brother."

"No, I didn't."

"Yes, you did."

"No, I didn't."

"Yes—"

"I did not kill my brother. It was an accident."

"See, now we're getting somewhere. You accidentally killed him."

"No, he accidentally fell out of the boat and hit his head on a rock."

Hilton felt cold metal against his forehead.

"What if I accidentally pulled this trigger?" the man asked. "Would your brains accidentally blow out the back of your head?"

"Why are you doing this?" Hilton fought back the terror in his voice.

"Because the good people of Mulberry Grove need to know what kind of man their new mayor is. I'm performing a public service."

"You think I might win?"

"Of course you'll win. Who the hell wants to be the mayor of Mulberry Grove? You got it in the bag."

"Do we know each other? Your voice sounds—"

"No. I'm just a concerned citizen."

"So what do you get out of this? Make me confess, and then what?"

"I'd be more than happy to keep your secret."

"There we go. I didn't kill my brother, but if I confess—let me guess—on video? Then I pay you money to not tell anybody? You must think I'm an idiot."

"You're the one tied to the chair."

"Only because you jumped me. Untie me, and let's discuss this like a couple of real men. I didn't murder Richard."

"Aha! I never said murdered."

"You said killed."

"Murdered. Killed. Two separate things."

"We can debate semantics all night. I'm not telling you I killed or murdered my brother, because I didn't," Hilton said.

"All right. I'll be leaving you here to think it over. See you in the morning."

"I'll freeze to death."

"Not my problem," the man said.

"How much do you want?"

"How much do you have?"

"How much do you want?"

"Christ on a bike, answer the question."

"Wait a second, I thought I recognized your voice. You're that detective," Hilton said. "La...La...something."

"No, I'm not."

"Yes, you are."

"No, I'm not," the man said louder.

"Yes, you are."

"Shut up. I'm not...whoever you think I am."

"Christ on a bike? Who says that? Two hours ago in my living room you said it. And you accused me of killing Richard. So I'm sticking with my theory here. You're that detective...La...Le... Deuce. Le Deuce."

Silence.

He knew he was skating on thin ice, but kowtowing wasn't going to save his life. He had to appeal to Le Deuce's better nature —if this man was indeed Le Deuce—and persuade him to set him free. He didn't believe the man he'd met earlier was a killer. The one skill set he'd always had in his back pocket was his ability to read people, and Le Deuce didn't have that killer instinct. He didn't have dead eyes.

"Maybe we can work something out?" Hilton lowered his voice to project confidence. "Do you really want to kill me? If you do, then nothing I say will change your mind. But if I'm reading between the lines here, seems to me you just want money."

The man didn't respond.

Hilton hoped he wasn't about to be tortured. He had an extremely low tolerance for pain. Just the thought of having his fingernails ripped out had him shaking.

"Hello, anybody there?" he continued. "Okay, maybe you're gone, maybe not, but I have a question. At what point did you get the idea to kidnap me? I mean, you showed up to question my wife about some guy she probably slept with—"

"Did sleep with."

"You don't know that."

"True, but you tell me what's going on. You know your wife."

"The Diane I know wouldn't have, but, well, I don't want to think about it. Question is, how do you go from talking to my wife to...hey, you just admitted you're him, right? Le Deuce."

He sensed a presence behind him, felt hands on the back of his head. The blindfold fell to the floor. He opened his eyes to a dark room.

His eyes got used to the darkness, and he noticed a kitchen countertop to his left and wires coming out of the wall in front of him. Space for a refrigerator? He looked down. The linoleum was ripped and pulled up. Above the counter—or was it the sink?—a shattered window. He fought back a scream. This was his worst nightmare: an abandoned house. His skin crawled. This place had to be full of mold. If this nut didn't kill him, the mold in this house would. He tried not to breathe.

A short man in a ski mask, a black shirt, and black pants pulled up a metal folding chair, sat down across from him, and in a muffled voice asked, "Why are you such an asshole, Hilton?"

"I'm not an asshole."

"Sure you are. You won the lottery, Hilton. You got it all. But like everybody else, it's never enough. Is it?"

"You don't know a thing about me."

"I know you got a nice house."

"So?"

"And a thriving business."

"Which I worked my butt off to build."

"And a sexy wife."

"Screw you." He pictured himself ripping the man's ski mask off and bashing his head into the dirty floor over and over again. The man was lucky Hilton was tied to the chair.

"That why you murdered your brother? Was he in the way? Was he keeping you from having an even more fabulous life?"

"My brother was selfish, okay? He was a narcissist. He could make you feel like the greatest person in the world and then turn on you faster than...why am I telling you this?"

"Guilt. It's a heavy burden. Eats at your soul."

"I can't have a serious conversation with a guy in ski mask. I just can't."

The man didn't blink an eye, just continued to pant like a thirsty dog and stare at Hilton through the slits in the mask.

"Take it off. You want my money? You want to make a deal? Show me your face," Hilton said. A minute passed. He thought they were going in circles.

Then: "Jackson Booth was an entitled prick. Much like you, Hilton. Thought the world was his oyster. Must be the kind of man your wife likes to bang. Where do you think they did it? In your kitchen? How about your living room? In your bed?"

The idiot was trying to goad him into doing something reckless, but it wouldn't work. Keeping calm was his only option if he wanted to survive.

"You don't know your wife at all," the man went on. "You think you do, but you have no idea who you married. Oh, she's sweet, and in that soft little voice she'll tell you how much she loves you, but give her a chance and she'll grab the biggest knife she can get her hands on and gut you like a fucking fish."

"Diane might, let me stress, *might* have slept with this guy—and I hope she didn't, because frankly she could have done a lot better—but you're mistaken if you think she'd gut me like a fish. That's a little extreme. Don't you think you're projecting a little there? Probably thinking about some woman who did you wrong. Look, you're not gonna kill me. I know that and you know that. My butt is freezing, and I don't want to spend the rest of the night on this hard chair, so can we work out a deal?"

The man groaned and pulled off the ski mask.

"Thank you, detective."

Le Deuce threw the mask on the floor. "Here's the problem, Mr. Hancock. Jackson had a quarter of a million in cash and coke in his car the night he disappeared."

"Who was this guy?"

"Jackson works for Fisher McAllister. Ever heard of him?"

"No."

"Didn't think so. Most civilians haven't. But he's one of the biggest drug dealers on the East Coast. Hilton, I'm not gonna lie to you, I've been working undercover the past year trying to build a case against him. Anyway, long story short, Jackson was supposed to meet me the other night and drop off the money and the coke. We were going to bust him, but he never showed. Now McAllister thinks I did something to his boy Jackson and took the cash and dope."

"Wow."

"Your wife got caught in the crossfire."

"Can't the police do anything?"

"Nah, see, I was deep undercover." He leaned back, rubbed his chin, and eyeballed the ceiling. "I gotta find that money. If I can't? I need to hit you up because I'm not staying here. I won't last the weekend. And if I'm going down, so are you and your wife."

58

———

NICOLE, still a little stunned at the ease with which she'd confessed everything, buckled her seat belt and plopped her cast on the center console.

Well, not everything.

She wasn't about to tell Diane that she and Timothy lost the money. No way in hell that confession was coming out of her mouth. How it went missing didn't matter. It was gone, and that was that. But the rest, overall, had been accurate. She smiled. This was a first. She and the truth often traveled different roads. Life was easier that way. Despite her rebellious nature, she had always been a peacemaker at heart, and in her experience the truth rarely, if ever, set anyone free. It certainly never set her free.

On her phone she googled "bail bonds Mulberry Grove," one-thumbed.

The door opened. She looked over.

Diane climbed into the car, sat her coffee and donut on the console and her purse on floor behind her seat. Rubbing her hands together, she said, "Brrr, it's cold. Time to start a new tradition—Christmas on the beach."

"With margaritas."

"I mean, since I'm blowing my life to pieces this week and all."

"Might get some snow tonight."

"Great, just what we need." She started the car and backed out. "Find anything?"

"Well—"

Diane slammed on the brakes. "Hey, come on..."

Nicole glanced at the rearview camera screen. From what she could tell, a car or SUV had stopped right behind them. With a row of bushes in front and a car on either side, she and Diane were boxed in. She wished they had parked next to Sophie's Donut Hole and not out here in the pitch-black boonies where the parking lot lights had a mind of their own.

"Thanks a lot, asshole," Nicole said.

Diane pulled back into the spot and put the Lexus in park. She grabbed her donut, took a bite, and washed it down with some coffee. "I haven't eaten this many donuts in years."

"Stress will do it to you."

For the next minute or two, they sat and waited in silence. Nicole scrolled through her phone, continuing her search for a bail bond service nearby. Normally she would be on the verge of getting out and explaining why somebody needed to move their damn car, but the image of Timothy sitting in that jail cell made her heart ache. Until a few weeks ago, she didn't even know she had a heart to ache. Except for her Papa, she hadn't met many good men in her life. In fact, now that she thought about it, he and Timothy were the only good men she had ever met.

"Can I stay at your place tonight?" Diane asked.

"Why?" Nicole gave her a sideways glance.

"I don't want to go home."

"A hotel would be better. Just to be on the safe side, what with all the weird shit going on. "

Diane turned and glared out the rear window. "Do you believe this? What is going on?" Then she added loudly: "We haven't got all night."

Diane's tone took Nicole by surprise. In the darkness, illuminated by the dashboard lights, Diane looked eerily like their mother. She had that same rage in her eyes Janice would manifest at the drop of a hat. It brought back memories she'd rather forget. She unbuckled her seat belt.

"What are you doing?" Diane asked.

"Going to tell jackass to move."

"No, you'll get us into a fight."

"With a broken arm?"

"Stay put. I got it," Diane said.

Before Nicole could protest, she had her seat belt off and was out of the car.

She left the door cracked open, and a bitter wind blew in. Nicole shook for a moment and debated reaching over and closing it. But she had neither the energy nor the will to climb across the seat. Besides, Diane wouldn't be more than a minute or two. The person in the car blocking them probably had no idea they were in the way. People were so caught up in their own tunnel vision today, they didn't even notice the most obvious inconveniences they caused.

"Everybody Wants to Rule the World" made her jump.

Looking around frantically, she spotted Diane's purse on the floor behind the driver's seat. She went to grab it, but the cast on her left arm made it impossible. She turned and leaned across the center console. Her fingertips only grazed the side of the purse. Did she really need to answer it? Was it life and death? With everything that had happened in the last forty-eight hours?

Yeah, it might be.

With a disgusted sigh, she practically climbed into the back seat to grab Diane's purse. Sure enough, the phone was in there. She yanked it out and flipped it over.

Dang, Diane really did a number on it. The screen was a spider's web of cracks extending from the top left corner to the bottom right. Still, she could see it was Hilton calling. She tried to answer, but the display wouldn't swipe. The call ended. She opened the purse to put the phone back.

"Oh, my, now that's interesting," she whispered. At the bottom of the purse was Diane's Glock.

Leave it to her sister to come prepared. She wanted to jump up and down and yell, "Hell yeah." Between the woman in the car and Le Deuce showing up at Diane's place, a growing sense of dread had gripped Nicole, and a little voice kept nagging in her ear, "*What's next? What's next? What's next?*"

Her door swung open. She looked up. "Aren't you on the wrong side?"

Diane leaned in, the overhead light hitting her face. The rage in her eyes was gone, replaced by terror. Nicole clasped the purse shut.

Diane mouthed, "Big trouble." Then she said loudly, "Get out of the car."

"Why?"

"Just get out."

Nicole showed her the purse and mouthed, "Gun."

Diane nodded and stepped back.

Nicole grabbed the purse along with her own phone, stepped out, and slammed the door.

The same Dodge from earlier was blocking them in. Damn it, she should have given the car a better look. Not that she could have done anything.

In the darkness it was difficult to make out the woman coming up behind Diane, but she appeared to be in her late twenties or early thirties, with short black hair with white streaks and an athletic frame. Her left hand gripped Diane's neck, and judging by her sister's reaction, the woman had just pressed a gun or knife against her back.

"You okay?" Nicole asked.

Diane nodded.

"Ladies, you have something that's not yours. I need it back," the woman said.

Nicole almost blurted out, "No, we don't. We lost it," but caught herself. Why play that card? The woman wouldn't believe it. And if she did, she'd shoot them right there in Sophie's parking lot.

She had a better idea. "You're not from around here, are you? What's that? English? Australian?"

The woman glared at her.

My guess is she's not a humorous person, Nicole thought. "Sorry, those Euro trash accents all sound the same to me. Look, um...I didn't get your name."

Nothing. Not even an eye roll.

"A name would really help," she continued. "It doesn't even have to be your real name, you know. I just don't want to call you 'lady' or 'ma'am.' It's awkward."

Her knees were shaking. And it wasn't just from the cold. Sure, this chick was in a whole other league, but this bravado bullshit had saved her ass before. It was worth a shot. It was all she had.

Except for the gun in Diane's purse.

"Okay, fine," Nicole said. "You don't want to be civil. Then how about Crazy Bitch? How about I call you Crazy—"

"Nicole?" Diane interrupted.

"Sorry, okay, I'm just not in the mood for this crap. We need to get Timothy out of jail. It isn't good for him to be there."

"Everybody Wants to Rule the World" blasted out of the purse.

"By the way, Hilton called a minute ago, but..." Nicole fumbled with the purse. "I couldn't answer because the screen is broken."

"Dreadful song," the woman said.

"Yeah, I used to hate it too, but it's kinda grown on me. There's some really nice guitar work at the end." She yanked out the phone. Held it up for Diane to see. "And it's your hubby again. Must be important."

Diane mouthed, "What are you doing?"

"You know what?" She ended the call. "We can call him back on mine."

"Ladies, it's getting cold out here. Let's go someplace warm where we can talk."

The woman pushed Diane toward the Dodge. Nicole lunged forward. The woman turned, revealing what Nicole already knew. She had a gun in her hand, ready to put a bullet in Diane's back.

"Miss Nicole, you stay right there."

Nicole stopped. "How do you know my name?"

With a mischievous grin, she opened the passenger door and motioned for Diane to get in.

Never get in the car.

Five words etched in Nicole's mind ever since that self-defense class years ago.

Never get in the car.

Ever.

You want to live?

Don't get in the car.

"Hang on, Diane."

Diane stopped mid-entry and turned, bewilderment on her face.

Nicole inched closer to the woman. "We can work something out. We can make a deal here, but we're not getting in your car."

The woman stared at her through cold eyes.

"If you kill us, how will you get your money back?"

"I don't need both of you."

"You're right," Nicole said. "You are absolutely one hundred percent right. Truth is, you don't need either of us. Because, ta-dah, we don't know where the money is, do we, Diane?"

Diane's mouth dropped. *Are you crazy?*

Why couldn't her sister play along? Just for once? Whatever, if she had to single-handedly save everyone's ass, she would. "There's only one person who knows where the money is. And he's sitting in a jail cell right now."

The woman got so close Nicole could smell the Captain D's. "You're lying."

"No, I'm not. Timothy took the money. We left it at Jackson's apartment. Timothy went back and took it, and he won't tell us—"

"Paranoid" cut her off. She rolled her eyes. "Can I answer that?"

The woman shrugged. *Whatever.*

Nicole pulled her phone out of her back pocket, checked the screen, and held it up. "Hilton. Again."

Diane stepped forward, her eyes begging the woman. *Please?*

The woman ripped the phone out of Nicole's hand and gave it to her. "Here. Jesus, you people are annoying."

"Hey, what's going on?" Diane said. "What? Who is this?"

Nicole watched Diane pace back and forth, listening intently to whoever it was on the phone. If it wasn't Hilton, then who could it be? She stuck her good hand in her pocket and longed for the warmth inside the car. It was getting colder by the minute. She pictured her cast upside Crazy Bitch's head and wondered if it would do any damage to either her arm or the chick's head.

"I want to speak to my husband...I don't believe you...let me speak to Hilton."

Her sister's panicked voice snapped Nicole back to reality. "Who is that?"

Diane shook her head, put her hand over the phone. "This guy's insane. Says he's kidnapped Hilton, and if we want to see him alive again, we better give him the money."

The woman grabbed the phone, forcing Diane backward. "Le Deuce, is that you? Le Deuce? Le Deuce? Damn it, the bastard hung up."

"You know him?" Diane asked, her voice breaking.

"Ladies, way I see it, we're in the same boat. You want your husband back. I want our merchandise back. What do you say we help each other out?"

Le Deuce kidnapped Hilton?

A black pit opened up under Nicole's feet, and the parking lot spun for a brief second. Why kidnap Hilton? And what about Timothy? Was he safe in jail? Obviously, Le Deuce knew people. Maybe they could get to Timothy. Either way, they were all screwed. At least if he was with them, it would be three against one instead of two. But that wasn't the real reason. She wanted him here. She needed him here.

"I'm not going anywhere until we get Timothy out of jail."

The woman smiled. "You look like a bullshitter to me. Diane, your sister a bullshitter?"

She shrugged. "Sometimes—"

"Sometimes?" Nicole blurted out.

"Nicole's telling the truth. He took the money."

"I find it incredibly hard to believe he hasn't told you where it is."

"If we bail him out," Nicole said, "he will take you to the money. Promise. I swear to God."

The woman glared at her with such ferocity, Nicole feared she was about to kill her.

Then she said, "Diane, give her your car keys."

"What?" Diane stammered.

"Give her your car keys."

"Why?"

"So she can bail her man out."

"Wait? What?" Nicole said.

"You just promised he would take me to the money, so go and fucking get him."

"By myself?"

"And then meet us at Frank's convenience store on Highway 92."

Nicole looked at Diane. She couldn't leave her alone with this psycho. Could she? No, no, she couldn't. That wouldn't be right.

"Can I have my purse?" Diane said.

"Huh?"

"My purse?"

Nicole handed it to her and watched her rummage through it. Suddenly she panicked. *Oh shit, she's about to pull out her gun.*

Diane gave her a key fob. "Here. Now go."

"I can't leave you."

"We don't have a choice," she whispered.

We don't have a choice? Suddenly they were in this together. She grabbed Diane's hand and squeezed it. Diane gave her a slight smile.

"We haven't got all night, ladies."

Nicole looked over. The woman was watching them like a hawk. "Can I have my phone back?"

"No." She slipped it into her jeans pocket. "I'm warning you— if you do something stupid, like get the cops involved or decide to run off with our merchandise..." She pointed at Diane. "It won't be pretty."

Head bowed, she charged toward Diane's car. *Wait a second...* She swung back around. "Uh...what do I bail him out with?"

Diane took her wallet out of her purse, ran over, and gave Nicole her American Express card.

Fighting back the shakes, Nicole got in the car and slammed the door. After buckling up, she adjusted the seat and waited for the Dodge to move, then she slowly backed out. Driving someone else's car for the first time was always odd, and Diane had never let her drive the Lexus before. She felt like a real shit leaving her alone with Crazy Bitch, but her sister was right; they didn't have a choice. Timothy might be the only hope they had.

The Dodge pulled out behind her, but when she took a right out of the parking lot, it took a left. She slowed and looked back. The taillights grew dim until they finally disappeared.

59

"CHRIST ON A BIKE!" Le Deuce screamed and kicked the metal folding chair across the kitchen.

It skidded into one of the broken cabinets in the corner and fell over, landing with a clang that rang out like a church bell.

"Shit, shit, shit..." He grabbed his foot and bounced around. He'd kicked the damn chair with his gout toe. Gritting his teeth, he closed his eyes as little drops of water dripped down his cheek.

How the hell did Miss Hot Chocolate find Diane? How could he have been careless? Of course she went to The Wicked Hand. Why wouldn't she? The woman wasn't stupid. He should have told Ian to keep his mouth shut. No, he should have paid Ian to keep his mouth shut. First she'd tracked his car, and now she'd found Diane.

This chick is fucking up everything. Hot or not, if it comes down to me or her...

Well, she better not miss. Because she won't get a second shot.

"Careful with the phone," Hilton said from behind him.

"What?" He spun around. In his rage, he'd forgotten about the man.

"You looked like you were about to throw my phone. Please don't."

Le Deuce hopped across the kitchen, his bad foot scraping along the rotting linoleum flooring, and got in Hilton's face. He waved the phone wildly in the air.

"You don't want me to throw this? You don't want me to throw your fucking phone? What are you gonna do, huh? What are you gonna do, Mister Crazy Chicken? I'll throw your fucking phone if I want. I'll go outside and drive over it with my car. Hell, I'll piss all over it. You don't call the shots here. Got it? You're the one tied to the chair. Not me."

"If you break my phone, how are you going to call her back?"

Le Deuce stood up straight. Damn, the dumb bastard had a point. "So you want me to call her back?"

"Yes, I want to get this resolved. I don't want to die in some old abandoned germ-infested farmhouse."

"Hey, we all have to go sometime, right?" He waited for a response. When he didn't get one, he yelled, "Right?"

"Right," Hilton said.

"You think you're too good to die here? What are you? Special? I've seen people die in every kind of place you can imagine. And most of them never saw it coming. At least you'd get to make your peace with God. At least you wouldn't go out like my Mama, just driving along, minding her own business, and boom—a semi comes across the center line."

"I'm sorry."

"Thanks. I appreciate it. Now shut your trap and let me think."

He hopped over to the kitchen counter, leaned up against it, and turned his back to Hilton. He didn't want his needy eyes staring at him.

He inhaled. To the lowlifes and scum he brought here, this kitchen smelled like rancid ass, but to him the aroma was intoxicating. When a bit of close-lipped interrogation was required, this was the place where he worked his magic. He'd found it years ago. Paid under twenty grand for it. It was desolate and creepy. Two things that always played well in his favor. He never had the power or the water turned on. What would be the point?

So Hot Chocolate had Diane and Nicole. And he had Hilton. Which left him where, exactly? And what about the boyfriend? Timothy? The throbbing pain in his foot was making it incredibly difficult to focus.

Something was missing. Some piece of the puzzle was staring him right in the face, but it was so small he couldn't see it. Where was the money? He could give fuck-all about the coke. He wanted the cash.

Who had the money?

The sister?

The boyfriend?

The wife?

He pulled his phone out of his pocket and discreetly propped it up on the counter next to an empty coffee can. Then he walked over to the corner, grabbed the chair, and dragged it back to where Hilton was.

Taking a seat, he looked Hilton in the eye. "You know these two ladies better than I do. Now maybe your wife wouldn't take that money, but your sister-in-law?"

"In a heartbeat. But you never said anything about Diane taking any money."

"I'm spitballing here, Hilton. That's how this detective gig works. Tell me about your sister-in-law."

He coughed and said, "Nicole is...well, she's a mess."

"A hot mess?"

"Always knee-deep in some drama. I never could keep track, and neither could Diane."

"You ever...?" Le Deuce smiled.

"No. Never."

"But you'd like to, I'll bet. Ever rub one out in the shower, dreaming about that tight little ass?"

"What is your problem?"

"Just trying to look at all the angles. You got some insane stuff going on here, Hilton. Think about it. You're running for mayor. You've got a very successful business with a bright future. Your brother died, what? Six months ago? And under very mysterious circumstances."

Hilton opened his mouth to object, but Le Deuce steamrolled him. "Your wife brings a rather nefarious man home while you are out of town. Said man disappears hours later with a quarter of a million in cash and cocaine."

"Why would Diane take it? She doesn't need it."

Le Deuce stroked his chin as he contemplated Hilton's question. "Unless she was planning on leaving you."

"She would not be hurting, trust me."

"My gut says she took it." He rubbed his belly. "And this baby is never wrong."

"I wouldn't know about your stomach, but she wouldn't do that."

"Just like she would never bring a strange man home? Do we ever really know anybody?" He let the question hang in the air. "She was the last person to see him. Trail ends at your house."

"You have his phone?"

"Yes."

"So wherever you found it would be the last place he was. And I know you didn't find it at my house."

"Technically, I found it at his apartment."

"So you found it at his apartment. What were you doing there?" Hilton asked.

"Whose interrogation is this?"

"What did you bring me here for? This doesn't seem too thought out."

"Why did you kill your brother?"

"I didn't—"

"Don't lie to me." He came up out of his chair. "This is what I do. This is my life. I know when people are lying to me. Why did you do it, Hilton? Why did you do it?"

Le Deuce was ready to beat him to death just for the hell of it. Who was this asshole to question him? Fuck the money. Kill the bastard, bury him in the yard. Fuck everything.

"It was an accident," Hilton yelled, voice cracking, spittle flying. "He was drunk and being an asshole. Getting nasty about Diane. We got in a fight, and I punched him. I punched him so freaking hard..." His voice broke. "He fell into the water and hit his head on a rock."

"And? I know that's not everything."

"I...I didn't jump in to save him. I just stood there and waited. I could have saved him. But I didn't." Hilton looked up, his blood-shot eyes on the verge of tears.

Le Deuce thought he saw regret in those eyes, but he didn't buy it. The son of a bitch got caught, that's all. Hilton didn't give a damn about his brother. Didn't give a damn about his wife either. Just another selfish prick who thought he was better than everyone else until you shined the light of truth on him and he melted.

He got up, walked back to the counter, and picked up his phone. He flipped the face toward Hilton and pushed the play button on the recorder app.

Hilton's face was clear despite the darkness, and his tin-can voice fought against the static echoing throughout the barren room. "It was an accident..."

Hilton buried his head in his chest.

Le Deuce laughed and stopped the video. "Man, these phones can do everything."

"Why are you doing this? What did I ever do to you?"

"It's not me you did anything to, Hilton, it's the world. You're a disease. A cancer. People like you infect everything. Destroy without remorse. Without reason. There's nothing inside you. You take and take and take until there's nothing left for the rest of us. I've been cleaning up the shit for people like you all my life and I'm tired. I'm wiped out, man. How come I don't get the nice house and the hot wife with the even hotter sister?"

"Maybe you didn't try hard enough?"

"Oh, I tried, believe me. But I'm a good guy. It might not seem like it in your position, but I am, and back in the day I wasn't even this fucking ugly. The world eats guys like me up and spits us out."

"What do you want? Money?"

"I want a lot of things. A lot of things. And you're going to help me get them. I've got you by the balls, friend."

He reached into his pocket and pulled out Hilton's phone. "We've got work to do."

60

———

HAD it dropped ten degrees since they'd locked him up? Timothy didn't know, and he didn't care. The bitter cold tearing into his bones meant freedom. He wiped a bit of snowy drizzle from his chin as he scanned the Lexington County Jail parking lot. Apparently Nicole had bailed him out.

So where was she?

When the deputy told him he'd made bail, he was speechless. He figured he'd be in for a few days, at least. Nicole didn't have that kind of money, unless she had a stash he didn't know about. With that girl, anything was possible, but he doubted it. Where did she get the money? Diane? It was the only thing he could think of. If so, he'd make sure to promptly pay her back. He hated to owe anybody a dime.

He tried to soothe his chapped lips with his sandpaper tongue, but it only made them worse. Damn it, he'd be home nursing a cold beer right now if he had his truck. There was no reason to impound it. That cop was just being an asshole. If there was even one little scratch when he got it back, he was getting a lawyer. It'd probably get tossed out of court, but it was the principle of the thing. He'd worked hard for that truck.

A Lexus pulled up, stopping inches from him. Who did he know with a Lexus? He took a step back. The driver's side window zoomed down.

"Get in," Nicole said, her face a blur of red and white from the one-two punch of the dashboard lights and the icy mist.

"Whose car is this?"

"Get in."

"This is Diane's car, isn't it?" He glanced at the passenger seat. "Where is she?"

"We don't have much time."

"Why are you driving? Is she all right? Did something happen?"

"Get in the damn car."

He rushed around to the other side, jumped in, and slammed the door. "What the hell is going on?"

Eyes forward, and her good hand on the wheel, she eased out of the parking lot like a student driver on their first lesson. After taking a right onto Jail Road, she put the wipers on high to combat the sludge suddenly pelting the front windshield and crawled along the pitch-black two-lane.

"Nicole?"

"Yeah?"

"Are you going to tell me what is going on?"

"You're not going to hate me, are you?" She kept her focus on the road.

He looked over. Her hand on the wheel was shaking. Not much, but he could tell. She turned to him. Their eyes locked. For the first time, he saw fear in them.

"What did you do, Nicole?"

Breathlessly she told him how some Australian chick—*I guess she was Australian. I mean, she sounded Australian*—had blocked Diane's car in the parking lot of Sophie's Donut Hole and about Le Deuce calling and claiming he was holding Hilton hostage and about the woman threatening to kill Diane if they didn't give her the money and cocaine.

Then she dropped the big bombshell.

Nicole had told the woman Timothy knew where the money was.

Son of a bitch.

And, to top it off, she'd promised the woman if she let Nicole get him out of jail, he would show her where he'd hidden it.

He closed his eyes and massaged his temples. A nasty headache was brewing.

"You okay, babe?" she asked.

"Where's Diane?"

"With Crazy Bitch."

"Crazy Bitch?"

"My little nickname for her 'cause she's crazy, and she's a bitch."

God help them. That was all they needed. If the woman was a professional, they might have a chance. Maybe a one-in-a-million shot, but still, it was a chance. But if she was a psycho?

He shook his head and opened his eyes.

What an absolute shit show.

"I know this is freaking you out," she said. "And maybe I should have left you in jail, but I couldn't. I just couldn't. So yes, I lied to her, but you weren't safe in there."

"It isn't Alcatraz."

"Le Deuce could pay a guard to push you down a flight of stairs or some inmate to shank you in the shower."

"Shank?"

"I'm sure he knows people."

"You've been watching too many movies. I was fine." That was a lie. He wasn't fine. Being in that cell was pushing buttons he didn't want pushed and dredging up memories long buried. But she didn't need to know that.

"I was terrified," she said, "and I needed you with me."

"So now we're both screwed?"

"I can take you back."

"Maybe you should."

He felt her simmering anger from across the car and said, "I'm sorry. I shouldn't have said that. I didn't mean it."

"Hey, if that's how you feel—"

"I appreciate you getting me out. I really do. If you were in jail, I couldn't leave you in there, either. And for the record, I'm the one who started this ball rolling, remember?"

She put her eyes back on the road. "It wasn't just you. It was a group project."

"No. This is my fault. If I hadn't taken that money…"

"But you did, so there's no point in going on and on about it. We need to worry about right now."

He watched her navigate the winding road, her beautiful face etched in shadow and light. He'd been with plenty of women before—some good, some bad—but nobody like her. She drove him crazy and kept him sane at the same time. He couldn't imagine his life without her. No way in hell would he ever let her pay for his stupid mistake. He'd take a bullet before that happened.

"We don't have a choice," he said, "we have to call the police."

"We do that and Diane is dead."

She's probably dead already. He turned to the window to avoid her eyes.

"Le Deuce is a cop," she said. "I'll bet Crazy Bitch is, too. We can't trust anybody."

Maybe she was right. Maybe they were on their own. He squirmed in his seat. His hemorrhoids were burning down the house. All he wanted to do was go home, crawl in a nice hot tub, and medicate with a bottle of Jack Daniels. He watched the darkness fly by. He could easily disappear into that black void. "Where are we going?"

"Crazy Bitch told me—"

"Can you not call her that?"

"Why not?"

"I don't like that word," he said.

"Crazy?"

"No."

"Bitch?"

"Yeah."

She cocked her head and looked at him. "Weird time to get all PC."

"I'm not getting PC. I've never liked it."

"All right, fine, whatever...you could have told me before."

"I'm telling you now. Look, growing up, my dad called my mother a bitch all the time. All the time. When he got pissed at her, he'd yell, 'Judith, you stupid bitch!' I can still hear his voice, loud as hell. That word brings out the fighting side of me."

"That's horrible. Did he ever hit—"

"No. She toed the line."

"I'm sorry."

He shrugged. "Where are we going?"

"Crazy told me to take Diane's car, bail you out of jail, and then meet them near that gas station on Highway 92. You know... um...that old one...kinda sixties looking?"

"Frank's?"

"Yeah."

"Which conveniently is out in the middle of nowhere." He crossed his arms and leaned back into the seat. "If this woman thinks I know where the money is, why did she let you bail me by yourself? That doesn't make any sense. I wouldn't trust you."

"Thanks a lot."

"No, what I'm saying is, she doesn't know you. Why would she trust you? She should be here. What's stopping us from taking the money, hitting the road, and never looking back?"

"Diane. She told me she'd kill her if I didn't come back."

"But she still wouldn't have the money. Maybe she didn't want to go anywhere near those security cameras in the jail parking lot?"

Nicole got quiet and seemed lost in thought. Finally she said, "She also thinks I'm lying and that you don't know where it is."

"She's right, but what if I do? That's a big gamble on her part."

"I told you she's crazy."

"Ruthless? Yes. Crazy? I don't think so."

"Why are you taking up for her? You don't even know her. First you don't want me to call her a bitch, which, hey, I understand, but now you say she's not crazy?"

"I'm trying to understand who we're dealing with. Odds are no matter what we do, she'll put a bullet in our heads—"

"Stop. You'll jinx us. All that negative energy is weirding me out."

"We have to face the truth, Nicole. That's the only way we even have a chance. You know what we need? A miracle. That's what we need, a freaking miracle. How about that guy...um...?"

"Mark?" she said.

"Yeah, you think he would—"

"No, absolutely not." The road split in two, and she veered right.

"Why?"

"I don't trust him."

"We're running out of options."

"We don't have a way to contact him. Crazy took my phone, and even if we did, we'd have to tell him everything, and I mean everything. And he still might be a dick and say, 'Tough shit.' And if he helped us? Oh, he'd want something for it. Trust me."

"Like?"

"A cut of the money."

He nodded. "And what else?"

"Me."

"You're right. That's a stupid idea."

He tried to think, tried to form a plan, but all the roads were littered with bright red signs: *Danger Ahead! Road Closed! Turn Around! Danger! Danger! You're All Gonna Die!*

"I've got an idea," Nicole said.

Motion in the side mirror caught his eye. Was somebody behind them? He glanced over his shoulder. Nothing but sleet and gloom.

"Are you listening to me?"

He snapped out of it. "Yeah, yeah."

"I have an idea. Tell Crazy you hid the money at the lake."

"And?"

"She'll take us to the lake."

"And?"

"Diane has a gun in her purse."

"She does?"

Beams ripped through the car, bathing them in a blinding white light. Behind them an engine roared—*VROOM! VROOM! VROOM!*—like a lion ready to pounce. Timothy swung around and looked out the back window, shielding his eyes with the palm of his hand.

A pair of blistering high beams, swerving side to side, bore down on them.

"Hey, dickhead, get off my ass," Nicole yelled, glaring at the rearview mirror.

He turned back. "Get over. Let 'em pass."

"Where? There's nowhere to go."

Straining to see through the murky drizzle, he spotted what looked to be a dirt road up ahead on the right. "Up there. Take that turn."

Nicole put the pedal down. "Is it a Dodge?"

"I can't tell."

"I'll bet it is. I'll bet she's been following us."

"Nobody's been behind us since we left the jail."

"Maybe she had the headlights off. I don't know." She took a hard right and tore down the dirt road.

After a few minutes, the trees thinned out, and a field emerged.

They came upon a locked metal gate blocking the road. She did a 180, stopped, and killed the lights.

He rubbed the fog off the windshield with his jacket sleeve. "We should wait a few minutes just to make sure they're gone."

"So you do think it was her."

"It could be anybody."

"I'll bet it was her."

No point in arguing. If it was the woman, they'd find out soon enough. They lapsed into silence, and despite the sleet dancing on the roof and the engine humming, it grew eerily quiet. He glanced over at Nicole. She was staring out the window, gripping her cast tight against her chest. In all the chaos, he'd almost forgotten about it. "How's the arm?"

"Itchy."

"Broke my leg in high school. The itching about drove me insane." A long pause. "You said Diane has a gun in her purse?"

"I know, isn't that great?" She sat up straight.

"Not unless we're prepared to kill this woman."

"Kill her? All we have to do is tie her up and get the hell out of there."

"Then the gun is useless. We might as well not even have it."

"What are you talking about?"

"When you pull a gun on somebody, you better be prepared to use it. Crazy's got a gun. You think she won't use it?" He stopped. "Wait, did you hear that?"

"No."

"Listen."

Tires rumbled across gravel. They looked up. Headlights appeared in the distance.

"Shit, it's her," she said.

Damn it, he wasn't ready. He needed a plan. The car crept closer, and he realized Nicole, of course, was right. It was the Dodge.

It stopped at the edge of the clearing, the high beams burning so hot he had to turn away. He heard a car door open and looked back. Through squinched eyes he saw someone walking toward them.

Nicole's "crazy" woman?

Beads of sweat dripped down his cheek. He swallowed. A knife went down his throat. He'd give anything for a drink.

"Tell her it's at the lake," Nicole said.

"What?"

"The money. Tell her you hid it at the lake. It'll buy us time."

The woman stopped in front of the Lexus and motioned for them to get out.

Nicole grabbed his arm. "Promise me you'll tell her it's at the lake."

"Nicole?"

"Promise me."

"Okay, okay, okay." He opened the door and slowly got out. Nicole did the same.

The woman moved toward Nicole like a panther, and he quickly sized her up. Attractive in an obvious sort of way, and possibly sociopathic by the gleam in her eye, she was most likely former military and/or private security.

But Nicole was wrong.

She wasn't crazy. He'd stared down crazy before. That didn't make her any less dangerous, but it did give him a glimmer of hope. Still, he had to tread carefully.

She stopped next to Nicole and, with a smirk, gave *him* the once-over. "Timothy, Miss Nicole here said you're the man to see. That true?"

"Yeah, I guess so."

"You guess so? That's not what I want to hear. Where is it?"

"Lake Howell."

"Where specifically at Lake Howell?"

"I'll have to show you."

"No, you'll tell me."

"When Diane's husband is safe."

"You don't get to make the rules, sweetie." Magically, a gun appeared in her hand. She grabbed Nicole by the back of the neck, forced her to her knees, and jammed the gun into the back of her head.

"Ow!" Nicole yelled. "Jesus."

"Imagine what a bullet through the back of her head would do to that pretty little face."

"Hey, whoa, whoa, stop! This is between you and me. Let her go."

She pushed the barrel in deeper and glared at Timothy, her eyes taunting him—*come on, come on, what are you gonna do?*

He didn't move a muscle. He wasn't about to take the bait. "Shoot her and you might as well shoot me, because I will never tell you where it is. Never."

Heart pounding, he wondered: *Will she do it?*

No. This was all for show, just to see how he would react. To see how far she could push him. Stay calm, he told himself. Stay calm and in control. Right now, he and Nicole were of no use to her dead.

"Take us to the lake," he said with the best confidence he could muster. "Once we know Hilton is safe, the money and cocaine is all yours."

Seconds ticked by. He kept his eyes off of Nicole and on the woman.

Suddenly she pushed Nicole away and kicked her in the back. Nicole fell facedown in the muck.

"If you're lying," the woman said, "I will make sure every fucking one of you dies an excruciatingly painful death. Understand?"

He nodded.

"I can't hear you, Timothy."

"Yes, I understand."

He'd won the first round. They still had a fighting chance. He reached down and helped Nicole to her feet. She started to open her mouth, but he shot her down with a look.

They walked to the Dodge, the woman following close behind, the barrel of her gun weighing heavily on his soul. He didn't want anybody to die tonight.

They stopped beside the Dodge. Diane was sitting in the passenger seat. She looked at them through the foggy glass, her face blank, eyes hollow. Timothy thought he caught a smile, but he couldn't be sure. At least she was alive, thank God.

"Get in the trunk of the car," the woman told Timothy.

"Why?"

"Just get in the damn trunk." She clicked the key fob. The hatch opened with an ominous pop that echoed forever.

He stared at the dark compartment, his breath coming in quiet, short gasps. A voice in the back of his mind whispered, "Don't climb in," but he did.

61

DIANE'S EYES followed the snow dancing downward. By morning it would be majestic, snowfall always was to her, but she couldn't escape a bloodcurdling thought—

Will I be alive to see it?

Somewhere, a little girl or boy was giggling with anticipation as they watched from the bedroom window their backyard turn white. She wanted to grab them by the shoulders and yell, "Make good choices."

She glanced up and caught the woman in the back seat watching her in the rearview mirror. An intense urge to climb over the seat, rip the gun out of her hand, and beat the living tar out of her swamped Diane.

Instead, she lowered her gaze and slid her trembling hands underneath her legs. She snuck a peek at Nicole. She was clutching Diane's purse for dear life and staring blankly out the passenger window. Discreetly, she reached across the console and touched her arm. Nicole snapped around.

Their eyes met. Diane mouthed, "Sorry."

She shrugged, gave her a lifeless smile, and turned back to the window.

Diane glanced at her purse, picturing her Glock tucked in there alongside her lipstick, wallet, tampons, and more. It was reassuring and terrifying. She had an ace up her sleeve. But if she played it?

"Hope for the best, plan for the worst, baby girl," Nana used to say.

It's one thing to shoot a wineglass, Nana. It's a whole new ball game to shoot a person who's shooting back.

Earlier, after the woman forced Timothy into the trunk, Le Deuce had called back. The conversation had been surreal—almost comical—until she heard Hilton's voice. It was as if someone had thrown hot coffee in her face. A police detective had kidnapped her husband, and in exchange, all he wanted was one little bag. A little bag filled with money and cocaine.

A little bag she didn't have.

Could it get any worse? Cancel that. Why press her luck?

They had agreed to meet at Lake Howell to make the exchange. Now here she was, waiting in the dark, watching specks of snow flutter to the ground and praying to God that she, Nicole, Timothy—or all three of them—weren't floating facedown in the lake when the sun came up.

An overwhelming urge to pee hit her.

"Hey, um, I have to go." She turned around and tried to smile, but her lips stuck to her teeth. "Too much coffee."

Nicole perked up. "Yeah, she's not kidding. Small bladder. There's a bathroom that way, Diane. It doesn't work anymore, but as long as you don't take a—"

"Actually, the woods over there are fine." Diane watched the woman and waited for a response.

"You can't hold it?"

"No, I can't."

"They'll be here any minute."

"Do you want me to pee all over your seat?"

Nicole chimed in, "Is this a rental?"

The woman rolled her eyes and got out of the car.

As she opened Diane's door, Nicole opened hers. "Now that you mention it, I need to go too."

"Stay," the woman said. "You'll get your turn."

Nicole slunk back down and shut the door.

Diane walked around the front of the Dodge and headed for the wooded area a few feet to the right. The razor-sharp wind sliced through her clothes, but the adrenaline rush she was riding was so intense it barely registered.

"Hey, Diane."

She jumped at the sound of her name and whipped back around.

"You might want this." Nicole was dangling the purse out the passenger window. The woman ripped it out of her hand and headed toward Diane.

Eyes on the purse, her mind ramped into overdrive. What if she opens it? What if she...? What if...? A million fatal scenarios played out in the blink of an eye.

They met halfway.

She held up the purse. "Quite heavy. What's in here?"

"My...um...insulin and...um...my shots and my meter."

She tilted her head and gave Diane the once-over. "You're diabetic?"

"Yes. Yes, I am."

"You don't look it."

"There's a diabetic look?"

The woman's eyes bore into her with such fury Diane thought, *This is it. She's going to kill me.*

"Hurry up and piss. Do anything idiotic and they both die."

Diane was shocked the woman believed her. The diabetes comment had come completely out of the blue. Nana had been diabetic, and she remembered having to give Nana her shots when Nana couldn't do it herself because her hands were too arthritic.

Shaking, she took her purse and headed back to the woods. She took her time. Any sudden movement might get her a bullet in the back. Just a few more feet...and then what? Pull out her gun, duck behind a tree, and blast away?

But as she stepped into complete darkness, she heard that smooth, bitter voice: "Wait a minute, Miss Diane, bring that purse back over here."

Her legs wobbled. She didn't have more than a second or two before the woman came charging over. She unlatched the purse, reached in, and wrapped her fingers around the handle of her Glock.

What if she missed? Hit Nicole?

She felt something next to the gun. Something she should have remembered but hadn't. It was a hell of a risk, but she grabbed it and closed her purse. Head down, she walked back to the woman like a good little schoolgirl.

"Is there a problem? I don't think I can hold it much longer."

The woman pulled her gun up, held out her left hand.

Diane gave her the purse.

The woman opened it and smiled. "Well, my, my. What's this?"

Diane made eye contact with Nicole and nodded—*here we go.* It was so subtle she wasn't sure her sister could see it in the blanket of snow flurries.

62

DAMN IT, she was almost to the woods. The skin under Nicole's cast itched like a thousand mosquitos had made a meal of her arm, but it barely registered.

The only chance they had just went to shit.

She plied her fingertips underneath her cast, scratched absentmindedly, and watched in disbelief as her sister handed the purse to Crazy.

I should rush her. Right now. Get out of the car and rush her.

With a broken hand?

She glanced back at the trunk. Timothy could take her. Six foot three and built for speed versus five foot two with one good hand? No contest.

She leaned over the console and found the trunk release button. The tip of her finger almost touching it, she froze. What was she doing? Timothy was safe back there. As soon as that trunk popped up, the bitch would open fire. He'd be a sitting target.

"In a minute, baby. I'll let you out in a minute," she whispered and sat back down.

She gazed out the passenger window. This was the longest minute of her life. Diane's eyes found hers through the snowy drizzle. The look on her face struck Nicole as odd. *Did she just give me a signal?*

Crazy let out a horrendous scream.

What the...?

Nicole tumbled across the console, reached out, and hit the button. The trunk opened with a clang, and she bolted out of the car.

Muzzle flashes tore apart the darkness like fireworks on the Fourth of July. Chunks of bark whizzed through the air. Small clouds of debris exploded at her feet.

Flinching, Nicole went sideways, tripped on a fallen tree limb, and tumbled into the snow-covered dirt. She grabbed her cast, rolled onto her back, and strained to see what was going on.

A few feet away, Crazy coughed and waved her gun around like she was fighting off a swarm of bees.

Nicole scrambled to her feet and tried to spot her sister. It was too dark.

She opened her mouth to yell "Diane" but shut it just as quick. One word and the woman would spin around and unload on her.

From the way Crazy was flailing about, Diane must have sprayed something into her eyes.

Pepper spray? Hell yes!

The chick was blind.

Nicole jumped behind a tree, struggling to breathe. Was an anvil on her chest? Where was Diane? Timothy? She shot a look back at the Dodge. The trunk was open, but there was no sign of him.

The gunshots stopped. She brushed the snow off her face and waited. The deathly quiet unnerved her.

Out of ammo or faking it?

Rustling in the grass.

Nicole froze. Listened.

Leaves crunching. Slow at first, and then something—or

someone—went from a jog to an all-out sprint. She peeked around the tree. A tall silhouette zoomed past her.

Timothy?

She stood up just in time to see the shape tackle the woman.

"Nicole? Diane?" he shouted. "I got her."

"I'm right here, behind you," Nicole yelled.

"Get her gun."

Nicole leapt forward, slid through the snow, and ripped the gun from the woman's hand. She got to her feet and took aim. "Stop moving, damn it."

"Don't piss her off," Timothy said. "Nicole's a hell of a shot." He pulled Crazy's arms behind her back and sat on top of her. She bucked like a bronco, but he didn't give an inch.

"Where's Diane?" Nicole looked left to right. "Diane? Diane?"

She took a step back and peered into the woods. It was a black mass. Where was she? Was she shot? Was she—*please, God, no*—dead?

"Diane?" she screamed. "Diane?"

"Over here," a weak voice came from the shadows. After a moment Diane limped out of the woods.

Nicole's mouth dropped open. This wasn't the same woman who had shown up two nights ago at The Wicked Hand, all poised and confident. Now her hair was a bird's nest and her jeans and coat decorated with patches of dirt and snow.

"What the hell did you do to her?" Nicole said.

"Pepper sprayed her in the face when she went for my purse. And then, like an idiot, fell and twisted my ankle as I ran away."

"That was a stupid thing to do," Timothy said. "She could have killed you."

"Well, yeah, but it wasn't like I had a choice." Diane leaned down, picked up her purse, and brushed the dirt off it.

"Baby, she was gonna kill us," Nicole said.

"Okay, okay, I get it. But what are we gonna do now? I can't keep her pinned down forever."

"I wanna know her name." Nicole leaned down and stuck the gun in the woman's face. "Who are you, lady?"

No response, just a look of rage.

"Get that out of her face," Timothy said.

Nicole stood up and backed off. "She kidnapped us. Got you arrested."

"I got myself arrested."

"This psycho was going to kill us."

"I heard you the first time."

"Stop it, both of you," Diane interjected. "Timothy, I agree with Nicole, we need to know who she is. We don't have the money—"

"Diane?" Nicole spun around and mouthed, "No, don't tell her that."

"We don't have it. There's no point in lying about it, and when we have to let her go—which we will have to do—this nightmare will start all over again."

Nicole walked back to the woman and stood over her. "Let's be realistic. You're gonna kill us, right? If we let you go, you're not gonna be like, 'Hey, guys, no money, no problem. Peace out.' Are you?"

The woman didn't look at her.

"You ever been pepper sprayed?" Timothy asked.

"No."

"It hurts like a motherfucker, and you can't see a damn thing. She's helpless right now."

"It won't last forever." Nicole turned to Diane. "We don't have a choice. It's her or us."

"We're not murderers," he said.

"You got a better plan?"

"Yeah, we call the police. Like you should have done two days ago."

"Don't lay that on me," Nicole said.

"You're right," Diane added. "We should have called the police then. But it's too late now."

"Knock it off. We are not killing her. End of story."

"Baby, what choice do we have?"

"We have tons of choices."

"She will kill us."

"She can't even see."

Diane moved closer to Nicole. "How about we just put her in the trunk until Hilton gets here, and then we can figure out what to do?"

Timothy thought for a moment. "That'll work. You two need to step back. I'm going to get her to her feet."

Diane pulled her gun out of her purse and aimed it at the woman.

"What are you doing?" Timothy asked.

"Making sure she doesn't do something crazy."

He shook his head. "Fine, just give me some room."

Nicole, her gun also aimed at the woman, stepped back a few feet. Diane followed.

"I'm going to stand up," Timothy said to the woman. "And then when I tell you, I want you to get up. Be smart, okay, because I've got two trigger-happy ladies here. We cool?"

She ignored him.

This won't work, Nicole thought. *Crazy is pissed.* If she wasn't planning on killing them before, she sure as hell was now. They couldn't afford one mistake.

"Are we cool?" Timothy said louder.

"Yes," the woman mumbled.

"Now before I do that, I need to see if you have any other nasty surprises."

He grabbed each hand and stretched her arms out in front of her, lying them on the ground. Starting near her shoulders, he slid his palms down each side of her body until he got to her ankles.

When he found nothing, he checked her boots and her pockets. He stood and hurried out of her reach.

"Okay, you can get up," he said.

Nicole watched the woman rise to her feet. The skin surrounding her eyes was red and splotchy. Nicole almost felt sorry for her. Then she realized the chick would slit all their throats in a heartbeat if she got a chance and felt stupid for the quick surge of compassion.

Timothy came behind the woman, grabbed both her wrists, and pulled her arms behind her. She winced.

"Can you see?" he asked her.

"Barely."

"Diane, you have any tissues in your purse?" He walked the woman to the lake shore.

"Where are you going?" Diane asked.

"I'm going to put some water in her eyes. I'm not sticking her in the trunk with this shit all over her face."

Nicole followed them toward the lake. "Babe, this is a terrible idea."

"It'll only take a minute."

"She doesn't deserve to have her face washed off. She's not a good person."

Timothy ignored her and continued directing the woman to the lake.

It was just like him to be nice to a cold-blooded killer. If only his brain was as big as his heart. She ran to catch up with them.

He stopped at the water's edge and glanced around, confusion in his eyes. Nicole could tell he'd gotten himself boxed in. He should have thought this through. When he relaxes his grip, she's gonna bolt.

She pulled her gun up to eye level. Her hand shook, and she propped her cast underneath her wrist. "Diane, we need you down here."

She heard her sister's footsteps behind her as Diane trudged through the grass and dirt.

"Hey, babe, hang on, let me do that," Nicole said.

"What?" He turned back toward Nicole.

The woman yanked her hands free, swung her foot back, and kicked him between the legs.

Timothy let out a hoarse, "Son of a bitch..." and fell to his knees.

The woman twirled around like a ballerina, one leg raised, and smacked him in the head with her heel. The blow sent him tumbling backward into the shallow water. She jumped into the lake after him, pulled him up to his knees, wrapping her arm around his neck in the blink of an eye.

"I'll break his neck. Swear to God."

Nicole stopped. How could he have been so stupid? She wanted to kill him herself.

She looked over her shoulder. Diane was standing in a combat-ready position: legs apart, arms extended, both hands on her gun.

Nicole mouthed, "Don't," but it was too late. The bullet whizzed past her.

63

———

Hilton glared at the highway racing toward him. Through the frosty windshield, snow and headlights were carving shards out of the night. A sudden belch moments ago had left the taste of vomit lingering on the back of his tongue. He cleared his throat. It didn't help.

Diane had the money? Had he heard that right?

Leaning forward, he tried to take his weight off his numb hands. The handcuffs were on so tight he was worried if he didn't get cut loose soon, his hands would have to be amputated.

Diane had the money.

The little turd had put her on speaker. Asked her point-blank. And in that innocent tone he knew oh-so-well she'd simply said, "Yes."

Despair tore through him. His eyes found the road again, and he took stock of the previous few days. First, his wife had screwed some random stranger she met at a bar? Then she'd stolen the guy's money? And cocaine? *Really, Diane? Cocaine?* And then what?

Killed him?

Who in the world was this woman? Not the same one he'd

married, that was for sure. Maybe Richard was right. What the hell was he gonna do? This was insane. This was—

Pull it together before you go all looney.

If only Peggy were here, she'd know what to do.

Peggy?

Damn it. He didn't get a chance to tell her it was all over between him and Diane and that he was flying back tonight. How long had he been out? Hours? Days? She had to be freaking out. He bet she'd called and texted him a hundred times. Might have even called the police. That gave him hope, but only for a second. What good would it do? They had no way of knowing where he was. No way of knowing one of their own was trying to kill him.

He took a quick look at Le Deuce, all smug and bloated behind the wheel. God, the man's pasty skin was as white as a shark. For a second, in the harsh glow of the dashboard light, Hilton thought he was being driven by a ghoul.

Despair turned to blind rage.

If only he could get these stupid handcuffs off. He'd bash that asshole's fat head into the steering wheel so fast he wouldn't know what hit him. He'd rip his heart out, fry it up and eat it with *—whoa, whoa, stop.* This was disgusting. What was wrong with him? Who was he? *What* was he?

A liar? A cheater?

A murderer?

That one he found hard to swallow.

For all he knew, Richard was dead the moment his head hit the rock. Sure, he'd punched him, but there was no intent to kill, and besides, his brother was plastered. Richard didn't fall out of the boat because Hilton hit him. He fell out because he was shit-faced drunk.

Murder? No. His attorney, Franklin Blum, would say it was manslaughter, if that.

Le Deuce took a sharp left without braking.

Hilton slammed his shoulder into the passenger door. The

taste of vomit overwhelmed his mouth and his stomach went into spasms.

"Stop the car," he let out in a sandpaper rasp.

Le Deuce swiveled, eyes crazed. "What?"

"I'm gonna throw up."

"So?"

"Pull over. I'm about to puke."

Le Deuce shrugged and turned back to the road.

"You want me to puke all over your car?"

"It's not my car."

"I swear to God, what is wrong with you?"

"You think I'm stupid?"

"I have to throw up."

"Let me tell you how it'd go down if I pull over. You'll beg me to undo your hands. Being the nice guy that I am, I'll take off the cuffs. Then you'll get a stupid idea to attack me, and guess what?"

Hilton, dumbfounded, marveled at his grotesqueness.

"I'll have to put a bullet through that oversized head of yours. Is that how you wanna go out?"

"You're not gonna kill me."

Le Deuce laughed like it was the funniest joke he'd heard in years.

"You need me. You need my money." A wave of nausea washed over him. Beads of sweat trickled down his forehead, and his damp shirt clung to his back.

"Open the window if you gotta hurl your cookies."

"You tied my hands behind my back. How can I roll down the window?"

Le Deuce tapped the switch on the door panel armrest, and the passenger window eased down. The cold air seized Hilton by the face, and he recoiled.

"I'm not sticking my head out the window like a dog."

"In or out, I don't care."

The little turd wouldn't budge, so Hilton leaned out the

window. The wind ripped through his hair as he closed his eyes and waited for the inevitable. It came like a volcano, spraying along the exterior of the car door before finding its way back to Hilton's face.

"Damn it," he yelled.

"What now?"

"I got vomit all over my face."

"Let me see."

Hilton turned toward Le Deuce and raised his eyebrows as if to say, "Is it bad?"

Le Deuce broke into a wide grin. "It's all over you."

"Can you pull over so I can wipe my face off?"

"Nope."

Hilton looked in the side mirror. It was too dark for him to tell where he was hit.

"I wanna see Diane."

Le Deuce started singing, "Come on down, come on down to Crazy Dick's Chicken Town."

"I'm not kidding. I want to see Diane now."

"Yeah, well, how about you wish in one hand and shit in the other and see which one fills up faster?"

Le Deuce swerved into the right lane, charged up the Vining Creek exit, and after a few minutes turned onto Howell Road.

Hilton watched the road sign speed by out of the corner of his eye. Almost there. Thank God. Maybe with Diane's help, he could reason with the little turd. This nightmare had to end. He wanted to be back in Peggy's arms.

No price would be too high for that.

64

––––––

Diane prayed for the splash. There would be a splash, wouldn't there? She'd aimed for the head. Despite the fog and the snow and the blanket of darkness, she'd seen those cruel eyes bearing down on her. Mocking her. Taunting her. Daring her.

Can you do it? I don't think you can.

She'd taken a tremendous chance—a horribly reckless chance—but the woman was going to kill them. She knew it, Nicole knew it, and Diane bet deep down, Timothy knew it too.

And he'd be the first. She would snap his neck the moment their guns touched the dirt. Diane had never been more sure of anything in her life.

Splash!

"What is wrong with you?" Timothy leapt out of the water.

Splash! Splash!

"Am I bleeding? Am I hit?" He stumbled around in the dirt, hands running through his hair like his scalp was ablaze.

Nicole raced to him and grabbed him by the shoulders. "Stop moving." She ran her fingers across his head, spun him around, and checked his back. "You're fine."

Diane rushed past both of them and came to a stop at the edge of the lake. She scanned the water churning toward her. "Where is she? Nicole? Timothy?"

"You could have killed me," he said.

"Did I hit her?" Diane turned and found Timothy. "Did I hit her?"

"She screamed and let me go, so yeah, I'd say you hit her."

"Then where is she?"

From out of nowhere, fingers gripped her ankle. Diane shrieked and yanked her leg back. But the fingers clung tight, and she went flailing headfirst into the shallow, blistering cold water. The force of the impact sent her gun flying from her hand.

The blows were nauseating—quick, gut-wrenching jabs across her back and head. She reached out to grab hold of something—anything—to pull herself to safety, but her frozen fingertips found only air and water.

BAM! BAM! BAM!

Gunshots?

The blows stopped.

She tried to raise her head, but it was like she had an anchor wrapped around her neck pulling her down.

This is it. I'm going to die.

She waited for the kaleidoscope to flash before her eyes—the mundane and the exhilarating, the heartbreaking and the breathtaking—but there was only a murky pit of darkness beckoning her.

HANDS—*TIMOTHY'S? Nicole's?*—grabbed Diane's arms and legs and ripped her from the water.

"Diane?"

The voice pulled her back from the abyss. Gasping, she sucked in as much cold air as her lungs could take. She was swallowing razor blades, but she couldn't stop.

"*Diane?*"

She opened her eyes. The murk swirled away and Nicole came into view, panic writ large across her face.

"Am I dead?"

"No, but that bitch gave it her best shot."

"Is she...?"

"Yeah."

"Who?"

"Me," Nicole said. "I still have one good hand."

Diane tried to sit up. A red-hot poker ripped through her. "Ow! Oh, that...hurts."

After a minute, she forced herself to her feet. She would be feeling this pain for years. She licked her lips. Her tongue was coated like she'd sucked on a penny. She needed some water.

"This is just a horrible nightmare, right, Nicole? A nasty, horrible nightmare. Oh, God, I don't want to go to prison."

"Nobody's going to prison." Timothy stepped out of the darkness.

Tires rumbled through the dirt. Light flashed across Nicole's and Timothy's faces. Diane glanced back. The pain in her shoulders hit her so hard she almost went down again.

A car had pulled into the clearing and parked. Engine breathing, headlights pulsating, exhaust fumes rising—it was a coiled snake ready to strike.

Hilton? Le Deuce?

Maybe they should call the police, Diane thought. Just get it over with. Prison would be better than this. Or would it? She'd never been in prison before.

She plied the sticky wet hair from her face, pushed it behind her ears, and tentatively put one foot forward. Going down face first in the muck wasn't an option.

"Le Deuce?" Nicole came up beside her.

"Anybody else and we're screwed."

"We're already screwed." She stifled a laugh.

"I'm sorry."

"Me too."

"I love you," Diane said.

"What?"

"I love you."

"Don't even. We're going to get out of this. We're going to be fine."

"I know."

They watched the car and waited.

Get on with it already. Diane's heart was about to explode. She rubbed the snow from her face. Her clothes were soaking wet and her teeth were chattering, but she didn't have to pee anymore. One small victory.

She turned to Nicole. "Where's your gun?"

"I've got it." Timothy came around Diane's left side.

The car engine died, but the headlights didn't. The door creaked open, and Diane could hear someone climbing—*or falling?*—out. They stepped into the light.

A short, round silhouette hobbled toward her.

"Detective Le Deuce?" Timothy yelled.

Diane reached down for *her* gun. Too bad it was at the bottom of the lake.

"Hey, the gang's all here," Le Deuce said, chuckling. "Christ on a bike. It's cold as balls. You people got my money?"

Diane bit her tongue and waited for one of them to answer, but they stood there: two deer in the headlights with a car coming a hundred miles an hour.

Nicole stepped forward. "Yeah, about the money—"

"We don't have it," Diane said, past the point of playing games. "And we can't get it."

"That's not what you told me on the phone."

"Where's Hilton?"

"Where's Hot Chocolate?"

"Hot Chocolate?" Diane and Nicole said in unison.

"The Aussie, goddamnit. Where is she?"

"In the lake. Facedown." Nicole smiled.

Perplexed, he looked them up and down. "You're shitting me?"

"She tried to kill Diane."

"It's true. Look at me."

"Well, that's a shame. She was damn easy on the eyes. So where's the money?"

"You took it," Diane said.

"The hell I did."

"Nicole and Timothy left it at Jackson's apartment after you moved his body. And now it's gone. Right, Nicole?"

"Right."

Diane glanced at her. Nicole gave her a wide-eyed smile and nodded. Was she telling the truth? She better be.

Le Deuce leaned hard on his cane. To Diane, it looked like the only thing between him and death.

"Are you people on drugs? I didn't move his body. That is the stupidest thing I have ever heard. If I had the money, would I be going to all this trouble?"

"Is Hilton in the car?" She tried to move past him, but he blocked her with his cane.

"Hang on, darlin'."

Darlin'?

She came within a heartbeat of shoving that cane up his ass, but pushed it away and trudged on toward the car. Just putting one foot in front of the other took everything she had. She got to the passenger side, looked through the window, and stifled a scream.

Hilton was hunched over, arms behind his back, his face smeared with God knows what. His puppy dog eyes found hers and he yelled, "Diane?"

She tugged on the door handle. Locked.

"Hey, get him out of here. What have you done to him? Le Deuce? If you've hurt him..."

"Shut the hell up. I can't think." He reached into his coat pocket and yanked out his gun.

Everybody froze.

Diane watched the barrel swaying in his hand. Was he about to topple over? Could she rush him? At this angle, she was in his blind spot. She moved but stopped. What was the point? She'd screw it up like she'd screwed everything else up the past few days.

"What do you want from us?" Nicole asked. "We don't have your money. We don't have your coke. We got zilch."

"You know what you are, honey? You're a goddamn liar. And I hate liars."

"Watch your mouth," Timothy said.

"Whatcha gonna do, Mister Guitar Picker?"

"I play bass."

"Whatever. I might be ugly, but you know what I ain't? I ain't pussy whipped."

It came out *pussawhapped*—one word.

"I don't let the little man do the thinking for the big man. You losers have completely destroyed my life. Like one hundred percent destroyed it, and it's time for some payback. So somebody better cough up some dollar bills unless they want to end up floating out in that lake with the Aussie."

"Liar?" Nicole screamed. "Who's the liar? We saw you, you and some humongous dude, move Jackson's body. Why did you do that? And where did you take it? We don't have your money, ass—"

"Enough!"

Diane's outburst slashed through the bickering. All heads swiveled toward her. "We're all liars, okay. Get my husband out of the car, please."

Le Deuce's eyes lit up as he tried to stare her down. She could feel the rage radiating from him. It shook her. She couldn't imagine that kind of fury driving her day after day. Whittling her down. Eating her up like a cancer. She'd made some stupid mistakes in her life, but at least she hadn't spent it living in a cesspool of anger like him.

Or her mother.

She almost felt sorry for them both. "You going to kill all of us? All four of us?"

"No, not all four. Just one. Maybe two. By the way, Diane, your husband killed his brother."

"Excuse me?"

"He confessed."

"I don't believe you."

"Yeah, he punched him in the face and knocked him into the lake. And then did nothing. Just let him drown. Maybe if he hadn't been such a coward and jumped in, Crazy Dick would still be getting crazy with some chicken or something."

"You're lying—"

He pulled his phone out of his pocket, fumbled with it for a minute, and then Hilton's crackling, tin-can voice fought against the hiss.

"It was an accident. He was drunk and being an asshole. Getting nasty about Diane. We got in a fight, and I punched him. I punched him so freaking hard..." His voice trailed off. "He fell into the water and hit his head on a rock."

"And? I know that's not everything," Le Deuce said in the background.

"I...I didn't jump in to save him. I just stood there and waited. I could have saved him. But I didn't."

Le Deuce stopped the video.

"Diane, don't listen to him. That doesn't mean anything," Nicole said. "I'm sure he forced him to say that."

Oh, it was true, all right. Deep down inside, she had always known. But how do you believe something like that? How do you truly believe it? Because to do so meant her marriage—her entire life—was a lie.

She walked away from the car. Hilton could rot in there for all she cared. "We still don't have your money."

"But *he* does. And if he wants to be mayor—"

"Oh my God, you're gonna blackmail him?" Diane surprised herself with a full-throttle belly laugh.

"Damn right. Mulberry Grove needs good public servants. Your hubby is a murderer."

"Can I see it again?"

Le Deuce pushed play and handed her the phone. Before it finished, she handed it back to him.

"He's tied up. You've got him tied to a chair, it looks like. I mean, who's going to buy this?"

"Everybody. People are morons."

"But you're torturing him."

"I never laid a hand on him."

"Fine, whatever."

Shivering, she limped past him. If she didn't get out of these wet clothes soon, she was going to catch pneumonia.

She stopped in front of Nicole and Timothy and whispered, "I don't know what to do. Clearly he's insane, but do you think he'd hurt us—"

Blam!

Nicole recoiled and went to the ground. Diane's hands found her ears as she spun around.

Le Deuce—arm in the air, gun pointed toward the sky—had fired a warning shot.

With lightning speed Timothy stepped between Le Deuce and Diane and Nicole, his gun aimed directly at Le Deuce's heart. "Drop it."

Le Deuce let his cane fall to the ground and brought the gun eye level, gripping it with both hands.

Diane peeked up at the night sky, waiting for the bullet to come back down.

"I'm sick of you people," Le Deuce yelled. "You're a bunch of leeches. You just take and take and take. You didn't need that money. I needed it. It's mine. I worked hard for it. That was my lucky break. And why did you kill her? I liked her. She probably would have never screwed me, but still. It's just not fair."

Diane stepped in front of Timothy. He shot her a *What are you doing?* look.

She mouthed, "Trust me" and turned her focus to Le Deuce.

"Give me the gun. Come on, give me the gun. You don't want to hurt anybody." She tried to make eye contact, but it was like getting the attention of a cat watching a ping-pong game. If only she could remember his first name.

William?

Wasn't that what police negotiators did in a hostage situation? Use the first name to gain trust.

Vinny?

She ran down a list of names until: "Victor."

He looked at her. "What's Jackson have that I don't?"

"What?"

"Jackson," he repeated. "He was such a pain in the ass, but they all loved him. The ladies...they just couldn't get enough of Jackson."

"Well..." One wrong word could set him off. "He was charming."

"Actually, he was kind of a jerk," Nicole said from behind Timothy. "I could tell right away."

"Then why did you let me...?" Diane looked over her shoulder. Pain shot down her spine. She rubbed her shoulder blade.

"The way he moved, I figured he might be good in bed. You needed that, so..."

"Thanks, I appreciate it."

"Hey, I did the best I could on such short notice."

"Was he good in bed?" Le Deuce asked.

Diane's jaw dropped. "I am not talking about this. Why are we talking about this?"

"I don't understand. I'm a nice guy. I'm a detective. I help people. I solve crimes. I make the world a better place, but I couldn't get a beautiful woman to look my way if I gave her a million bucks. I can't even get an ugly woman to look my way."

"You're not a nice guy," Nicole yelled.

"Nicole?" Diane stammered. Was she trying to get them killed?

"He's not. He's holding us at gunpoint and threatening to kill us. Nice guys don't that."

"Okay, this conversation isn't getting us where we need to go. Everyone take a deep breath, and let's start over." Diane shook off the cobwebs. "Victor, please, can I have the gun?"

"If you tell me how he was in bed, I'll put the gun down. If you tell me what he had that was so damn special, I'll get in that car and get the hell out of your life."

"I'm not doing that."

"Diane, you've already done it," Nicole said. "Just tell him what he wants to hear."

"Not what I want to hear. The truth. I want the truth. Everything. How he kissed you, how he touched you, how he made love to you."

"So you're going to humiliate me?"

"This isn't about you, Diane," Nicole said.

"Apparently it is. I'm done. This is too creepy for me. I'm a grown woman and I slept with a grown man, and it's nobody's damn business what we did. I'd rather you shoot me than tell you what that night was like. It's my night. It's my memory, and you can go to hell, you little freak."

"Thought so." He jerked the pistol up and took aim.

Diane watched the barrel of the gun zoom slowly into focus, crowding out everything else in her field of view—Le Deuce, the car behind him, and even the snow on the trees disappeared.

She wanted to run, wanted to fall to her knees and crawl. She wanted to do anything to get away from that barrel, but her body, paralyzed with fear, resisted her at each turn.

65

———

THE TERROR in Diane's eyes brought a smile to Le Deuce's lips, and his finger tightened on the trigger.

She deserves this.

Hell, Diane *and* Nicole both deserved it. Had they ever suffered a day in their pretty little empty lives? Had they ever known pain? Or fear? Or the sheer terror of being alone? Of course not. How could they? These chicks had won the most important lottery in the world, the beauty lottery. The one that opened every door with ease.

And they had no clue.

No stinking clue.

He'd known far too many women like them over the years, all of them to a T weak and needy and utterly worthless. Oh, they promised a good time with their sultry lips and tight asses and luscious tits—*"Hey, honey...here you go, darlin'...well, hello, hand-some..."*—but they'd stab you in the balls without batting an eye and laugh while they did it. He'd seen it too many times. Men hopelessly ensnared like a fly in a spider's web. Dumbasses paying for that slice of heaven with their money and their life, while the bimbo just kept licking her lips and shaking her ass as she moved on to her next conquest.

He hated his desires. Detested his lustful thoughts. Hated the blood flowing between his legs like a volcano about to erupt every time he got around a hot woman. Hated wanting something with every fiber of his being and knowing he would never, ever get it.

God may have created Adam, but Satan sure as shit created Eve.

And even that son-of-a-bitch Timothy had won the lottery—tall, rugged, and probably hung like a horse. Le Deuce would give his left nut to look like that. And if he did, you could bet he wouldn't destroy his body with all those stupid tattoos. The guy looked like an idiot. A total idiot. And yet, Le Deuce was certain the douche had gotten more prime pussy than he could even dream about.

Lucky bastard.

On second thought...

Le Deuce pivoted, bouncing the barrel from Diane to Timothy.

66

GUNSHOTS ROCKED the car and rattled the windows. Hilton went sideways, slamming his forehead into the passenger window.

"Ow! Ow! Ow!"

The rancid smell of vomit already had him on the edge of puking again, and for a split second he thought whatever was still left in his stomach was taking the elevator back up. He closed his eyes. Breathed through his mouth.

He couldn't take this anymore. It was too much.

"Why me, God? Why me?"

He broke out in a loud sob and shook as tears gushed down his cheeks. He'd tried to be a good husband, a good brother, a good person. How had he allowed himself to be conned by Diane? Why had he followed her down this rabbit hole? They could have been happy together. They could have had a good marriage, but she pushed him away. Could she blame him for turning to Peggy when she didn't even want him to touch her anymore? He should have left years ago. But he was weak. A stupid, sniveling little weak loser.

Hang on.

Maybe it wasn't gunshots he'd heard. Maybe he'd imagined it. Maybe the stress overload was making him hallucinate weird sounds. It could have been a train. Or fireworks. Could have been anything but gunshots. He peered out the frost-covered windshield hoping what he saw would reassure him but found instead the hazy reflection of his own vomit-caked face. It was a pathetic sight. If only Richard could see him now. He'd laugh his ass off.

Screw you, asshole.

Using his right shoulder, he rubbed a circle in the fog on the passenger window. It wasn't much, just enough for him to make out a body lying in the snow.

"On my God, oh sweet Jesus," he whispered. He banged against the door with his shoulder and screamed, "Let me out of here. Diane? Nicole? Somebody? Open the door."

He struggled with his handcuffs. Kicked the dashboard with his feet.

I'm going to die. Right here. Right now. I'm going to die, and there's nothing I can do about it.

He had to get out of the car. He couldn't breathe. He had to get out right this second.

But how? His hands were tied behind his back. The doors were locked.

Or were they?

He spun around in the seat, putting his back against the passenger door. He ran his fingers along the side panel until he found the door handle. He pulled on it.

His fingers slipped off.

He tried again.

Slipped off.

Again.

Slipped off.

Again.

The door swung open, and Hilton tumbled out of the car, landing on his side in the snowy dirt and grass.

"Ow! That hurt."

His face burned from the bitter cold. He rolled over and

looked up. It was too dark to make anything out. Who was that on the ground? Nicole?

Diane?

No, please...

Not Diane.

$$67$$

Le Deuce felt something wet hit his face and opened his eyes. Snow was raining down on him like buckshot.

What happened?

He tried to sit up, but every inch of his body screamed, "Stay down, motherfucker."

Where am I?

Lifting his head an inch or so off the ground, he saw snow-covered branches swaying in the wind but nothing beyond. With a Herculean effort, he tilted his head to the right.

A dark shape charged toward him.

He tried to pull his gun up. His arm wouldn't budge. What the hell? He looked at his hand. It was empty.

Christ on a bike!

Where was his gun?

The rocks underneath him dug into this spine. He was on his back? The brutal wind tore into his face. He snuck a peek at his stomach. Blood oozed across the bottom of his shirt.

Oh, shit. Oh, shit.

Shot? How did I get shot?

He wheezed and fought back tears. The burning in his chest spread like an out-of-control wildfire, and he came close to blacking out. No, he couldn't black out. He had to get up. He had to get help. He wasn't going out like this.

"Why did you make me do it? Why?" The dark shape hovered over him, his voice echoing as if in a large tunnel.

"Do what?" The sound of his own voice surprised him. Scared and weak, it couldn't be him.

"I told you to drop it. I told you to put it down. I didn't want to shoot you, goddamnit." The shape morphed into Timothy.

"You're an asshole," Le Deuce said.

"You tried to kill us."

"I missed?"

"Completely," Timothy said.

"Seriously?"

"Yeah."

"Well, you stole...my...money."

"It wasn't your money."

"Whatever. Get away from me."

"Nicole, call 911," Timothy yelled.

Le Deuce wished he wouldn't yell. It was like nails on a chalkboard.

"Why?" she yelled back.

"We can't just let him die," Timothy said.

"I'm not going to prison for that piece of shit."

"Fine. I'll do it." He jumped up and ran off.

Le Deuce was glad. The prick was getting on his nerves. If only he could crawl to someplace quiet. Someplace where he could think. All their whining was hurting his head. He just wanted to sleep for a few minutes. Get his strength back. Then he'd get up and drive himself to the hospital. The gunshot wound couldn't be *that* bad. Nothing a few stitches wouldn't fix, right?

Why did it suddenly get so dark? He couldn't see the trees

anymore or the snow or the three musketeers. Their voices dimmed until they were like flies buzzing in the distance. He closed his eyes. But only for a minute, he told himself. He wasn't about to die. Not here.

Not tonight.

He deserved better.

68

Nicole stumbled backward as Timothy barreled straight for her. Her foot sank in the mud and she sidestepped to the right, losing her balance. Quickly catching herself, she scurried past him.

"Gimme the phone, Nicole," Timothy said. "Gimme the phone."

She zigzagged back and forth, keeping her distance. She'd never seen him this wild-eyed before. He was twice her size. If he got those big paws on her, it'd be over in an instant.

"Babe, what are you doing? We can't call the police. That would be suicide."

"We can't just let him die."

"You want to go to prison? You want *me* to go to prison?"

"I'll go. Not you."

"You really believe that? Stop, okay? Just stop. Use your damn brain for once."

"Why are you trying to save him?" Diane blurted out. "He's a monster."

Timothy froze, the blood draining from his face, and turned to her. "He's a human being."

"Who tried to kill us a minute ago. You didn't have a choice."

"Yes, I did. When I took that money, I had a choice." He tugged at his hair. "Now that woman is dead. He's bleeding out. We took it back. I swear to God we tried. And then I had to mess it all up and lose—"

Nicole grabbed him by the arm. He spun around. Their eyes locked—

Whoa, babe, don't let that cat out of the bag.

"Calm down and listen to yourself, okay?" she said. "You're getting hysterical. He's not worth it. Trust me. It's better this way."

Tears welled up in his eyes. She couldn't believe it. He was serious. He really wanted to save the little rat. It was so sweet, and so completely stupid.

"It's too late to call the police, babe. He'd be dead by the time they got here. It'd all be for nothing. If he hadn't missed..." She trailed off. "I'm sorry, but I will not lift a finger to help that bastard."

He looked over. She followed his gaze.

Sprawled out, Le Deuce was already covered by light patches of snow.

"You know I'm right." She touched his hand.

"Excuse me. Hey, excuse me," Diane shouted. "Lose what exactly?"

The rage in Diane's voice shocked Nicole. She sounded so much like Janice it was scary. She peeked around Timothy.

Diane—clothes sopping wet, hair matted and stringy, hands on hips—was walking toward them with that dagger in her eye Nicole had seen only a few times before. Her sister crossed was a hell of a thing.

"Nothing. He's babbling." Nicole wrapped her good arm around him. "Right, babe? You're confused."

"Nicole," Diane pressed.

"What?"

"Can somebody please tell me the truth?"

"The truth? We took the money back, and we left. That's the truth."

"Timothy?"

"Why are you asking him?" Nicole arched her back. If her sister wanted a fight, she'd gladly give her one.

"Timothy?"

He didn't respond, just continued staring at Le Deuce. Nicole wanted to slap him in the face and scream, "Snap out of it."

"What happened?" Diane asked again.

After a minute he said, "We took the money back to Jackson's apartment. But we changed our mind and didn't leave it."

"Changed your mind?"

"It was too dangerous to leave it. After we saw them take Jackson's body, we realized we needed leverage."

"So where is it?" Diane said.

"Somebody stole our car," Nicole said.

"Stole your car?"

"We stopped at Waffle House—"

"Huddle House," Timothy said.

"What?"

"It wasn't Waffle House. It was Huddle House."

"Okay, so who cares? Waffle House? Huddle house? We stopped, like, you know, to eat, and when we came out, the car—with the money in it—was gone."

Nicole stared Timothy down. When he hung his head, she turned her eyes on Diane. *Happy now?*

"What car?"

"A rental," Nicole said.

"Why don't I believe you?"

Nicole threw her hands up. "We're wasting time."

"It just seems awfully convenient to me. One minute the money's here, the next minute it's gone." Diane snapped her fingers. "Poof."

"I don't care. Believe what you want. I'm sick of you calling me a liar."

"But you did lie to me, Nicole."

"I told you we didn't have the money, which is the truth."

"Saying you left the money at Jackson's apartment and the money actually being stolen because you were stupid and left it in the car are two very different things. Why couldn't you be honest with me?"

"Because you wouldn't have believed me. Admit it. You wouldn't have. You would have thought exactly what you're thinking right now—I stole the money and put all of us in danger—"

"You almost got us killed," Diane shot back. "If we'd had that money—"

"They would have killed us anyway," Timothy shouted.

"He's right."

Diane shook her head and walked away.

"You know," Nicole said. "Maybe instead of arguing, we should figure out what to do. We have life-changing decisions to make and very little time left. Once you moved his body, it was always going to end like this."

Diane ignored her and kept on moving.

In the awkward silence, Timothy looked at her. *What now?*

Nicole shrugged. Hearing the wind whistling through the trees and the water quietly lapping at the shore, she noticed it was the first time tonight the sounds had registered. She loved this lake. Over the past year it had become her lake. She'd couldn't remember how many times she'd sat out here strumming her acoustic guitar, writing songs. Now that was all gone. Lake Howell would forever be a black pit of hell.

She'd never come back here again.

69

WEIGHED down by her wet clothes, Diane limped through the snow, careful not to trip. She had to get away from Nicole. Get away before she said something so horrible she could never take it back.

Sticks and stones may break my bones, but words will never hurt me.

Wrong. Words kill. Little invisible bullets, they rip through the soul, slicing and dicing with machine-like precision. Better to walk away, cool down, and find a way out of this nightmare.

Is there a way out?

She closed her eyes, rubbed her neck, and winced. Her hands were freezing. A few more hours of this and she'd be in the ER for hypothermia.

Swimming in the lake? In December? In the snow? Doesn't make much sense, ma'am.

Well, doc, you see, this lady—and I use that term loosely, by the way—this lady tried to beat me to death.

What an absolute mess she'd made of the past few days. How did this happen? Did her inner Janice come out? Had it been lying dormant all this time, waiting for the right spark? Apparently she *was* mama's girl. Mama's girl all the way. Nicole had nothing on her.

"Diane?" a ragged voice called out. "Diane, please help me."

She spun toward the sound of the voice and was blinded by the car lights. She shielded her eyes with her palm and saw a silhouette crawling on the ground.

Hilton?

As she moved closer, her eyes adjusted and she saw it was Hilton. He was crawling on his stomach, hands behind his back, through the muck. She couldn't believe she'd forgotten about him. How did he get out of the car? Pausing, she studied him with a mixture of wonder and disdain. What had possessed her to marry him? Had it ever been good? It must have been, right? It had to have been. But for the life of her, she couldn't remember when. He wasn't always an asshole, was he?

She hobbled over, stopping a few feet in front of him.

Hilton raised his head and gave her a crooked smile. "Thank God you're okay."

His face was mud caked, his hair straight out of a light socket. Not much of a politician right now, she laughed to herself. The urge to step over him, get in the car, drive away, and never look back was strong.

"Help me up," he said.

"Richard. Tell me what happened with Richard."

"Diane, come on. Help me up. Get these handcuffs off of me."

"Did you murder your brother?"

"What?"

"You didn't hear Le Deuce's video?"

"No." He hid his eyes.

"You said *you* killed him."

"I told him what he wanted to hear. I had to. He's crazy."

"Can anybody around here tell the truth? Am I asking too much for a little honesty?"

"I didn't kill him."

"Did you push him into the lake?"

"No. Absolutely not."

"Hilton?"

"He was my brother."

"And he drove you around the bend. You seemed to get over it pretty quickly."

"That doesn't mean I killed him."

"I have to know."

"I don't know, okay?" The sobs came fast. "I don't know. I can't remember. He was drunk. We were arguing. He said nasty things about you, Diane. Nasty things. You know how he could be when he got drunk. Mean. Mean like a snake. Next thing I know, I'm pulling him out of the water. Blood everywhere."

Suddenly she felt sorry for him. Sorry she'd never given him the love she'd promised. Sorry they wasted each other's time. Because that's what it was. Thirteen years of wasted time. Was he telling the truth? Who was she to judge?

She leaned down, grabbed his hands, and helped him to his feet. She turned him around and looked at the handcuffs on his wrists.

"How are we going to get these off?"

"Le Deuce must have the keys."

"I think he's dead."

Hilton looked back, eyes wide. "So that's what those gunshots were...what do we do?"

"His key ring?"

Diane made her way to the car, opened the driver's side door, leaned in, and turned off the lights. She removed the car keys from the ignition, looked for a key to the handcuffs. There wasn't one. Damn. Now she'd have to search his pockets. Oh God, this was getting too creepy.

She stumbled through the darkness, slipping on the snow back to Hilton. "It isn't on his key ring."

"We have to get these off."

"I know."

"His pockets?"

"Ugh. Seriously?"

"Please," Hilton said.

"I think he's dead."

"Well, I can't do it." He pulled his cuffed hands away from his back.

"Yeah, I get that. Who is she?"

"What?"

"I know something's going on. Who is she?"

"Do you have to do this right now?"

"Yes." Diane stared at him.

He looked at the ground for what felt like a thousand years to Diane before the words came out. "Peggy. Her name's Peggy."

"Have I met her?"

"No."

"She have a last name?"

"Ramone."

"Does she work for you?"

"Well...she's my campaign manager."

Diane laughed, shook her head, and walked away. "I didn't even know you had a campaign."

She headed over to Nicole and Timothy. They were wrapped in a tight embrace. It seemed an odd thing to be doing under the circumstances, but they lived in their own little world.

As she got closer, she could hear Nicole whispering, "Babe, it's okay. You're not a bad person, really. I love you."

"I just feel terrible," Timothy said through what sounded like quiet sobs.

"Don't, babe, don't ever think—"

Diane cleared her throat. They stopped talking. She felt horrible eavesdropping, but it was time to make up. Sorta. "I'm sorry. I'm being a bitch."

Her head buried in Timothy's chest, Nicole looked up and gave her a death glare.

"You're right, no more arguing," Diane said. "We need to pull it together to get out of this mess."

Nicole let Timothy go and faced Diane. "What's up with Hilton?"

"Handcuffs. We need to get them off. I think Le Deuce has the key."

"What do we do with those?" Nicole pointed at the body floating in the shallow part of the lake and then to Le Deuce.

"Guys, if we cover this up, we're going to be living with it for the rest of our lives," Timothy said.

"Yeah, we get that," Nicole said.

"Do you? Always looking over our shoulders, and not just for the police. We don't know who she is. We don't know who she works for and what they know. I mean, we don't know anything."

"So what are our options?" Diane asked.

"Call the police, tell them the truth. Hire a good lawyer and hope for the best."

"Nobody will believe this," Nicole said. "I wouldn't believe it, and I've lived it."

Timothy continued, "Get the hell outta here and hope we leave no incriminating evidence behind."

"Just leave them lying out here in the open?" Diane thought that was a crazy idea.

He nodded. "Or find a place to bury the—"

"Can somebody get these damn things off?" Hilton yelled.

Diane looked up. Hilton was chugging like the little train that could toward them.

"You might want to slow down," Nicole yelled.

Suddenly his foot slipped, and he went flying, landing on his ass and sliding.

Nicole giggled.

Diane shot her a look and hobbled past Hilton without

helping him up. She stopped a few inches away from Le Deuce, stood on her tiptoes, craning her neck from side to side.

Was he dead? She felt like grabbing a big stick and poking him with it. Was he breathing? It was dark, and she couldn't tell. All she had to do was go through his pockets. How hard could that be? She looked him over.

What if he isn't dead?

She shuddered. The moment she went rummaging through his pockets, he could grab her by the hair, pull out a knife, and slash her throat. She looked back at Nicole and Timothy.

Help.

Please.

No, this was on her. With a groan, she inched closer. "Victor? Victor? Can you hear me?"

She rubbed her brittle, frozen hands together. She looked back again. Did Hilton need those handcuffs off right this second?

Just get it over with.

She knelt down beside Le Deuce. Wincing, she slid her hand into his left pants pocket. It was empty, of course. Who keeps their keys in their left pocket? She leaned over him and quickly realized she would get his blood all over her clothes. She struggled to her feet, limped around his body, bent back down, and avoided looking at him as she stuck her hand in his pocket. Going through the pockets of a dead man? She had sunken to a new low.

Finally: a handful of change and some gum. Great.

"What are you doing?"

Diane jumped back and looked up, her heart about to explode.

Nicole was standing on the other side of Le Deuce.

"You scared me to half to death," Diane whispered. "I'm trying to find the key to those handcuffs."

"Why are you whispering?"

"I don't know."

"I think we should leave them on him," Nicole said.

"No."

"Have you tried his coat?"

"I'm getting there."

After a minute or two of ferreting through his coat pockets, Diane pulled out what looked to her like a tiny skeleton key and held it up.

Nicole nodded.

"You sure?"

"Trust me, I've seen a few handcuffs in my day."

"I'll bet." Diane got up and followed her sister.

70

Diane parked the car and checked the time on the dashboard: 5:16 a.m. The sun would be up soon. Their luck, if you could call it luck, only had to hold out a couple more hours.

"More like the rest of your life, sweetie. No statute of limitations on murder," Nana's voice whispered in her ear.

Put a sock in it, Nana.

Dragging the woman out of the lake and putting both bodies in the trunk of Le Deuce's car hadn't taken more than half an hour. But to Diane it seemed like forever. It didn't help that the thought of someone catching them red-handed had her heart racing ninety miles an hour the entire time.

The long drive was even worse. Convinced flashing blue lights would appear in her rearview mirror at any moment, she could barely keep a grip on the wheel. The wet and icy roads didn't help. But it was all wasted energy, worrying over something that didn't happen.

She killed the engine, along with the lights, and waited a few minutes until the Ford pulled in behind them before allowing herself to breathe again. After getting the door open—the cold making it stick—her boots crunched the snow-covered ground as Hilton climbed out of the back seat and Nicole the passenger side.

Hilton was right, this place was deserted. Not a house or street-light for miles as far as she could tell. She eased the door shut, stretched her pain-riddled back, and listened to the wind howling. Rubbing her hands together, she watched her breath drift away. A hot shower and a warm bed seemed like something from another life.

Eyes adjusting to the dark, she could make out bits and pieces of the farmhouse. It was obvious it hadn't been occupied in years. With its boarded-up windows, rickety old porch, and knee-deep grass, the place was straight out of every bad horror movie she'd ever seen. No telling what nastiness Le Deuce had gotten up to in there.

At the lake, after Diane had gotten Hilton's handcuffs off, the four of them fought over what to do. Should they go to the police or cover the whole thing up? Three to one, cover-up was the clear winner. But how? Leave the bodies where they were? Bury them? Throw them in the lake? Take them someplace else?

Hilton suggested Le Deuce's farmhouse—the place Le Deuce had held him captive. Nicole and Timothy were hesitant. Thought it too risky. Could Hilton find the house again? What would they do if he couldn't? Toss the bodies in the woods?

Ultimately, they decided it was the only option.

Timothy insisted on driving Le Deuce's car by himself. Told them if he got pulled over by the police, he would take all responsibility for the bodies. Nicole was not happy, but she understood. Diane kind of admired Timothy's backbone. She wished Hilton had one.

"You sure this is it?" Nicole came around the front of the Dodge Avenger.

"Yeah," Hilton said. "This is it."

"You're sure?"

He looked the place over. "I'm pretty sure."

"Pretty sure?" Diane asked.

"Yes, damn it, this is it," he yelled. "Jeez."

"Hey, not so loud." Timothy joined them.

"See that big red barn way over there?" Hilton pointed past them.

All three turned.

"Where?" Nicole asked.

"Right there. I distinctly remember driving past that barn when we left. I'm telling you this is the right place."

"Well, let's hope so." Timothy walked around to the back of the Ford.

Nicole and Hilton joined him. Diane lagged behind.

At the trunk, the taillights were bathing everything in neon red. It was creepy as hell and reminded her of that scene in *Goodfellas* when De Niro and Pesci stabbed the guy in the trunk.

This night couldn't be over soon enough.

Timothy popped the trunk. The loud clank made her jump. She looked at Le Deuce and the woman, rag dolls intertwined, and wondered why she wasn't running screaming into the darkness. The Diane of three days ago would have turned tail in a heartbeat, but she wasn't that person anymore. Or was she? It was hard to know who she was anymore. She missed her old self.

"So what now?" Timothy asked.

"Throw them in there and then burn the place down," Nicole said.

She looks crazed, Diane thought, her face awash in red, mascara running, blond hair frizzing out. "Toss them in there? Burn the place down? What is wrong with you?"

"They were trying to kill us. Sorry, but I don't give a shit. And hey, it would destroy all the evidence."

"Yeah, and the fire department and the police would be here lickety-split," Hilton said. "We should—"

"Lickety-split?" Nicole giggled.

Hilton gave her a perplexed look.

"What are you? Like, nine years old?" Nicole asked.

He threw his hands up. "Can you take this seriously?"

"Guys, it's going to be daylight soon," Diane said. "Give it a rest."

Timothy turned to face them like a professor about to lecture his class. "Well, first off, we don't have any gas, so setting the house on fire isn't an option. Unless we want to go get some gas, but at five o'clock in the morning, putting gas in a container is going to be very suspicious."

"We bury them, then," Hilton said.

"You know how cold and hard that ground is? Unless there's a shovel—or more importantly, *shovels*—inside, we're not burying them in the yard either. So I suggest we leave them in the house."

"Lying there? Out in the open?" Diane asked.

"Could be months or years before somebody finds them, if ever."

"What if we make it look like they shot each other?" Nicole broke in.

"Huh?" Diane asked. Was her sister losing it?

"You know," Nicole continued. "Use Le Deuce's gun to shoot the chick and her gun to shoot him. So it looks like they had a shootout."

"We could. Of course, someone might hear the gunshots and call the police." Timothy paused, his face getting very serious. "Are we sure we want to go through with this? This was self-defense."

"Hey, I didn't kill anybody," Hilton said.

Diane shot him a look. *Excuse me? Richard?*

"Accessory to murder. And do you really think the DA will care? You're involved, so deal with it," Timothy said. "Point is—"

"Point is, we've already moved the bodies," Diane said. "We've already made our choice."

"She's right," Nicole added.

With a resigned shrug, Timothy reached in and grabbed Le Deuce by the shoulder and pulled him out of the trunk. Hilton leaned in to help. Nicole took out her cell phone and activated the flashlight app, showering them with light.

"Turn that off," Timothy said. "You trying to wake up a bunch of rednecks? Have 'em running out here with double-barrels?"

"Babe, this is like the Antarctic of Georgia. There's nobody out here. See how dark it is? You want to trip and fall and break your neck?" Nicole said.

"We'll figure it out."

"Fine." She shut off the light.

"You know, maybe we should get the door open first. Before we carry them over," Hilton said.

"Good point." Timothy let Le Deuce go, and he tumbled back into the trunk.

Diane trudged around to the driver's side, turned the ignition off, and removed the keys. *Enough with the red taillights, already.*

They were creeping her out.

DIANE WATCHED Hilton and Timothy slowly carry the woman's body down the basement stairs. Hilton, legs trembling, looked like he was about to topple over. She'd offered to help, but they'd made it clear: "We got it."

Fine. Bust your ass, see if I care.

Besides, the thought of touching a dead body again made her want to throw up. That rancid smell wasn't helping either. It had hit her hard from the moment she'd stepped into the house. Musty boiled cabbage? Dead skunk? Imagine how bad it would be in a few days with the smell of a couple of rotting corpses added to the mix.

Rotting corpses? Would this nightmare ever end?

Out of the corner of her eye, she caught Le Deuce's body lying on the concrete floor and turned to Nicole.

Her sister was holding her phone high above her head, using the flashlight to illuminate the concrete basement. Cobwebs and dust covered the tiny room. Broken wooden shelves, a few falling or about to fall, lined the wall to Diane's right. All empty except for a couple of paint buckets and some rusted gardening tools. To her left, a tarp covered a gigantic pile. Something about it looked ominous, and she wondered what was under it. Old furniture? Kindling? Spiders? Oh, there were spiders all right, large, creepy ones. She was sure of it.

There was only one small window. And it was so dirty no one could see in or out.

"Kind of anticlimactic," Nicole said.

"How?" Diane asked.

"I don't know. Guess I was expecting something more dramatic...considering all we've been through."

"Dramatic?"

"You know, the house going up in flames as we drove away, explosions touching the sky behind us."

"Why are you being so flippant about this?"

"Why are you being so calm?"

"I'm not."

"Gotta laugh or you're gonna cry...right?" Nicole paused and then almost to herself added, "Our fingerprints are going to be everywhere. We have to wipe both cars down."

"What are we going to do with them?"

"We can't leave them here. Park them in different parking lots around the city? I'm not sure."

Hilton and Timothy laid the woman's body across from Le Deuce. There seemed to be no rhyme or reason to the placement. Sort of like everything that had happened the last three days.

"Who is she?" Diane asked.

They turned, all eyes on her.

"We don't even know her name," Diane continued. "What if somebody comes looking for her? Not knowing who she is leaves us—"

"Vulnerable," Hilton said.

"Exactly," Diane said.

Timothy bent down and went through her pockets. Pulled out a wallet and thumbed through it. Held up what looked to be a driver's license, letting it catch the light from Nicole's phone. "Name's Ava Walker."

"Ava? She doesn't strike me as an Ava," Diane said.

"Okay, then." He pulled out another license. "How about Jenny Miller?" And another. "Or Vicky Beale?"

"How many are there?" Nicole asked as she moved closer to him.

"Let's see. One...two...three...four...five. Five fake IDs."

"Lot of good that does us," Diane said.

"Keep them. We might need them later," Nicole said.

"Later? For what?" Diane asked.

"Insurance. We're in the dark here. There might be people out there who know who we are, but we have no clue who they are. Try saying that twice."

Diane shook her head. Her sister was losing it.

Hilton paced in a circle, chewing on his thumbnail. "I'm trying to remember what Le Deuce said, something about the money and coke belonging to some guy named McAllister," Hilton said. "Anybody heard of him?"

They shook their heads and muttered a collective "No."

"Claimed he was working deep undercover to bust this McAllister."

"You believe that?" Timothy asked. "Le Douche was a total scam artist."

"I'm just telling you what he said."

"We can discuss this later. We need to get out of here. Sun will be up soon." Timothy crossed his arms and surveyed the room.

Diane couldn't take it another second. She dodged past Hilton and charged up the stairs, not bothering to look back at the bodies on the floor. There was no point. They were burned into her memory.

They'd haunt her for the rest of her life.

SATURDAY

71

NICOLE STARED at the shadows on the ceiling. They were slithering like snakes. *Is this a dream?* She closed her eyes, counted to ten, and opened them again. The shadows had stopped moving, but something still wasn't right. Was that her ceiling? The room was so dark she couldn't tell. Terror gripped her. Where was she? How did she get here? What happened?

Calm down. Just calm down.

She raised her head slightly and looked around the room. She was in her bed, thank God. She rolled over, hoping to wrap her arms around Timothy. But the unmade bed was empty. Did he leave? Had he even been here? She couldn't remember. Everything was a blur. She peeled her tongue from the roof of her mouth and rolled it around her gums. It tasted like she'd sucked on a car battery.

She shot up. What time was it? Where was her phone? The room spun, and she flopped back down. After a minute she slid out of bed with a defiant, "Screw it."

A glance in the full-length mirror in the corner stopped her cold. Tattered Black Sabbath T-shirt, pink socks, pale white legs, arm in a cast, black mascara under her eyes, and light-socket hair—Jesus, she looked worse than ever.

"Timothy?" she yelled at the top of her lungs. "Timothy?"

Loud footsteps and then: "Hang on, hunny bunny, I'm coming."

A moment later, the door creaked open and Timothy, backlit by the hallway light, entered, a cup in each hand. "Coffee?"

"What time is it?" She took one of the cups. The hot brew warmed her throat, washing the nasty metallic taste away in one sip.

"Six twenty, six thirty? I don't know. Six something."

"At night?"

"Yeah."

She glanced up from her cup and caught him staring at her, that puppy dog look on his face. "Don't look at me. I look like shit."

"No, you don't." He kissed her forehead.

"Don't lie to me either. I look like shit and I feel like shit."

"Oxycodone and Kentucky bourbon..." He shook his head and grinned. "You started babbling, so I put you to bed."

She took another sip and tried to jump-start her brain. The past twelve hours crept back in: driving the cars to the junkyard; the icy roads; her broken arm growing so painful she absolutely had to take a pain pill when they got home; washing a piece of toast down with a glass or two of bourbon.

A thundering growl escaped her stomach. She burst out laughing.

"Hungry?" he said, smiling.

"Sounds like it."

"I'll fix you something."

Ah, he was so damn sweet. She looked into his blue eyes and wondered: What did he see in her? Didn't he know she was no good? Didn't he know she wasn't always honest with herself? Or the people closest to her? Didn't he know she wasn't to be trusted?

Maybe he did and loved her anyway.

"How about I fix us both something?" She grabbed his hand and pulled him toward the door.

Hand in hand, they walked down the hallway and into the kitchen. He went to the refrigerator, opened the door, and peered in. She looked in the pantry and found a can of chicken noodle soup. One lonely can. She checked the expiration date. Still good. *Yeah!*

He closed the refrigerator. "Time to make a Piggly Wiggly run."

"We did the right thing, didn't we?" She watched him refill his coffee and sit down at the table. "Are you listening to me?"

"What are you talking about? Leaving the cars at the junkyard?"

After getting Diane's car from the field, they had driven to a junkyard, wiped down the two cars—Le Deuce's Ford and the woman's Dodge—and left them there, hidden among the old and rejected.

"No, everything," she said. "Everything we did. The bodies...everything."

"If we get away with it, then yeah, we did the right thing. If not, well, I guess we'll find out."

"You're not helping."

She checked the cabinets until she found a saucepan. She wasn't much for cooking and was surprised she had cookware. She emptied the can into the saucepan, added some water, placed it on the stove, and turned the burner on.

"Well, one thing worked out in our favor." She sat down beside him.

"What?"

"If they find the bodies, all the bullets are from Crazy Chick's gun, not Diane's."

"Are you sure? I thought Diane shot her."

"She missed."

He looked confused for a moment, then nodded. "I think you're right."

"Maybe we'll get lucky and nobody will find them."

"Let's hope." After a long pause: "What about this guy Mark? He concerns me."

"That idiot doesn't know anything."

"When it becomes clear Le Deuce is missing—"

"Nobody will give a shit," she said. "Trust me. Everybody hated Le Deuce. You did the world a favor."

"Don't say that."

"It's true. For all we know, he could have been a serial killer. That house was a serial killer house, babe. A serial killer house."

"Yeah." He stared at his coffee. Then he looked up and forced a smile.

"You can't keep beating yourself up." She touched his hand.

"Sure I can."

"You saved Diane's life. You saved my life."

"That's like setting your house on fire and congratulating yourself for saving the cat. I knocked the first domino over."

"Bullshit. If Diane had called the cops like I told her to, then none of this would have happened, okay? I could have forced her, but I didn't. There's plenty of blame to go around. We all made stupid mistakes."

"Two people are dead."

"Three, if you want to be accurate."

"Yeah, but we had nothing to do with that," he said.

"We did introduce him to my sister, who fucked him to death."

"Nicole?"

"What? Apparently she hadn't had sex in a long time."

"You're terrible."

"And you love me."

He pushed his chair back and stood up.

"Where are you going?" she said.

"The bathroom. You mind?"

"Leave a dollar on the counter."

As he shuffled down the hall, she yelled, "You know you love me."

The door closed with a soft click. She shook her head. If he went in the bathroom to cry over Le Deuce, she was gonna bust his balls. That prick wouldn't have shed a tear over him.

She got up and checked on the soup. It was in the "Will it ever boil?" stage. She watched the bubbles popping up, slow at first, and then faster and faster. Suddenly the smell of chicken noodle soup made her want to puke. She shut the burner off, grabbed the pan, and poured the soup down the sink.

She had to get out of the house. No, out of the city. No, out of the country. She wanted to run like hell and never look back.

Timothy came up behind her. "What are you doing?"

She jumped and dropped the pan into the sink. She turned around. "You scared me."

"Sorry."

"Were you crying in the bathroom?"

"What? No."

"Don't cry over him. He doesn't deserve it."

"I wasn't crying," he said, eyes wide, brows up.

If that was his intense look, she thought, it wasn't working. She wrapped her arms around him. "Let's get out of here. I'm in the mood for something hot and spicy."

"I'm hot and spicy."

"Ha, ha."

NICOLE FINISHED her cigarette and tossed it out the open window. Three crunchy tacos and a Diet Dr. Pepper had hit the spot. Strands of hair flittered about her mouth. She brushed them away and looked over at Timothy. He hadn't said much since they left her house. One hand lazily on the wheel of her RX-7, he seemed lost and heartbroken.

"You're not the only one, you know," she said.

"What are you talking about?"

"I killed somebody last night, too."

He shot her a look. "Don't sound so proud of it."

"I'm not. It feels really weird saying that."

"It is weird. Sad and fucked up, too."

"Yeah, but I'm not crying about it."

"I'm not either," he said, a chill in his voice she'd never heard before.

"Please. You look like you could burst into tears at any moment."

"Forgive me for having a conscience."

"She was trying to kill my sister. I don't give a fuck. I did the right thing, okay? I will lose zero sleep over that bitch."

"Give it time."

"I know I should feel bad. I get it, but I just don't. I guess that makes me a terrible person."

"No. You're not a terrible person."

"Thanks."

He got quiet.

She wished she felt guilty. Maybe then she'd understand what he was going through. Right now all she felt was relief. Relief that bitch was dead. Le Deuce too. What a couple of freaks.

"After Afghanistan I promised myself I would never kill another human being," he said. "I broke that promise."

"To save Diane's life. You didn't just shoot him for the hell of it. He made you do it."

"That doesn't make it any less painful."

"We're alive."

"Yeah, and..."

"It's a big fucking deal."

"But we're always gonna be looking over our shoulders," he said. "This won't ever end."

She sighed. "Let's not worry about the future right now, okay?"

She turned on the radio. Marvin Gaye was singing "I Want You." God, what a voice, she thought. The icy wind danced through her hair. She closed her eyes and embraced the cold. The fact that she, Diane, Timothy, and Hilton—well, maybe not Hilton—had come so close to death freaked her out. And yet, in a way, she felt free; like a fog had lifted and she could think clearly for the first time in years.

She thought she heard him mumble something about "married people and testifying," and swung around. "What?"

"Married people can't testify against each other," he said, loud and clear.

"Really? What are you saying?"

"Just making an observation."

"Are you proposing to me? That sounds like a proposal."

He flashed that big, goofy grin, melting her heart.

"Oh my God, you are proposing."

"No, I'm not. Don't put words in my mouth," he said, laughing. "I'm just saying, it's something to think about."

"You're so romantic." She leaned over and kissed him. "Can we get away from here? Get away as far as possible."

"What about the band?"

"We can find a new band."

"We're a great band," he said.

It was true, they were, but she'd had it with this place. She didn't even know if she'd ever be able to play guitar again.

He thought for a moment. "I've always wanted to live in Alaska."

"Oh, babe, that's too cold for me. How about Italy?"

"Italy? That's a whole other continent."

"Might as well go big."

"Any news on your mom?"

Crap. She couldn't believe she'd completely forgotten about Janice. Now she felt like a real shit. "No. I'm sure if there was problem, the hospital would call. I'll check on her in the morning."

"I hope she's okay."

"Yeah. Me too." She grabbed his hand.

"Hey, you think Piggly Wiggly sells Christmas trees?"

"Christmas?"

"Yeah. It's, like, two days away."

Damn, she'd forgotten about Christmas too. "Maybe? I don't know."

"Let's find out."

"Okay, babe. Whatever you want."

She cranked Marvin up and, hand in hand, she and Timothy rode into the darkness.

SUNDAY

72

THE EGG SIZZLED when it hit the pan, and a splash of grease popped Diane's wrist. *Ouch!*

She jumped back and rubbed the burn for a minute. Satisfied the damage was minuscule, she added a second egg and tossed a bit of salt and pepper on each. After a long, deep sleep—her longest in years—she'd woken up famished and, for some odd reason, craving fried eggs and toast, a specialty of Nana's when Diane was a little girl.

She grabbed a spatula and tried to slide it under one egg to flip it, but the little sucker resisted her every move. It didn't help that her hand was shaking. *From hunger?* she wondered. *Or stress? Or both?* It was hard to tell. Finally she flipped it, but the yolk broke and it flowed across the pan. Damn it, she knew she should have gone to Panera.

Behind her, wheels rumbled across hardwood, and she glanced back, surprised to see Hilton trudging into the living room, pulling his suitcase like a dead man walking. They'd barely spoken to each other since coming home yesterday morning, and she'd almost forgotten he was here. He'd offered to stay at a hotel last night, but she'd nixed that with a curt, "Don't be silly," and he'd slept in the guest room.

She turned back to the egg disaster on the stove and flipped the other one. That yolk broke too. God, she was terrible at this. But, in her defense, she hadn't fried eggs in years. Her usual breakfast was black coffee and a bagel, and maybe a smoothie when she was in the mood.

"When's your flight?" she said.

"Around noon."

She glanced up at the clock. Eight forty. Great. He probably wouldn't be rushing out the door anytime soon. She caught herself about to ask him if he wanted some breakfast and stopped. There was no way in hell she'd ever cook for him again. Not that she was much of a cook; like her mother and her sister, that was not one of Diane's gifts. Still, he didn't deserve her cooking, good or bad.

"Any news on Janice?" he said with a sympathetic *I-still-care-about-you* tone.

"No. I'm going to check on her after I eat," she said in a *I-don't-want-to-talk-to-you-right-now* tone.

"Hopefully, she's doing better."

"Yeah, let's hope."

She scraped the eggs out of the pan and onto a plate, turned the burner off, and marched to the kitchen table. As she sat her plate down, she realized she'd forgotten to make some toast and headed back to the counter.

Walking across the kitchen, she could feel Hilton's eyes following her. He seemed to be chomping at the bit. Was there something he wanted to say? If so, he needed to spit it out or scurry off to his new life. *You probably should get going if you want to make your flight, dear.*

She was pulling a couple of pieces of bread out of the bag when he said, "I don't like leaving this way."

She slowly turned. "You really want to talk about this?"

"I think we should."

"Why?"

"To clear the air."

"Okay, so how do you want to leave? Should we part as friends? Should we cry it out together? Maybe ask Alexa to play something soulful and have one last romantic slow dance? I'm confused, Hilton. This isn't how you envisioned the big finale?"

"You make it sound like it's all my fault."

She stared him down, forcing him to look her in the eye. "You did start seeing someone else, um...months ago, if I remember."

"Which was a terrible, foolish mistake."

"Was it? Or do you feel bad just because you got caught?"

"I feel horrible. I never should have lied to you, but I have to say I never slept with her in our house."

"Slept with? Don't you mean had sex with?"

He rolled his eyes.

God, she wanted to punch him. "What an honorable man you are. Sorry I didn't live up to your high moral standards. Sorry I'm just a common floozy."

"At least my mistake didn't get people killed."

She slammed the bread in the toaster, pressed the lever, and glared at him, her blood boiling. *Screw you, you jackass.*

"We killed two people, Diane. And I'm not sure I even know why at this point."

"*You* didn't kill anybody. Except for Richard, it sounds like."

"That's a low blow."

"Hey, now you have an excuse to run for mayor."

He looked confused.

"So you can make sure nobody finds out what you did to your brother," she said, suppressing a laugh.

"Is that supposed to be a joke?"

She shrugged.

"It doesn't matter," he said. "I'm not running for mayor anymore."

"Great. I'm sure the world will mourn."

"This is pointless."

"You had all the time in the world to talk to me. But no, you found somebody else and hung me out to dry. When did you plan on telling me about her? Never, I'll bet. You were probably gonna string us both along, weren't you?"

"That's not true."

"When were you going to tell me? After you won the election? After I stood by your side like a good little woman?"

"The other night. I flew back home to tell you only to find out you'd gone crazy."

"Crazy?"

"Yeah, in a manner of speaking. You were being pretty weird. And in case you've forgotten, I was kidnapped. I could have been killed."

"It's always about you, isn't it? Always." The conversation, like their marriage, had hit a brick wall. "Go. Just go. Just get out of here. Run off to your dream girl and your fantasy life, okay?"

Clearly flustered, he grabbed his suitcase and stormed toward the foyer, only to stop and turn back. "You can have the house."

"I don't want it."

"I built it for you."

"You built it for yourself. I wanted to renovate a Victorian."

Ching! The toast popped up.

"I don't even know who you are anymore," he said and stalked out, the suitcase wheels clacking on the marble floor.

She waited for the front door to slam. When it did, she felt like screaming, "Hallelujah," but refrained. Instead, she methodically took the toast out of the toaster, buttered it, and put it on a small plate. Then she got some orange juice out of the fridge and poured herself a glass.

She carried the toast and juice to the table, sat down, and took a bite of her eggs. *Yum.* They were tastier than she'd expected. As she ate, an earworm burrowed into her head.

"Come on down, come on down to Crazy Dick's Chicken Town..."

She laughed.

***

Mulberry Grove Regional Medical Center was eerily quiet for a Sunday afternoon, Diane thought as she pushed the elevator call button. Footsteps echoed on the tile floor, and she looked over. A nurse rushed by, the white pompom of his Santa hat flopping wildly about.

Christmas?

This wasn't Christmas. Not to her. This was Halloween. One long, never-ending nightmare. The door opened, and with a heavy sigh, she got on the empty elevator and hit the button for the eighth floor.

Earlier, after finishing her breakfast, she'd called to check on her mother. The nurse on duty said Dr. Bernstein wasn't convinced Janice was out of the woods just yet, and that it would probably be tomorrow or Tuesday before she could go home.

During a scalding hot shower, reality reared its ugly head. For the foreseeable future, someone—either her or Nicole—had to take care of Janice. She was too fragile right now to live by herself. Nicole clearly was in no shape, financially or mentally, to do it, and while Diane had the financial resources, the thought of she and Janice living under the same roof for a day, much less a few months, was overwhelming. Could she do it? Maybe it was time to grow up and put the past behind her.

After her shower, she'd sent Nicole a text suggesting they meet at the hospital later that afternoon. A reply never came, and Diane could only assume her sister—a notorious night owl who rarely got out of bed before lunch—was asleep. Still, the lack of a response made her uneasy, and she had to temper the feeling something was wrong.

The elevator stopped on the second floor. The door opened and a short, heavyset, balding man hustled in, flashing a hurried smile. Diane returned the smile and watched him out of the corner of her eye as he moved to the back of the elevator. The door closed with a harsh clang, and a random thought sent a chill up her spine.

She was alone in an elevator with a stranger.

Which shouldn't be a big deal, she'd done it a million times over the years, and yet...

She glanced back. He was engrossed in his phone and didn't look up. She made a quick study of him. He could have passed for a less attractive middle-aged Danny DeVito and obviously wasn't a threat. She felt foolish for her rush to panic. Rubbing her clammy hands together, she watched the floor numbers climb higher.

Ping. Third floor.

On second thought, who made her an authority on assessing a threat? Just because he looked like an out-of-shape, middle-aged loser didn't mean he was one. He might be a hit man, or an undercover detective keeping a tail on her. Or—*God forbid*—Le Deuce's brother. They did kind of favor one another. No. She shook her head. That would be one plot twist too many.

Ping. Fourth floor.

What if he'd been watching her house all day and followed her to the hospital? Was he after the money? Or revenge for Le Deuce and the woman? She wanted to look back, but she couldn't move. Her knees shook. A lump stuck in her throat. She pulled her purse tight and straightened up. *Stop. Stop. Stop. This is insane.*

Ping. Fifth floor.

The elevator lurched to a halt. The door slid open, and a blinding light poured in. Gasping for air, she pushed through an older couple trying to get on, almost knocking them over. "Excuse me, excuse me. I'm sorry. I'm so sorry," she said, stumbling into the hallway.

Behind her, she heard the elevator door close and hurried down the hallway, too terrified to look back to see if he was following her. When she got near the nurses' station, she slowed her pace and glanced back.

The hallway was empty.

Was she losing her damn mind? She fought back tears. What was wrong with her? She was freaking out over nothing.

She spotted a bathroom, went in, and locked the door. Trembling, she leaned against the wall. Was this her life now? Watching over her shoulder everywhere she went? Having a panic attack any time someone looked at her twice? She splashed some water on her face and took a moment to regain her composure.

She left the bathroom, walked till she found the stairs, and trudged up to the eighth floor, the elevator off-limits for now. Approaching Janice's room, she saw a group of nurses and technicians spilling out the door and into the hallway. *What is going on?* She took off.

A nurse looked up, saw Diane rushing toward her, and put her hands up. "Hang on, hang on."

"Janice Robinson? I'm her daughter," Diane said, panicked. "What's going on? Is she okay?"

"Ma'am, you're going to have to wait down by the nurses' station."

"Why? I don't understand."

"Ma'am, please, the doctor will be with you as soon as possible."

Diane leaned up on her tiptoes and tried to look in but couldn't see past the people in the doorway. Something was wrong. But what? Her hand fell to her side, fingers gripped her dress. *Oh God, did she have another stroke? No. Don't even go there.* She turned and staggered back down the hall. She found a chair and sat down. Her phone buzzed. She yanked it out of her purse.

Nicole had finally texted her back.

NEW YEAR'S EVE

73

WITH FROZEN FINGERS, Diane took a handful of Janice's ashes from the urn and scattered them across the water. The metallic-gray clouds parted momentarily and a golden beam came down, setting the murky water ablaze. Diane thought it looked like the hand of God touching the lake. Or maybe—she fought back a laugh—aliens beaming Janice up to their starship. Never in her wildest dreams did she imagine her mother's final resting place would be the lake behind her house.

"We could have launched these as fireworks." Nicole took the urn from her.

"People do that?"

"Yeah, I read about it online."

"You should have said something."

"I knew you'd never go for it."

"Maybe you don't know me as well as you think you do," Diane said.

Nicole grabbed the remaining ashes from the urn and scattered them. They landed in the water, sending tiny ripples across the lake. "Poor Janice, your heart never stood a chance. You rode that baby hard and put a lifetime into fifty-eight years."

"She died from a stroke."

"Well, she rode something hard and it killed her."

Diane pulled the scarf tight around her neck. A little melodramatic, but her sister did have a point. She grabbed the flowers Nicole and Timothy had picked up on their way over and tossed them into the water. The flowers, according to Nicole, were so they could follow the ashes as they floated away.

In the distance a crow cawed, and she glanced back at her house. Timothy was standing near the fire pit, watching. He had respectfully declined to be a part of the ash-scattering ceremony, saying that it should be a private moment between them.

Nicole put the lid on the urn. "Well, that's that. Thank God there wasn't any wind. I'd hate to have Janice all over my face."

"What is wrong with you?"

"Jeez, I'm just stating the obvious."

Diane turned and, crunching through dead leaves, trudged up the hill toward her house. She stopped at the fire pit and warmed her hands over the dwindling flame. Christmas had been a lonely, drunken bust—she really needed to lay off the Pinot Noir—and getting Janice cremated over the holidays had been more difficult than it should have been. All in all, a fitting end to the worst year of her life.

Nicole walked up and wrapped her arms around Timothy. He kissed her forehead.

"How you doing?" he said.

"Hanging in there," Nicole said. "I'll be all right."

They were a good fit, Diane thought, two crazies taking on the world. She hoped it worked out. Somebody in this family deserved to be happy. "I'm assuming we're safe, right?"

"Safe?" Nicole looked at her.

"Do you think anybody will come after us?"

When neither one of them immediately responded, Diane's stomach clenched. "What are you guys not telling me?"

"Nothing. I'm not worried about it," Nicole said.

"Me either," Timothy added.

"Why don't I believe you? Does anybody else know about this? About the money? About the lake? About any of it?"

"No," he said.

That he seemed to be avoiding eye contact didn't calm Diane's nerves. "Nicole?"

"I swear. We didn't tell a soul."

"Okay." She grabbed the poker and separated the logs in the fire pit to keep the fire from reigniting. "How about some lunch? Anybody hungry?"

"Thanks, but we need to get going," Nicole said.

"Yeah, we have a flight to catch," Timothy said. Nicole elbowed him in the ribs. "Ow!"

"A flight?" Diane said. "Where are you going?"

"We're just getting away for a few days," she said.

"Where?"

"The Bahamas," Timothy said, smiling.

"Skipping the country?"

"We want to get out of here before the shit hits the fan," he said.

"What are you talking about?"

"Don't listen to him, Diane."

"Haven't you heard about the virus in China?"

"What virus?"

"That bat virus out of Wuhan."

"Time to go, babe." Nicole grabbed his hand. He brushed it away.

"People are dying in the streets, like, literally keeling over dead, and they're locking the city down. It's like *Dawn of the Dead* or something."

"Oh my God," Diane said.

"Timothy, that is total nonsense. You're scaring the shit out of my sister. You've got to stop reading those stupid conspiracy websites. They're turning your brain to mush."

"Hunny bunny, I'm telling you this is going to be the big one."

She grabbed him by the arm and dragged him onto the veranda. "Ignore him, Diane. Seriously, he's gotta get off Reddit."

Diane shook her head, turned, and looked back at the lake. The trees at the water's edge were gaunt scarecrows, clinging on for dear life, and the barren grass surrounding it, withered and yellow. Not a fitting burial ground now, but by spring it would be beautiful. A gust of wind nipped at her face, bringing with it the smell of decaying wood and rotten eggs. She squinched her nose up. On the horizon, billowing clouds gathered like an army, turning the pearl-gray sky black as coal.

DIANE WAVED bye to Nicole and Timothy as the RX-7 backed out of the driveway. Bat virus? What the hell was that boy talking about? He was sweet but a bit loopy in the head.

The car disappeared around the corner. Something low and ominous rumbled in the distance, and she looked up. Watching the enormous black cloud move slowly toward the house, she waited for the crack of lightning. When it failed to appear, she turned and went inside.

She walked into the living room and made a beeline for the cozy chair near the fireplace. Before she could plop down, she flashed on Jackson's last moments on the floor in front of the hearth and, with a quick pivot, went to the couch. She sat down, kicked off her sneakers, pulled her legs underneath her, and tried to suppress a yawn. She'd barely slept all week, and yet she held her eyes open as if the lids were propped up with toothpicks. The nightmares—every night since Hilton left—were relentless. She kept waking up in a sweat, a scream on the tip of her tongue.

She marveled at the large room and all the work she'd done to it over the years. Most of it practically by herself, as Hilton was little to no help. The man couldn't paint his way out of a paper bag.

He was right. This *was* her house, and she'd made it beautiful. And a small part of her didn't want to leave, but there was a darkness creeping in. A black hole she couldn't mend.

The house deserved better.

Her eyelids grew heavy. She closed them, promising herself it would only be for a moment.

Thunder exploded.

She awoke with a jolt. Rain pounded the windows, coming down in sheets. How long had she been out? She looked at the clock on the wall. Half an hour?

She pushed herself off the couch, went over to the kitchen table, sat down, and opened her laptop. When she finished reading the pages from yesterday, she smiled. They were good. Really good. Finally, her drought was over. The words were flowing.

She made herself a cup of coffee and got to work. Hours passed, and when she could write no more, she got up to stretch her legs. She poured another cup of coffee and went to the kitchen window. The rain was over, but a dense mist lingered. Streaks of saturated red and orange lit up the sky as the sun went down.

Was somebody out there? she wondered. Was somebody watching her right now? Waiting for the perfect opportunity? Perfect opportunity to do what? She closed the blinds, blew the heat off her coffee, and took a sip. Maybe she'd get a dog—a big guard dog, like a pit bull—to start the year off right. Or a concealed carry permit. Or hell, maybe she'd get both.

AUTHOR'S NOTE

Books are magic.

You string together a bunch of words and the next thing you know, if you're lucky, you've made someone laugh, or cry, or stay up all night because they had to know what happened next.

We are all storytellers in one way or another. It's just that some of us—*the crazy ones?*—painstakingly put our stories down on paper. And, even crazier, send them out into the world, on a wing and a prayer.

So, if you took the time out of your busy life to read this book, thank you.

Hopefully, you just had to know what happened next.

ACKNOWLEDGMENTS

I'd like to thank my parents, who have always been there for me. They will forever have my gratitude and love.

A special thanks to Kate Schomaker, who did an excellent job of editing this book.

And finally, a big thanks to my beautiful wife, Shannon, who read every draft and told me the truth.

ABOUT THE AUTHOR

Steven R. Brooks is a screenwriter, songwriter, and novelist. He lives in Athens, Ga with his wife, son and two pugs. *Dead Bedroom* is his first novel.

www.stevenrbrooksauthor.com